A GINGERBREAD HOUSE

Catriona McPherson

SEVERN
HOUSE

First world edition published in Great Britain and the USA in 2021
by Severn House, an imprint of Canongate Books Ltd,
14 High Street, Edinburgh EH1 1TE.

Trade paperback edition first published in Great Britain and the USA in 2022
by Severn House, an imprint of Canongate Books Ltd.

severnhouse.com

British Library Cataloguing-in-Publication Data
A CIP catalogue record for this title is available from the British Library.

ISBN-13: 978-0-7278-5001-0 (cased)
ISBN-13: 978-1-78029-799-6 (trade paper)
ISBN-13: 978-1-4483-0538-4 (e-book)

All Severn House titles are printed on acid-free paper.

Typeset by Palimpsest Book Production Ltd.,
Falkirk, Stirlingshire, Scotland.
Printed and bound in Great Britain by
TJ Books, Padstow, Cornwall.

A GINGERBREAD HOUSE

Also by Catriona McPherson

* available from Severn House

This is for Kristopher Zgorski,
with love and thanks.

PROLOGUE

There was no mistaking the smell. Except, come to think of it, that's not true. It was all too easy to mistake the smell, to miss that one crucial note in the putrid bouquet. For a start, it was damp and there was a years-deep rind of mould coating the bricks, eating into the mortar, softening the cheap cement that, once upon a time, had been used to pour the floor.

In the damp, rot had come along and worked away at the joists and beams, at the stacks of softening cardboard boxes and yellowing newspaper. The drains were bad too, always had been; a faint drift in the air like a sigh of sour breath. Cats, of course. Or maybe foxes. *Something* had got in and stayed a while. And why wouldn't a cat or a fox stay, out of the rain, with a buffet of little scurrying things laid on? Little scurrying things that must have thought they were safe in here. They added their bit to the chord too, but in such tiny dabs it would take a bloodhound to find them.

No bloodhound needed for the bottom layer. Under the damp and rot, under the drains and vermin, there was something else, sweet and soft as a whisper. And what it whispered was a tale of death. Unmistakable, inescapable death. Not the snuffing out of a mouse either, nor some gasping stray, nor a proud wild fox brought to broken, whimpering nothing. This was something much bigger.

There were three of them actually; curled together, as close in death as they were in life. Stopped short, they were a snapshot of themselves, their little vanities there in the coloured hair, covering grey, that lay in hanks near the scalp that had held it, in the good shoes well-polished and cared for, always stored on trees, now buckled and cracked around the bones of the feet inside them, in the pretty lingerie, rotted down to clips and hooks, stained and rusting, sinking through fragile skin. Hopes and triumphs were gone, disappointments too. All their stories were lost except one: the stark truth of what they really were, under their dreams and shame. What they were was meat. And when meat spoiled it stank, worse than old eggs, worse than fresh vomit, worse than shit and sweat and terror, until eventually that truth faded too, the last story told.

Dear ———

I hope it's OK that I'm writing to you. It was my doctor who suggested it. It struck me as selfish but she said there was no harm.

All I really wanted to say was sorry. ~~I'm sorry I was too late to save your loved one.~~ I'm sorry I didn't put two and two together ~~a lot quicker.~~

I wasn't trying to be a hero. I was trying to do the right thing. But I'm not cut out for saving the day. I'm a worker bee. Even as the boss's daughter, I was never really one of the bosses. ~~My dad's old-fashioned, so I learned the business but I learned payroll in HR, monthly accounts in financial, ambient supply chain in logistics, and maintenance in the fleet.~~

So, you see, I didn't go looking for trouble; I stumbled over it like an extra stair in the dark. Only that's the wrong way to say it. I'm sorry. I didn't mean to make your heartbreak sound like something that happened to *me*. And it wasn't trouble. It was evil. It wasn't a surprise either. ~~It was more like finding out that something you always thought was a fairytale, something to scare children giggly round a campfire on a dark night, was real and was never going to stop unless you, worker bee, no way a hero, stopped it.~~

I'm sorry. That's more like it but still not right. ~~I knew vampires, werewolves, trolls under the bridge and poisoned apples weren't real. If I suddenly met them all one dark night, blundering into their private party, I'd still have known they weren't real. I'd have known I was ill. I'd have gone to a doctor and got myself a nice wee prescription and a note for a couple of weeks off work.~~

I knew it was real. I knew things like that could happen. I just didn't know it was close. Maybe it was the same for you. I watched the news, sometimes. I heard it often enough anyway, when I was driving. ~~And I heard your tearful pleas. Maybe not yours literally (or maybe I did) but parents like you, siblings, repeating a name, begging anyone who was listening to help.~~ I'm sorry I didn't pay attention until it was too late.

Because I'm still not being honest. I'm so sorry. It wasn't a coincidence. It was more than "close to me". ~~But if my dad hadn't got a stomach bug last spring,~~

From: Tash Dodd <TDodd4reals@gomail.com>
To: E.S. Norman <DrENorman@nhslothian.scot.nhs.uk>
Doc N – this is pointless. I don't know what to say to them. I don't even know who I'm writing to. Every time I get going I end up talking about me, me, me and I have to cross it out. Thanks for the suggestion but seriously look at what I wrote! I can't send that. Sorry.
Thanks anyway.
See you next week.
Tash. xxx

From: E.S. Norman <DrENorman@nhslothian.scot.nhs.uk>
To: Tash Dodd <TDodd4reals@gomail.com>
Tash, you misunderstood me. That's on me – last session was very hard for you. I didn't mean for you to send a letter. I still think it would help you to write it though. Please write it down. Write it out of you.
See you Thursday,
Ellie Norman

Dear ———
I am writing to say I'm sorry I was too late.
Tash Dodd.

From: Tash Dodd <TDodd4reals@gomail.com>
To: E.S. Norman <DrENorman@nhslothian.scot.
nhs.uk>
Dear Doc N,
That's what I managed to come up with after I fired
off that last email to you and started again. Better,
but still hopeless. I get it now. You want me to write
what happened? OK.
See you Thur,
T xxx

ONE

'm not cut out to be a hero. I'm a worker bee. Even though I'm the boss's daughter I was never one of the bosses. Not really. My dad's old-fashioned, so I learned the business but I learned payroll in HR, monthly accounts in financial, ambient supply chain in logistics, and maintenance in the fleet. Hiring and firing, nursing the big corporate accounts, wrangling chilled chains and screwing bargains out of dealers? Big Garry Dodd, the BG of BG Solutions, BG Connections and BG Europe, while it lasted, did all of that.

The name makes him sound worse than he is, or was, or seemed anyway. But what else would he have called his 'company' back when it was one van with a hand-painted logo on both sides and a stack of business cards from a machine at the service station? BG was what he'd scratched into the teak veneer of his desk at school when he was bored, and what he'd scratched into the clouded plastic of the fag machine at the Coach when he was waiting outside the girls' bogs for Little Lynne to stop moaning about him to her friends and come back out again. It was BG who loved LM in the tattoo he got when they broke up, to show her and win her back, and it was BG he'd tried to get her to have tattooed on her bikini line when they went on their engagement trip to Tene.

'Jesus, Mum!' I remember saying, the first time I heard this. I left the table and stamped upstairs to my room. 'Nice story to tell the kids!'

My mum just smiled and went back to pecking at her calculator. She took care of the money – every penny, from investing the pension fund to setting the Christmas bonus for the jannies – and she took good care of Big Garry too. Never nagged him, never laughed at him. The perfect wife. Too perfect, if you ask me. I'd hear them in the afternoons, crooning away in the master suite across the landing and then I'd stamp *down*stairs. One time, I passed Bazz on the way.

'Doesn't that bother you?' I said.

'What does?' Bazz said.

'That's not even the right way to turn it into a ques— Never mind. Jesus!' Bazz just looked at me out of red eyes and shrugged. I grabbed my car keys and left the house, aimlessly driving until I was sure they would be finished, showered and up again and Bazz would be out on whatever thrilling stoner night he had planned. He *was* one of the bosses. His childhood in video games and adolescence on the dark web had turned him into a tech wizard. But he was usually off his tree, not fit to be in charge of a Ms Pacman. So his official title was 'outreach and PR manager' and God knows what he actually did to earn it, except that he was in the *Herald* most weeks, handing over a giant cardboard cheque to someone and grinning.

Anyway that's who we were. Four Dodds – Big Garry the boss, Little Lynne with the pound signs in her eyes, Bazz the wasted hacker, and me. The worker bee, best behind the wheel of a van out on the road, or a forklift in the warehouse, back straight and buds in, grafting at what Big Garry called 'the coal face' for every day, 'the family empire' when he was trying to hide his pride under a joke, and 'the reason I missed your childhood' when he was at the teary stage of hammered. End of a wedding, kind of thing, Christmas night with his fifth brandy, last dinner of a holiday, over the grappa.

It used to make me angry, make me think why *shouldn't* he be proud, why should he be guilty about the life he made for us? He'd come from nothing, although my granny hated hearing *her* life summed up that way. A council house in Grangemouth though, skiving in the back row right through school, flirting with a bit of trouble when he was bored, till his mum took her hand to him and skelped the sense back in. And so maybe my granny was right; he'd started with *that*.

The council house was long gone but he was still in Grangemouth. 'Makes sense, Lynne,' he used to say. 'Nice and central. Halfway to Edinburgh, halfway to Glasgow, handy for everything.' 'Handy for the refinery,' she'd say. 'Nice view of the Young Offenders.' This was when my mum was going through her property phase, egged on by the telly. She spent a good couple of years leaving schedules for estates in

Perthshire and mock castles by the sea lying around. He built her a house on an acre plot with a kitchen island and two sinks in their en suite, and she stopped moaning.

Maybe that was what she wanted all along. I didn't have a very clear view of my family. All I saw was Lynne being greedy, Big Garry being successful, Bazz being as jammy as get out, and me? I was lucky. Ordinary and lucky and just sort of fine, the way lots of people can only dream of being. The way – it turned out – that I was only dreaming of being too.

A late outbreak of stomach bugs in the middle of May had brought the warehouse to its knees. And the logistics contractor up in Dundee was going to have to recreate an entire set of forecasts because Big Garry had gone meddling in an online projection he didn't have the competence for and wrecked everything. So, while he was at home, propped up in bed sipping flat Coke, and his assistant was staying away in case she caught it too – she'd mumbled something about a suppressed immune system, no details, and I couldn't be bothered arguing – I was alone in his office on a Saturday morning. The mess on Big Garry's desk was legendary, but if I knew my dad he'd have printed out that forecast beforehand. The print-out was sure to be somewhere deep in this mulch of paper, and I was determined to find it.

I started by sorting into piles by broadest category, but no matter how I cut it there was a growing heap of paper I couldn't put anywhere. There were figures and numbers and jotted notes. I couldn't work out whether the figures were weights or prices, whether the long numbers were for international dialling or invoice tracking, and the notes might as well have been Greek.

'*Dad!*' I muttered to myself. 'All this *paper!*' I heard his voice in my head and smiled in spite of myself. 'Paper and ink, Tash. That's the way.' It was one of his favourites, along with 'Belt, braces and glue.' Because belt and braces between them still left too much to chance.

He'd listened to people selling the paperless office, back in the day, but a desktop computer with outsize monitor, keyboard stored on a little tray that slid out – occasionally – from underneath, hadn't helped, on account of the printer that came with the rest. The photocopier *definitely* hadn't helped. It was right here in his private office and he used it every day. So the paper mountain grew and grew and grew.

I knew there were probably sandwich plates and coffee cups living underneath it, so when a muffled phone rang it was no kind of shocker. This wasn't the confident bell of Big Garry's mobile. He had that at home with him, charging up on his bedside table. It wasn't the discreet beep and flash of his internal landline either. And it wasn't an outside call because he didn't get them; they went through the outer office to save him being hassled.

I started hunting but hadn't found the handset before the ringing stopped. Maybe it wasn't a phone at all. Had my dad finally got himself a step-counter? Was that his alarm going off to tell him to stand up and stretch? I grinned at the thought and laid another piece of paper on the miscellaneous pile. The ringing started again. And it *wasn't* a step-counter. It was definitely a phone: a second phone – that marriage ender, that respect shredder – and it was somewhere in this jumble of paper on my dad's desk. I could feel it thrumming as well as hear it ring.

Who knows what induced me to do what I did next? Maybe it was the timbre of the vibration, too deep and solid for the sound a little burner would make if it was sitting on a desktop shifting as it rattled. I wheeled the chair back, bending to look underneath. And there it was, in a nifty little pocket made out of gaffer tape. Without thinking, I plucked it out and flipped it open.

'Garry?' came a voice, as I was saying hello. 'Oh, Lynne,' it went on. 'Good enough. Where's the big man? No matter. Tell him I owe him a bottle of forty-year-old single malt and a round at St Andrews. Talk about getting out in the nick of time.'

'Wh—'

'Never mind asking why!'

'I never asked why,' I said. Was I hoping whoever it was would realize he wasn't speaking to my mum? Maybe. But he only laughed.

'Good girl.'

'Who is this?'

He cackled, making the cheap phone buzz. 'That's it, Lynne-dee-hop! Exactly. "Never met you in my life." "Name doesn't ring a bell." That's the idea.' He paused and blew out a huge breath. 'I'm man enough to admit when I'm wrong. I thought Big G was crapping out early but if we'd been in the game when this broke? A fucking *lorry*! A *lorry*-load of them!'

'What lorry?' I said. If this was a business matter, I should know about it. 'Lorry-load of wh—'

'Just turn on the ten o'clock news tonight and you'll see.'

The line went dead.

The guy had said 'lorry-load' like it was a big fat deal. One lorry. A burner phone taped under a desk for one lorry? It was hard not to think he was kidding. But still, I opened the call history, deleted the record of the conversation and put the phone back in its little black tape nest, wiping my fingerprints off it as I did, feeling stupid to be so melodramatic, but not quite stupid enough to stop. Because if I was being honest, there were lots of things that were no kidding matter, even in single lorry-loads. Drugs, guns, the stuff for making bombs. I didn't believe it yet, but I wiped my prints anyway.

I left the office then, walking away from my five piles of sorted paperwork, and checked in at the loading dock. Egger, the warehouse foreman, was stressed by the number of men off sick but he was fine himself.

'Lump of granite I am, Tashie,' he said. 'I never ail a day.'

'Lucky,' I said.

'Ach, it's easy if you're not the one wiping bums and noses,' he said. 'My wife goes down like a skittle whenever one of the weans brings something home. No luck about it really.'

A nice man, I thought. I always had. I'd always thought the same of Big Garry. Or close anyway. Not 'nice'. But good. Straight. An open book. Not many words on the pages but an open book. I hadn't *really* believed it was a cheater's phone or I wouldn't have answered it. Was it drugs?

When I got back to the house, my mum was on her knees in the kitchen raking through the deep bottom drawer of the freezer.

'You're early,' she said, twisting round. 'Don't tell me *you're* feeling rough.'

'I'm fine. How's Dad?'

My mum sat back on her heels and huffed out a laugh. She was wearing stretch trousers with net sections in them, and she sat comfortably on her folded legs, her posture perfect, the picture of the sweet life that comes when a well-to-do man loves you. Big Garry and Little Lynne had come a long way from that hand-painted sign on a single van, Bazz and me on bunk beds in a box room, all set with our aspirational names: Sebastian and Natasha. They'd arrived at a liveried fleet, giant cardboard cheques and this kitchen floor she was kneeling on in her black leggings, spotless because someone else swept and mopped it twice a week. It had been her one condition when he talked her into the flow-through family kitchen dining entertaining space. She'd muttered about the Sopranos and insisted someone else clean it.

'He's fine too,' she said. 'Right on the border between taking it easy and milking it, if you ask me. He's said he could "probably manage" some fish tonight, and a rom-com.' My mum bent over the drawer again. 'I've got some of that prawns with ginger and spring onion in here somewhere.'

'Prawns? Really?'

'I'm not poaching white fish in milk for a man with a packet of Hobnobs hidden under the covers. I'm not his bloody mother.'

'He's never!' I said. 'He's chancing it, isn't he? State he was in this time yesterday.'

'The one good thing about a stomach bug, to my mind, is it gets you off to a roaring start for a new diet.' My mum had a habit of lifting her top and grabbing a roll of flesh above her waistband, tugging at it. She did it now.

'Mum!' I had always hated the sight, her fingers pinched white as she pulled at her own flesh, the raw dough look of the stretched skin.

'You empty out at both ends then you're off your feed for days after. He's wasting a gift. Tell him from me if you're going up.'

'I'll take him a cuppa. Check for chocolate round his mouth.'

My mum winked and turned back to the freezer drawer. I heard the voice again. *You're a good girl.* Then I filled the kettle and put bags in two mugs, one for my dad and one for me. I'd hang out with him for a bit. He must be getting lonely. Was it guns?

He was definitely better. He had sheets of the newspaper strewn all over his bedcovers and the remote in his hand, his glasses shoved up his head to let him focus on it. The French doors were thrown open to the Juliet balcony and the back windows were open too, so the air had freshened and it no longer smelled like a sickroom.

'Thank God!' Big Garry said, not quite his usual bellow but far from feeble. 'I haven't seen that besom since she cleared my dinner tray. She's keeping out the road in case she catches it.'

'I don't blame her,' I said.

'She slept downstairs last night.'

'I don't blame her!'

Big Garry patted the bed beside him but I snorted, handed over his tea mug and retreated to the rocking chair. My mum had breastfed me and Bazz in this chair – 'Best way to get your waistline back even if it kills your boobs' – and there it still was in their bedroom.

'Egger's on his feet and taking care of everything,' I said. 'He's a nice man, isn't he?'

Big Garry shrugged. 'He's a good worker. Never gave me a minute's worry so far.'

'No sign of Her Ladyship in the outer office.'

'Now, now.'

I took a sip of tea and used the pause to look at my dad over the edge of the cup. I wished it *was* a bit of a flutter with another woman, even the missing assistant. He would blow it soon enough, then my mum would sack the bitch, tear a strip off him, get some new jewellery and settle down again. At least, that's what I suspected. Who knew, really, about the inside of someone else's marriage, even a marriage that had made you.

'Anything else?' he was asking me.

I took a moment as if I was thinking – was it bombs? – then

shook my head. 'Nope. Ticking over. The contractor's pretty pissed off with you for wrecking the projection output.'

'I'll cope,' my dad said. 'He'll have to.'

'You shouldn't go digging around,' I said. 'Or if you want to, you should get yourself on a course and learn to do it without making a hash.' I knew there was no chance of it. He would never think it worth the effort.

'Paper and ink, Tash,' he said, like clockwork.

'But if you'd *stick* to paper then,' I pointed out. 'Instead of meddling online as well as killing the world's forests to keep up with your printing out.'

'He should never have had just the one copy. You'd never catch me with one copy of something that mattered. Belt, braces and glue, Tash.'

'It wasn't a document you screwed up. It was a—'

'Belt, braces and glue. Anyway, he's getting paid for redoing it.'

Irritation distracts you. I was bugged by my dad still not understanding what he'd stuck his spanner in and why it wasn't the consultant's fault. And I was worried about the call too. Only later would I remember that he wasn't beating himself up about having to pay for the same logistics twice. I asked myself when that had started. Back in the days when I was wee – waiting in reception with my colouring book instead of in the after-school club, or later – waiting for a free driving lesson instead of buying ten from a proper driving school – Big Garry watched every penny. He was already prosperous by then, but he was still careful. Somewhere along the line to the flow-through entertainment space he got lazy about money, careless about wasting it, almost as if he knew he had too much of it and regretted that, wished some of it would go away. But a whiff of guilt didn't square with a few other things he'd always said, about honest reward for honest toil, about there being no shame in enjoying what you'd come by fairly, about never stopping anyone else from climbing the ladder alongside him, so he wasn't going to feel bad about how high he'd reached.

I ate my ginger prawns across the breakfast bar from my mum, sharing a bottle of white wine while we had the chance.

Big Garry could be a bit of a face-ache about midweek
drinking.

'You sure you're OK?' she asked at one point. 'You're
quiet.'

'Fine. Just thinking.' Drugs, guns, bombs.

'You don't want to be doing that,' she said, as I knew she
would. She always did. It was part of what made living at
home so comfortable and so infuriating.

'I'll clear up,' I said when we were finished.

'Three plates and a wipe round the microwave!'

'It's the least I can do,' I said. 'Literally.'

Even such a tiny attempt at a joke reassured her. She wrinkled her nose at me and disappeared into what they called 'the
messy room' to watch the kind of junk television she'd never
get away with when Big Garry was on his feet and in charge.

At five to ten, I went upstairs. I never watched the news
normally and didn't want to raise suspicions. There was
national politics, international politics, and some scandal
about corruption. I didn't see how any of that could relate
to my dad and a phone taped under a desk. My mind was
drifting when I caught '. . . have uncovered what appears to
be part of an operation stretching overland from eastern
Europe and the Near East all the way to the French ports
and into Britain . . .'

I heard my parents' bedroom door banging open and my
dad's voice shouting down the stairs. 'Lynne! Lynne, get up
here.'

'. . . although the UK collaborators in what police are
describing as the most ambitious single attempt ever discovered
have thus far evaded detection.'

Of course, I thought. Of course. Not drugs or guns or bombs.
People. I turned the volume down in case he could hear it
through the walls and gave my attention back to the
newsreader.

Now he was saying: 'Seventeen of the forty individuals are
being cared for in hospitals in Calais while French
officials—'

And just like that my life was over. Oh, I kept breathing in
and out, and I kept eating, burning calories, eliminating waste.

I kept sleeping and waking. But my life as the lucky daughter of a good man and his loving wife, heir to his solid business, resident of his comfortable house . . . all of that was done. No more worker bee. Hero or villain now. Black hat or white hat. I didn't think my life was going to have decisions like that in it. Probably no one does, eh?

TWO

Ivy had waited outside as long as she could, standing in the plume of light from the open door, looking up and down the street through the fog of her own breath, glancing at the sparkle of frost around her feet whenever a car passed her. She remembered Mother whispering, always in the larder cupboard, as if she waited for Ivy there.

'Don't look into passing cars, if you're stood on the pavement ever.'

'Why?' Ivy had stared up into Mother's face.

'Why do you think?' The voice was so sharp it rang, even in here with stacked shelves on three sides, sacks of spuds and onions over half the floor.

At seven years old, Ivy didn't know. She knew now, so she looked down at her feet in their short boots as the cars went by. There was a six-inch gap between her coat hem and boot tops but legs never seemed to register cold. She had her sheepskin mittens on. And at least it was dry. Someone even said that, hurrying past her on the step.

'Brass monkeys! But at least it's dry.'

Ivy still hadn't managed to find an answer by the time the woman had thrown open the door and disappeared inside. 'Brass monkeys' was an expression she always wondered about. There was nothing obviously coarse in it, but the sort of people who used it and the sort of chuckle they got when they did made her doubt. That woman, in her body-warmer, parking her little car in such a neat twist of reversing, locking it with such a jarring toot, breezing past Ivy with a casual word, she was just the sort of person to use vulgar slang to a perfect stranger.

Unless . . .?

Ivy turned and looked in through the half-window. Unless . . . She peered past tattered notices and bits of leftover tape, just in time to see the tail of the body-warmer whisk out of sight.

Unless that was Myra? But they had agreed that whoever got there first would wait outside. 'Hook up at the door' Myra had written in her email. And now Ivy was sure. Because when she'd read that, she felt her mouth purse in that way Mother's used to, that way she'd found her own begin to as the years rolled by. Years of uncouth boys on the late bus, sniggering girls passing in the street, nasty jokes in every sit-com and innuendo everywhere. Even on the news these days. Of course a woman – she'd laugh to be called a lady, her with her little car and her body-warmer – who said 'hook up' would say 'brass monkeys' too. But if that was Myra why had she walked past? Ivy could feel the tightening at the back of her throat that meant tears were coming. She heard Mother's voice again, not a whisper this time and not behind the larder cupboard door. She'd sing this out across a room. 'Someone ring the plumber! The tap's dripping.' Little Ivy would swallow the tears and smile, or run away and hide if she couldn't help them spilling.

She wanted to run away now. She should have known better than to try to change her life. For a while there it had seemed easy. She wanted a friend and she wanted a cat. She knew how to get a cat – you go to a pet shop – but how did a woman in her fifties who lived alone and worked at home get a friend? 'Join a club' was the answer she kept reading. But she didn't want to learn salsa or slog up and down hills in the rain. When the solution arrived in her mind she laughed out loud. And her first few days as a member of I Heart Cats and Cats, Cats, Cats online were the happiest she could remember. It was only very slowly that she realized her new friends were all in Texas or Adelaide. She was down to checking once a day when she met Myra. Right here in Scotland and inviting Ivy to meet tonight, at this very gathering.

'I don't go out much at night in the winter,' she had told Myra, in the chat column.

'Oh, I know!' Myra typed back. 'You always think after Christmas, spring's round the corner. February gets you every time, eh?'

So Ivy had agreed to wrap up and venture out to meet, 'irl', as Myra said. And now, after she'd been stood here for – she struggled at one cuff with the other mitten until she uncovered her watch – twenty-five minutes, her so-called new friend had walked right by. Of course, the twenty-five minutes wasn't Myra's fault, strictly. Ivy liked to be punctual and, with the buses the way they were, that meant early. It was just gone half past now.

On that thought, the tears dried up. Of course Myra went rushing by and straight inside. She didn't want to be late. She'd assume Ivy was inside too by now. She'd never think Ivy would stand here like a lummox while the clock ran down, would she? Myra would be thinking this stupid woman standing on the step was here for something else: waiting for a lift, or on her way to an eight o'clock start.

Ivy wrestled the swing door open – these mittens made her hands next to useless – and trotted, almost sprinted, down the corridor the way Myra had gone, the thick soles of her short boots squeaking on the tiles.

She burst into the room, already apologizing.

'—sorry I'm so late. I was waiting outside and I never noticed the ti—'

But for once she had caught a bit of luck. She *wasn't* late, because it wasn't that sort of do. The meeting room was laid out in rows, with a flyer on every seat and a podium at the front, but the women were hugger-mugger at a table on the far side, inspecting something – was it cats? – and helping themselves to coffee from a sloping cardboard can the like of which Ivy had never seen.

Myra, if it was Myra, was deep in the huddle – it was gift baskets they were looking at – and Ivy's luck had run out. She couldn't get near her. When they all had their coffees and buns and were drifting towards the seats for the presentation, she was trapped behind three huge women – immense they were – swapping phones and scrolling through pictures, and when she turned to go the other way she found the row of chairs behind her was full, everyone's bags on the floor. She'd have to clamber to get out, so she sat, sweltering in her big coat, with no cup of petrol-can coffee, never mind a bun, and she couldn't even see Myra now.

She didn't like to keep searching; there was a very odd little woman sitting a few rows back whose eyes were fixed on Ivy

every time she caught them. So she sat forward, tears close
again. She'd look a fool if she stood up so soon after sitting
down. But she'd never get her coat off struggling with it in
her seat, and she'd catch her death later if she went back out
with none of the benefit, not to mention she could already feel
a sheen on her lip from the heat.

A short, square woman with a no-nonsense haircut was
climbing the podium and it was too late to do anything, because
the meeting had begun.

'Welcome to the first Grampian Nine Lives League meeting
of a brand-new fund-raising, cat-defending year,' she said, to
a ripple of not quite excitement but definitely enthusiasm
'We've got the worst of the winter by, although you wouldn't
think so tonight!' There were a fair few scattered titters. This,
Ivy thought, was an easy crowd. 'We're delighted to see so
many new faces. Angie's going to go round with membership
forms while I'm doing my little bit of housekeeping. So if
you're new, just put up a paw – claws in, please – and we'll
furnish you.'

Ivy put both hands in her coat pockets and slid down in her
chair. The words of the squat woman washed over her. It was
so warm in here, typical community hall. They used to be
chilly and dank, but you'd never get away with it now, with
Health and Safety. Now, a heating system pumped hot water
through under the floor – Ivy could feel the warmth stealing
up through the thick soles of her boots – and she wasn't the
only one growing drowsy as the dry voice wore on, talking
about kitten fostering now.

She couldn't foster kittens. She'd never want to give them
back. But she could – she *would* – buy one big comfortable
cat to keep for her very own, even though there were none
here tonight and she felt foolish now for thinking there might
be. She had always wanted one. As a child she had begged
for one. A cat would have spared her. Don't, she told herself.
It's all a long time ago. She shook the thoughts away and
listened. The voice had taken on a new note to go with a
strange phrase.

'What's a "kill shelter"?' Ivy whispered.

'We've got an absolute beginner here, Carole,' Ivy's

neighbour piped up, turning to give Ivy a wide smile. It wasn't a kind smile, she thought to herself. 'What's a kill shelter? For the newbies.'

'At least they don't dress it up,' the squat woman – Carole – said. 'Homeless cats. What we used to call feral. What some people still call *stray*. As if it's a *choice* they've made!' She shook her head at the folly. 'First, they trap them.'

'No!' said Ivy, imagining the snap of a spring and the crunch of bones. Except it would be more than a snap, wouldn't it? In a trap big enough for a cat. It would be like a thunderclap.

The memory surged back and overwhelmed her. When Mother told her that, aged nine, she was old enough to empty the traps now, Ivy couldn't help the tears and couldn't run away in time to hide them. 'Ring the plumber!' Mother said, staring down at her daughter's streaming eyes and wobbling lip. 'What's wrong now?' Ivy, too upset to bide by her usual rules of saying nothing, blurted out, 'Can't we get a mouser? I'd feed it and I'd groom it.'

'Why should we keep a cat when we've got you?'

'But, I can't, Mum. I can't stand the sound of them crying when they're stuck in there. I can't empty them. I can't do it.'

'You little fool,' Mother said. It passed for affection. 'They can't cry with their necks broke. Even *you'd* stop crying if your neck was snapped in two.'

Ivy did stop crying then, the shock of the words working on her like a slap.

Carole had finished speaking.

'So,' Ivy said, 'the humane shelters trap the cats, take them to the vet, knock them out, spay them and then release them again?'

'They do. The cats go back to live out their natural lives.' Carole was beaming.

'And die their natural deaths,' said Ivy.

'Exactly,' said Carole, although her smile dimmed.

'Hit by a car or caught by a fox,' said Ivy. 'Or starving to death in a hedge somewhere, injured.'

Carole opened her mouth but nothing came out. Behind Ivy, muttering had begun and, in front of her, the rows of backs and heads looked wooden. No one turned to see who was speaking.

'So, really,' Ivy said, 'if they're captured and injected – to be spayed – they'd be better off if the anaesthetic wasn't anaesthetic at all. They'd be better off being put to sleep then and there. They'd never have the trauma of coming round in a cage and the pain of the stitches. They'd be free of all cares and their deaths would be . . . what did you say? . . . humane.'

She was thinking aloud more than arguing. She thought aloud a lot. Only this time there were people listening.

'Our name,' said Carole, with a quick glance at the front row and a quick shake of her head. Ivy wondered if someone was taking minutes and had just been told to skip a bit, 'is the Nine Lives League! Not the Quick Death League.'

'But I always thought "nine lives" meant eight near misse—' Ivy got out.

'Were you hoping to join us?' said Carole. 'Or were you actually hoping to adopt a cat of your own? Because we can't be too fussy about membership fees but, I can assure you, we're very selective about who we let enter into the adoption process.'

'Neither,' Ivy said. 'I just came to meet a friend.'

'Oh?' Carole lifted her head and scanned the seats, all the women silent again now. 'Well, either your friend hasn't turned up or else she's decided not to claim you.'

The silence lengthened. Then someone towards the back said: 'I wouldn't, if it was me.'

Ivy stood up, swaying a little. 'Sorry,' she said, shuffling along the row. 'Sorry. Excuse me.' She couldn't see Myra anywhere, just row after row of blank eyes, and that one avid pair: that same little woman, still staring.

She was out in the cold hallway when she realized she was being followed. She felt a hand on her arm and turned to see her, tiny beside Ivy, as slight as a bird, with pale soft skin and dry lips. The lips were parted and her breath came quick and harsh, just like a scared bird when it gives up and waits to die, its heart fluttering.

'Who *are* you?' she said, breathy little sounds.

'Myra?' said Ivy, relief and anger mingled. 'Why did you just sit and stare? Why didn't you wave or come over?'

'Who's Myra?' the woman asked. Ivy opened her mouth, to try to explain. 'And who are *you*?'

'What do you mean?'

The woman's hand fell away from where it had been clutching Ivy's sleeve. 'It's all right,' she said. 'You don't need to answer. I know who you are. I'm looking right at you.' She took a staggering step to one side.

'Are you all right?' Ivy looked around urgently for someone to come and help. She was no good with ill people, or upset people, and this little woman was as white as milk, smudges jumping out under her eyes as her cheeks drained and she sank down on to a bench underneath a row of old-fashioned coat pegs.

'How old are you?' she asked Ivy. 'Sorry to be so blunt, but how old are you?'

'Why?' said Ivy, sitting beside her.

'I'm fifty-four,' the woman said.

Ivy nodded. 'So am I.'

'I was born on the twenty-ninth of October.'

Ivy felt her eyes open wide. 'Me too.'

'At the cottage hospital in Fraserburgh,' the woman said. 'The midwife unit, they call it now.' She was talking very fast, as if to get the words out before they burned her mouth. 'I'm a twin. Not identical. Obviously. Not that we ever had a test. Obviously.'

'Obviously?' Ivy said. Still there was no one else in the cold hallway who could help, and a stranger making no sense was just as bad as them being ill. Ivy couldn't cope with that sort of thing.

'My sister doesn't look anything like me,' the woman was saying.

'Oh?' said Ivy. Why did no one come? This peculiar little woman was going to faint. No one could be that colour all the time.

'No,' she said. 'But she's the absolute dead spit of you.'

THREE

Ivy didn't go to pubs, except maybe for lunch once a flood, and certainly not a pub like this one, with men three deep at the bar and a snooker table in the back room, but when the woman, still pale and trembling, had steered her towards it, Ivy had followed. They couldn't sit forever under the coat pegs and they couldn't stand outside. The wind had picked up and it drilled through Ivy's thick coat. A pub would be better than freezing to death.

'My name's Kate,' the woman said, once they were seated. 'My sister's Gail.'

'Ivy.' She paused a moment. 'Is this real? It seems too . . .'

'It is!' Kate said. 'Far "too"! I'm not even a member of this branch! I don't even live here! It's just that I'm up visiting my aunty and she's driving me nuts. I needed to get out for a bit and saw the poster. I don't even *live* here.'

'I'm not a member either,' Ivy said. 'Of any branch at all. I was supposed to be meeting my friend but she never turned up.' She had caught Kate's excitement and she decided to join in with her exclamations, even though they were unlike her. 'I nearly didn't come in!' she said. 'I nearly went home before it started!' Then she stared Kate for a moment. 'Are you sure?'

'Sure?' Kate reached across the corner of the table – they were in a booth, on a cracked green leather-effect banquette – 'Ivy, you are my sister's double. You are my sister's twin.' She stared until her eyes dried and she had to blink them. 'I'll get us both a drink and then— Look, take my phone.' She slapped it down on the table, solid and shiny in its case, nothing like Ivy's scratched screen and finger marks. 'Scroll through my photos while I'm getting a glass of what? White? Red? Or brandy? I might need a brandy.'

'I can't go snooping through your phone!' Ivy said to the narrow back as Kate made her way through the three-deep fringe of men and put her elbows on the bar. She's done that before, Ivy thought. She stared at the little legs above the high heels, the smart hem of the narrow skirt. Were those Mother's delicate ankles she was looking at? Mother had always been proud of her legs, always wore tights and a skirt and had a little heel to her shoes even for every day. Even for home. Ivy had always believed her broad calves and splayed feet came from her father but now . . . Well, maybe they did.

Kate was coming back. 'Did you see?' she said, sliding a glass towards Ivy. 'Oh. You didn't look? Here, let me.' She took a sip of brandy. Ivy thought it must be brandy. It was too dark for whisky and the wrong glass for sherry. She brought her own glass to her lips, tilted it and let in a silken tongue of liquid, cold round the edges but fiery as it spread across the back of her throat. Kate was scrolling so fast through her photographs that the pictures themselves were no more than a blur. 'I'm bound to have a good one of her somewhere,' she said. 'Last summer we went on one of those— Or you know what? Why don't we phone her? Why don't we FaceTime with her? Right now! What am I like, looking for old photos!'

'Do you think?' said Ivy. 'Should you spring it on her?'

'I can't keep it to myself!' Kate had hit speed-dial and Ivy could hear the notes of the saved number and then the trill of the other phone. Kate flashed her eyes and smiled, managing a second sip of her brandy while she turned the phone to speaker and slid up beside Ivy to share the view of the screen. Ivy could feel her heart start to pick up like when crowds of boys got on the bus and sat near her, or when someone had too many items in the express lane and she had to tell them. Only this was bigger.

'A twin,' she said. 'I've been an only child my whole life. I've been so alone. That's why I started thinking about a pet. That's how I met Myra. Online. She was thinking of getting one too. I thought they'd have them there tonight, to choose from.'

'You'll have to settle for a sister,' Kate said. 'A sister!' Then she took a breath so sharp it was almost a gasp and put the phone down, throwing it away from herself. It skidded a few inches across the polished top of the pub table before the bumper stopped it. It kept vibrating along with the ringtone.

Ivy dragged her eyes away from it at last and towards Kate's face. Her pale top lip was trembling and when she lifted her glass it made a hard clink as it hit her teeth.

'Are you all right?' Ivy said. She took the glass – tipped so far there was a danger of it spilling – out of Kate's hand and set it down. 'What's wrong?'

'Stupid,' Kate breathed. 'I was so excited to see you. My twin's twin. My sister's sister. I'm so *stupid*.'

'Don't say that.' Ivy took her hand and held it in both of her own, engulfing it. 'What's wrong?'

'Well, we're not *triplets*, are we?' Kate said.

The game of snooker had ended, with the sharp crack of cue ball against black and a bray of triumph and scorn from the men watching. Ivy wished they were anywhere but here. Maybe if they were somewhere nice, with a pot of tea, or even a wine bar and soft music playing, she'd be able to think of what to say. But this rough, beer-steeped cave unsettled her.

'You are my twin's twin and I'm not,' Kate said. Her words came out clipped and bitter and for one wild moment Ivy thought of Mother again, a harsh laugh and that edge of triumph always in her. 'You're my sister's sister,' Kate was saying, 'And I'm no one.'

For a beat, for a breath, for a blink, Ivy felt a surge inside. It was power and she could wield it. She could find that edge for herself and drape a sweetness over it that left just a glint out in the open. Then she took another breath and it was gone. She squeezed Kate's little hand tighter. 'That's not true. Of course you're your sister's sister. You've been with her your whole life. Did you share a room? Did you have a twin pram? Nothing can take that away.'

'Thank you,' Kate said. 'Thank you for saying that, Ivy. You're a very kind person.'

That was when Ivy started to cry. 'I've never—' she said, scrubbing her face with her hanky. 'No one's ever said— You're thanking *me*?'

'Don't do that,' said Kate. 'The skin under your eyes is too thin to be scraping at it like that. Blot. Like this.' She took a cotton hanky out of her own pocket – a cotton hanky, ironed and sweet-smelling, like Ivy's own – and pressed it against

Ivy's closed eyes, as if it was a blessing. 'Gail's just the same. She shows it under her eyes if she's tired and yet she rub-rub-rubs at them as if they've offended her. All summer long with her hay fever. Do you get hay fever?'

'I do,' Ivy said. 'Do you?' Kate shook her head and Ivy watched the light shining through her cloud of light hair, like thistledown, so different from Ivy's coarse hanks. 'How did it happen?' she said. 'In a cottage hospital, not in a great big place. How could you be mistaken for me? Look at us!'

'But Gail and I were like two peas as newborns,' Kate said. 'We even weighed the same. We both weighed— Well, you *know* what we weighed.'

'Six pounds six,' Ivy said, nodding. Mother used to tell her she'd been a lovely baby – 'very neat and pretty' – and then she'd wonder aloud what had gone wrong.

'Can you roll your tongue?' Kate was saying.

'I can,' said Ivy. She stuck her tongue out, tightly rolled like a new leaf.

'I can't,' said Kate. 'And Gail can. My mum and dad could too. How about yours?'

'Could?' said Ivy. '*Could?*'

Kate put a hand out and clutched Ivy's sleeve. 'I'm sorry!' she said. 'I should have led up to it. They're gone. I'm so sorry.'

I'm not, Ivy thought but managed not to say. Instead she gave a small smile of her own, hoping it looked like Kate's. 'Mine too,' she said. 'My father years back and Mother last Christmas. I'm sorry.'

'I'm not,' Kate said. Then she put both hands over her mouth and let her eyes drop wide above them. 'I don't mean that how it sounds,' she added, when she took her hands away again. 'I mean . . . there would have been such . . . parents – mothers anyway – are more . . . I think it would have been . . . Oh, I can't explain what I'm trying to say! I need to phone Gail. She's the clever one. Are *you* clever, Ivy?'

'But I know *exactly* what you're trying to say.' Ivy ignored the question. 'You've got your mother and that's that. Another one's just going to make hurt feelings all round.' Kate was nodding, drinking it in, so Ivy felt bold enough to keep talking.

'A sister's different. You can have as many sisters as there are beds in your house and you can just love all of them the same.' Kate beamed. She didn't seem to have noticed that word, like a bombshell, that Ivy had said without thinking. A word not used in their house, except for malt loaf and some quiz programmes that were not to be interrupted.

'Where do you live?' Ivy asked hurriedly anyway.

'Hephaw,' said Kate. 'Down in West Lothian. We've lived there since we were tiny. Since right after we left here.'

'And do you live close?' Ivy said. Kate frowned and shook her head, not understanding. 'To each other. Oh! Here's me never asked if you're married. Either of you. If there are children.' She felt a little dip in the warm feeling that had bubbled up inside her and was bobbing along under her collarbone, like laughter that might break out, or a burp if she was honest. What if there were husbands? She rubbed Kate's hand in hers again and couldn't feel a ring. Or what if Kate was on her own and Gail had a husband and big children in ripped jeans and trainers like the boys on the bus, and she was too busy to care about Ivy and she talked Kate out of *her* excitement too.

'We live together,' Kate said. 'We always have. We shared a bedroom till we were thirty. We've never married, Gail and me. And we work together; our own little business. And oh! I can't wait to show you the house. It's a fairytale cottage. Our pride and joy. You'll love it too – I know you will. As soon as I've told Gail, as soon as you can swing it, you'll have to come down and stay for the weekend. Or it doesn't have to be the weekend. What about *your* work? There's so much we don't know about you!'

'My own little business,' said Ivy, 'just like you.' It was nearly a lie, now she only had two clients, now that everyone could do their own online. Who needed a bookkeeper these days?

She thought she saw a sharp look in Kate's eyes then. She was probably wondering about money and property. Well, no shame in that for Ivy was thinking exactly the same.

She was still thinking about it lying in her bed that night, close to midnight, looking up at the lamp shadow. *A fairytale cottage.* In Hephaw. She wasn't familiar with the town but she knew the central belt of Scotland didn't get on many calendars. *Can't wait to show you.* It was sweet, how proud Kate seemed to be of the place, despite the location. And, besides, Aberdeenshire wasn't the misty glens either. So Ivy was glad, all in all, that there was one of her and two of them, that it made sense for *her* to travel, for *her* to visit. She wouldn't have wanted to see disappointment in their eyes at the sight of this flat, with the heavy old furniture saved from her parents' place and the cheap new curtains she'd hemmed herself. Hemmed to the sills because the cost of floor-length was a slap when she'd checked.

You could tell a lot from a voice, of course. The almost forgotten Myra with her 'hook up' and that strutting bit with her car keys and her 'brass monkeys' – Ivy thought of both with scorn now. Kate had not a trace of a local accent, none of the sayings or sounds Mother had dinned out of Ivy as a child. *You're not a tattie farmer,* she'd say. *So don't speak like one.* Potato, Ivy would breathe, too quietly for Mother to hear. Hypocrite.

She turned over again, flipping her pillow to the cool side. Kate was a lady. She had the nerve of a lady, not the worries of someone like Ivy, never saying boo. There was that moment as they were leaving the pub. One of the men at the bar had happened to turn and see them sliding out from the banquette. It was nearly closing time and they were probably all half-drunk, getting that way men get. Certainly this one saw the chance of some fun.

'At bloody last!' he said, nudging his friend and jerking his head at the two women. 'You getting a room?'

Ivy said nothing and Kate only frowned.

'Been sitting there holding hands and pinching cheeks for two hours.' Now four or five men had turned and were grinning.

'Get your mind out of the gutter!' Kate said. The size of her, but she spoke up clear and steady. 'This is my sister.'

'You're so . . .' Ivy said, when they were outside. The wind stung, whipping her hair across her hot cheeks.

'Coarse,' said Kate. 'Uncouth. I know.'

'Lovely,' said Ivy. 'Grand.'

Kate's kisses, pecked one on each side as she reached up on her tiptoes, kept tingling all the way home. And, as Ivy washed her face, she smiled again. 'Get your mind out the gutter!' she said to her reflection in the mirror. She would say that, in just that voice, the next time a teenager said a foul thing to her face or behind her back. If there was trouble on the train down to Hephaw, for instance, when she went to meet her twin. Her twin! Or rather, the other triplet, as they'd decided. Her sisters! Her sisters were sitting rows behind her, in a darkened room watching as someone – who *was* that? – on a podium pulled mangled creatures from a trap. They were right there behind her, but she couldn't turn her head, and didn't know why. She scrolled through a phone for pictures and couldn't find any.

Ivy tossed around in her narrow bed, twisting the sheets, and making soft moans in the back of her throat with no one to hear.

FOUR

I was sitting in my van on Fraserburgh High Street, skipping through my music for something I wasn't sick of, checking the time far too often, telling myself it wasn't cold enough to start the engine, even though my hands were wooden and I knew they'd sting later when they warmed through again. I braced my feet as the van rocked in the biting wind. Straight off the North Sea it was. 'Straight from the Baltic' Big Garry always said, no matter how many times I told him to look at a map. I found myself smiling at the memory and then felt a jolt – one that was growing familiar – as reality hit me. He was two people in my mind now: the people smuggler that I was going to bring down; and the man in my memory with his sayings and his ways.

A yawn racked me and, when it passed, left me shivering. 'Oh, give it up, Tash,' I said. I often spoke to myself, usually in just this scornful cajoling tone, undercutting whatever I'd decided, convincing myself I was wrong about some little thing or other. Not the big thing, funnily enough; I was dead sure about that.

I put my foot on the clutch and turned the key, trying not to hear the struggle of the engine coming to life from a cold start. Two women who'd just left the pub together turned round and gave the van a wary look.

My interview was set for midnight and I'd even remembered to pretend to find that strange. 'Don't worry,' the guy had said when I'd queried it, laughing through his nose. 'That's normal in this line of work. The switch from back to night shift's the only dead time in the day. We always do interviews then. 'Sides from owt else, it flushes out the time-wasters, if you get my drift.'

'Right,' I had said. 'Yes, I suppose so. If someone won't stop up till all hours to get the job they won't stop up till all hours to do it.'

'That's about the size of it,' the guy had said, sounding disappointed I'd worked it out and stolen away the chance for him to explain it to me. 'Only it's not a job. You did know that, right? It's a partnership.'

I checked my watch again. If I drove slowly and went through the streets instead of out to the bypass I'd be in nice time. Meaning ten minutes early. Five minutes to brush my hair and gather my nerve, five minutes ahead knocking on the door. Perfect.

I slowed in case the two women wanted to cross the road and get out of the wind, but they were standing in the pool of yellow from the lamppost, hugging each other. They were local, probably, born and bred in this merciless granite town, well used to that freezing gale off the North Sea. They might be daughters of trawlermen, granddaughters of gutting women, totally impervious. Or maybe it was a date and the cold didn't matter. They were dressed too different to be friends on a night out – one as plain as pudding in warm boots and a quilted coat and one in high heels with a sparkly scarf – and they were made too different to be sisters. A blind date, I reckoned. Was a kissless hug a bad end to a blind date or a good sign for the next one? I wouldn't know. I'd never had to go online for a fella or wait for one of my pals to press-gang someone.

Not that I'm pretty. Bazz won that lottery, a perfect mix of Dad's Scottish thing of black hair, black brows, black lashes and pale blue eyes and Mum's English thing of golden skin and rosy cheeks like a peach. Bazz was a blue-eyed peach and everyone he met believed that all the good stuff went deeper than his dimples. I got Big Garry's white skin and solid middle, Little Lynne's sharp nose and cankles. But they'd made me wear braces and do ballet so I had straight teeth and an even straighter back and I knew men looked: I could feel their eyes on me.

There's more humiliating things than being chosen for your looks anyway. My family was known in Grangemouth. Known to have money, that is. And money without class is the perfect mixture to snag the interest of absolutely everyone. At least it struck me that way. The Bo'ness Road poshos had been whisked away to boarding school at twelve, but they came home for Christmas and hung around in their rugby shirts, assuming I'd be grateful for the attention. There was a pool at my house, heated, and a cinema room. Even as they laughed at how naff it was, they made sure to bring a pair of trunks and ask what films were on offer.

The Kerse Road boys – Kerseholes, they called themselves – as down-to-earth as the Dodds and none of the cash? Well, they had a go too. They knew my granny still lived in her four-in-a-block on Wallace Street. They knew Big Garry Dodd had started where they still were and they reckoned sidling up to me was one way to follow him all the way to where he was now.

When I took the Saturday job in the front office – that was my dad over the back; no hand-outs for his girl! – the boys who looked up to him came round like dogs to deer shit, hanging over the desk, even pretending to need packing boxes, pretending they didn't know they weren't free. So the girls who came round were nearly welcome, just as a contrast, even though I knew girls weren't my cup of tea. I didn't understand what vibe I was sending out. Maybe no more than how I treated the boys – poshos and yobbos – with the same disdain and so the girls reckoned they might as well have a go. I'd found friends that way, but no lovers.

I was glad of it now. No strings, no ties. It made it that much easier to do what I was doing. What I was starting to do, with this first step, easing in at Icarus Overland. If I was really going to go through with my plan and not just call the cops on a burner then throw it into the sea. But that would bring down an empire, destroy a life's work, collapse the coalface. I didn't want to do quite as much as that.

I was well out into the suburbs now, the winter night not quite so bitter away from the sea, so my hands were a bit warmer and sat relaxed on the wheel, my foot steady on the pedal. I knew I was a good driver. How could I not be? But it still sometimes unsettled me to realize I had zoned out, following the satnav as if the voice had gone straight from my ears to my hands and missed my brain completely. Paying attention again, I thought suburbs was the wrong word for these streets of light industrial and remnants of retail, just the odd house stranded amongst the plumbing supplies, logistics software, and electronic components. Outskirts, that was the word I was after. BG had been born – the one van and a pre-fab – in the outskirts of Grangemouth, on a patch of weedy tarmac between the bonded store and a timber merchant, and every BG centre was still in the outskirts of somewhere. I was a connoisseur of burger vans and doughnut stands, from the years of working wherever I was needed. I knew which DIY stores sold crisps and Coke at the check-out and which car dealerships couldn't care less who helped themselves to the coffee. I had given up asking my dad to put in snack machines. Costs to the bone, cash in the bank. That was Big Garry's way.

I glimpsed the sign for Icarus Overland: an outsize plastic board hooked on the chain-link at the far end of a cul-de-sac. *Down To Earth Delivery*, it said. Grudgingly, I admitted that was clever and wondered how much they'd had to cough up to a branding firm for it. Then I was swinging in at the open security gate and heading for the boxy little office to one side of the warehouse, swerving the men on the loading dock and the growling, idling vans, their exhausts still belching as they warmed for the night shift. They were half-and-half fleet and privates, thank God. If Icarus was maxed out and already letting drivers use their own vans, they wouldn't blink at me doing the same. And if I used my own van I'd need much less checking.

The office door was glass and a harsh blue light shone out on to the tarmac. I could see someone stand up from behind a desk and come to meet me. Trouble. If he could tell my van wasn't one of the usuals, if he was that sharp, I might have to abandon this attempt and try again. Another name, another phone, another Gmail account. I'd been driving for hours and my shoulders slumped at the thought of it.

But the man I'd seen moving was slouched in the doorway now, with his phone tucked into his neck as he lit a fag with a match he scraped on the harling. He wasn't even looking at me. I had slowed, parked and jumped down before he turned my way. When he did, he gave me no more than a lazy once-over.

I walked right up to the foot of the metal steps and gave him a smile I hoped was bright enough without being a challenge to him.

'I'll have to go, doll,' he said. 'Customer.'

Doll. He was a Glasgow man! I felt my breath pick up and wondered if I should turn and walk before he got a better look at me. I had come all this way up to Fraserburgh to get away from anyone who'd know Big Garry and might, at some function or other, have met me. Glasgow was far too close to home. But I managed to get a decent squint at the guy in the light, while he finished up the goodbyes and stowed his phone back in its holster, and I was pretty sure I'd never seen him before. I tried to slow my breath again. He'd definitely never worked at BG anyway. I knew the face of every guy who'd ever passed through there.

'I'm not,' I said, climbing two of the steps and then sticking my hand out. 'A customer. I'm here for an interview? I spoke to the day-shift manager, I think.'

He lifted one eyebrow and turned his head to the side as if he was running through all the possibilities of a girl working for him. I pretended I hadn't noticed and climbed up another step. 'Nate Dewar.' He rubbed his hand on the bum of his trousers before he shook mine.

'Jamie Morton,' he said. Then: 'Nate?'

'Oh!' I said. 'I never thought. Short for Natalie, not Nathan. You were expecting a man, weren't you?'

'Twenty-first century, sweetheart,' he said, no irony intended, I was sure. 'Come in and let's have a chat. That your van, is it?'

I was cheering inside but I kept my voice calm as I answered. 'Three years old, just passed its first MOT, zero excess, refrigeration unit already installed.'

'Is it now?'

'And I've got the inspection report for it. I've been driving seven years, no points, and I don't drink.'

'No use offering you a wee whisky to keep out the cold then, eh?' The floor of the office bounced as he crossed it and the filing cabinets lined up against the back wall slammed against each other like cymbals. He threw himself into the big

padded chair behind his desk and immediately put both feet
up on top of the paperwork that littered the top. 'Just kidding,'
he said. 'But how about a cup of tea?'

'I'm fine,' I said. 'You go ahead.'

He had a fancy black carry-out cup beside his laptop and
he flipped the stopper and took a swig of it. 'Coffee
and butter,' he said. 'Half a litre a day. I've lost two stone,
carb-free since last Christmas.' Then he did that thing of
nearly crossing his arms but, instead of threading his fingers
through to rest his hand, he kept it behind his other arm to
bunch both sets of biceps forward.

'Good for you,' I said. 'To be honest, that's the only thing
about a driving job – gig – that's putting me off. Trucker's butt.'

His eyes flicked to my hips and back up again.

'Here,' I said. 'Here's my stuff. Application form. DBS
check. That report on the chill unit. I've got plenty experience
for multi-drop but only casual, seasonal.'

'And what's got you interested in medical delivery?' he
said.

'Sick of handing people crap they don't need and know
they shouldn't have bought,' I said. 'I want to do something
worthwhile.'

'And why was it casual seasonal?' he said. 'What were you
doing the rest of the time? Here! You weren't actually *doing*
time, were you?' Then he said 'heh-heh', to show he was
joking.

'College,' I said. 'Bloody waste of money.'

'What did you do?'

'Film.' This was no time for pride. I welcomed the pity,
even the hoot of laughter, since it might get me in the door.

'And you don't mean plastics engineering, I'll bet,' he said.
I had been laughing along with him and my smile didn't dim
but it took more work to keep it on my face as the thought
that he was no fool struck me again. 'But what makes you
want to be a driver at all?' he said, when he'd recovered from
his joke. 'Girl like you, no offence, you could be on a reception desk somewhere. Bringing in punters.'

'Drivers get better money,' I said, then held up my crossed
fingers. 'I hope.'

'They do,' Morton said. 'If they're willing to work hard, and work quick. You decide if it's worth your while to make this profitable. It's completely up to you, though. Lost and late items, if you don't bother to keep up? Well, that's going to cost you. Your choice. But I will say, you're joining a good team. We've got some of the best delivered rates in the whole of the country.'

I left a pause as if I was mulling over his words. 'Do you all know each other then? The different companies.'

He hooked a look as if he didn't understand me.

'Otherwise, how do you know your rates are better?' Morton sliced a glance away to one side. It might have been the side that people looked to when they were lying. But it might just as easily be the side where they searched for genuine information, to retrieve it. I could never remember. 'Or is there a league table?'

'That's it,' Morton said. 'But it's complicated. And confidential. Management-level access only.' He *was* a fool after all, I thought. There was no such thing and if there was it would be public.

I puffed out a sigh and raised my eyebrows. 'Rather you than me, pal,' I said. 'Film diploma, remember?'

He was smiling again. 'Have you got any questions yourself?' he said.

I nodded. It was part of the game to have questions. I knew that from sitting in on interviews at BG. Minimum wage and minimum perks but everyone pretended that the drain clump of beer belly and bad breath trying to snag the job really just wanted flexible hours and the chance to use his own initiative. If any of them had ever asked what the overtime rate was and how the boss felt about hangover sickies, I'd have started him at a premium for honesty.

'I have got a few questions, as it happens,' I said to Morton, and saw him crinkle up his eyes and lift one side of his mouth in something that wasn't quite a smile. He'd be wondering what crap I'd manage to dredge up.

'I know I'd be delivering from the pharmaceutical suppliers—'

'Sometimes Aberdeen RI,' he cut in.

'But I'd be based here, right?'

'Your tracer's based here. You've got your deposit for the tracer with you, I hope? Expensive bit of kit. And you'll be fuelling up here. Yes. Why?'

'Are there showers?' I said. 'Changing facilities?'

'Just lockers,' he said. 'You'll have to stand up with a flannel if you come straight from Zumba.'

I gave him the laugh he was waiting for. 'And the lockers? Are they just for the shift or can I iron a load of polos and leave them there for the week?'

'Your locker's yours for the duration,' Morton said. 'And then some.'

Bingo! My heart leapt but I managed to frown and quirk my head as if I didn't understand.

'Worker privacy laws,' he said. 'Nae such thing as a master key, unless we want our arses sued off us. Over the pond, you know, they spot-test for drugs and booze, spot-search every damn locker whenever they feel like it. Different story here. Folk have retired and left all their clobber, taken the only key with them, and here's me terrified to break the lock and bin it in case heid-the-ba' pops up with an inventory.'

'Bit mad,' I said, cheering inside. The lockers at BG were always stuffed with leftover crap for months while HR made 'all reasonable efforts' to contact the ex-employee and shake the key out of him. I'd counted on it being the same at Icarus. I didn't know what I'd have done otherwise.

'Bit *pointless*,' Morton said, nodding at his laptop. 'That's where everyone keeps their dirt these days. Not wrapped in brown paper.' I glanced at the back of his monitor and hoped my face showed nothing. He cleared his throat and hurried on. 'Any other questions?'

'Is there an iron? A washing machine?' It would do no harm for him to believe it was clothes storage I cared about.

'Oh aye,' he said. 'The washer and dryer are in with the massage chair and the mini-gym.' His smile was broader than ever as, giving his thumb a lick that was just one notch too extravagant, he turned the top page of my application and bent his head to read it.

*   *   *

Ten minutes later, I had myself a contract with the subcontractor to the Grampian Health Trust, doing the kind of specialized work we'd never got into at BG. And, since I wasn't employed, and I'd coughed up a hefty deposit for the tracker logger, not to mention I was using my own van, there was nothing else needed. I patted myself on the back for my choice of company, big enough to go looking for serious sub-work, small enough to be panicking that they'd got it, green enough not to question me too much.

'Just one thing, doll,' he said as we were heading out of the office to take a tour of the warehouse and meet the foreman. 'I'm Mr Morton. Not "pal". OK?'

I flushed but luckily he took it to be embarrassment instead of fury and he swatted me on the behind with my own application in its folder as I passed through the door. I kept walking, teeth clenched and head high. I'd have put up with a lot worse than that to get my feet under the table and that locker filled.

Of course, none of the shirts in any of the BG offices, much less the polos on the warehouse floor and behind the wheel had ever messed with me. They looked. Sometimes they took their sweet creepy time looking and even sucked their teeth too, but they knew if a cardboard file ever hit Tash Dodd on the bum, there'd be a sacking and a punch in the gob to go with it. Nate Dewar wasn't going to be so lucky. 'Eyes on the prize, Tash,' I told myself. 'Eyes on the prize.'

The foreman, an Indian man in his fifties, blinked once or twice when Morton introduced me, but he said nothing.

'Own van?' he said.

'And she's going to be working on the meds,' Morton said. 'Got her DBS check and a refrigeration unit.'

'Good. Saves me a lot of juggling. Is it white, your van? Even better. We've got cling-ons. You'll not mind cling-ons, eh? Decals. Turn *your* wee van into *our* wee van. You don't need to keep it on when you're not logged in. We can't insist on it. But we prefer it, don't we Jamie-boy? Good advertising.'

'I've got a decal on my Beemer,' Morton said. 'Unless Herself's on board. She forgets where the money comes from.'

'Mine won't peg out my work clothes,' said the foreman.

'Puts them in the dryer with a perfume sheet in case the neighbours see. Women. No offence, Natasha.'

'Natalie!' I said, far too loud and far too bothered. Both of them stared at me for a moment, but then both of them concluded I was pissed off at them making their wee jokes about wives. 'Nate, for short. Nate, if you want me to answer.'

'You'll need to get used to a bit of joshing,' said Morton. 'And you'll need to answer to whatever.' The two of them shared another look and I made myself nod and try to look sorry.

'Speaking of which,' said the foreman. 'Come and say hiya to the dregs of the night shift. It's always the same few at the coo's erse.' He was talking louder and louder as he led the way into the bowels of the warehouse, past high cages of discarded packing plastic and towers of pallets ready for return. 'No matter the routes, no matter the loads, these are the boys you'll find having one last wank in the bog before they put the rubber to the road. Aye, I mean you!' This last was in answer to a shout of denial from somewhere deep in the avenues of loaded pallets.

I snorted and fell into step behind him. The crudeness didn't bother me. I'd grown up on porny calendars and page-three girls littering the vans and the loading docks. I'd heard more graphic accounts than that of what the drivers got up to on the lonely road and in the Portakabin toilets before they set out. And anyway, despite everything, the smoky whiff of shredded cardboard from the recycling compactor, the oily perfume of the thick pallet wrap and the nutty smell of bio-degradable packing noodles felt like home.

I was in. They didn't suspect a thing, and all I had to do now was keep my head down and shovel the days past me like a tunnelling mole. I was going to get a month's dedicated experience in a new field – the perfect cover story for what I was up to if anyone from home found me – and I was going to write a statement to leave in a locker:

'Garry Dodd, of BG Solutions, BG Connections and formerly BG Europe is the UK collaborator in the people smuggling operation uncovered at Calais on the fourteenth of June 2017. Attached find—'

Only I didn't know how to describe the papers I was going to stash here: dockets, statements, memos, emails, invoices, delivery notes, drivers' logs, clients' names. It was everything I had managed to copy in the long months of planning between the day of the late stomach bug and the burner phone, and the day, in the pits of a filthy winter, when I walked away. It was every piece of documentation I could lay my hands on, and that meant plenty, what with his commitment to, belief in, paper and ink. I had no idea what mattered and what didn't, because I'm not an accountant – never mind a forensic accountant – but somewhere, I told myself, some time, in some mammoth session of printing or copying he must have produced at least one page that should never have seen the light of day.

Could I have lied? Could I have *pretended* that I'd stashed evidence and then bet on my own bluff? Maybe, but it wasn't worth the risk. Also, I didn't trust myself not to chicken out. Real stuff really stashed was me throwing my cap up and over the wall.

I still thought I was doing the right thing. Atonement, reparation, justice – I had so many names for it. At the same time, I told myself it was a project, a puzzle to be solved, a game to be played and, if I was lucky, won. I didn't think about losing the game or what the forfeit might be.

FIVE

Ivy stepped off the train with bubbles of . . . well, she would have said trepidation if she was being honest, but excitement was a better word. Either way she swallowed hard and drew a deep breath as she made her careful way along the platform to the footbridge. West Lothian, she said to herself, trying to make it sound romantic. Hadn't Walter Scott written about the Lothians? And wasn't there an ancient stone palace in one of the towns? Didn't earls and marquesses live in castles dotted all over the county? Didn't people live in houseboats on the old Union Canal? But nothing she'd seen from the train windows was romantic in the least. She had seen cars, mostly, when the railway track ran alongside the M8, and she'd seen enough industrial storage to last a lifetime, certainly no palatial grandeur and nothing so quaint as a painted houseboat moored by a towpath.

'Alight here for Livingston East,' a voice had said as the train was slowing. Livingston! Mother had had a friend there and her scorn was always bottomless. 'A glorified shopping centre,' she said. 'An overgrown carpark. All roundabouts and carveries. Not a High Street in the place.' Ivy had thought it sounded lovely, mistaking 'carveries' for 'carnivals', because of 'roundabouts' probably. She was sick of Fraserburgh High Street where nothing ever changed. A glorified shopping centre sounded like fun, especially if it had a pictures upstairs, with ten screens and plenty popcorn.

Maybe we could go tonight, she thought, the three of us. Watch a film. Or maybe they would stay in, at the fairytale cottage. She hadn't seen any cottages from the train window either. She'd seen bare fields and waste ground, the backs of factories and a guddle of sheds and shacks that could have been anything. Allotments maybe. Lock-up garages for the people who lived in the high flats? Well, it's never the best of a place that backs on to the railway line, she told herself sternly.

She was determined to have a lovely weekend, now she was finally here; it had taken so much more time than she'd expected to get it organized. Phone calls and texts and an email with an attachment. That was because she didn't understand Kate's instructions.

'Bring your photos,' Kate had said. 'I'm dying to see pictures of the rest of the family and Gail wants to see what you looked like growing up. You know, to compare.'

'I'll have to sort through the box,' Ivy said. 'Most of them aren't in albums, apart from my parents' wedding.'

'I didn't mean hump a load of old snaps!' Kate sounded as if she was laughing, so Ivy said nothing. 'Aren't they on the cloud by now? Scan them in and we can see them when you get here.'

'I wouldn't know where to start,' Ivy said. 'I got myself in a mess trying to install something just last year there and had to pay a fortune in computer repair.'

'OK, well not scanning then. Take a picture with your phone, email them to yourself and then download them into a gallery.'

'I don't use my phone for that sort of thing. I couldn't even follow what the fix-it lady was telling me. I had to give her my passwords and let her take over my account and do it herself!'

'You shouldn't do that, Ivy,' Kate said. 'Are you sure she was trustworthy?'

'Of course! She told me straight out to change all my passwords once she'd finished. She made sure.'

'Yes, but . . . never mind,' Kate said. 'I tell you what: have you got a buggy? A shopping trolley?'

'I've got Mother's old one somewhere.'

'Bring your photos *and* your laptop and I'll scan them in for you while we're going through them. I'll make a montage for you. It can play on a loop.'

'Won't that drain the battery?' Ivy asked but she did what Kate was suggesting, lifting down the familiar boxes, seeing again the familiar moments captured there in black and white, in faded Polaroid, and finally in colour.

She had meant to go through and weed them out a bit. Gail and Kate wouldn't care about her dad's golf pals or her school trips to Balmoral. But, as ever, looking at all those smiling faces, the men in shirts and ties, the women in hats and gloves, made her feel a strange mixture of wistfulness for something she once had and melancholy for something she never would have. She started trying to decide how old Mother was in all of these snaps, gauge where Mother had been in life at fifty-four, the age Ivy was now. She had been married, with a teenaged child, and a car. A whole house, rather than a flat. A crowd of friends who came round in the afternoons to drink tea. A different crowd of friends who came round at night, in couples, to smoke and laugh and drink Gaelic coffee. Ivy could still remember rummaging in the After Eights box, the empty sachets like the gills of a black mushroom, and then her fingers hitting that one remaining chocolate. She would stand amongst the greasy plates and clouded glasses in the kitchen, nibbling it in quick tiny bites like a hamster stuffing its cheeks.

And so, in the end, she ran out of time to sort the pictures and put names on the back. Instead, she just dusted all three boxes and slotted them into the wheeled tartan buggy she used to use for shopping until one day she had seen herself reflected in the scored plastic of a bus shelter and been shaken by the sight of an old woman. She had snatched the hood of her coat down and smoothed her hair and she had tried to stand straighter and look like the girl she still thought she was. Only, that stupid trolley rumbling along behind her made it a futile effort and before she was halfway up her own street she pulled the hood up again, clammy and unpleasant now on top of her wet hair in the drizzle.

So she worried about arriving at Kate and Gail's house with it. It and the boxes of snaps. She wondered if they had theirs in stiff albums with little holders at the corners, like her father's boyhood stamp collection. She had even looked in the back aisle of the ironmonger's to see if there was a wicker trolley with a hooked handle like an old umbrella. She had a feeling, never examined, that wicker trolleys were smarter; that they went with cotton aprons and long wellingtons with straps, instead of the PVC and short red rainboots Ivy wore, like Mother before her.

But then she worried about arriving at the house at all. The fairytale cottage, supposedly, although the address seemed wrong.

'Did you say *1a* Loch Road?' she had asked, her biro poised over the pad ready to write down whatever Kate told her.

'That's right,' Kate had said. 'It's out of the station, down to the main street, turn right and then first left. You shouldn't need to ask anyone. But there's plenty shops to bob into if you do get lost. A bookie and a nail bar that should both be open. And Adim's.'

Ivy had said nothing. She didn't understand why Kate and Gail weren't meeting her off the train. As for the suggestion that she'd go into a bookie's to ask for directions? She'd never been in one in her life. Somehow the thought of the bookie's bled into the idea of the nail bar and made that seem, in Ivy's imagination, just as disreputable, just as much a place she'd stay away from. And Adim's sounded like one of those nasty fly-by-night places one step up from a market stall. She was determined to have nothing to do with any of it.

It was a newsagent's, mind you, she saw as she walked past it minutes later. Small ads in the windows and hoardings propped up against the outside wall. But the pavement near the door was freckled with chewing gum and cigarette ends and Ivy felt her mouth pursing as she moved to the edge of the pavement and trundled her shopping trolley past at a clip.

So this was Loch Road, opening between a shuttered Chinese takeaway and the nail bar Kate had mentioned. Ivy peered up it, telling herself nowhere looked its best in February, then felt her shoulders drop. Detached Edwardian villas. That was perfect. If she had ever thought where she'd like to find a long-lost sister it would be in a quiet street of detached Edwardian stone villas. Here was solidity and respectability but nothing so posh that Ivy would feel unequal to knocking on the front door. She knew this world. She'd had her nose pressed against it since she was a child, going to tennis parties but never with her own racquet, accepting invitations but never repaying them. She set off up the street, telling herself to stop worrying.

She'd been telling herself that all week. Truth be told, all the fuss about the buggy and the boxes, the bookie's and the house number were distractions. What really bothered her was that she had still, in the two weeks it had taken to organize this visit, not spoken to Gail.

'She's thrilled,' Kate said. 'I mean, obviously she was shocked at first. But she's absolutely delighted. She's just shy. She doesn't get about much. She's' – Kate dropped her voice here – 'what people *might* call a recluse. And then there's still grief. It's not so long since our dear father passed. But she's absolutely dying to meet you. Don't worry.'

Ivy was beyond the end of the brick wall that marked the back yards of the main street shops. Now she was walking past a stretch of fancy railings, fleur-de-lis at the top, a yew hedge bulging behind them. Yew, not even plain old privet. And here was the gate, with '1a' in gold on a medallion.

Ivy stared. The house sat well back from the street at the far end of what was more an orchard than a garden. There was a path through the middle, made of very workaday concrete slabs and edged with bricks set diagonally so they stood up like shark teeth. But on either side there were apple trees she could tell were of great antiquity. They were gnarled and bowed, propped up with crutches here and there, looking like hunched-over crones. Like enormous dead spiders, Ivy thought, some of them so misshapen their trunks had split and showed thick orange fungus growing in the scars.

The house itself, beyond the orchard, was just as startling. It was tiny and joined on to the side wall of the house next door. It had one deep bay window with a turret on top, one small bay window, and in between them a double door with black iron hinges and a stone surround. A carriage lamp above was lit and blearing orange out into the dull day. A fairytale cottage, Ivy thought, nodding. It was even in a sort of a forest, nearly.

She looked for a doorbell or knocker. Finding neither, she rapped on the wood and waited, half turned away, half inclined to trot back down the path and catch the next train home.

But when Kate opened the door, she was beaming and she came right out on to the step and hugged Ivy tight.

'You came!'

'Of course, I came. Did you wonder?'

'I'm just being silly,' Kate said. 'Come in. Gail's having a nap but that means you can look around and get settled before you meet her.'

Ivy was already looking around. Inside the front door was a small vestibule and then, through an inner door, a broad, short passageway. The floor was polished stone and the walls were panelled wood to head height, plain plaster above. On the left-hand side a pair of glass doors were lying half open. Ivy left her trolley in the hallway and followed Kate through them. This room was the one with the big bay window. It also had a fireplace with a high marble mantelpiece and a picture painted right on to the wall above, framed with a plaster relief of fruit and ribbons. There was no furniture beyond a piano in the far corner.

'This is the ballroom,' Kate said. 'Isn't it lovely?'

Ivy was noticing the parquet floor under her feet, pungent with the sun beating in the window and drying it, and noticing too the pair of chandeliers over her head, clouded with dust. She nodded.

'And through here is the supper room,' said Kate, throwing back a pair of painted panel doors that disappeared into the wall. More parquet, better preserved on the shady side of the house, as well as another, smaller, marble fireplace and a little more furniture: a long table – or maybe it was a lot of little ones pushed together – but it stretched down the middle of the room with wheel-backed dining chairs neatly tucked under it. At one corner was a silver tray with a bottle of wine and three glasses on it. Ivy knew the bottle had only just been opened because she could hear it fizzing and she thought she could see a vapour rising from its neck. Kate must have popped the cork when she heard the knock at the door.

'Champagne!' Kate said, pouring three glasses. She lifted one and held it out. So Ivy lifted another and clinked. 'Welcome home!' Kate said.

'It's a very unusual house,' Ivy said, when she had taken a drink. She managed not to shudder, but it wasn't very nice wine. It tasted as if it had had an aspirin tablet dissolved in it. Beecham's maybe.

'Through there is the kitchen,' Kate said, pointing. 'Well,

scullery. And across the hallway . . .' She went clip-clopping back through the two rooms, the sound of her high heels ringing out in the emptiness. Ivy thought she could hear the droplets on the chandeliers setting up an answering tinkle as Kate passed underneath. Certainly some of the dust motes came showering down in the disturbance, swirling like snow-flakes or fireflies against the light until they fell below the level of the windowsill and passed into shade again.

'The card room,' said Kate, opening a door at the far side of the vestibule. This room was carpeted in rich red and panelled in wood so dark it was almost black. There were three green baize tables set up with chairs around them and packs of cards and dice laid out as if a party was about to start. Against the back wall, a chaise, made up as a single bed with a white counterpane and a nightdress case on the pillow, lent an odd note.

'I use this room to sleep in,' Kate said. 'And the gentlemen's cloakroom is just behind. It doesn't have a bath, of course, but it has a lavatory and a nice big basin. Lots of hooks for my clothes.'

'I see,' said Ivy, politely.

'Gail has the ladies' withdrawing room,' Kate said, going back out into the hall and opening another door farther along the passageway. 'And the ladies' powder room adjoining.'

'Should we disturb her?' Ivy said. Then: 'Oh, isn't this pretty?'

The ladies' withdrawing room was painted blue and white with a pale carpet and two more chaises, both made up as beds, with pillows in striped cases and wool blankets. One of them was untrammelled but the other one had its covers pushed back as though someone had just climbed out. Ivy could see the neck and stopper of a hot-water bottle amongst the covers.

'Is that . . .?' Ivy said, pointing to the neat chaise. 'That's not . . . for me, is it?' Surely the two sisters, the two *lifelong* sisters, would share this room and she would have the single in the card room. Surely.

'No!' Kate said. 'That's not your bed.'

There was a long silence while the echo faded. Kate had spoken very loudly.

'Well, thank you for giving up your room,' Ivy said, at last.

'The powder room through here really *is* pretty,' Kate said, throwing open a frosted-glass door. She was carrying on with the tour as though nothing had happened. Ivy followed her and peeked in. The room was quite large, although broken up by toilet cubicles set across the far end. Around the other walls, gilt-framed mirrors sat above little bandy-legged dressing tables with powder-puffs in glass bowls and bottles of coloured liquid Ivy could only guess about.

'It is,' she agreed. 'Has Gail got up and gone straight out?'

'Oh, no,' said Kate. 'Sleeping or awake, she's downstairs.'

Ivy hadn't been aware of the knot in her shoulders until it loosened. 'Ah!' she said. 'Have you got a flat down there?' Of course. They didn't really live in this . . . what would you even call it? A museum? They kept it as a showpiece and lived in a basement flat. But why would they be staying here tonight? Why would she?

'Not really,' Kate said. She hesitated.

Haltingly, Ivy asked: 'What *is* this?'

'The house?' said Kate. 'You mean the house?' Ivy hadn't meant the house, but Kate sailed on. 'It's on the feu as "Doctor's Ballroom". That tickled our father. We girls always called it our fairytale cottage. But really it's an annexe. The doctor's house – the old doctor's house, I should say because he's been dead a hundred years and none of our family have ever been doctors, but these things stick, don't they? – well, it's next door.'

Ivy's shoulders dropped away from her ears again. The big stretch of blank wall that this little fairytale cottage was joined on to was the real house where they actually lived. They just used this as an escape. Or maybe they'd always played here, from when they were girls together.

'I'll go and bang on the floor for Gail,' Kate said and left the room, almost trotting.

Ivy looked around again. If the hospital hadn't made the mix-up, *she* would have spent her childhood playing here. She would be at ease here. At home.

As if to make it come true she wandered across to the tumbled chaise to straighten the blankets. As she flapped them, a little leather case that had been tucked into the folds dislodged itself and hit the hard floor, its gold clasp falling open. Ivy caught her breath and listened for rushing footsteps, but the house was silent. She bent to pick the case up, praying it wasn't broken. A drop of wine spilled out of her glass as she stooped.

It was a double photograph frame, she saw, and it had survived the fall. In her relief she forgot to worry about being caught snooping and opened it right up. On one side was a studio portrait of a couple in the stiff Sunday best of the 1950s. On the other side was a snap of three little girls. They were dressed for church too, in white gloves and white shoes along with their summer frocks. One of them was Kate; it was obvious even down all these years, so Ivy peered at the other two, looking for her own childhood face in either of theirs. They looked vaguely similar to one another but they looked nothing like her. Nothing at all.

'Our cousins,' said Kate's voice suddenly behind her. Ivy snapped the photograph frame shut and put it down on the smoothed blanket. 'Our favourite cousins, actually. They spent every summer here. Gail keeps those photographs of her loved ones with her always. Sleeps with them under her pillow as you see. Our parents. And me. And our favourite cousins.'

Ivy didn't have any cousins, and no one had ever stayed a whole season when she was a child. She imagined herself here in the long larky summers, with Gail and their favourite cousins. Imagined Kate in *her* place, learning to tell Mother's mood from the sound of her breathing, springing mousetraps in the larder.

'I thought you'd have a cat,' she found herself saying, the memory putting the thought in her head.

Kate frowned.

'Because you're in the Nine Lives League. The branch down here. Not the branch up by me.' She was prattling. She always did when she was uneasy. But why was she uneasy?

'I didn't tell you I was in the NLL,' Kate said.

'Didn't you?' Ivy said. 'It doesn't matter.' And it didn't. Nothing much seemed to matter, all of a sudden. She took another sip from the glass and it didn't taste so bad this time.

'Thank you,' Kate said. 'I'm nervous.' But Ivy would have said, if anything, Kate had relaxed. 'I want it to go well when you meet Gail. And she's . . . I told you she was . . . I've been struggling with her lately, you see. I maybe should have told you more. Been clearer. Talked plainer.'

More plainly, Ivy thought. 'Couldn't your auntie help?' she said.

Somewhere else in the house a door opened and closed. And Ivy couldn't say for sure whether the fixed look suddenly on Kate's face came as a result of that or whether the blankness had already settled across her beforehand. She found herself thinking, just for a moment, that she could turn on her heel and make it to the front door before Kate in those court shoes could catch her. She could grab at the handle of her shopping trolley on the way. And if she missed it, she could live without a lot of old photos. The moment passed. Don't be so daft, she told herself. Why are you making trouble where there's no need? They're eccentric. So what? Nine out of ten people looking at you would say you'd fit right in.

Kate spoke again. 'My auntie,' she said.

'Your Fraserburgh auntie,' Ivy said. 'Is she the mother of your favourite cousins?'

'Yes, I did say I had an auntie, didn't I? In case you wondered what I was doing all the way up where you live. Fancy you remembering a little thing like that.' Kate was smiling, grinning ear to ear actually. 'Here's to your excellent memory,' she said, raising her glass. It was much fuller than Ivy's. *It* – after this last slug – was empty.

Ivy could hear footsteps, soft and shuffling, moving through the house, coming closer. Once again, she thought of the route to the front door, forgetting all about the shopping trolley this time. She thought of the length of the front path and the design of the catch holding the gate shut. She thought of the distance to the mouth of the street, to the nail bar and the newsagent's.

'Don't call her Gail,' Kate said, in a hissed whisper.

'What?' Ivy's voice had dried to a croak. She cleared her throat. 'Why not?'

'In fact, don't talk to her.'

'*What?* Why?' Ivy wished she hadn't drunk the glassful now. She couldn't seem to catch the start of the thought she knew was nearby.

'Unless she talks to you.'

The footsteps were right outside the door now. The handle was turning.

'Come in, darling,' Kate called, as the door began to open. It was so quiet Ivy could hear a clock ticking in the hallway. 'Come and see who's here!' Kate said, and it seemed that she spoke extra-loud, ostentatiously loud. The clock stopped.

'Is it her?' The voice from behind the door was no more than a breath. 'Is she back?'

'It's her, darling,' Kate said. 'She's back.'

'Who's ba—?' Ivy was asking as the door swung wide. Then she screamed.

SIX

Martine smiled. If you smile at people it makes them kind. She took the name badge the woman held out stuck to the tip of one finger, and pressed it against the lapel of her jacket. 'I probably don't need this,' she said. 'I've been coming for months.'

'Have you?' She wasn't really asking. She was already looking beyond to the next people, an elderly married couple who were waiting to sign in and take their stickers.

Martine kept smiling. The poor thing was harassed, that was all. Sitting there in a draught at the entrance to the function room, taking subs and ticking off names on a sheet. Not everyone had the right kind of mind. A lot of people, herself included, would far rather stay at home at a screen than come out and deal with the rough and tumble.

When she got inside, she looked around with her smile just beginning to calcify, just threatening to make her cheeks ache. She recognized some of them and she was sure some of them recognized her. Be funny if they didn't. She stuck out. In Lockerbie. She was the only Black attendee in this room, like she was the only Black resident on her street, like she'd been the only Black kid in her class.

One time in year ten, one of the teachers had told the story of how Robert Burns, stranded in Dumfries and working as an exciseman – 'stranded in *Dumfries*?' one of the boys, one of the wags, had said. 'Bright lights compared to the Locks, Miss' – but the teacher had shushed him and carried on. Stranded in Dumfries as an exciseman, he said in a letter to a friend that the townspeople would as soon recognize a hippopotamus in their midst, as a poet. And as she said the word, the teacher, young and still earnest, had looked right at Martine. She meant to be kind. Of course she meant to be kind. She was trying to make Martine see that to be different was to be special, like a poet among farmers. But why did she have to say 'hippopotamus'?

Why did *he* – supposed to be poetic – have to say 'hippopotamus'
when he could have said 'bird of paradise' or even 'tiger'? The
kids had started calling her 'Hippo' that very day. And she had
smiled and smiled and smiled. Because if you show them they're
not getting to you, they stop.

'Hippoooooo!'

She turned. She didn't know who it was but he looked about
the age to have been just above her at school. All the boys
above her at school looked the same now. At least the ones
who were still in Lockerbie did anyway. The ones who were
stranded here, headed for forty, no poetry about them. They
were balding by genetic accident and actually bald by design.
Shaved in denial, the way the girls were dyed in denial, so
that instead of a collection of grey and pink, they were a
collection of blond and bristles. And all of them were fat too.
All the ones still in Lockerbie. The women dressed carefully,
their blouses cut away at the shoulders but draped in folds
across the front, their control-top trousers boot-cut over high
heels to add length to their legs. The men took a different
tack. Football tops left untucked and jeans worn low were how
they imagined they hid what had happened to the wiry boys,
or willowy boys, or even stocky boys they once were.

'Pig!' Martine said, matching the tone of triumph disguised
as pleasure. 'How are you?' She had no trouble keeping *this*
smile on her face. It was hard not to let it turn into peals of
laughter as he got even more pig-like in his confusion: his
pink cheeks flushing and his little eyes, deep in the overhang
of drooping eyelids, shrinking as he pinched them up in an
effort to understand. 'Sorry!' Martine said. 'I thought you
were Pig. But you're not, are you?'

'Pig who?'

'He wasn't in our year,' she said. 'I knew him from choir.
Oh . . . what was his second name?'

'Can't believe you've forgotten *me*!' the man said, back to
full strength again, grinning at her. His teeth hadn't survived
the years of smoking and crashing out drunk with bits of kebab
still stuck in them. Martine was only guessing, but the spongy
texture of those eyelids and the straining belly under the
Rangers shirt were strong clues.

'Remind me,' she said, grinning back, wondering what he'd make of her perfect white top row. 'I'll kick myself.'

'Gogs,' he said, pointing to himself with both thumbs. 'Gogsie. Gordon Rae.'

'Gordon!' she said. 'I *will* kick myself.'

'Don't do that,' he said. 'Let me.' He made a feint, with his fists up, as if he'd threatened a punch instead of a kick. 'We're over there,' he added, jerking his head.

'Who's we?'

'Me and the missus. Just you, is it?' He was still jabbing his fists and bouncing on the balls of his feet.

'Well, it was nice to see you,' Martine said. He dropped his hands again and, after giving her a look she couldn't decipher, he walked off to join a woman with blonde hair and a slit-shouldered top, who was sitting over a fat lever-arch file at one of the middle tables, a glass of wine at her elbow. That, Martine thought, was Nicole Mackay; Nicole Rae it looked like, these days.

Nicole gave Martine a look she was used to, up and down, clocking the way her cinched belt told the truth about her waist and her lack of make-up proclaimed that she had nothing to hide about her skin. Martine waved and smiled and Nicole managed half a smile and a crabbed twitch of a hand that might have become a wave if she'd had a gun to her head.

'Hippo.' Nicole was too far away for Martine to hear it but she saw the glossed lips form the sounds.

'Cow,' she mouthed back, thinking it was close enough to 'Nicole' that the woman would never know. She turned away. *Was* that a half-hearted sort of a wave, she found herself wondering. Or was Nicole trying to beckon her over? Had she just been invited to come and sit with them and refused? Maybe. But if she went over and found out otherwise she'd just have to trail away again.

Instead, she chose an empty table at the side, sliding in, facing the room, to unbuckle her own lever-arch folder and start leafing through her slips. She wasn't there to socialize.

When she'd decided to do her family tree, she'd assumed – as you would – it was all online, and that suited her well enough, but truth was she spent too much time on her own and most of that staring at a monitor. So when they all started nagging her she didn't have a leg to stand on.

'It's more efficient to do it in writing and send the questions to a list where people can search by keyword,' she had said – or rather typed – to @DescentofMe, one of the most frequent contributors to the group she'd added herself to.

'Nah, nah,' came the answer. 'That's where you're wrong. You get stuff in the chit-chat – asides, throwaway remarks – that can turn out to be gold. And it's not like you have to choose. You can still keep up with your online peeps.'

'If you're lucky enough to live in a town with a Family Forest and you don't go, I'm going to get the ferry and the train and the bus to Lockerbie myself and slap you. You don't know you're born!!!!!' @VikingGrl never let any of them forget she was in Shetland and Shetland was quite remote.

Martine gave them the benefit of the doubt, since they'd been right about the extra excitement you got from original documents. She had even taken to sniffing them, like the total fanatics. She had thought people were praying, in the library, the first time she saw them bending so very deeply over an open register and burying their noses in the valley of the binding. But when she tried it herself, alone in an empty study carrel, checking over her shoulder beforehand to see if anyone was passing, she understood. It was mostly dust, but not all. There was a faint tang of what might be ink, familiar from the days when she'd stooped low over homework, the blots of a cheap biro on the paper inches from her nose. And besides the ink and dust, there was something living. It should be disgusting by rights. Because it could only be the oil and sweat from the hands of whoever had written the entries all those years ago and the oil and sweat from the hands of everyone who had turned the pages in the decades and centuries since. The residue of their sneezes, the smears of fingers used to wipe noses then trace entries, the spit from a licked thumb turning a page. If you thought about it too long, you'd heave. But somehow – she bent again and took a deep breath – it was exciting. It brought them all to life, these people – the hat trimmers and housemaids, the coalmen and cowmen – who would otherwise just be names in a book, ink and dust.

So, wrong about the documents, she was ready to believe she was wrong about the social club too. And she was more than ready to admit that she had to change *something*. She wouldn't go as far as to say she was unhappy, and she'd never let the thought that she was lonely form in her head. 'Lucky' was what she said, whenever she took stock: a good job as a freelance grant-writer, her own boss, no overheads except a decent Wi-Fi connection that she'd want anyway and one good black suit for meetings that was so anonymous she'd been wearing it for years, dry-cleaned and hung on a padded hanger between times. She could take holidays when she felt like it, plan her days and weeks around small rewards, go to the gym when it was quiet during the school run, order online knowing she'd always be there to sign for deliveries. Lucky.

But the work itself was deathly dull and she could only stand it with a podcast on. So, little by little, between her work podcasts, her treadmill podcasts and the fact that she had no chance of getting to sleep at night unless someone was burbling in her ear, she sometimes felt as if she spent her whole life plugged in to the conversations of strangers who didn't know she was there. Often, recently, she'd wondered if it was doing something that shouldn't be done to her brain. She worried she might not be laying down short-term – or did she mean long-term? – memories, since half her mind was always listening instead of sifting her day.

It was when she started dreaming about the podcasters that she finally joined the Family Forest, coming along to the function room of the Cross Keys the second Tuesday of the month to share her passion, as @QueenofScots1 put it. 'Share your passion, Martine,' she'd said, on RoyalBlood. They had moved beyond handles to first names now, histories shared, problems halved. @QueenofScots1 was a surgery receptionist called Myra who truly believed she was descended from the House of Stuart, even though she had traced four lines back to the eighteenth century and found them all petering out into cart makers and bricklayers. Now she was trying a fifth contender.

Despite the delusions and wishful thinking, Myra and the rest of RoyalBlood were ninjas at the actual process of tracking down records and Martine couldn't quite drag herself away.

She couldn't quite drag herself away from the Family Forest either, even though she thought she'd be more . . . bedded in? Was that the expression? . . . by now. She didn't mind walking in the first time to not much of a welcome, because it stood to reason that this lot were family-minded rather than friend-minded. But she had, after all, lived in this town her whole life, moving from her gran's house to a studio, then an ex-council with new doors and windows, then a semi-detached, and finally her executive dream home, where pale grey carpet started at the front door and went all the way to the back of her walk-in wardrobe, where the fridge texted her that her milk was near its date, where the automatic garage door was as quiet as her Cherokee tyres on her Monoblock drive.

Not that Martine was materialistic. Not at all. The carpet, the texts and the driveway had meaning far beyond the price she paid for them. And what they meant was dignity. Because she *hadn't* actually lived here her whole life through. Every so often, in her childhood, she'd move back in with her mum in Dumfries, where clean floors, like dinner money and bus fares, were far from a given. She'd lie in bed at night, ignoring the smothered giggles and shushing after closing time, pretending to be asleep until after the bloke had gone in the morning. She threw out spoiled meals and sour milk and never complained until, every time without warning, as though she were a bucket that was strong and sturdy as it filled with hurts, she'd overflow and find herself back at her gran's, weeping into her pillow without making a sound. The second night she'd sit down to eat at the table with the wrinkled plastic stuck on top. By the third she'd be playing a round of crib after the dishes were dried and put away and meeting the same questions with the same answers.

'Why'd you bother, Marty?'

'Because *you* don't know who he is.'

'Well, no. I never met him.'

'And she does.'

'She does, she does. But if she hasn't told you by now . . .'

'She might. One day. She will.'

'Aye, she might at that.' Then her gran would reach over

and pull on a pinch of her hair, not so hard it hurt, but hard enough to straighten it out and let Martine see it from the corner of her eye.

Then, at seventeen, suddenly, a lot of things that had been hidden came into view. For a start, she realized that Alesha Dixon wasn't just lucky and perfect. She'd had someone to teach her what to do. As soon as Martine went to a decent hairdresser in Glasgow and spent her ice-rink money on products, she stopped looking like a burst mattress – her mum's words – and had curls instead of kinks for her gran to pull on, curls that would bounce back when she let them go. That was one thing.

The other was a realization, slow at first, then in a rush that left her shaking: her mum didn't have a *clue* who he was. She wouldn't have been able to name the men from last year never mind eighteen years back and, even though her dad must have been remarkable in whiter-than-white Dumfries – a hippo in their midst, she more than likely never heard his second name and couldn't dredge up his first after all this time. Martine had never seen her mum on a third date.

The final thing she saw now was that her gran was protecting her. Every time she explained why she went back to her mum's flat – to hear his name, because her mum might tell her his name, because her mum knew his name – and her gran agreed and pulled her hair . . . she was lying. She didn't want to take away her little granddaughter's hope, maybe. Or she didn't want to admit out loud what her daughter was. Or she liked an easy life.

So, at seventeen, Martine gave him up. She gave up on the student who'd been travelling from the Highlands back to London and broke his journey in the Station Hotel in Dumfries one night when her mum was behind the bar, carrying on back down south the next day, never guessing what he'd left behind him. She gave up every version of his London life too. The one from when she was tiny, where he lived in a garret with a view over rooftops to the dome of St Paul's. That was from a Disney film, probably. The Richard Curtis one from when she was twelve, where he lived in a tall house with white plaster like the icing on a Christmas cake and two bay trees on the doorstep. The one from when she was fifteen and had him living in Croydon, or Brockley – somewhere real – in bunk beds with a bus pass. She even gave up on him being a student, qualified now and working in a children's ward, or a sheriff's court, or a city bank. But she never gave up on the crowd of faces she always saw around him. A mum who stood no nonsense, a dad who took him boxing, two grandmas in church hats and two grandpas with allotments. And brothers and sisters and cousins and aunties and nephews and nieces. White girlfriends and white boyfriends, babies every shade, all the tooth-sucking done with years ago, so that when *she* arrived, off the train from Lockerbie, golden-skinned and curly-haired, she'd blend right in. The more the merrier. She'd even change her name to his, whatever it was. She'd be Martine . . . something wonderful.

Then she turned seventeen and, like a soap bubble with one breath too many blown in, the whole shimmering, billowing dream was suddenly gone, with a spit of cold truth in her face and nothing but plain grey life in front of her eyes. She stopped smiling. Stopped for long enough that her gran started calling her 'Misery-guts' and talked about the wind changing.

'That's better,' she said, when Martine stretched her lips wide and crinkled her eyes up. 'Costs nothing.' But she was wrong. It cost her every day.

That was all more than ten years back, and Martine told herself it was cold ash now. She never asked herself, certainly never answered, why she stayed round here when she could go anywhere. What she gained from being right here where her mum had been, visible, findable, unmissable. She even told herself this family tree she was researching, all down her mother's side, was nothing to do with it. With him. Not a reaction, not a corrective, not an attempt to fill up on cousins dangling from a dozen branches, so she'd forget the imagined noisy London house, all that unheard laughter and those unknown names.

And look! Myra was right. It *was* a good way to meet people. Someone was standing by her table right now, reading Martine's name badge. She broadened the smile she had on her face anyway and made a ceremonial little shift to one side, pulling her folder closer so it took up less room.

'Sit down,' she said. 'I'm not expecting anyone.'

She was a pale, slight little person, late forties Martine reckoned, neatly dressed in uncomfortable-looking clothes, not that different from Martine's own – a fitted jacket, a tight skirt – but maybe these clothes had been chosen for different reasons. Martine's uniform showed off her figure and declared her attitude. This woman, inside the tailoring, was soft-looking, wispy-haired and downy-cheeked, as though the clothes might be holding her together, as though without them she'd have trouble standing.

Martine was still holding out a hand in welcome, but the wispy woman looked around herself at the other tables. Martine's smile stayed just as wide but it took a bit more effort.

'I'm sort of half-looking for someone kind of,' the little woman said. 'But maybe she's not here.'

'She can join us if she turns up,' Martine said. She knew her voice was starting to sound grim. One more chance, she thought. One more. 'Plenty space for another one. Another two, actually!'

'Thanks,' the woman said and she sank down with relief. But Martine had noticed that she wore high-heeled shoes with her trim little pencil skirt so she didn't let herself believe that it was companionship causing the smile and the relaxing.

'Lovely,' the woman said, once she was settled. 'I'm Kate.' She held out a hand and Martine shook it, trying not to react to how clammy it was. But Kate had noticed her expression changing. 'Sorry,' she said. 'I'm a bit nervous.'

'I was just the same first time I walked in,' Martine said. 'But there's no need to be. Can I get you a drink? The white wine's usually nice and cold. I'm Martine, by the way.'

'So I see.' Kate nodded at the badge. 'Martine . . .?'

'MacAllister.'

'Oh!' Kate said, sitting back sharply. 'You *are* Martine MacAllister?' She bent forward again. '*You're* Martine MacAllister? I don't—'

'What?' said Martine.

'I didn't—'

'What?' said Martine.

'Just that, the thing is, if you're Martine MacAllister, then I'm sort of half-looking for you.'

SEVEN

The acoustics in the function room of the Cross Keys would have been perfect in a recording booth, but they were notoriously bad for parties. They didn't book many bands – Lockerbie wasn't that kind of town – but even wedding DJs over the years had given up trying to mix a decent sound and settled for the easy womp-womp of a deafening bass line. The thump of the bass was what drunks danced to anyway and the thump of the bass was what tipsy mums felt in their bellies, what got them snuggling up to their husbands, forgiving years of disappointments in hopes that the new love being celebrated would spread out from the happy couple and head their way.

Some of trouble came from the thick carpet over good honeycomb underlay, everywhere except the tiny dance floor. Some of it was down to the velour seat covers and deep cushioning, the matching velour curtains with deep fringed pelmets. The ceiling was made of fire-retardant polystyrene tiles, which didn't help, and the walls were papered in flock. All in all, the function room soaked up noise like a sponge. It made the claustrophobes who happened to spend time there check the exits and take frequent breaks outside in the carpark, pretending to cool off, and made gossips forget that they'd better check over their shoulders before they prised the lid off some can or other.

Tonight, the muffled deadness made Martine feel – as she stared at Kate, in the silence after the statement was made – as if her ears were ringing.

'You're looking for me?' she said, at last. '"Sort of" anyway?'

'That wasn't true,' said Kate. 'I was just playing it . . . cool? Down? I'm absolutely looking for you. I think.'

'Absolutely, you think?' Martine said. And when Kate hesitated again, she went on: 'I'll get you that white wine while you work it out, eh?'

She was trying for a wry tone, an air of worldliness, but inside she was buzzing with curiosity as she made her way through to the bar. Someone was looking for *her*? Why would anyone be looking for *her*? Maybe someone online had said she came to this meeting and would help a newbie get started. But in that case surely whoever it was would have e-introduced them. She asked the barmaid for another glass of wine and ignored the look. Even if she *had* necked the first one, it was no one's business.

Or maybe Kate was after a grant-writer and had come to do an impromptu interview. If so, it was the most interesting thing that had happened in twelve years of grant-writing, hands down.

Martine shared a word with the barmaid, as if to show she wasn't what she dreaded becoming: the sort of person who would ponder and ponder a tiny moment in an ordinary day, like she was doing with this Kate person, right now.

Only, if she was looking for a grant-writer, why was she so gobsmacked to find one?

There was the usual explanation, of course. There was *always* that. She'd had it only yesterday, with a client from Lancaster, meeting him at some scummy café near the bypass, for his convenience. He'd heard her Scottish accent half a dozen times and he checked and rechecked the café customers looking for the face to match it. When she finally went over and introduced herself he blushed, apologized and practically told her he loved Beyoncé.

She paid for the wine and squared her shoulders to go and find out what Kate wanted, planning to smile all the way through whatever the explanation might be. Maybe Myra or someone else on RoyalBlood had sent Kate to meet her, as a nice surprise. Only now Kate was worried they wouldn't be using the same resources; that Martine would be deep in immigrant ship lists and churches in Jamaica. And she was scared to look rude by asking. Martine could put the poor woman out of her misery, go back to the table and say, 'It's my mum's family I'm tracing, and she was as white as snow.'

'Thanks for this,' Kate said then took a slug and set the

glass down firmly. 'Right. Here goes.' She hauled in a breath and let it go again. 'Here goes,' she repeated, gazing at the table. The silence stretched.

'It's my mum's family I've been researching,' said Martine. 'And she was as—'

Kate looked up so fast Martine thought she could hear a snap in her neck. Did necks snap, like ankles and knees, if you stressed them?

'Right, right,' said Kate. 'Well, yes. It would be.'

'Would it?' Martine said. She kept the smile, just.

'Because your dad,' Kate said, 'never acknowledged you. Never contacted you. But he did know about you.'

Now the smile sank from her lips as if it had never been. Martine MacAllister, who had been grinning non-stop since she first learned that it was the best way to make people like you or at the very least leave you alone, felt her cheeks drop until they felt heavy, like two saddlebags, on either side of her mouth. She felt her mouth fall open. She stared.

'You were born on the twenty-second of July 1983,' Kate said. 'Weren't you?'

Martine nodded.

'Your mum phoned him. From the labour ward. She called him to tell him about you. A little girl, seven pounds five ounces, healthy except a bit of dislocation in your right hip, wasn't it?'

Martine nodded again, then found her voice. 'I wore a Y brace, to correct it. Till I was five months old. I can't remember it of course, but I saw pictures. How do you know all this? Did he tell you? Do you know him?'

He! Him! The him she had given up on so many years ago. This woman was surely too young to be his wife. If he was a student then, he'd be . . . And this woman, Kate, couldn't be more than . . .

'He didn't get the call,' Kate was saying. 'He was out. She left a message on the answerphone. And he kept the tape.'

Martine took a sip from her glass and put it down. She thought she was being careful but as she let go, a little splash of wine fell on the table-top, landing in three distinct drops, high and round on the sealed polish. She stared at them, imagining herself taking the napkin from under the glass and wiping them up, but doing nothing.

'He kept the tape his whole life,' Kate said then her eyes flashed. 'Sorry! He died. About a month ago. And we were clearing the house and found this little tape. You remember those tiny little cassette tapes like from a doll's house? No one could work out how to play it. My brother-in-law, Leo, took it to work and turned it over to the nerds in the end. We're all so savvy with the new stuff now but the old stuff is beyond us.'

'Speak for yourself,' said Martine. 'I'm only OK till it goes wrong. Then I just phone the fixers and hand over my passwords.'

'You do? You don't worry that they'll hide in there forever watching what you're up to?'

Martine opened her eyes wide. 'I might now!' she said. Then she laughed. 'Nah, better things to worry about than James Bond super-spies.' She took a drink. 'So your brother-in-law got the tape working?'

Kate nodded as she sipped her drink then put it down and went on. 'Of course, we had no idea what it was going to say. He came back in from work with this look on his face like I've never seen and he just put his phone down on the table and pointed to it, then went out. You know? To let us hear it in privacy.'

'Us?' said Martine.

'My sister and me. Gail. His wife.'

'And what *did* it say?'

'I've listened to it so many times, I know it off by heart. "It's Karen. I'm at the pay-phone in the hospital. Just letting you know I had a wee girl. She's fine. She's perfect. Except for a clicky right hip, but they said that's easy fixed. Seven pounds five ounces. I'm not asking you to come. In fact, I'm telling you not to come. And I don't want anything from you. But I thought you'd want to know."'

'Clicky hip,' Martine said. 'That's exactly what my mum always called it. Why didn't she want him to come?' She searched Kate's face and it didn't take long. 'Oh,' she said. 'He was married?'

'Yeah,' said Kate. 'He was married. He never got in touch again. And neither did your mum, I don't think. Not in writing anyway. He'd have kept it.'

'And how did you know it was me?' Martine said. 'I mean, how did you know it was me you were looking for? There must have been more than one baby born that day in Dumfries? Did you . . . Do you work for the NHS? Did you find a medical record? About my hip?'

'No!' said Kate. 'Heavens, no! I don't work for the NHS and neither does Gail. If we did we'd lose our jobs for that. We run our own little business, as it goes.'

'Did you check the register?' Martine said. 'Was I the only one with no dad on her birth certificate that day?'

'Poor little baby,' said Kate. 'Was he not? Really?'

'Well, no,' said Martine. 'He'd have had to be there to go on it, since they weren't married. You learn that quick enough at this genealogy caper.'

'Right,' said Kate. 'Makes sense, I suppose. Otherwise . . .'

'Yeah.' Martine smiled to show she wasn't offended. 'Otherwise . . . We'd all be putting "Idris Elba", wouldn't we? So, how *did* you know?'

'That it was you?' Kate said. 'Because of your name. Martine.'

'What about it?'

'And his name.'

'What was it?'

'Martin Ellis. Martin E.'

Martine took another slug and mopped the three drops with the napkin while the glass was off the table. 'Martin,' she repeated. 'Ellis. It seems obvious now. It would have been quite easy to find him. If I'd been looking. But it never crossed my mind.' She set the glass down again. 'And what's his connection to you? And your sister?'

Kate's eyebrows rose up until her brow was crinkled. 'Didn't I say already?' she asked. 'Did I really not say? He's my dad. Was. My dad. Our dad. Gail and me.'

Martine felt her cheeks sink down again, her bottom lip turned out this time. 'I don't get it,' she said. 'How can he be?'

'Why not?' said Kate. 'Did you think we'd be angry? Maybe some people would be. Maybe my mum would have been, if he'd gone first, and she'd found the tape. But not Gail and me. We just wanted to find you.'

'Her,' said Martine. 'You want to find *her*. I agree the name's a bit of a coincidence, and there's the fact that my mum was single, and her name was Karen – it's a massive coincidence, actually – but it must be someone else you're looking for, who was born in Dumfries that day.'

'Why?' said Kate. 'What do you mean?'

Martine stared at her. Then she pushed her jacket sleeve up and stretched her bare arm across the table, laying it beside Kate's bone-white one.

'I can't be your sister,' she said. 'Obviously.'

Kate didn't move. She just stared and stared, goosebumps lifting on her arm. Martine could feel the tickle of the tiny blonde hairs.

'So . . . your mum was white?' Kate said, at last. 'Is that what you mean? Are you showing me the colour of your skin?'

'And my dad's Black,' said Martine. 'Obviously. Whoever he may be.'

The dots on Kate's forearm were so pronounced now they made Martine think of that phobia, those people who couldn't look at beehives or pomegranates. She didn't share the aversion but she'd heard a podcast about it and under-stood it. Right now she felt her own hackles rise in sympathy.

'"Whoever he may be"?' Kate echoed. 'He was Martin Ellis. Of course he was. I mean, what are the chances of two little Black girls being born in Dumfries to single white mothers on the same day?'

'I don't understand,' Martine said.

'Me neither,' Kate said. 'I can't work out what's bothering you.' Then her head jerked up again. 'Wait! Oh my God. Didn't I tell you? Didn't I?'

'Tell me what?'

'We're adopted. Gail and me. We were adopted when she was three and I was a baby. We never knew who it was that couldn't have them. Dad or Mum. Never knew till after he was dead and we found the cassette. Obviously it was Mum, right? And that's why he always kept the recording – you're the only one that's actually his, biologically. And it explains why he would never try to add you to the family, doesn't it? It would have broken my mum's heart. It would have destroyed her. He was a nice man. A really good man. A great dad and a good husband. One lapse doesn't change that.'

Martine nodded. A good man, a good husband, with two little girls at home, went out one night and knocked up her mother.

'I'm sorry it's too late for you to meet him,' Kate said. 'But we've got photos.'

'With you?' Martine couldn't help the leap in her voice. 'On your phone?' She darted looks at Kate's bag and her pockets. Surely the woman would have at least one picture of her beloved late father with her always. It was probably her wallpaper.

'Not on me, no,' said Kate. 'Sorry. But at home. Albums full of pictures and home videos too. You will come, won't you? Come and spend the weekend with us? Come and stay? We're only up in Hephaw. You know where I mean?'

'Hephaw?'

'West Lothian. You'll love our house. Seriously, wait till you see it. Come for the weekend.'

'The weekend,' said Martine. 'Videos?'

'Are you OK?' said Kate. 'I know this is a lot. We couldn't think how to approach you. This was my idea. Just going for it. But are you OK?'

'I'm just,' Martine said. 'It is.' She took a deep breath. 'It *is* a lot. I don't understand . . . How did you find me?'

'What?' Kate said. 'Birth records are public—'

'No, I mean how did you find me here. Tonight. How did you know I'd be here?'

Kate chewed her lip for a while before answering. 'Sorry,' she said. 'I hope this doesn't make you feel uneasy. We hired a private detective. I'll show you his report.'

'It doesn't,' Martine said. 'Make me feel uneasy. It's practical. It's . . . it's flattering actually. It's amazing. Someone trying to

find me. My mum's dead, you see. And my gran, who practically brought me up, died. And I'm an only child.'
      Kate reached over the table now. 'No,' she said. 'You're not
an only child. You've got sisters. You've got Gail and me.'

EIGHT

I wasn't sorry to be out of Fraserburgh, and away from the exciting world of sub-subcontracted medical delivery. I definitely wasn't sorry to hand back the tracker-logger and know that I wasn't a moving light on Jamie Morton's driver-location app. Leaving my locker stuffed with treasure, I packed up and moved the operation south to Lockerbie. 'Belt cinched,' I said to myself. 'Time to twang the braces.' Did it trouble me that I was still following his rules? Not at all. He was right about some things and I'd be a fool to deny it. Besides, it was more than a back-up plan. It was a calculated move in a game I still couldn't believe I was playing. It was a great big 'try me; I dare you'.

But the big picture was too scary to look at for long. I made myself turn away and concentrate on the details instead: another name for another job. I couldn't believe it was this easy, but it turns out life in a free country is not nothing. The Protection of Vulnerable Groups form asked for 'previous first and last names, if any' and even two of each – Tash Dodd and Nate Dewar – didn't trip a switch, maybe because neither of them had ever been in trouble. So when Trix Depp – with her no experience but a lot of enthusiasm, her clean licence and that PVG clearance – turned up for interview, RoundnRound Special Pupil Transport Services bit her arm off.

Once I had started the job itself, I was nearly ready to jack in the plan, forget my vow to bring Big Garry down, and just be a pupil transport assistant for the rest of my puff. Do this very job, get a promotion, mount a takeover, make changes. Do it better, make it the best it could be. For now, I just did *my* best, and got a name for it.

'You'll settle,' said Ken, my driver. 'Stop making us all look bad.' I could see his eyes in the rear-view mirror, cold as gum in a puddle. Not a twinkle in them anywhere.

'I'm not trying to make you look bad,' I said. 'If you've got a guilty conscience, that's on you.'

We were right at the start of the new run, on our way out to the flats beyond the bypass, to pick up Janelle, in her wheelchair, with her oxygen tank, and her service dog for her fits. After Janelle came two brothers with low-functioning autism who needed to be in the van with their noise cancellers before the rest of the seats filled, then Olivia, blind and palsied, wee Freya in her three braces, one for her back and one on each leg, and Jack in *his* wheelchair, even more fancy than Janelle's, who couldn't manage a long trip without stomach trouble, and all the embarrassment a ten-year-old boy in a full bus could feel about it. Ken had kicked up about that, when I showed him a different route and pointed out that Jack could be last on first off, saving us both a lot of mopping.

'You're not supposed to complain about personal care,' Ken had said, rootling the last scrap of a fried egg piece from between his back molars. 'That's the job.'

'I'm not complaining for me,' I said. 'I'm thinking about the lad. Can't be very nice, every morning in life.'

Ken shrugged, as if it was nothing to him whether a kid was sick or well. But he could see the point of it.

'Ha'way then,' he said, slurping the last of his grey coffee that had to be clap cold by now. I shuddered, drained my water glass and got to my feet, re-Velcroing my Hi-Vis as I edged out of the café into the cheerless Monday morning drizzle.

I met Ken at the same greasy spoon every day and every day I had a glass of tap and a banana and ignored the girls behind the counter glaring at my thermos cup, daring me to take a sip from it so they could chuck me out. I had no idea how Ken had got out of the morning staff meeting and managed to stick me with picking up the day-sheets and specials; all the other drivers were there with their PTAs, only me on my own. I was careful to complain about being left with the paperwork, not giving him even a whisker of a clue that I was thrilled. But thrilled I was. I had thought it would take weeks to build up enough trust with my driver before he'd let me file the sheets without him checking them over.

Ken dinked the lock open and climbed up into the driver's

seat with a grunt. He had a driver's figure, and no mistake. Trucker's butt. When I was a wee girl I thought that's what men looked like. Short-legged, with a belly that rested on their lap when they sat, round shoulders over ham-shaped arms and no neck to speak of. I had thought that was what happened to boys, like girls getting extra chins and bunions. I had been eighteen before I realized it was self-fulfilling; that no one rangy or bony could stand to sit in a lorry cab all day and no one who minded junk food could stand to eat in service stations the way the drivers had to. My dad was different. He still had the ham-arms and the short legs – for his height anyway – but his shoulders were square, at least when he wore a decent suit, which he usually did, and his belly was as flat as it was on his wedding day. As he always said. I would cringe in advance of the punchline. 'And Lynne's is a damn sight flatter!' he'd say, his voice rising to a shout. My mum laughed like she didn't mind and if Big Garry caught sight of my stony face, he'd shake me if he was close enough, chuck something at me if he wasn't and say, 'Come on! We wouldn't have it any other way.'

In the back of the accessible bus I was unwinding a string of fairy lights and draping them over Freya's seat.

'—hell's that for?' Ken was saying.

'It's her birthday.'

'How d'you know?'

'Because their dates of birth are on their consent forms. I put them in my phone.'

He stared at me in the mirror, eyes slightly narrowed. He was dying to find fault.

'I wouldn't,' he said. 'When it comes round to Olivia, she'll kick off. You know what she's like.'

I knew exactly what Olivia was like. Nearly completely blind and so wobbly on her pins she needed a walker. 'Tell me!' she'd cry out, when the rest of them saw something out the window. She sounded like a baby bird, like a kitten. 'Tell me! Tell me!'

'It's a rainbow, Livvy,' I would say. 'It's a horse.'

'Clippety-clop,' said Freya. 'Pop-pop.'

Simon and Damon, the twins, said nothing, but sometimes

they picked up on the excitement of a flock of geese against the sky or a vintage sports car overtaking and then they would shoot side looks out of the corner of the eye and enjoy the sight, so long as no one caught them at it.

'When it's Olivia's turn,' I said to Ken, 'I'll give her a feather boa and put a bit of music on. Better than fairy lights for a blind kid.'

Ken said nothing. He was still silent when we pulled into the designated parking space at the foot of Janelle's building and I jumped down to go up and fetch her.

The sky was still rosy, as early as this on a spring morning, and the flats were quiet, no more than a burble of telly coming from behind their front doors. The lift wasn't just working, it was pristine, smelling like the Magic Tree hanging from the emergency stop button and only faintly of the vinegar and grease from someone's carry-out the night before. I stepped off on to Janelle's landing and stood a moment, taking in the view. The sky had faded already, while I was in the lift. Now it was pale and pearled like the inside of a shell, dazzling where the sun showed behind thinning cloud. Dumfries looked like a toy town, with Matchbox cars on its tangle of streets, dolls' houses lining them.

There weren't many moments like this but sometimes, when dawn and goodness chimed, I could feel myself expanding, as if sheer resolve, growing inside me, could make me into Wonder Woman.

Behind me, a front door opened. Janelle's mum put her head round it.

'Thought I saw the bus. And I heard the lift. You having a fag?'

'Just dreaming,' I said, turning to face her. 'I love it how no one ever vandalizes this lift because they know Janelle needs it. Like how no one ever nicks the poppies.'

'What poppies?' Deeta was busy poking Janelle's hair into the sides of her anorak hood, such thick hair.

'At the cenotaph. The wreaths sit there for months till they're bleached in the sun and no one ever nicks them or kicks them to bits. Like Janelle's lift. Good morning, sunshine!'

Janelle rolled her eyes and whipped her head back and forth

across the back of her wheelchair. Most of the hair Deeta had
poked in came bouncing out again.

'If we could harness that, and spread it . . .' I said.

'What you on about?' said Deeta. 'What's she on about?'
She bent low over Janelle, kissed her eyes and nose, kissed
her cheeks and lips, lifted first one hand and then the other,
prising them open and planting a kiss in each palm. 'For later,'
she said. 'Here, Mutt!'

Janelle's alert dog, a chihuahua called Muttley, came
prancing out of the living room, already in his little jacket
with the built-in pouch for his poo-bags, carrying the end of
his lead in his mouth. He jumped up on to Janelle's lap,
trampling and snuffling and making her writhe against her
restraints and let out a string of high-pitched squeals and
uncomfortable-sounding short groans.

'The first time I saw her I thought "she bloody hates that
dog",' I said to Deeta. 'I'm starting to learn her noises now.
See you tonight, eh?'

The dog kept both its bug eyes trained on me as I rolled
Janelle back to the lift. It didn't trust me yet. Or maybe it
knew I didn't care for it.

'It's nothing personal,' I told it. 'I'm just not a dog person.'
Although it didn't help that Muttley had crust in the corners
of his bug eyes and brown stains at the sides of his snappy
little mouth. 'Who's a good boy?' I said. He recognized that
sentence and he curled up facing the other way. 'Your dog's
a pillock,' I told Janelle. 'Hey, wait till you see what's in the
bus for Freya's birthday!'

The lights and crown were a huge hit with all six of them.
Simon and Damon scowled and adjusted their headphones
as if they were trying to get a better seal between their ears
and the unbearable cacophony of the world. They really did
need the seal but it had become code for huffs too now. I
even wondered sometimes if they were communicating
through it, like courtesans with their fan semaphore. I would
ask their dad what he thought when I dropped them off
again.

'Can I keep it?' Freya asked. 'Trix. Trix. Trix. Can I keep it?'

I had meant to store the crown and lights in the bus for the

next birthday, but I shrugged. It was from the pound shop. I
could buy a stack of them.

We made it to Jack's school gate without mishap.

'Better luck tomorrow, Ken,' I said as I locked the chair
wheels into the lift, strapped them and checked the barriers.

'Eh?'

'Oh come off it! You took the Heathhall roundabout on two
wheels.'

But Ken's eyes in the rear-view looked genuinely troubled.
Maybe I was being cynical. Maybe just because he never
washed his uniform and the sight of the dandruff collected
under the epaulettes of his jumper sickened me, I was unfair
to him. Like I was unfair to Muttley with his crusty eyes.
What kind of man would want to make a kid sick just to stop
a colleague being proud of a good idea?

He revved the engine as the hydraulics let go and settled
Jack's chair on to the ground.

That kind of man, I thought. 'Oi! Exhaust fumes! Cut it
out. You shouldn't even have the engine running when there's
a kid on the lift,' I said, then muttered, 'Twat!'

'Twat! Twat!' Olivia shouted, flapping her hands.

'Ears like a bloody bat,' I said. 'That's supposed to be a
myth.'

I lifted the barriers and rolled Jack out, kicking his brake
once he was clear, delivered him to his classroom assistant,
then jabbed the buttons to raise the lift again.

Simon and Damon's class had swimming today, so there was
no time to go back to the office after the morning drop-off.
Instead, I went with Ken to his choice of venue to while away
forty minutes. The guy must know every budget café in a
ten-mile radius, I thought to myself, squirming as the split
leatherette on the seat pinched my bum. It was better than the
other seat, with the duct-tape mend that rolled back and stuck
to you, but only just.

'Piles?' Ken said.

I stopped squirming. The guy wasn't fifty; he had to know
that was harassment. He was carefully piling a soft fried egg
on top of the split sausages he'd already laid on a slice of

bread. He added another slice and pressed the sandwich together. I had to hand it to him: the sausages stayed put and the yolk seeped up into the top slice, not out on to his plate. He lifted it tenderly and tore off a third with his first bite.

I wound the string of my teabag round my finger and dipped it in and out of the cup, watching the water swirl pink.

'What is that anyway?' Ken said. 'Bloody honking.'

'You're kidding,' I said, pointing at his sandwich. 'It's blackcurrant. It's nice. It's refreshing.'

'Don't stain the sheets,' said Ken, nodding at the clipboard by my place as he took another gargantuan bite. Fat dripped out on to his plate and the table around it and Ken mopped the drops up with the crust.

'Are they sticklers?' I said, glad of the opening.

'Is who?'

'Records,' I said. 'Finance? I dunno. Who is it that reads them?'

'Reads what?' Ken had stuffed the last of his sandwich in and was chewing on both sides of his mouth.

'The logs,' I said. 'All this lot. Who is it that says I can't get a wee pink spot of blackcurrant tea on them? Make a change from butter and bacon, wouldn't it?'

Ken made a scornful noise and blew out some half-chewed sandwich with it. '*Read* them? Nobody *reads* them. We're in trouble if anybody ever *reads* any of them.'

'What? Trouble how?' I said. 'I'm doing my best to fill in what they're asking for. Is there something else?'

'Calm down, calm down,' Ken said. He had put his cake plate on top of his empty sandwich plate and was slicing open the iced bun. 'I'm sure you've dotted all your Ts. I *meant* the only time anyone ever opens the files and starts hoicking out forms is if there's a case hearing and the social workers are in arse-covering mode.'

'Wait. What?' I said. 'You mean none of this lot I'm killing myself to keep up with is ever going to see the light of day until someone comes checking up on us?'

'Bingo.'

'And does that ever happen?' I said. His eyes narrowed. Did he think I was accusing him of something? I covered it

by adding: 'Tell me you're not really going to butter that thing
and clap it back together.'

'It's helluva dry without a wee scrape,' Ken said. He was
wrestling with the butter pod, trying to work out what corner
of the foil top was meant to be the opening. His fingers, meaty,
nails bitten to the quick, looked unlikely ever to lift the tiny
little cow-lick of gold. I watched him, buggered if I was going
to help an obese man add more fat to the sugary treat that
rounded off the second meal of his morning. Then, remembering that I was crawling, I held my hand out.

'Give it here. Jeez!'

'Ta,' Ken said. And as I had hoped, in gratitude, he started
up again. 'Not in my time. I have had a clean record since
they put it out to contract. And I did fourteen years for the
council direct before that. Nothing ever happened on my bus
to make any of the busybodies call a meeting.'

I nodded. 'And none of the parents ever ask for
record-sharing?'

'Naw. Calm down.'

'Do they actually keep them?' I said, flicking the sheets in
front of me. 'Bet they get binned.'

'What?' said Ken. 'You've got a lot to learn. Binned?
Nothing, ever, gets binned, Trixie lass. Not one single sheet.
This lot'll still be in a box-file in long-term off-site secure
storage when . . .'

'The sun burns up the Earth?'

'Exactly.' He took another bite and I took another sip.

'I'm glad about the parents,' I said. 'I mean, I know they're
in their rights but I don't think I'd feel the same about them
if they were always checking up on me.'

'They're not likely to come checking up on *you*,' Ken said.
'You're up the lift instead of waiting at the foot. Laying on
birthday treats. You're flavour of the month, you are.'

But he said it friendly enough, I thought. He was the perfect
partner for me. He truly did not care.

'What about you?' I said. 'Have they been arsey to you?'

'Me?' said Ken. 'I'm an institution. I'm in with the bricks
and I'll leave in a box. Never a day sick, never ask for leave
in term-time, never late when it's icy or early when the footy's

on. See, that's what you need to learn, hen. You don't need to go sooking up to them. Just do your job, no more and no less.'

I couldn't help the smile. I had landed in clover here. I would fill in the sheets all by myself. I would file them all by myself. And I was partnered with a driver who'd never been checked up on in all his long years of service.

'What's with the smirk?' he said.

'Just thinking,' I said, buying time. 'I'm glad I'm paired with an old-timer to keep me straight.'

'Seasoned alpha,' Ken said. 'Not old-timer. But yeah, I'm coasting now. I've got three years to go till my lump sum.'

'You're looking well on it,' I said, recalculating his age.

Ken finished the bun, sat back and slapped both sides of his stomach. 'You have to choose between your face and your figure when you get to my age,' he said. 'Liz Taylor knew that.'

I could almost feel sorry for him, thinking about the trouble I was going to cause him, down the line. Maybe I could do what I was here to do quickly, in the next couple of weeks, and then annoy Ken so much he'd ask for me to be shifted to a different driver. I'd miss our kids, though.

'Can I choose where we go for our lunch?' I said. 'Near the swimming pool.'

'How?' said Ken. 'What's wrong with Mickey D's?'

'You've got to be joking,' I said. 'You've had two breakfasts. You can't have a burger at dinnertime.'

'Me and Liz Taylor know better,' Ken said. 'Where is it you're dying to go?'

'Tapas bar,' I said. 'I'm kidding! Upstairs in Tesco'll do me. Anywhere there's a vegetable that's not pickled.'

It was the high point of my working relationship with Ken, that swimming-day morning at the greasy spoon with the split seats. I decided he wasn't so bad after all and he let me drag him to a café just beyond the bypass, minutes from the leisure centre, where we'd never been before. It had lorry bays in half of the carpark and slot machines by the front door but I managed to get a salad out of them. Ken deigned to try the ham and Swiss panini with home-made crisps and grunted

that it was passable. Then he took a look around the rest of
the clientele and nodded towards a light-skinned Black woman
sitting alone at a table working on her laptop while she spooned
soup carefully.

'Rougher crowd than Mickey's,' he said.

I tried and failed to think he meant something else. He kept
chewing, a leer on his face, daring me to say something. I ate
my salad with my head down, managing to stop feeling sorry
for myself only by thinking how it must feel to be a Black
girl in Dumfries, sticking out like a sore thumb everywhere
you went. When I passed by the woman's table on my way
to the loos, I smiled at her as if we were long-lost friends
and then felt a flush as she looked right through me. Ken saw
the smile and the look and snorted.

I really *had* flushed, I saw as I looked at myself in the
mirror, an angry stain spreading over my neck and up my
cheeks. Even my ears had darkened. 'Snotty bitch,' I muttered,
banging into the cubicle. 'Smile costs nothing.' Then I caught
myself. Chances were condescending smiles from people like
me were harder to stomach than flat stares from people
like Ken. That girl didn't owe me a thing. So when I'd washed
my hands and I came back out again, I kept a neutral look
on my face and strode by, only realizing once it was too late
that *this* time the woman had turned to smile back. Maybe she
was shy. Or maybe she reckoned her in her business suit with
her laptop out on the table didn't have to respond to the likes
of me in my Hi-Vis unless she felt like it. Or most likely, she
hadn't noticed me at all because she was watching for someone.
He was here now and it was him she was smiling at.

But he stayed by the door, looking around. His eyes drifted
over the three women with pushchairs in a huddle by the big
windows, the retired couple whispering together over a shared
scone, and the woman with the laptop, before his gaze came
to rest on me.

He started forward uncertainly. 'Martine?' he said, flicking
a look at the logo on my polo-shirt.

'Over here,' said the laptop woman, standing and starting
forward with a huge smile on her lips now but a look in her
eyes that could take down a charging bull. She was dressed

in the female version of the guy's get-up, maybe better quality, but otherwise identical: a black suit, black shoes and a white shirt. 'Are you David?' she asked him.

'Oh!' the man said, wiping his hand on his trousers before sticking it out, maybe as if it might be clammy. But just maybe as if the idea of cleanliness was on his mind suddenly.

I tried another shared look, in light of this fresh outrage, but 'Martine' was staring at the man who'd come to meet her and didn't notice. 'I like your hair,' he was saying.

'Snotty cow,' Ken said, nodding at the pair of them as I rejoined him. 'Face like a skelped arse. You'd think she'd be happy.'

'About *what*?' I said.

'Being welcome. And don't start on me.'

'Welcome where?' I said. 'She's obviously local. She sounds just like you.'

'Better than sounding like you. Edinburgh, is it? Morningsaaiide?'

I wanted to slap him with the truth – Grangemouth, over from the dockyard, great view of the refinery – but if he thought I was from somewhere else, I wasn't going to argue. 'Yep, Edinburgh,' I said. 'The posh end, obviously.'

'You did something wrong to wind up here then,' Ken said, and even he slumped as he looked around, at the sticky floor, the grime on the windows, the belching exhausts of the lorries outside restarting in the cold.

A wave of homesickness passed through me like the first shudder of a flu bout and I turned my mind away from the stark truth, that home was gone. Instead, I pictured files – unguarded and unread – lying forgotten behind the grey fronts of a wall of drawers like my own private bank vault. I found myself smiling down at the first few that lay crumb-strewn and smudged on the table before me.

NINE

Martine had never been in Hephaw before. She had never been in any of the string of workaday towns that meandered, one into the next, through this scarred, tired county. The buckle of the Bible Belt was a title claimed by the oddly proud burghers of many a hick town in the American South, with their megachurches and their huge houses for wholesome blond families of nine, perfect smiles and terrible clothes. Martine knew that. She'd become somewhat obsessed by the South, a few years back, before the genealogy. She had wondered for a while if 'he' maybe wasn't a Londoner at all, but American, and in her ignorance she thought all the Black people in America lived down there, in the humid shade of those raggedy trees she couldn't name. So she'd watched documentaries and reality shows, expecting *Gone with the Wind* and Alice Walker, finding megachurches instead.

That one phrase had stuck. The buckle on the Bible Belt. She remembered it now, driving through West Lothian. 'The buckle on the Central Belt,' she said to herself. 'Ingliston, Livingston, towns that could have been anywhere. Newbridge and Avonbridge, English-sounding somehow. Dechmont and Pumpherston, exotic in name, drab in reality. Then three towns all named Calder – East, Mid and West – as if even the town planners couldn't be bothered.

And now Hephaw. Martine caught sight of the sign announcing it or she wouldn't have known she had left the last town behind. There were no outskirts, no suburbs, certainly no fields between one and the next. Just this endless road, with shops and flats, cheek by jowl, then depots and garages, spread out in space unwanted for anything else, the odd pub with a carpark and maybe a skittle alley tacked on, as the speed limit rose to forty. Then there'd be a proud sign, announcing twin towns and claims to fame and the speed would go back down to thirty, the traffic lights for pedestrian crossings would start up and the garages and depots would give way to strings of shops again.

Hephaw was no different from all the rest of them. Cheap clothes shops and charity shops, because sometimes new clothes couldn't get cheap enough; bakers and butchers with names picked out in gold on painted backgrounds; burger, kebab and pizza joints, with plastic sheeting bolted over the original shopfronts; pub after pub after pub; closed phone shops and computer repair – remnants of short-lived hopes; open nail bars and tanning salons – current hopes still afloat, but always with signs saying 'walk-ins welcome'.

Martine's satnav showed the red pin worryingly close. Kate had said she'd love their house but she hadn't said anything about the area and 1a Loch Road looked to be just off this straggling High Street of newsagents and saver stores. Martine indicated, turned and began peering out of the passenger window for her first glimpse of the place.

'Your destination is on the right,' the satnav told her. She pulled in and parked by an iron gate between hedges, thinking *here goes.*

She had seen endless photographs now since that night at the Family Forest when her life changed. She'd seen faded snaps of a young man in his twenties, bell-bottom trousers and a striped V-neck T-shirt. He wore sunglasses and beamed out of the picture. Martine tried to see her face in his – her smile, her nose, her chin – but the original was overexposed from the start and had faded over the years, the flash on Kate's phone doing the rest of the work of hiding him. There were more: he was there in the back row of a school photo, with a thick black ring round his face that had smeared until it nearly obscured him; he was there at a party with a crowd of drunk friends, all of them with open shirts and shiny faces. Useless, Martine thought. He didn't even look like the same person in all these photos and in the one of him with two little white girls, she would never have said either was Kate.

She shouldered her messenger bag, gripped her overnight bag, and let herself in at the gate. The garden was long and uncared-for, scrubby old trees standing in tussocky grass and a long straight path that led to a wooden door, its varnish starting to lift and flake. Martine was sensitive to disorder. Who wouldn't be, after her childhood? Between the chipped veneer and thin carpets in her gran's flat, clean enough but worn through long before Martine arrived on the scene, and the smeared chaos of her mum's place, greasy dust on every ledge and stains on the wall above the open bin where lobbed teabags had missed, an endless line of black bags outside the front door waiting for the day that never came when someone would take them away, Martine sometimes thought that, even more than her new car and her good job, her bank balance and her credit rating, the solid ground in her life was the gleam on her polished taps, the Hoover swipes in the thick pale nap of her whole-house carpet, the sparkle of her windows, washed every month inside and out, reflecting her headlights in an unbroken streak of pure shine without a single fingerprint whenever she came home after dark.

Sometimes she wondered if dogs' noses and children's hands messing up her perfect windows would have been nice too, then she stepped inside, threw her keys in the bowl, hung her coat on a hook and stepped out of her court shoes, breathing in lemon polish and hearing nothing but the soft surge as her heating came on.

Whatever lay behind this peeling door was something quite different. She knew that before it opened and Kate peered round it, beaming at her.

'Come in!' she said. 'You made it. Is that your car at the gate? The navy blue one? Lovely. We can move it round later, can't we? It's fine for now. Come in, come in.'

She pressed Martine into a hug and Martine hugged back, guessing from the slightly vinegary scent coming off the shorter woman's hair that she was nervous enough to be sweating. Again, Kate was dressed in clothes far too old for her actual age: a cardigan on top of a round-collared blouse, with a pleated skirt and pale tights. She had tartan slippers on and kirby grips holding her hair off her face. Martine was touched to see all this evidence of intimacy. She was family, Kate's bare face and tea towel over the shoulder seemed to say. No need to be putting on airs and graces.

'How do you like our fairytale cottage?' she said. 'I'm in

the scullery. Come and keep me company. But do you need . . .? I mean, how long was your drive?'

'I'm fine,' Martine said.

'Because the gentlemen's cloakroom is through the card room there—'

'The what?'

'And the powder room is off the ladies' withdrawing room at the back.'

'The . . . what?'

Martine looked at the closed doors leading off the wood-panelled hallway and then back at Kate, frowning, but with a smile too – that smile that was her core policy, her best defence.

'It's a ballroom,' said Kate. 'The Doctor's Ballroom. Georgian, you'll see – if you care about architecture or interiors at all. See. This is the ballroom itself through here.'

Martine left her bags in the hall and followed.

'And this is the supper room.' Kate's slippered feet thumped softly on the patterned wood floors. Martine followed her silently, her flat crepe soles not even squeaking. 'Let's have a toast!' There was a tray already set out, three glasses and an open bottle of something fizzy. Martine took a glass and clinked it against Kate's. She took a polite sip. It wasn't flat, as she'd expected from it sitting there open, but it wasn't good.

'The scullery is our kitchen,' Kate said, making her way through a frosted-glass door in one corner. Martine followed. It was a long narrow space, stone-floored and brick-walled, surely an offshoot from the main building. There was a dull metal box on legs with brass taps sticking out over it, a sink apparently. Martine gave it a close look, wondering if it was lead and if the dishes washed in it were safe. Besides the sink, the 'kitchen' consisted of wooden boards with shelves below and hooks above. In the far corner a two-ring hotplate sat beside a little bar fridge. The flex they were plugged into snaked across the few feet of floor to where it was fed through under the propped open sash of a barred window next to an outside door, the gap stuffed all around with rags.

Kate went back to the task Martine had interrupted, stirring a pot so broad it stretched over both rings of the hotplate and so tall she had to reach up over the side.

'What are you making?' Martine said. She was sure that pot was aluminium. Did people really still use aluminium pots to cook in?

'Stovies,' said Kate.

'I'm a—'

'But I remembered you're a vegetarian,' she added, cutting in. 'So it's just potatoes and onion. And Marmite for a bit of flavour.' She balanced her wooden spoon on the edge of the pot and turned back to face Martine again. 'It really is lovely to have you here. You're the answer to my prayers.'

Martine smiled at the start of this speech then found her face falling sombre again as she repeated the end of it to herself. 'You mean . . . finding me?' she said. 'After you'd found out I existed? And all the time looking?'

Kate took the tea towel from over her shoulder and folded it carefully in half then half again. And again. She kept folding until the cloth was a fat roll that wouldn't fold any more. 'Yes,' she said. 'Exactly.'

'Is Gail coming?' Martine asked.

'She's here.' Martine looked over her shoulder towards the rest of the house. What had Kate called those other rooms on the far side of the hall? And why hadn't Gail come to greet her?

'She's downstairs,' Kate said. 'She'll be up soon. Or I could get her up now.'

Martine shifted her feet. 'Don't disturb her if she's busy. Do they live down there?' Kate hesitated. 'Gail and Leo.' She hadn't heard another word about Leo since the fact that he took the tiny cassette to work and went away discreetly while the sisters listened to the message. Maybe that meant he'd give them space today.

'There's no one living down there,' Kate said.

Martine looked towards the floor, at the stone slabs that were worn slightly concave in front of the wooden counters, from generations of feet shuffling and scraping as women stood there.

'Do you work down there? You said you run a business but you didn't say what it was, did you?'

'Tech support,' Kate said. Martine couldn't understand why those two words, or the combination of the words and the

look on Kate's face, should trouble her. Kate lifted a broom
from where it was hooked on two nails on the back of the
door and banged it on the stone in three raps, hard enough to
jolt Martine out of her thoughts again.

Kate cocked her head. 'She's on her way.'

Martine had heard nothing. 'Thank you,' she said. 'I'm
dying to meet her. And talk. We've got so much to say, the
three of us, haven't we? Well, the two of you. I'm dying to
hear all your memories of . . . him. Martin. Your father. Our
father.' She gave a breathless little laugh. 'I don't know what
to call him. What would you like me to call him?'

'Dad,' said Kate. 'If you like. Or anything you want to. But
I would just say, maybe when Gail's here, don't talk too much
about dying.'

'Dying?' Martine said. 'Martin dying? Of course n—'

'You, me, anyone,' said Kate. 'Dying to meet, dying to talk.
You'll see.'

Martine could feel the word 'sorry' starting to form but she
bit her lip on it. That was bonkers. In fact, everything about
this place was just slightly . . . what was the word she was
reaching for? 'Dying' was only an expression. She took another
drink to help the awkward moment by.

On the other hand, she could remember what new grief felt
like from when her gran died. How unreasonable it could make
you. And besides, she should be grateful for 'bonkers'. An
interesting family, a quirky home, was cause for celebration.
She had spun so many tales to herself about her dad – the
African student, the Deep South preacher's son (he had become
a preacher's son, over the years, somehow), the London lad
with all the sisters – that she had sometimes thought the truth
would be a disappointment.

Hardly. She smiled at Kate, at the tall pot of stovies with
the spoon balanced on top, at the weird, slummy kitchen. This
place and her two adoptive sisters were anything but dull. She
held the glass up in a sort of toast to that thought, as she drank
again.

'Here she comes,' Kate said again. Martine still couldn't
hear anything. This stone-floored room with its bare-brick
walls was like a tomb around her. The first she knew was the

snick of the latch on the outside door and the creak of the hinge as it swung open, letting in a gust of cold and making her shiver. She took a step back. She could even feel a catch in her throat as if she was going to let out a cry, but she managed to hold on to it. Framed in the doorway was a woman a head and a half taller than Kate and broad across the shoulders. She was dressed in a long purplish-grey tunic that hung to her ankles and her feet were bare, her toes red and white in patches from the cold. As she stepped inside, she left wet footprints on the stone flags. But it wasn't the strange dress or the bare feet that had set Martine's pulse rattling. It was the veil. The woman wore a veil of thin grey gauze dropped over her head and falling beyond her shoulders all around.

'H–Hello,' Martine said, with a quick darting look to Kate, whose face was unreadable. 'You must be Gail. I'm Martine. I've been so very much looking forward to meeting you.' She held out her hand to shake.

'Ssshh,' the woman said, so quietly Martine might have believed she'd imagined it if she hadn't seen the veil moving. Gail's right hand stayed by her side, holding something Martine couldn't quite see hidden in the palm. Probably a phone, she thought. That was probably the curve of a metallic phone cover.

'Look, darling,' Kate said. 'Look who's here.'

Gail shook her head. 'Ssshh,' she said.

'Go and sit down, darling,' said Kate. 'I'll bring a plate of food for you.'

Gail shook her head again and there was a twist to her mouth this time. 'No,' she whispered. 'You have to stop.'

Then she turned and left, gliding silently on her cold bare feet. The wet prints ran out before she stepped on to the patterned wood of the . . . dining room, Martine wanted to say, although that wasn't what Kate had called it.

'Is she OK?' Martine whispered, once she judged the woman was out of earshot.

'She's fine. She's just having trouble with feelings of grief. Natural enough. She's better every day and you being here will help no end.'

Martine nodded. She hadn't traipsed around a garden in bare feet or covered herself with a veil when her gran died but she remembered those early nights when sleep felt a thousand miles away. If someone had been there to see her they might have found her as odd as she found Gail.

'And she's having trouble eating, is she? Upset at you for trying to make her? That can't be easy.'

It explained the huge pot of potatoes and onions, she reckoned. If it was Gail's favourite food maybe. Or if she wasn't going to eat anyway and Kate was sick of thinking up nice meals just to see them wasted.

'She's fine!' Kate said again.

Martine saw a fleck of spit hitting the surface of the pan and noticed a tendon standing out on Kate's neck. 'Are *you* OK?' she said.

'I am fine, fine, more than fine,' Kate said. 'Go and talk to *her*. She needs you. I'm fine. She's the one who needs you here.'

Martine stared at Kate's neck, at the pulse visibly pounding. She couldn't walk away from this much distress, but what could she say to help?

'Can't Leo help her?' was what she went for. 'Or, has her doctor seen her?'

'Leo!' It was a howl. 'Yes I did, didn't I? Leo. A man with a job. I said "Leo". Like I said "auntie". Like I said "cat".' She was stabbing her spoon into the pot as if to kill something lurking in there.

'OK, OK,' Martine said, like she would to an animal injured and snarling. Like she had, once, to a drunk with a broken bottle neck in his hand. Slowly, she backed away and, as light on her toes as she could be, she flitted to the hallway, to the place where she'd left her bags. Her overnight, her messenger, her keys and her phone. And she stopped dead, feeling a whimper grow in her throat. They were gone.

For one moment, just one, she saw herself opening the front door and running down the path, leaving her bags behind her. She could go to the newsagent's over the road, or the nail bar on the corner and say . . . what?

The whimper turned into a groan and from behind the half-open door across the hall she heard Gail again. 'Ssshh.' Relief flooded her, annoyance at its back.

She tapped and then entered a pretty blue and white panelled room, empty like the rest of the house, except for a couple of chaise longues. Gail had lain down on one and was leaning back, lifting her feet. They were filthy, Martine noticed, with lines of mud between the toes and bits of grass stuck to the insteps. And the hem of her dress was muddy too, clinging round her ankles. It was thin material, almost transparent, and the underneath layer looked like silk. She still held the phone in one hand and was clutching a little leather case with a gold clasp in the other.

'Gail?' she said.

'Ssshh.'

'Gail, have you put my bags somewhere out of the way?'

'Ssshh.'

'Look.' The annoyance was growing but she tried to keep her voice gentle. 'Look, I'm sorry for what you're going through and obviously it was far too soon for me to turn up here. So if you'll just tell me where my bags are I'll— Don't shush me again. I know you're grieving but—'

'Grief,' said Gail at last, in a stronger voice than Martine had heard from her, 'is the last act of love.'

'That's right,' Martine said. 'Someone once told me grief is the bill we pay for the love we knew.'

'Tell *her!*' Gail had turned her head and was facing Martine full-on now. She pointed with the hand holding the phone. *Was it a phone?* Her chest was lifting and falling rapidly and the gauze in front of her face was fluttering with each snatched breath.

'Is that why you're wearing a veil?' Martine said. 'Is it mourning?'

'I'm not *wearing* a veil,' Gail said. Her voice had risen with her quickening breath and was as high as birdsong now. 'The veil is between us, before your eyes.'

'Oh darling, don't say that!' Kate's voice came from the doorway, a sudden wail in the silence.

'She's hidden my bags,' Martine said.

'Ssshh,' said Gail.

Kate had a shallow plate of food in each hand, steam curling off them in the cold air as she advanced into the room. 'I've brought you something to eat, my darling.'

Gail pressed herself back into the chaise and raised both

hands in front of her. Now Martine could see that the little rounded object wasn't a phone after all. It was a knife, one of those old craft knives, probably illegal now – what were they called? Stanley knives! As Kate took one more step, Gail's thumb moved and the blade slid out with a sharp tick.

As silently as she could, Martine set her glass on the floor and got to her feet.

Kate bent over the chaise with her neck stretched, inches from the glinting blade. 'Stop it,' she said. 'We both know that's not for me.' The plates had tipped and thin streams of liquid were pouring on to the floor, chunks of potato thudding down and splashing in the puddles. Martine felt her stomach rise as she edged towards the door.

Tock. The blade flashed as it slid back inside the handle.

'Look,' Kate whispered. Her voice was coiling and gentle but as she swung her hand towards Martine an arc of hot liquid sprayed over the floor, catching the front of Martine's legs. 'Look!' Kate's face was inches from Gail's now. 'She's right there. She's right here. I brought her for you, just like—'

Tick.

Martine stood frozen for one long empty moment, looking between the two of them, Gail stark-eyed behind the veil and Kate yearning forward as if to peck holes in the air in front of her face. Then she turned and fled, her crepe soles squeaking on the hall floor. She lunged for the front door handle, fumbling and twisting it this way and that until she couldn't deny it.

'Did you lock this?' she shouted. 'Am I locked in here?'

'Just till you settle,' said Kate. 'I'll move your car round and you stay here with my sister. She needs you. You're exactly what she needs.'

Martine went racing through the house to the kitchen to twist and rattle the door handle there. She shouted and pounded on the solid panels. She took a pan from a shelf and threw it at the window. It smashed the glass but bounced back off the bars.

As she fell back against the wall and let herself slide down to squat on the floor, she could hear the thump, thump, thump of Kate's slippers and the slap, slap, slap of Gail's bare feet, and very faintly the tick-tock, tick-tock of the knife blade going in and out in time, as they approached her.

TEN

The trouble with most people was that they didn't sculpt their lives. Oprah had said that, used just that word, and the sound of it in her smoke and honey voice – '*sculpt* your life', had made Laura shiver with a delight sharp enough to feel indecent. It wasn't the sort of thrill you should feel all alone in your own living room watching daytime telly with the curtains drawn over. It was like when your hairdresser suddenly started massaging your scalp in the middle of an ordinary hair-washing, as if giving that much pleasure – enough to lift all the hairs on your arms and wring a groan from your throat – was the sort of thing that happened any day of the week. And it was everywhere: even food adverts that followed the glossy swirl of chocolate sauce round the meek white mounds of ice cream in a way that made her think of ice dancers, swooping and whirling, speeding up in tighter and tighter spins then bursting free into a long low lazy loop again, still panting. She couldn't watch it, couldn't watch any of it, couldn't look at herself in the mirror after.

Laura didn't like to lose control. She liked to plan. People didn't plan, not in detail anyway. They dreamed. They hoped, long after they should know better. But they didn't *plan*. Laura planned. She wanted a baby, just one, and a house. She saw it so clearly she could have drawn a blueprint. And she wanted a business, with no fewer than three employees and no more than six, in a modern building, with a carpark and a reception desk.

So first she needed a man. That was exactly the sort of clear sight most women she knew would shy away from. They'd tell themselves they'd do it alone, they were goddesses and wonderful, and then when it was wine o'clock, they'd admit it wasn't working and they were beginning to think it never would.

Laura was different. She knew if she concentrated on getting the man and then pegging him down with the baby, he'd be on the hook for her business plan whether he stayed with her and called it love or moved on and called it alimony. She didn't mind which.

She didn't mind which man either. So long as he was tall, with good hair and all his teeth, and earned a decent six figures, she could cope with just about anything. And she knew how to snag him too. It was mostly diet and exercise. Even if they were canny enough not to say it out loud any more, at least in mixed company, every man wanted a fit body. She knew plenty girls who spent a fortune at the hairdresser's and the beauty parlour, even the perfume counter – the clueless fools, when the fact was that ninety-nine men out of a hundred couldn't tell the difference between a five-hundred-smacker highlight job and a packet from the chemist. As long your hair was long and clean and you didn't mind him holding it like a rope, it was all the same. And none of them liked that caked-on look with the boxy eyebrows and ten tones of shading, never mind the thought of kissing wet-look glossed lips. She laughed up her sleeve at them all on a Saturday night, circus clowns. They were out on the pull, and they might as well be wearing signs on their heads telling men to stay away. The perfume was worst of all. They came home from Magaluf laden with duty-free, loving themselves for it, and even that one man in a hundred who cared about hairdos and didn't mind bronzer, even *he* couldn't stomach the guff of them. They were like gardens sprayed with cat repellent telling themselves the cats would be rolling up any minute now.

Laura had long blonde hair she washed every day and left loose. She wore no make-up at all, ever, as far as any man would know. And she smelled of Pears soap and baby powder. She wore heels she could walk in, jeans that fitted her with no rolls bursting over the top, and the best push-up padded bra she could afford under a low top with a pendant necklace that gave them an excuse for looking. And they did look. Then they looked up, cowering with guilt, ready for a frosty stare or even a rude word. But she kept on listening to whatever they were banging on about with exactly the same happy smile on her face, as if she hadn't noticed.

If she'd smirked at them, making out she didn't mind, they'd have backed off. No one wanted a slapper who wore a low top and loved it when men looked down her cleavage. But a sweet, fresh-faced girl who smelled like their wee sister after bath time, and didn't even know when men were taking liberties? Probably didn't realize how low the neckline was, or even how perfect the rack was? That was the sort of girl who needed someone to look after her.

Not that she seemed to be searching. She was always happy to hear of an engagement, hen night, wedding, even baby shower. She was delighted at the news and thrilled to be included. She loved her job, as far as anyone could tell. She'd drop it if a city-break came up, but she was just as happy to suit herself for three weekends in a row if the man of the moment got a better offer. She was a good driver and kept her car immaculate, but she handed over the keys automatically and let herself be driven without a murmur. She liked a drink, but she never got plastered, never got sloppy. She was great in bed. She knew it and wasn't ashamed to congratulate herself. She was absolutely bloody great. Responsive and willing, no matter what they asked her to do, but she never pushed it. Never asked *them* for anything they hadn't at least hinted at already. And – this was her secret weapon; this was what set her above all the other women she knew and all the other women she heard men moaning about – she didn't want to talk about it afterwards. She didn't want to talk about anything. She didn't talk.

Laura Wade, in short, was the perfect woman. She was forty years old too, which was the perfect age to attract a man who wanted to settle down.

'You're the perfect age,' she told herself out loud, in the bathroom mirror, on her birthday. It was less intimidating for a man of the right age – which was forty-five – to ask her out. He didn't need to worry about music and late nights. He knew she'd understand that he had responsibilities at work and friends he wanted to spend time with.

So why was the memory thudding so solidly in her mind of when she'd been looking at herself in this mirror and telling herself she was thirty now and needed to get a move on because if he didn't turn up soon, she might as well call it a bust and shift to plan B.

Not that she actually had a plan B. She didn't have time between all the different tentacles of her budding business empire.

'I'm a content designer,' she'd say on first dates. Normal men didn't want to hear any more than that. They looked at her posh watch and her posh car and drew the conclusion that whatever content she designed, she did it well enough. She never talked about it again, unless they asked. And they never asked.

The truth was that she wrote greetings cards, two hundred quid a poem and fifty for a one-liner. Gal pals and wine was her speciality, but she could knock out an exhausted new parent or a second chance at love often enough to keep her options open. She'd stolen the idea of writing messages in sand from somewhere or other too and that was a sweet little sideline, but it took half a day and only when the weather was good. Selling phone cases online was her bread and butter. She designed them herself so she wasn't lying, but it was retail. Not that she had anything against retail. She kept trying to move into dog accessories, where the big money was, but she'd been stung.

'Sand to Arabs and snow to Eskimos,' she told herself in the mirror each morning. She had offloaded the six boxes of dog coats to a market trader, cutting her losses, and rarely thought about them these days. At least she wasn't doing carpets any more. She hadn't got rid of her steam-cleaner. It sat there taped up in black plastic in the back corner of the garage, just in case. When she parked the S-Class she looked at it the way you'd look at the handrail in a hotel bathroom, thinking 'never' and hoping it was true.

All in all, Laura was the last person to go forking over her hard-earned and hoarded cash to buy services from anyone else. She washed her own car and her own windows. She cut her own fringe and did her own ironing. She'd designed her own website and made her own windscreen fliers.

But something had tipped her over the edge on this one. Match, eHarmony and Elite Singles between them hadn't coughed up anything worth a second date in the six months since she'd offloaded Gareth.

He had seemed promising at first. Early on, she'd made sure to get a squint at his bank statement, and she'd seen the monthly total of his child support. If that was how fatherhood took him, she thought, then she could put up with his split fingernails and kayaking anecdotes. Then, on the way back from a Valentine's weekend at a Highland hotel, he dropped the bombshell. No more kids. He was committed to the two that his marriage had produced and he didn't want to be split between them and any more.

'I'm guessing you'll be OK with that,' he'd said. He couldn't look at her, not on that twisting country road in the near dark, but he must have picked up on her reaction somehow. 'Laura?' he said after a minute. 'I mean, you've never mentioned kids and you're so . . .'

'So *what*?' Laura said, the harshest words she'd ever spoken to him. No one likes a shrew.

'So professional,' he offered after a moment's thought. 'Slick. Not slick. Polished, though.'

Slick, she repeated to herself. Slick.

She broke up with him, by text, the next night. When that didn't bring him to her entryphone promising to match the Waltons if she'd just buzz him up and let him apologize, she couriered his sad little collection of possessions round to him and blocked his number. There was no time to waste on no-hopers, she told herself, trying for upbeat. But the truth of it – the hourglass running out, and that little fold in the corner of her mouth that didn't disappear these days even when she smiled – were like a dash of cold water.

Which was where 'Fairytale Endings' came in. She'd stumbled on the website late one Saturday night when she'd watched herself awake again on a whole painfully slow series of Swedish murders. At two o'clock, with a dull headache and gritty eyes, she'd searched dating, introductions, matchmaking and singles, clicking through the early pages she knew so well until she was back in the weeds, hating herself for even looking, despising the clunky prose and ill-advised fonts of these home-made little websites. It hadn't been that long since she'd caught a virus from one of these crappy-looking sites, such a bad one she couldn't get rid of it herself and had to cough up to a professional to do it for her. Laura hated being defeated and having to pay an expert to take over.

Fairytale Endings was different. She knew a decent photograph when she saw one and the picture on the home page, of an elegant room with little tables laid for supper, candles and crystal both twinkling, had not been snapped on an iPhone.

We are not a dating service, the blurb began. *We are not a singles service or an introduction portal. We are matchmakers as matchmakers used to be. Our clients are gentlemen between the ages of twenty-five and sixty who desire to meet financially independent, educated, interesting ladies with a view to marriage.*

'In other words, you're a dating service,' Laura said, but she closed the other windows on her laptop and got herself a refill of wine to read some more.

We host monthly dinner dances in an exclusive, private and safe location, the blurb went on. The sidebar photograph, black and white, was of a woman in a Hitchcock-era evening dress perched on a stool powdering her face in an ornate mirror. She held the powder puff in a hand wearing a long white evening glove and Laura wished she hadn't thought of Hitchcock's heroines. The smear of face powder on the white glove was an anonymous dark grey, like Janet Leigh's blood in the shower.

'You're drunk,' she told herself. She snapped shut the laptop, poured away the wine and swallowed half a pint of water and two ibuprofen before she went to bed.

Maybe she dreamed about it. (Laura rarely remembered her dreams.) In any case, she found herself looking for the site again the next day. They had a menu posted – scallops, pigeon, rhubarb fool – and a list of dances they 'suggested' an acquaintance with. Laura googled 'social foxtrot, easy waltz, minuet'. It was the minuet that undid her. Too many six-part miniseries with men in breeches and women in muslin.

She kept clicking and found the testimonials. They were discreet – no faces, no second names – but two of them were wedding photos. In one a slim bride in a sheath of cream satin was walking under an honour guard with a tall groom whose bald spot shone as if the photographer had focused his lens on it deliberately. Laura felt her pulse quicken. That had to be real. If they'd been models they'd have picked a man with a full head of hair. The other wedding photograph was from the neck down, two hands in brand-new rings clasped over a white lace pregnancy bump. And the caption 'Only human!' Laura laughed and scrolled on.

The enrolment questions were generic enough. They wanted to know her age, salary range, marital status, and aspirations. 'Marriage to a bachelor, divorcé or widower,' she wrote. 'Must want children.' She looked for another page where weight and height ranges might be hiding, where she could specify a flat stomach and a non-smoker, but there was nothing.

'Meat market,' Laura told herself. 'Or a cover for something.' Maybe it was a swingers' club and she was too green to decipher the code. But the two wedding photographs – bald, pregnant – wouldn't leave her. The next night, sitting with another glass of wine, she refilled the boxes and this time submitted the information.

In the morning, there was an email in her inbox telling her, with regret, that they had a full complement of ladies for the next two monthly dances, but would she like them to keep her name on file for later in the spring?

Laura bristled, wondering what troglodytes they were shoving at these gentleman clients, if there was nowhere to describe your looks on the submission form. She didn't reply.

Another day passed and then an email came warning her that her data would be disposed of in twenty-four hours unless they received instructions to the contrary.

'Please keep my information on file,' she wrote back. She couldn't help adding an attachment, a photograph of herself standing outside a German Schloss, crisp and sunny in white trousers and ballet flats, with huge sunglasses and a scarf tied over her hair. Her bag, from the angle in the photo, looked just like a Birkin. Gareth had snapped that and she knew it was tacky to use it but they weren't to know, were they?

Then she forgot about it. She was trying to decide whether to add earbuds and stands to her phone-case line or whether that would cheapen her brand. Her brand was all she had and she would protect it like a mother bear with her cubs. When the day came that she had a little shop in Glasgow and one in Edinburgh, a little concession here and there in the foyers of the best hotels, when she was thinking about London, one cheap set of earbuds with her name on them could drive off an entrepreneurial sponsor like a dose of anthrax.

When the email came two months later, there was no spark of recognition in Laura. She swept it away to spam and carried on with her costings. It was only at lunchtime, standing in her kitchen, waiting for one of her tubs of frozen soup to finish thawing, that her mind wandered to men, dates, dancing and then, as the microwave pinged, Laura's brain pinged with it. She pulled her phone close and fished the email back to her inbox.

'Our May event is rose-themed,' it began. 'Please let us know your favourite colour of rose when you accept this invitation. Allergy sufferers please alert us and we will make every attempt to ensure your comfort.'

It wasn't very informative but as she stood puzzling at the lack of details, another email arrived. 'Dear Laura, I'm delighted to announce that we have several gentlemen attending next month who are keen to meet a woman just like you. One in particular has been disappointed by the company at his monthly dances so far, and we have taken the liberty of forwarding your photograph to him in advance. He has requested your presence at his table for the third rotation.'

Laura narrowed her eyes at that. 'Third' sounded a bit indifferent. On the other hand, her experience with speed-dating had shown her that the last of the night was often the one you pursued, from sheer exhaustion. You were sitting opposite some guy when they finally stopped hitting that damn buzzer and so you gave him a shot, because it was either that or stand up again.

Maybe 'third rotation' was to give this gentleman who'd seen her photo a decent chance.

So she accepted. She composed a terse email saying she was free and would attend but needed more information, for her own peace of mind. The response came in twenty minutes, completely different in tone – gushing, she might have said.

'We can furnish you with any information you need on our gentlemen, except surnames. If you would be happier with a phone call, let me know when you are free and someone will ring you. For now, let me say that seven of our fifteen gentlemen attending in May are new to Fairytale Endings. The other eight are returning gentlemen who have not yet found that special someone. You will dine with three, moving between courses, and then are free to dance with anyone who asks. We have found that ladies prefer not to take responsibility for approaching dance partners and our gentlemen know that dancing is expected of them.'

Nicely put, Laura thought. Reassuring.

'Your three dining companions are as follows,' the email went on. 'Piers is forty years old, a businessman from Glasgow, he is divorced without children, and is looking for a companion who will cope well with his frequent long absences from home due to overseas travel.'

That was a possibility she hadn't considered yet: a man she could stay married to, avoiding all the hassle of a divorce, but who didn't get under her feet. He'd probably be guilty enough to invest in her business too and he wouldn't resent her putting in the hours because he wouldn't be there.

'For the main course, you will join Robert. Robert moved to Scotland from his native Ghana as a postgraduate student, and is now working in the tech industry. He is thirty-five years old and is a never-married singleton. His intention is to remain here indefinitely.'

In other words, he needed residency and thought a wife was the way to get it. That didn't necessarily put her off. There was money in tech and weren't Ghanaians all ten feet tall with perfect teeth and those sexy breathy voices? She could learn to cope with a tall, gorgeous husband whose English wasn't good enough for arguments.

'Over dessert and coffee, and on into the evening if you choose to remain together, your companion will be Grant. Grant has attended four Fairytale Evenings in the last year and has enjoyed each one. He is an enthusiastic dancer and a true conversationalist, but he has not yet met the girl of his dreams. Grant is looking for a woman in her late thirties, who is ready to settle down and is keen on a small family, but who is independent enough to steer her own ship while he concentrates on the expansion of his growing business. We showed Grant your photograph as an incentive for him to attend a further event, after the recent disappointments, and he was favourably impressed.'

Grant, Laura said to herself. She was standing at her breakfast bar charging her laptop before she took it to her study for a sprint. This was one of Laura's most productive little life hacks. She ran her laptop battery down while completing a task, demanding of herself that she finish it before recharging.

Grant, she said, leaving the kitchen and padding through to the spare bedroom, the one she had turned into a wardrobe for herself. She never had people to stay and she liked to see her clothes properly stored.

Grant and Laura. She leafed through the 'cocktail dress' section, wondering what Grant would like to see her in. She owned nothing black. You were already ahead of the pack if you walked into a party in a colour when all the other women had crapped out. She always took care to compliment them, of course, on their beautiful sequins, or beading, or chiffon, or fringes, as if any of those token efforts made up for the acceptance of defeat that was the little black dress.

Should she go sleeveless? Her arms were in perfect shape. But there was nothing to show on a second date if she went sleeveless on the first.

Grant and Laura . . . what? Would she change her name? She had always thought 'Wade' would make a good element in a double-barrel. It would depend on his, she supposed. If he was called Foxworth or Montague she would dump Wade like a poo-bag. But if he was called McGuffin or Burke or something, she'd weigh up her options. Briefly, she wondered what the Ghanaian's second name would be and whether an exotic touch would be good for business.

She plucked an emerald-green dress off the rack. She'd send it to be dry-cleaned before the dance. Not that she had put it away dirty. But the truth was she hadn't worn any of her cocktail dresses since a year past Christmas, her last weekend away with Gareth, so it might have got stale.

Somewhere in Laura's future, she firmly believed, there was a real walk-in wardrobe waiting, cedar-lined and air-filtered. There would be lights under the shelves and round the mirror and she wouldn't need to keep an exercise bike in it. She had a niggling little worry that she'd seen this wardrobe in a film and wasn't being realistic dreaming of it for her own future, but she batted the thought away. Even divorced Piers from Glasgow, dragging his failed starter marriage along behind him, couldn't object to his wife – his keeper wife, mother of his child – wanting some decent hanging space and a few shelves for her shoes.

When she wrote back to Fairytale Endings she didn't stand on her dignity. She loved the sound of Grant and was also very interested to speak to Robert, since she had never been to Africa. She was glad to have Piers as an ice-breaker. Perhaps she was fulfilling that function for him too? In any case, she was looking forward in great anticipation to May and to what promised to be a rewarding experience as well as a treat.

It was . . . concerning . . . not so much as troubling, but certainly concerning that Fairytale Endings didn't want her to talk about them on social media or share details with non-members. Discretion, they said, confidentiality, exclusivity. She could see the point of it. Piers, Robert and Grant didn't sound like the sort of men who would want their private lives plastered all over the internet. But still, it was concerning.

Laura thought of what all the other dating sites advised. Tell someone where you're going. Meet on neutral territory. Go in the daytime the first time, not in the evening. But then there were going to be thirty people at this dance as well as the organizers. She was being too cautious. She had suffered so many sharp falls that she couldn't accept something pleasant coming easily to her and offering a smooth path. Besides, she wasn't talking to a strange man online, arranging to meet. She was talking to a professional woman, like herself. Myra, from Fairytale Endings. Laura had a good feeling about this one.

ELEVEN

She didn't wear the emerald green in the end. She had pored over the photographs on the website long enough, by the time the date came round, to know that something lighter and sweeter would set her off against the pale panelling of the dance-floor room and the picked-out plasterwork of the little supper room. Not to mention toning with her chosen roses. She wouldn't have admitted to the organizers that her favourite roses were blood-red. Surely *no* woman would have said so. They would all know what Laura knew, that the first red roses of a new relationship were heavy with meaning.

No one would say purple, would they? That nasty shade somewhere between soot and liver. No, the other fourteen – Laura had got to imagining them, when she was on her exercise bike, all of them pitting against her for Grant, the prize of the night – they would all have said what she said, more or less: yellow, pale pink, pure white. And so she dressed herself up like a sweet pea, in ruffles that winked – now peach, now cream – as she moved. She made up her face with the lightest of touches, cheeks dusted pink, a few freckles painted on as if she'd tried to cover them but not very hard and just a little Vaseline on her dyed lashes and her lips. She would find an excuse to rub her eye at some point in the evening, sending the signal to Grant (or Robert, at a push) that she wasn't wearing any muck on her face, that this was the real thing sitting opposite him, smiling.

Pearls were a step too far, she thought, sitting at her dressing table and casting her eye over the jewellery at her disposal. Jewellery was tough for a single woman, before she gave up and started buying herself the 'I'm worth it' defiance pieces. Costume was pathetic once you were over twenty-one. Funky, quirky earrings and big bangles made her shudder. But until there was someone to put a diamond on your finger, any diamonds you put on your wrist or in your ears or hanging from a chain around your neck only served to highlight that empty finger even more. Pearls were the answer for a few years, but at forty, still to wear your pearls in the evening – such an obvious present from parents instead of more recent tributes – invited unkind looks, or, what was worse, kind looks. Kind comments, even. These days, Laura wore her pearls with a jumper and jeans, with a shirt for work meetings sometimes, and that was the end of it.

There was always the option of loading herself up with good gold chains and bangles, a garnet here, an opal there. It looked like cheap finery at first glance but then she would mention one of them. She could say the bangle with the sapphires and tourmalines was her granny's, or claim that she had only just got the flat platinum chain back from the menders. Let everyone know, in no uncertain terms, that all this clobber she'd flung together carelessly was worth a bundle.

But not with a peaches and cream ruffled dress for a dance in a room full of roses.

What if everyone except her *had* said red roses were their favourites? What if the other fourteen women had nailed their colours to the mast and she was going to look like a coward? Or an original? No man wanted an original. Not for keeps. Grant was looking for someone to settle down with, and Robert must be sick of sticking out in every crowd.

Laura lifted her hand mirror and looked at the carefully messy bun she had put together. Tonight was an exception to hair down, she was pretty sure. She didn't want to look disrespectful, like a soap star on the red carpet, clueless and scruffy. She had secured the twist of hair with a diamond hat pin she'd bought online, a real bargain. No one wore hat pins. But *she* wore it as a brooch, stuck through her dress, or like tonight as a hair clip.

No rings, she decided. Any ring at all was a joke for a single woman of forty. Her manicure was perfect and that meant more than baubles. Nothing round her neck either. Just a tendril of hair curling from behind one ear to rest against her collarbone. The diamond hat pin when she turned round, and through her ears . . . Oh sod it all. Her diamond studs were a carat each and she was bloody well wearing them. Anyway, when she put them in, she was surprised to see how titchy two carats' worth of diamond looked. Would she ever have a necklace – a whole necklace; not just a pendant on a chain? Would she ever have a tiara? A real one? She regarded herself with a look any witness would have called steely. If she didn't start paying attention and getting this right she wouldn't even get the chance to wear a plastic tiara for her hen-do.

It was quite a drive from Ayr. At first, she'd assumed Hephaw was some classy suburb of Glasgow she'd never heard of. Like most west coasters, she tended to think of Glasgow first. And last. When she punched in the postcode to time her journey and saw the road snaking all the way to the middle of the central belt, to the pits of West Lothian, she wondered for a moment if she'd found the catch. It sent her back to the website gallery and all the pictures of candlelit tables, marble fireplaces and gleaming parquet floors. What if it was like those hotels in Spain that used stock photos and, when you arrived, they were round the back of an abattoir?

Then she reconsidered it. Actually, it made perfect sense to put a business that would draw car drivers right in the middle somewhere. Edinburgh and Glasgow equidistant, and the bridges over the Forth bringing punters from the north. Should she think of that for herself, when the time came? Not that she was considering a destination premises like a supper club (or whatever this was) but she hoped for some foot traffic when her shop opened. Surely it was still better to have it in Glasgow though. Her empire might expand – *would* expand, and fast if she had anything to do with it – but her flagship store would be right there in the West End, where people with a bit of spare put it on their backs and flaunted it. Laura understood them and admired them. Ayr might be her birth-place, and house prices might keep her there awhile, but Glasgow was her true home.

She pulled the door closed and checked it, then tripped down the stairs to her covered parking space, feeling irrepress-ible bubbles of hope rising inside her. She had to stop while a patient transport bus backed in to the pavement dip to drop off one of her elderly neighbours. Niamh, Laura thought her name was. She remembered because it seemed a young name for such a frail old lady. But she was probably Irish and Niamh had probably been an Irish name since forever. Laura waved through the bus window at her and Niamh gurned back and shook her fist, which was as close as she could get to waving, since arthritis had bent her hand up into a claw. She did manage to poke her index finger almost straight and jabbed it down towards Laura's feet, her strong horny nail hitting the window with a pock-pock-pock. She frowned.

'I know!' Laura mouthed. 'They're for driving.' She opened the shoe-bag thrown over her shoulder and showed Niamh the frivolous strappy sandals with the spindly heels that she'd swap for the ballet flats when she got to Hephaw.

Niamh smiled and nodded and then grimaced as her chair lurched against the stops on the lift and her head jerked back. Laura crossed to her car and slid in, smoothing her dress and fastening her seat belt under her bosom to stop the ruffles at her neckline getting crushed.

An hour later, she was crawling along the main street of the kind of town she never thought she'd have business in. Ayr had its rough corners, of course; Laura avoided the bottom of the High Street and the Sandgate leading off it. Not that they were dangerous, but they were depressing. There was no way to avoid the depressing bits of Hephaw. The town, like so many Scottish towns, was just one long street with a few council estates tacked on behind it on each side and even fewer desperate attempts at gentrification squeezed in here and there, like this development of townhouses she was driving past now, whose weedy flower tubs gave away the fact that they hadn't attracted Yuppies in the end, as their builder must have hoped.

Laura stuck her chin in the air, refusing to recognize the echo of her own townhouse in her own affordable town. There was no danger of recognizing herself in any of the people lining the pavements this late Saturday teatime. Flipflops, leggings and a double buggy seemed to be the uniform for the women of Hephaw, tracksuits and pool slides over socks for the men. Laura kept going, past a pub that advertised Sky Sports, a Farmfoods freezer shop and a combined kebab and pizza takeaway.

'If there's a Payday Loan, I'm leaving,' she said aloud to

herself. She hadn't seen one by the time she reached the turn-off for Loch Road. The newsagents with grilles on the windows and the pitiful nail bar with its aspirational name had been bad enough.

'Where's the bloody loch, I don't wonder,' she said, pulling in beside a gate with '1a' picked out in gold paint on black iron. From habit she looked at the other cars parked up and down the sides of the street. A Skoda, a Hyundai, an Escort, for God's sake, with a mismatched wing and a missing hubcap.

These couldn't be the cars of Grant, Robert, Piers and the rest of them. Was she early?

It was just ten past seven. The invitation had been for seven o'clock. Maybe there was a carpark round the back. But when she peered through the bars of the gate, 1a Loch Road looked to be a house. A cottage. And it was joined on to its neighbour on one side and a high brick wall on the other. If there was a carpark then it was off a back street.

Laura wriggled out of her flats and into her sandals. She checked her tendril and her ruffles in the driving mirror, then rubbed her lips together to spread the remaining Vaseline over them. Perfect, she told herself, and opened her car door.

She couldn't see much of what was inside as she walked up the path. The bay window in what – from her study of the website – she knew was the dancing room had lace curtains, although she could tell from the points of brightness that the chandelier was lit. Candles would have been better with the roses.

She took a deep breath and knocked on the door, hearing the hollow echo of it reverberate inside the house. Then there was silence for what felt like a minute, but couldn't have been. Laura put her ear close to the wood, ignoring the peeling varnish. If the band had started up already, maybe no one could hear her. Maybe she should just go in.

She turned the handle and pushed, surprised and not entirely pleased to feel the door give way and start to open. She knocked again, in case just walking in was wrong, but again no one appeared in answer and she could tell now there was no music drowning her out. There wasn't a sound from inside the house.

She took a step back and glanced down the path and through

the gate at her car. She could be home in another hour, out of these torturous heels and this flimsy dress that was always wrapped round her wrong no matter how she plucked at it. Then she shook herself, pasted an innocent smile on her face and stepped inside.

The quiet was unnerving. To her left, through a pair of half-open double doors, Laura saw the real-live version of the photographs she'd been poring over. The floor was polished and the fire at the far end was lit and crackling. She stepped inside.

'Hello?' There was another set of double doors halfway along the side wall of the dancing room and through there a cluster of little tables was set with white cloths and empty vases. Where were the roses? Where were the *people*? 'Hello-o?' Laura called.

She checked her phone, even though she knew she was here at the right time. Maybe there was a garden and they were all out there enjoying the pleasant evening. (But where were the roses?)

She stood in the middle of the supper room, wondering whether to sit. Some of the tables were for two and some for four. She hoped she sat with Piers and Robert when there was another couple there to dilute the awkwardness and she hoped on her third rotation, when she met Grant, it was at a table for two.

If Grant was coming. If any of them were. Was it possible for everyone except Laura to have cried off for some reason? But wouldn't the organizers have let her know? She took her phone out again and opened Chrome, wondering if there had been some catastrophe that she alone had missed, from listening to her music instead of the radio.

But someone *was* coming. At last. She could hear footsteps, metalled heels on stone, then the sound of a door opening. 'Hello!' she sang out. 'I let myself in. I hope that's OK.'

A woman appeared around a door in the corner of the supper room, a colourless little thing with lashless eyes and wispy hair. She was carrying a deep plastic tray, the kind used to lease out glasses for parties.

'Can I help you?' she said. She was tiny and slender, with

ankles like a little bird and wrists that looked too fine for the weight she was carrying.

'Are you Myra?' Laura said.

'No!' said the little woman with a panicked look over Laura's shoulder. 'Who are you?'

'I'm Laura. Wade. For the dance?' Laura said, feeling irritation start to gather under her ribs. She had done herself up like a flower fairy and driven an hour to get here and this stupid dishwasher with her rented champagne flutes was just boggling at her.

'Oh, love!' she said now. She went to set the tray down on the nearest table then thought the better of it and bent, groaning, to put it on the floor. She wiped her hands on her apron as she straightened. 'Oh Laura, love!' she said. 'It's tomorrow! The dance is tomorrow. Oh, and you look so lovely too in your pretty dress.'

'Tomorrow?' said Laura. 'No. No! It's today. It's tonight. The rose ball. Saturday the twenty-fifth of May.'

'It's the twenty-fifth of May right enough,' the little woman said. 'But that's tomorrow. Sunday. We always have our dances on Sunday. It's . . . well, it's nicer, isn't it? We think so.'

Laura blinked a couple of times. Could that be right? Had she just assumed it was Saturday, because Saturday night was date night? She fished in her bag for her phone to check the calendar and the little woman put her head on one side, and twisted her face up into a rueful half-smile.

'You still don't believe me?' she said. 'But look: no one else is here. Everyone else is coming tomorrow.'

Laura let her phone slip out of her hand again and gave an answering smile.

'Promise you won't tell them all,' she said. 'When I come back.'

'Oh, I am glad to hear you say that.' The woman literally clapped her hands. 'I'm so glad this hasn't put you off and you haven't got another appointment. That would have been awful.'

'See you tomorrow then,' Laura said. All she wanted was to get out and get home. She couldn't rock up again the next day in the same dress and she needed time to think about another one. Maybe she'd even need to go shopping.

'See you.' The woman seemed to hesitate and then went on: 'You won't tell anyone, will you? It makes us look bad to have a lady make a wasted journey. I'd be really grateful if you didn't put it on social media.'

'Of course not!' Laura said. 'I honoured your request. There's nothing anywhere about me coming here. I didn't even tell friends. Not that I'm embarrassed. There's nothing to be ashamed of. But . . . well, you must understand. Or you wouldn't have asked for confidentiality yourselves.'

'You didn't tell anyone at all?' The woman's smile was hard to fathom. She seemed too pleased, somehow. Perhaps she felt pity. Perhaps she'd decided if Laura hadn't told a soul it was because she didn't have a soul to tell. Laura found herself hoping that was it, but feeling a flicker of understanding that it was something else entirely, something she didn't want to name.

The woman was looking over Laura's shoulder now, and quite intently. Laura felt the hair on the back of her neck lifting, and was sure that someone else was there, standing silently behind her. She half-turned but could see nothing except shadows, a half-open door leading back to the hall, a half-open door on its other side, darkness beyond. She strained her ears but heard nothing except the tick-tock, tick-tock of a clock that she hadn't noticed until now.

'You're *forty*, Laura, aren't you?' the woman said suddenly.

Laura turned back to face her. 'Yes. I didn't lie about my age.'

'And that's exactly right. That's exactly the right age. You're a perfect match.'

'Who for?' Laura said. She couldn't help a little leap of excitement inside her. 'For which one?'

'The only one that matters.' She was beaming. 'I thought the same age was the best idea, then I thought very young would be best, but you're just right. And you *look* just right.' She was still gazing over Laura's shoulder. 'This is going to be wonderful.'

'Are you talking to me?' Laura said. The clock had stopped. How could a clock just suddenly stop though?

The woman blinked and then she did look straight into Laura's eyes. 'Who else?' she said. Then, 'Before you go, can I ask you to do something? And then to say thank you, I'll show you something? Can you say "show" if it's a smell, not a sight?'

'A smell?' Laura said.

'It's the roses, for tomorrow. They're downstairs in a little flower room we've got down there and the smell would make you drunk. It's glorious. I mean, they'll be sweet enough tomorrow when they're up here, but the rooms are bigger and we'll have the windows open and scented candles and food, so they're bound to be diluted. I'd love to let you experience them all massed together today. I know you're a true rose fan, from the ones you chose. A named variety, not just a colour.'

Laura smiled, flattered. The truth was she had asked for Princess Elizabeth to see how far this outfit would go to please a guest.

'I'd love to,' she said. 'Thank you. And what is it you want me to do?'

'Oh!' said the woman. 'I nearly forgot. We've changed our wine supplier and I've just opened a bottle to check it out. For tomorrow. And I'm not sure. Now, I know you're driving, but would you take one sip and tell me honestly what you think?'

'Happy to,' Laura said. 'I bet it's fine. But it's good to pay attention.'

'This way,' the woman said, beckoning her to the open door in the back corner of the room. 'I'm Kate, by the way. You'll meet my sister Gail tomorrow and we'll have some servers too. Sixth-year students from the high school, but we've trained them properly. This way.'

'Your sister?' Laura said. 'So this is a family business?'

'Just us sisters,' she said. 'Think of us as *your* sisters. We do. The gentlemen are our clients, our customers. But the ladies are sisters.'

Laura opened her mouth; she usually had a ready answer for pretty much anything. But not this time.

Kate laughed a tinkling little laugh. 'You caught me,' she said. 'I'm the fanciful one. The dreamer.'

She had led Laura into a stone-floored scullery that looked too old-fashioned to be a working service-kitchen. There was an open bottle of prosecco sitting on the draining board, and a glass, almost full, the bubbles still rising. Kate took a second glass from a shelf and poured a healthy measure, much more than a tasting sample.

Laura sniffed and then sipped. If she'd been nearer the sink she'd have spat. 'Good news and bad news,' she said. 'Your palate is excellent. But that wine is not good.'

Kate put her own glass to her lips again. 'Not nice?' she said. 'But OK for Kir Royales? Or actually not good?'

Against her instincts Laura took another mouthful. 'It's not corked,' she said. 'And it's not rancid. But I don't think liqueur would cover it. Sorry.'

'I'll return the case,' Kate said. 'And hit the offy before it shuts tonight. Thank you. And now, for the flowers.'

She beamed at Laura and opened the back door, leading the way out into the garden. It was even longer than the front, but with no apple trees or paths. It was just a stretch of close-mown grass crisscrossed with washing ropes.

'My sister says we should have silk flowers and she thinks it would be easier to tumble-dry our tablecloths and napkins,' Kate was saying. 'Hand towels too. But there's no substitute for line-drying, I always say. You take a good deep lungful of your napkin tomorrow night and tell me I'm wrong.'

Laura looked around the drying green, to be polite, and as she was turning back she saw a movement at the window above her. She couldn't be sure; the glass had net curtains over it. Maybe they had moved in a draught. Or – Laura squinted harder – was there a face there? Just there where the net seemed thicker? Was there a blurred, grey face? She shook her head and blinked. Could two mouthfuls of wine really have made her feel this woozy?

Kate had doubled back on herself and was now picking her way down some mossy steps that led to a basement.

'Mind how you go in those lovely shoes,' she said.

Laura put her hand against the cool stone wall beside her and edged down, setting both feet together on each tread before reaching one down to the step below. Her head was definitely not as clear as it should be, but looking at her feet made it worse.

Kate was opening a door now, a door surprisingly well locked if it was only keeping a few flowers safe. It juddered and scraped on the stone step as she wrenched it. 'We need to get this sanded off a bit. But when you work in hospitality, you do tend to focus on the public face and let the rest go. Do you work with the public, Laura?'

'Not really,' Laura said. 'Not physically. Online. But I suppose I make sure and have nice headed paper and decent packing materials. You don't want to look small even when you are small. The eBay whiff, you know?'

'Exactly,' said Kate. 'You understand. You really are one of us. You're perfect.'

Laura found herself frowning and again wondering what to say. Then, although she wouldn't have been able to account for it, she looked down the long garden to the back wall, wondering if there was a gate, a back way out of here. She could see a door, but also a padlock glinting.

'Oh! I can smell the flowers already,' Kate said. 'Can't you?'

Laura took a sniff and couldn't smell anything except crushed grass and damp stone.

'No?' Kate was inside some sort of anteroom to the cellar now, lying under the scullery, just a little vestibule with another door at the back of it. 'Maybe my nose is attuned. They're through there. Breathe all the way out and then take a deep sniff when you go in.' She was unlocking the inner door now.

Laura thought about the way back to her car, up these stone steps, in at the back door, through the house and out the front, down the path to the gate. She half-turned, but she could still see Kate, with her hand on the inner door, just about to open it up and let her drink in all those beautiful flowers. One sniff, Laura told herself, then I'm out of here. A little voice inside her said: and I'm never coming back.

What harm would one sniff of some roses do?

She breathed out, blowing the air out of her lungs until her throat croaked, then, when Kate swept the door open, she stepped inside.

The inner door slammed shut behind her, as she choked on the stench and the sound of clamouring screams filled her ears.

She stood in the dark, gagging and stumbling, and didn't hear the sound of the outside cellar door banging shut and the bolts going home.

Then the screams died down to ragged breaths. Laura stood stock-still keeping her own breathing silent and shallow.

'She's gone,' said a voice.

'She left something though,' said another.

Laura licked her lips, but her tongue caught on them, suddenly dry and sour. 'She did,' she said. There was a sharp burst of scrabbling, like small creatures taking cover. 'She did leave something. She left me.'

'And then there were three,' said one of the voices, with a queer kind of relish in it, a crack in it that was almost a cackle.

Laura felt for the wall at her side, leaned one hand against it for support as her head reeled and her legs trembled. She managed to stay on her feet, managed not to buckle and fall. She stood breathing deeply through her mouth, trying not to taste the smell, waiting for her eyes to adjust before she felt her way towards whoever it was in here with her. Wherever she was. Whatever this was. For over a hundred careful shallow breaths, she simply stood there waiting.

TWELVE

I knew I'd be in trouble if I took too long dropping them back home and getting the transporter to the depot, but we were like a little pirate ship, the six of us, and it was unanimous. Ahoy for the ocean wave! Or at least the Irish Sea. Actually, only the prom overlooking it, but it did them a power of good in my view, as much good as the chemo in a different way.

And on a day like this, a perfect May afternoon, with a fresh breeze sending just a few cottonwool clouds scudding across the sky, the gulls squabbling, kids with bare feet and coat sleeves pushed up to let them guddle in the shallows, you'd need a heart of stone to take someone straight from the hospital pick-up bay back to their houses for the start of the fall-out. I'd even got them ice creams. Good Italian ice cream from Renaldo's, out of my own pocket.

'You don't need to finish it if you're feeling dodgy already,' I said, handing the cones round, 'but it's not the seaside without an ice cream.'

'You're a good lass, Nettie,' said Bobby the Bum-pincher.

I'd been warned about him. 'Old goat,' my trainer had said. 'He plays the cancer card like it's going out of business – *I'll not do you any harm these days, hen* – but what do you bet he's been the same his whole life and this is just his latest excuse.'

'Of course, *you* don't belong here,' said Suzanne, or Mrs Brierly as she preferred to be called. She lived off Racecourse Road and it thrilled her to bits that she got dropped off first so everyone else on the Cancer Express got to see the size of her house and the length of her drive. 'When you're Ayr born and bred, you don't think of it as the seaside. The seaside is Cornwall, or Lake Como.'

'Wouldn't that be the lakeside?' said Siobhan, half under her breath.

'*We* call it the sands,' Mrs Brierly went on. 'We used to exercise our ponies on the sands when we were girls. Did I tell you we had ponies?'

'I think – wait, yes, I *think* you mentioned it,' Bobby said, catching my eye in the driving mirror and winking.

'And we actually used to promenade on the promenade,' Mrs Brierly said. 'Dressed up in our best after lunch on a Sunday afternoon.'

'Nothing like a walk after all that rich food,' said Art, Bobby's friend. He'd had part of his jaw taken out and his days of rich food were suspended for the duration, if not for good.

'It was nothing like now,' Mrs Brierly said. 'Look at *them!*' She waved her cone at a string of teenagers huddled on the seawall, all of them puffing on ciggies and taking drags of fizzy juice, hoods up, shoulders hunched, crowing laughter breaking out regularly as the wags in the line-up took the piss, and took the piss, and took the piss, as relentless as the waves hitting the sand.

'But then look at *them,*' said Mrs Brierly, turning away from the hoodies, her voice softening. Down on the beach a huge family was making the most of their Saturday, the big kids digging deep into the wet sand, the mums and dads swinging wee kids high over the waves, making out they might dunk them, laughing at the squeals, trouser bottoms and sari hems getting soaked and nobody caring.

'You could be worse, Suzanne,' said Bobby. 'You're not mumping about immigrants anyway.'

'My grandad worked under the last viceroy of the Punjab,' Mrs Brierly said.

Bobby caught my eye again and twinkled. 'Work that one out with a paper and pencil, eh hen?' he said.

'Does anyone want to get out for a wee stagger around?' I said. 'Or a wheel up and down?'

That sobered them all. Siobhan and Bobby kept licking at their cones but a cloud passed over their faces, and the faces of Art and Mrs Brierly, plus Mrs Cooke who never spoke, and the youngster, Lawrence, who kept his earbuds in and wouldn't meet your eyes. They didn't want to get out and walk on the prom, much less go down on the sands. They were tired and they knew they'd get even tireder before the latest course was done.

'Actually, hen,' Bobby said. 'I can hear the cavalry coming over the hill.'

Bobby had a hundred different expressions for what chemo did to his insides.

'Aye, let's go,' said Siobhan. 'It's Saturday night and Nettie doesn't need any special cleaning.'

'I keep telling you I don't care,' I said. 'I don't mind, I mean. Of course, I *care*, but I've got a cast-iron stomach and it's part of my job.'

'It's embarrassing,' said Mrs Brierly, in a small voice. 'It was unheard of in my day. Not like the Sandgate at chucking-out time these days.'

'Chucking-up time!' said Bobby.

'Let's change the subject,' said Siobhan. 'Nettie, love, goan take this cone away, please. There's a wee star that you are. Quickly!'

I gathered all the half-eaten cones in a carrier and dumped them in the nearest bin. As early in the season as this, at least there was room. Come August the bins would be invisible under a mound of chip papers and nappies. I'd have to take my band of pirates along the far end, away from the swings and kiosks, or they'd be scunnered from the start and not want a single lick. If I was still here. Which I wouldn't be. I kept having to remind myself that driving the Cancer Express was only the glue in my plan, like the kids on the special bus had been braces, after the belt of the medical transit. Wait, no, that wasn't fair. It was important to be racking up the experience and gathering clearances too. It would all help me weather the stink, when the shit hit the fan. As I knew it would, because I was personally going to switch the fan on and lob the shit at the blades. I was more determined than ever to do it. This lot had had such a bum hand dealt out to them and they were so endlessly bloody decent in the face of it. Just like Janelle's mum, and Steven's dad and the classroom assistants.

'Off we go with a ho-ho-ho,' I said. 'Slow and steady. Soon have you home, my hearties.' I swept a look over all of them as I drew away, comparing them with Big Garry: a perfectly respectable business, plenty money and no real cares, and yet he'd dipped his hand into that filthy business, trading on misery, totting up the profits on units of stock as if they weren't people just the same as him. 'Seventeen of the forty individuals are being cared for in hospitals in Calais.' If I ever started to chicken out of what was coming, I only had to repeat those words to myself to make my spine regrow.

'Ho! Nettie?' Bobby's voice brought me back. I was startled to find myself parked at the ramp at Mrs Brierly's house, with Mrs Brierly's husband waiting outside the van in his slippers.

'You were miles away,' Siobhan said. 'You're were on total autopilot there.'

'It's a wonder we're not all on our way back to the hospital, on stretchers,' Mrs Brierly put in.

'Ocht, no,' said Art. 'You're not a driver, Suzie-Q. If you were a driver you'd know you can zone right out and still be as safe as houses. I used to come home on the M6 over Shap and never know a thing about it. Never so much as hit a rumble strip.'

'Thanks, Art,' I said, trying to keep the giggle out of my voice. Suzie-Q! Mrs Brierly's mouth had pursed up like the neck of a duffel bag. I tugged the handbrake on, killed the engine and slipped round to the back door to start manhandling her wheelchair on to the lift.

'Piece of bloody nonsense,' Mrs Cooke said. It was the first time she'd spoken all day, on the journey out or, now, on the way back. Mrs Cooke used a wheelchair all the time and it irked her to see the others delivered home on wheels when they could all have walked off the transporter on their own feet.

'Elfin safety,' Bobby said, like he usually did.

'There's my angel!' said Mr Brierly, when I had released the chair and handed it over. 'There's my bride, as pretty as a picture.'

'You're a lucky woman,' I told her, tucking her bag on to her lap. 'He hasn't got a brother, has he?'

Mrs Brierly smiled, but it was wan.

'She looks the same as the day I met her,' he said. 'Never lost her girlish figure and look at that cloud of red curls!'

He meant well, but I wondered how Mrs Brierly managed not to scream or whack him with her good crocodile handbag. Her girlish figure was courtesy of a double-mastectomy and three rounds of chemo. And her cloud of red hair had been bought online with a prescription discount.

'That man's a twat,' said Siobhan when the bus was underway again.

Bobby tutted. 'I hate to hear a lady swear. You're right, though.'

'Oh I love to hear a game old girl whip up a blue cloud,' said Art.

'Less of the "old",' said Siobhan. 'I've got ten years on you and your colostomy bag.'

'Good guess but wrong,' said Art. He had never told the rest of the patients on the transporter where his cancer was, which of course made them all assume it was somewhere in the lower middle. I wished he wouldn't hide it. I reckoned life was better now people talked about their cancers. Siobhan asked for a puke bag if she needed one and Bobby had a change of incontinence pad in a carrier bag on his wheelchair handles, just in case. Never turned a hair if I saw it when I was fishing out his house keys. And the middle-aged nurses at the chemo centre kept their wee fans round their necks for blowing away hot flushes too. Couldn't care less. Not like my granny who had hidden in the house, weeping from the shame of it. And the pregnancy bumps sticking out, belly buttons like pumpkin stalks, instead of that stupid way women up the duff used to wear flowery dresses and Peter-Pan collars, trying to look virginal, which was completely nuts any way you spun it.

I tuned back in to the chat on the back of the bus and found that my thoughts and their talk had run along the same channel.

'. . . go too far the other way,' Siobhan was saying. 'Tinder and Grinder and Xtube.'

'Who are they when they're at home?' said Art but Bobby hooted with laughter. *He* knew.

'There's no romance,' Siobhan said. 'No courting. No

wooing. Nettie, what do you do with your young man of a Saturday night? What are your plans this evening?'

'I've not got a young man, Siobhan,' I said.

'Or a young lady. I didn't mean to presume.'

'No young man *at the moment*.' I was navigating the narrow entrance to Siobhan's row of townhouse apartments. I hadn't had a man, young or otherwise, since I'd put the white hat on my head and gone to Fraserburgh. Too complicated.

'But look at that!' I said, as we pulled into the disabled parking space right by the door. A woman had stepped out of the next-but-one townhouse. She was wearing a floaty dress in smudged shades of peach and cream like a watercolour and she had her hair up in a bun and sparkly earrings on. She had driving shoes on her feet but she was carrying a shoe-bag that she opened to show Siobhan a pair of ridiculous sandals, with hardly a strap to hold them on, soles like paper.

'Aye,' said Bobby. 'She's not away round the bars to see if some bloke'll swap her a kebab for a stand-up trembler.'

He was shouted down by everyone else save Lawrence, who'd missed all of it. But even Lawrence turned his head as he caught sight of the dress-ruffles or maybe the sparkling earrings. He watched the woman – who must be twice his age, thirty-odd to his seventeen – until she stepped into her car, aggressively clean outside and suspiciously tidy inside, I could see from my vantage point in the driver's seat. Bit different from the van, although that was deliberate. With my treasure still safe in my locker at Icarus Overland, and the Easter eggs tucked in the student transport records down in Lockerbie, there was just this one last stash to be squirrelled away in South Ayrshire County Council's Patient Transport Service, Unit 11. And the way I saw it was, if I left things tidy, whoever came after me might go through the crate of boring-looking official papers in the luggage store, to make it their own, kind of thing. But, if I left a midden of receipts and wrappers, elastic bands, odd gloves and scrunchies, they'd tidy down *to* the crate and leave that sitting.

'You're a good girl,' Art said suddenly, behind me.

'What's that in aid of?' I asked him.

'No matter what you're up to,' he added.

'Who's up to anything?' I said. I flushed. My skin had always been my let-down when someone caught me out.

'*What's* she up to?' said Bobby. 'You on the skim, Nettie hen? Are you Ubering your wee arse off in our ambulance after hours, are you?'

'Ha!' I said. 'I only wish I'd thought of it.'

'You'd have to cover the logo,' said Bobby. 'But you could easy get a clinger online. We could all chip in.'

'This took off fast!' I said. 'What are you like, the pair of you? I'm keeping my job, if you don't mind. I'm not going to start running a bent taxi on my off-hours.'

'I suppose Ayr's a wee town and there's a lot of hospital and council workers might recognize the number plate,' Bobby said. 'You'd have to get yourself up to Glasgow to be on the safe side.'

'See what you've started now!' I said to Art, shaking my fist at him but softening it with a wink.

'Not me,' said Art. 'I'm just picking up on whatever you've started.'

'What are you talking about?' I said, but I knew my cheeks were darkening again.

'You never asked what it was I did, before I retired, driving up and down the M6.'

'So I never. What did you do?'

'Insurance fraud investigator,' Art said. 'I could always tell when someone was up to something.'

'That sounds interesting,' I said. 'What did *you* do before you retired, Bobby?'

'I was a copper,' Bobby said. His voice had changed. I had never heard him so sober-sounding. 'Finished up a sergeant. What is it you've sniffed out, Artie?'

'Purpose,' Art said. 'Never mind if it's a warehouse boy, a driver or a dinner lady. If somebody's on the skim you can tell from how they've got an extra dose of purpose about them, on the side of what they need to do the real job. You've got it, Nettie. You've had it from day one.'

'Now you come to mention it,' Bobby said.

'Give it a rest.' I hoped my voice sounded steadier than it felt. 'That's just my way. That's how I was brought up. You do what's on your plate the best you can. You dance with the boy that brung you.'

But Bobby and Art were both looking at me with the same expression now, eyes slightly narrowed and mouths slightly twisted. They'd forgotten about their chemo and the rough night they were in for. They both thought they were on to something.

'Your meds have addled your minds,' I said.

'That's a low blow,' said Bobby. 'That's not like you.'

'They're right, you know.' I looked up. Mrs Cooke had spoken, the second time she'd piped up today. 'I was a teacher, Nettie. Forty years of primary six. I've got radar on my radar, even if they're carving out every other spare bit of me.'

Bobby and Art both pushed their lips forward and nodded, Art ending with his chin on his chest. There was a pecking order to cancer, like everything else, and Mrs Cooke with her one kidney and her long-gone gall bladder and spleen, her colostomy to make up for her missing gut, was the survival queen. She had radiation burns she had to be careful about, padding out her seat belt with a cushion, and the kind of sparse, melted candy-floss hair that came from endless chemo and wrecked nutrition post-stomach cancer.

'And what's your radar picking up?' I said, going for a tone of kindly indulgence and a smile to match.

Mrs Cooke didn't narrow her eyes or shake her head, or make any other gesture or change in her expression. She didn't bother. Instead, she gave me a measured look and said: 'Can't you just tell us? Maybe we could help you.'

'Help me do what?' My voice was a yelp, which didn't add much to the act of innocence. 'Even if I *was* up to something, what makes you think it'd be the kind of thing you'd want to help with?'

'Radar,' said Mrs Cooke again.

'Well, I'm not.' I put the bus in gear and dropped the handbrake. 'So you can give your radar a rest.'

'It's nothing to do with us then?' Art said. 'It's something else? Something at home?'

'Is someone hurting you?' said Bobby.

'What the hell?' I said. 'What do you know about my home life?'

'That's another thing,' Bobby said. 'We don't. You're not from here. That's not an Ayr twang. And you've never said why you came. It can't be your boyfriend's job if there's no boyfriend.'

'And you could have picked up a driving job anywhere,' Art added. 'Why did you move to the end of the line for this, Nettie?'

I pulled the handbrake on again and slipped the gearstick back to neutral. I swivelled round in my seat until I was facing them. Lawrence had plucked out an earbud by now, wondering why we were still parked outside the townhouses when Siobhan was long gone. He raised one eyebrow, silently asking some imaginary peer of his what they were up to now, these pathetic ancient losers he had to share a bus with.

'The line carries on down to Girvan,' I said. 'Don't insult your own home town. Why wouldn't I want to live here?'

'Where did you come from?' said Bobby. 'What did you do before?'

'Back in the interview room, eh Sarge?' I said. 'What *is* this today?'

'Fine, fine, have it your own way,' said Art. 'Mrs Cooke learned nothing from all the years with her wee toe-rags. I'm as ignorant as a newborn babe and Bobby's as thick as mince.'

'No, you're not,' I said.

'No,' said Art. 'I'm not. I'll get to the bottom of it, if I just take my time.'

'If you take your time?' Bobby said. 'We're a bus full of cancer patients. You better bloody hurry.'

'I've got less time than anyone,' said Mrs Cooke. 'You could tell *me*, Nettie.'

'There's nothing to tell!'

'Or maybe the whole thing'll be done and dusted soon enough,' said Art. 'Are you renting or did you buy?' He turned to the others. 'I used to be able to tell a lot about the size of a scam from how deep the roots were that folk put down.'

'I'm renting,' I said. 'How could I buy on the pay I get from carting you lot about?'

'Ah, but you've got money behind you somewhere,' Art said, making me blush again. 'Insurance investigators never miss the whiff of money. You don't splash it about, but it still shows.'

I was shaking my head. No way he could know that. But Mrs Cooke and Bobby leaned in, keen to hear more.

Art started ticking items off on his fingers. 'You didn't want to go in on a lottery syndicate when the jackpot went through the roof. Rich folk don't need money. And you've got a watch you don't wear.'

'What?'

'Oh yes. You don't look at your phone to tell the time, Nettie. You always look at your wrist then remember you're not wearing it and check the dash clock.'

'So what?' I tried to keep my voice even but it was disconcerting.

'So, obviously you've got a watch but you don't want to wear it at work. What is it, a Rolex?'

It was a Cartier. My eighteenth birthday present from Big Garry. He had put it at my place on the breakfast table the day after my birthday. 'I didn't want you smashing it last night on your first night out on the lash, ho-ho,' he'd said. 'Try it on and tell me if it fits.'

'Not a Rolex,' I said to Art. 'A Timex and it's busted, so I've stopped wearing it. Any other signs I'm a princess disguised as a lowly bus driver? Just out of interest.'

'Your teeth are perfect,' he said.

'I'm lucky.'

'No,' said Lawrence. 'My dad's a dentist. Your mouth's too small to have such straight teeth naturally. I bet they were all bunched up when you were a wee girl.'

I folded my lips down over them, remembering the groggy afternoon, coming round from the anaesthetic once my 'crowded mouth' had been thinned out, and remembering the feel of the stiff braces and the sour taste of them if I missed a brushing. I did have a small mouth. He was right about that. Big Garry could eat a hotdog sideways, and when he sulked he looked like a toad, his big top lip flumping out over the bottom one. Bazz had inherited it. I had my mum's little bud of a mouth, except that I left mine alone, swearing I'd never plump it up with injections or paint it twice the size it should be.

'Jesus,' I said. 'It's 2020, folks. A decent dentist isn't a luxury item.'

'Touched a nerve, have we?' Bobby said.

'Will we have ringside seats when it "goes down"?' Art said. 'Is it local?'

'And are you sure we can't help you?' said Mrs Cooke.

I gazed at them all. They deserved respect. 'Sorry about the language,' I said. 'Yes, you touched a nerve. No, it's not local. And you're best off out of it, Mrs Cooke, but thank you.'

'Is this for real?' Lawrence said. No one answered him.

'When?' Bobby said.

'Soon,' I said. But I couldn't stand lying to them again now I'd stopped. 'Actually, anytime at all. Only I'm scared. It's time for action and I'm not acting because it scares me.'

'Oh Nettie,' said Mrs Cooke. '*You're* scared? I'll swap you.'

THIRTEEN

Laura's eyes adjusted before her breath had recovered, long before her stomach stopped heaving. She tried a small sniff anyway and, although the air was still rank, it was bearable. It had only been because she was expecting flowers that the stench had almost done for her. She breathed silently, looking around herself. The room appeared to be sizable, but awkwardly shaped, with odd angles and corners. Supporting walls, she supposed, holding up the house above. It was dim but not completely dark, which she didn't understand, since there was nowhere for the light to be coming from, no windows and only a chink of twilight seeping in the crack around the locked door behind her. The ground under her thin soles was chilling damp. When she shifted her feet she thought it might be stone, or concrete anyway. The main walls were stone, certainly. She could smell the metal of them, the minerals blooming out of them, even on top of that animal stink that came from far away in front. Something was surely dead down here.

But something was living too. She hadn't imagined those voices, and the silence began to pound at her. Why had they stopped speaking? What were they waiting for? As quietly as she could, she spread her feet to get a solid stance and she settled down to see what would happen next.

Later, much later, it would strike her as odd that she didn't bang on the door or shout for help. Perhaps it was because she'd have to turn her back on the two voices and, if she made a noise, she'd never hear their owners approaching. Or perhaps it was that she had known, all along, somewhere deep down, that Fairytale Endings was too good to be true. Picking your own roses for a dinner dance where you didn't have to pay a penny, to meet successful single men who wanted to marry? All that was missing was a pumpkin coach. She had the stupid shoes, and they might as well be made of glass for all the use they were on this cold floor. Her arches ached in them but her bare feet would freeze, even if she could kick them off quietly.

Who knows how long she stood there. In the end it was a throat-clear that spurred her to talk. It sounded so homely and familiar, like someone in the next seat of a quiet carriage.

'Who are you?' she said at last. '*Where* are you? Can we put a light on?'

'Who are *you*?' said one of the voices. It sounded like an old woman, her voice dry and cracked.

'How long have you been down here?' Laura said. 'Did you come for the dance? Did they tell you it's tomorrow? Did you find them through the websi—'

'Who *are* you?' It was the younger voice. 'What website?'

'And what's that terrible smell?' Laura said.

'Don't be rude.' The first voice again. The older one. 'She can't help it. Wait till you've been in here for weeks on end.'

Laura felt a skirl of vertigo. 'Weeks?' she whispered. Then she felt relief flood through her. 'Oh, I get it. It's a game! Right. An escape game? Well, I'm not going to stand for it, because I didn't sign anything. How long have you *really* been here?'

'I don't know,' said the older voice. 'Depends what date it is. It was February the twenty-third when I came. And then you came in March, didn't you?'

'March the twenty-third,' the other said. 'I came for the weekend.'

'But it's May,' said Laura. 'It's the twenty-fifth of May! You're kidding, right? It's a role-play game. It's a hoax. It's some kind of test.'

'If you say so,' said the older voice.

Laura breathed in and out, trying to calm herself. This was insane. It was an outrage. It couldn't be legal. She always read small print and there had been nothing about any escape games anywhere on the Fairytale Endings page. Besides, the escape room she had been in on a weekend away one time was spotless 'What *is* that smell?' she said. 'It smells like death.'

'It's blood,' said the younger voice. 'I can't help it. Two months with nothing to use for the blood.'

'So we left the rags by the door where she'd have to smell them when she comes in,' said the louder, stronger, older voice. The voice of the woman in charge. 'It's worst there. Better back here with us.'

OK, Laura thought. I'll play along. And when I get out I'll sue them for every penny they've got. Because there's no way this is legal.

'Are there any steps?' she said. 'I can't see.'

'It's flat.'

'Because I've got heels on. I don't want to fall.'

'Best take them off. It's uneven. Did you drink the wine?'

It was definitely a game then, if they knew about the wine. That *had* to be illegal: tricking her into swallowing alcohol. She bent and eased the jewelled straps of the sandals, setting her bare feet down. It *was* concrete, but softened with some kind of fungus, she decided, feeling her soles sink in, feeling the squeeze of water she forced out. Was that moss? Could moss grow in a cellar? It didn't feel fleshy enough to be those glistening black ears that grew in bouquets, that people used to believe was witches in disguise. She felt her way steadily forward, ignoring the feel of her feet squelching. Anyway, as she got further away from the door the floor underneath her dried out and grew dusty. But they were wrong; the smell didn't get better. It did get a little less dark, though. There was a tiny fanlight, near the ceiling in here, ground level outside probably. It was thick glass, reinforced with bars although only six inches square. By its light, she could pick out sturdy posts, buttressed at the top and set into concrete at the bottom, holding the cellar ceiling up like the props in the tunnels of an old coalmine. And she could see the far wall, what must be the front of the house, less frightening to walk towards it than to be edging into sinking darkness with only two voices to depend on.

Another couple of steps and she could see the women as well, although she wouldn't have thought those two dark lumps were people if she hadn't just heard them talking. They were sitting on the floor, close but not touching. She walked towards them until she heard their breath, then stopped.

'You're not doing a very good job of it, you know,' she

said. 'You sound far too calm. If you're paid actors you're not earning your crust. You should be screaming and banging on the door to get out.'

'We did our screaming,' the older one said. 'I did mine and then you did yours too, didn't you? No one heard us and we hurt our hands. I ripped a nail out at the bed. So. No more screaming.'

'Even so,' Laura said. 'You're miles too casual. You don't sound traumatized enough.'

'See?' said the young voice. 'That's what I said when I got here. You sounded . . . muffled.'

'Muffled!' said Laura. 'Exactly. *Are* you trained actors or are you amateurs?'

'You *did* drink the wine,' the older voice said. 'You're slurring. Well, wait till you taste the water.'

'What's wrong with it?' Laura said.

'Don't know. But the bottles are never sealed, are they?'

That was a nice touch, Laura thought. Clever. An extra twist in this game. No, not a game. A prank, played by a sadist. A joke, told by a madman. Madwoman. Performance art. Trolling. Gaslighting. What a lot of words there seemed to be for the senseless ways people enjoyed messing with each other.

That was what she still believed, deep down near the middle of her, close to the pip of her life. And a little bit further down, if someone could crack the pip and look inside it? Down there, already she knew it was true. So, her mind retreated from the knowing. She floated above the knowing, telling herself words like prank, joke, game, trick, hoax. Telling herself *no*.

Martine was floating too. The story that kept *her* safe above the unbearable knowing was taking place outside this cellar, far away from this house, this town. In Lockerbie, her neighbours and clients and all her friends from school and work and the Family Forest were campaigning hard, organizing themselves, raising reward money. They were homing in on her. They would find her soon. They might be turning into Loch Road right now. And when they did, when they found her, she would walk out of this cellar and she would tell the police who came to arrest Kate and Gail that she didn't need to go to the hospital. But she wouldn't go home either, to her neat little house with its boxy rooms and its tacked-on garage. She couldn't imagine ever making herself go into that dark garage again, with its bare walls and its cold floor. She dreamed of it, whenever she managed to sleep deeply enough to dream at all. She was in the boot of her car in the dark of her garage, and the door that should lead to her bright kitchen had been bricked up. She'd start awake, and three waves would break, in turn, so fast that she gripped the edges of the sleeping pad to stop the world spinning. First came relief. She had escaped from the dream. Then came the fact, like a slap, of where she was instead. And third came the ache to return, to be safe in a dream that couldn't hurt her, even in the boot of a car in the dark of a bricked-up garage. Anywhere but here.

So, she wouldn't go home. When she talked herself out of the hospital, she'd go to the best hotel she had the energy to drive to, Glasgow probably, and she'd book their best room, so long as it had a bath. A bath in the middle of the floor would be best. She never wanted to feel cooped up again. A slipper bath in the middle of a huge room and she'd fill it with bubbles until the foam surged over the rolled edge and broke off to float around the room in scented clouds. She would sink under the perfumed water and feel the dirt lifting off her in oily ribbons that floated to the surface and . . . popped all the bubbles.

She edited the daydream. She would step into a shower first. A rainforest shower where a hot stream fell from the ceiling like a torrential tropical storm. And it would have glass walls she could see right through so it felt as if she was standing in open space. She would wash herself, scour her hair with three changes of shampoo and then slick it with a whole bottle of conditioner. She would scrub her body with a rough mitt, dollops of gel turning it slidy. She would screw the corner of a flannel into her ears, and her nostrils and her navel. She would straddle the showerhead and turn the dial to a jet instead of a rain, then she'd squat and she'd shut her eyes against the flakes of dried blood from two shameful months of soaking through her meagre rags and paper, two shameful months of strained chalky shitting from the starvation rations those two witches were keeping them on. She'd shut her eyes as all of it ran away down the drain, then she'd sit down on the clean tiles and rub soap between her toes, running a fingernail under her toenails and flicking the worms of dirt and skin down the drain too.

Then, clean, she'd step into that free-standing bath, with a table nearby, a glass of champagne and a box of—

'Chocolate?' Ivy's voice rose to a squawk. 'Chocolate? You've got to be kidding.'

'Why?'

'Constipation,' Ivy said. 'There's no roughage in chocolate.'

'Fine,' Martine said. 'A glass of champagne and a box of dates. A champagne and prune juice cocktail.'

But Ivy wasn't always listening. She wasn't listening now. She had gone on her own favourite journey, a trip away from the fetid air around her and the rough concrete under her. An excursion inside herself. She took herself between her lips and down her throat, deep into her own belly. It started with a cold glass, taken out of a freezer and spangled with glorious fractals of ice, glittering like jewels. Into it went a smoothie of strawberries, blueberries, mangoes, and pineapple. Thick, full-cream yoghurt and a splash of rum and she would drink it down in one long gulp, ignoring the ache in her head and the cramp in her stomach from the cold. Then she would eat a salad of the crispest, greenest lettuce leaves, and the nippiest, pepperiest rocket leaves, and the softest, sweetest spinach leaves, so succulent she had to swallow their juice as she chewed. There would be pomegranate scattered on the leaves, like a cooking programme on the telly, and capers that burst in her mouth, flakes of chili that made her sneeze, little pickled mustard seeds that popped on her tongue and, when she was finished, she would lift the bowl and drink the remnants of black balsamic dressing. And when she had drunk the dressing she would wipe her finger round the bowl and lick it.

Then she'd eat a skate wing, brown and buttery, and a heap of tiny potatoes dredged in flecks of mint and a corn-sheaf of blackened grilled asparagus with hot lemon butter. And she'd sip ice-cold, sweet white wine, just the way she liked it and she'd never let anyone sneer her into ordering dry again. And when she had stopped gasping and burping and her stomach had quietened, she'd take a whole pavlova, the serving plate just for herself, balanced on her lap, and she would dig her spoon into a pistachio-coloured splat of passionfruit and down through the cloud of cream, whipped thick and sharp with sherry, and she'd smash the sweet toffee-brown meringue and lift the first spoonful, the very thought of the tart fruit making her mouth squirt water as she opened her lips.

It was the fur on her teeth that always brought her back again. She ran her tongue along them, dreaming of passionfruit, pomegranate and brown-buttered skate, and felt the rough coat of plaque that had softened them like lichen on gravestones. Then she'd taste her tongue, the dark, sour pelt it wore. She would feel the cracks at the corners of her lips and the flat puckered scab of her last cold sore.

But even when she was back, on the pad, on the floor, in the dark, her stomach stayed lost in the daydream, growling and gripping, whining like a child. At least this time there was a distraction. There was another woman standing there. Ivy could see a suggestion of frills as if, whoever she was, she had dressed for a party.

'Sit down,' she said. 'There's plenty room for sitting. It's a squash when we lie down to sleep but come and sit.'

'We'll have to make another pad,' said Martine. 'Sacrifice a cover.'

Ivy couldn't imagine sleeping under one of the thin blankets instead of two, even if they rolled up together. Even if she was in the middle with a body on either side to keep her warm. 'We'll see,' she said. 'Did you say you had heels on?'

'Ohhhhh!' said Martine.

'What?' said the new woman.

'Just that there's an edge of something. It might even be a trapdoor but we can't get it up. Maybe one of your heels would do it. Jam it in and hit it with the other one. Who knows what's under there.'

*   *   *

'They're good shoes,' Laura said, then she felt the foolishness of it and bit her lip. 'I've left them over by the door. I'll go and get them later. Like you said, right now, I need to sit down. I might *fall* down.'

'You're one step from the edge of the pad,' Ivy said. 'Come on. Sit and put your head between your knees till you feel a bit more like it.'

'This isn't really happening,' Laura said, as she squatted and felt for the edge of the 'pad' the two women were sitting on. It was a thick platform of flattened cardboard boxes, six or seven layers deep, and she felt the edge of a wool blanket spread on top of it. She hadn't felt that stiff matted wool of an old blanket since she was a child.

'What's your name?' said Ivy, when Laura raised her head again.

'Laura Wade. I came to a party.'

'I'm Martine. I came to a family reunion.'

'And I'm Ivy. I came because I haven't got the sense God gave drunk monkeys. However stupid you feel, Laura, I've got you beat.'

Ivy stretched out a hand and patted Laura on her shoulder, her hand making contact half with the fluted sleeve of her dress and half with the clean smooth skin of her shoulder.

Laura finally believed then. She knew it. She could smell the months that Ivy had spent in this place. They stayed stamped on to her sleeve and her skin, like a nightclub pass, when the woman took her hand away.

FOURTEEN

No one saw me walk back in. I hadn't expected drivers to be hanging around in the middle of the day, well after the start of the back shift and long before the end of the day shift, and I parked in the clients' spaces right in front of the main door, far away from the loading bay and anyone who might catch sight of me from the warehouse.

But I'd reckoned on a few shirts and skirts. There was usually someone crossing the foyer, or looking out of one of the office windows, whiling away a phone call. Sales, marketing, tech, HR, payroll, operations . . . Big Garry moaned about how many of them he employed and it was him that came up with the nickname for them, but I had always suspected he was proud, on the quiet. Oh, he still talked the butch talk about his success: number of vans, number of rigs, number of drivers; miles covered, countries, tonnage of freight. But if he wasn't proud of his shirts and skirts, then why didn't he let them all wear BG polos and fleeces, like they wanted to and for the branding?

Just like the carpark, the foyer was deserted when I pushed my way in through the smoked-glass doors. I stopped dead, arrested by the familiarity of it all. The smell never changed. Floor polish and glass cleaner and a trace of garden centre from the peat that the houseplants grew in and the mist the receptionist sprayed them with to keep them shiny. There were two red couches facing each other across a glass coffee-table fanned with trade magazines. On the far wall, a coffee-maker that had cost more, ten years later, than the two couches put together. There was still a box of Krispy Kremes. Big Garry, who would never feed his men for free, knew how to court clients.

I had sprawled on the old couches, colouring in and doing the puzzles in my Saturday comic, waiting for my mum to finish the books and take me and Bazz swimming. I'd sprawled on these new couches waiting for my dad to come and give me a driving lesson. I'd even sat behind the desk on the swivel chair, learning the ropes. 'Every bit of it from cracking pallets to firing skivers,' Big Garry had said, although Bazz had never stuck a crowbar in a pallet or fired some scally after a third warning. Plus he was too big a lout to answer the phone without losing business. He'd bunk off and leave the desk unattended, like whoever was supposed to be there now.

I glanced up at the camera in the corner, but I knew there would be no one at the security kiosk in the middle of the day. So I slipped away to the foot of the glass and chrome staircase that rose through the foyer to the office level, climbed up, feeling dizzy and knowing I was pale, then punched in the unchanging security code – my parents' anniversary – at the top door.

I made my way down the corridor not glancing to left or right, not wanting to catch anyone's eye through the little windows in the office doors. At the end, I paused, steeling myself to bat open the swing door to his outer office and breeze past the assistant's desk. But I caught a second break. The woman my dad still insisted on calling his secretary was AWOL too, a dozen tabs open on her monitor and the fan whirring.

I could hear his voice, through the half-open inner door, and my legs threatened to buckle. 'Aye, aye, aye and Mexico'll pay for it,' he was saying. 'If you want to make an offer, I'm ready to hear it.' He paused. 'No,' he said into the phone with that patient voice that his intimates knew was more dangerous than shouting, 'that wasn't an offer. That was an insult.'

With my guts churning, I edged into the room and stood looking at the back of his head. He had spun his chair round to face out the window, like he always did, looking down on the loading bay, the van ballet of arrivals and departures, his empire. He was wearing the same stupid uniform as ever – a striped shirt with a plain collar. A pair of cufflinks, one B and one G, too heavy and too gold. His suit trousers were sharply creased top and bottom but bagged at the knee and his jacket was hung on the back of his chair where its bright lining – chosen to match the stripe in today's shirt – could be seen.

That jacket had had a starring role in my imaginings about today. In my mind's eye I'd seen my legs giving way, this pale dizzy feeling turning into a full-on faint, my guts letting go as I lay on the floor, and Big Garry putting the jacket on, cracking it over his back like a ringmaster's whip, like a bull-fighter's cape, then stepping over me.

His desk was the same chaos as ever, I was glad to see. Nothing had happened while I was away to reduce Big Garry's respect for 'paper and ink'.

'I know you're trying to make a splash,' he was saying into the phone, 'and I get that somebody must have told you this was how to make it, but when you've been in the game as long as—'

He had seen me. Swinging in his leather chair he had finally turned far enough to glimpse me standing there.

'I'll have to go, Dave,' he said. 'I'll get back to you.' He put the phone face down on his desk-top.

'Hiya,' I said. 'How are you?'

'"How are you?" she asks!'

'How's Mum?'

'How do you think?'

'And Bazz?'

'How do you *think*?'

'Useless and cushioned,' I said. 'He'll go far.' I walked towards him and took a seat in the client chair on the opposite side of his desk. I folded one leg under me to sit on, so I didn't sink down. No trick was too pathetic for Big Garry to play, including looming over whoever came into his room to bug him.

'Where have you been?' he said. He wasn't breathing hard. He wasn't even talking loud. He was saying the right words but his heart wasn't in it.

'It doesn't matter.'

'It matters to me.'

'Did you go to the cops?' I said. His eyes slid away to the side. 'No you wouldn't have gone to the cops, would you? Because they would have asked too many questions. About enemies and associates. They would have snooped around far too much. So . . . no cops. Did you get a private detective?'

'Your mum was worried sick,'

'Oh, I'm sure.' I was getting angry now and it was helping me. 'If you had a detective, Dad, you should get your money back.'

'You think you're funny?' There was always a line with Big Garry. It was fine to wind him up, up to a point. The way he was talking to me now told me I'd neared the point but not passed it. I'd heard worse when I was critiquing his wardrobe or being ungrateful for a present.

'So let's cut the crap,' I said.

And just like that we were over the line. Clear over. 'You think you can talk to me like tha—' he began.

'That's nothing,' I said, interrupting him. 'I think I can talk to you like this. Listen carefully. Here's what's going to happen. I'm taking over.'

'Taking over what?' He sounded genuinely puzzled.

'BG Solutions, BG Connections.' It still felt strange to say the two names, without BG Europe to round off the trio. Like when someone dies. I'd said 'Granny and' for years before I broke the habit. Big Garry watched me for a couple of slow breaths, but he wasn't thinking. He's not a stupid man but he can't hide it when he's thinking. 'I'm going to be the CEO,' I said. 'And majority shareholder. You're going to buy Bazz out and give his shares to me. Dangle something shiny in front of him and he'll bite your hand off. You know that as well as I do.'

There was a flash of amusement but it passed. 'I don't get it,' he said. 'What's the punchline?'

'No punchline,' I said. 'You're retiring, Dad. And you're emigrating. Here's the story: Mum's health is going to take a nose-dive and you're both going to drop everything and go somewhere warm where she can enjoy the time that's left and you can devote yourself to her. Got it? I'm going to run BG now.'

'Have you fallen and hit your head?' Garry said. Again, they were the right words but his delivery was off. There was no outrage, just a half-hearted parroting of the sort of thing he imagined someone would say.

'It makes perfect sense,' I said. 'I'm not going to embarrass you. I'm not going to tank it. People will be surprised but no one will be suspicious. We wouldn't want to be raising suspicions, now would we?'

'What are you on about?'

'You didn't tell *anyone* I'd gone, did you?' He shifted. 'Did you, Dad?'

'We said you were travelling.'

'Perfect. I have been. And I've been training. I've been working incognito for a rival operation up north, delivering medicine, and I passed probation as a vulnerable student transport assistant in the Borders and as a patient transport driver on the west coast.'

Garry laughed. 'What for?'

'Because it's not the sort of work you can do without a clue,' I said. 'And I've got clearance now. I've had two police checks and an advanced security check. I'm golden.'

'What *for*?' he repeated.

'You can tell people that I was off doing some research for our expansion into vulnerable and high-risk transport. That's the future, Dad. But you're too old – no offence – to be learning new tricks. So I went off and did some hands-on research and now you're handing over.'

'Vulnerable and high-risk?' Garry said.

I stood and walked forward until my hands were resting on the edge of his desk. I bent over until my face was inches from his own. I'd rehearsed this in my head so many times, wondering if I'd have the nerve to do it, hoping I'd see genuine bewilderment in his eyes and then he'd explain the mistake I'd made. Now it was happening, my voice was calm, completely under control, and Big Garry's hands stayed in his lap without even twitching. 'You heard me. The guaranteed delivery of controlled, perishable, and/or hazardous essential items. That's honourable work. But as well as that we're going to be known for the safe and respectful transport of vulnerable people with complex needs. And that's *God's* work, because nothing is more important than humane and appropriate support and service towards all people in need of transit. Right, Dad? *Right?*'

'Tash,' he said. 'I've no idea what this is about. I've got nothing to do with whatever you think is going on.'

'I know you don't,' I said. 'I know you're *out*.' He shook his head almost fondly at me. 'I saw the news.' He frowned. 'I saw the news the night you were in bed after you'd had that bug. You shouted for Mum to come upstairs and watch the news with you.'

He nodded, remembering. I was remembering too: 'uncovered what appears to be part of an operation stretching overland from Eastern Europe and the Near East all the way to the French ports and into Britain.' Then he shouted down to my mum and the newsreader said 'although the UK collaborators in what police are describing as the most ambitious single attempt ever discovered have thus far evaded detection.' Then I turned the volume away down and just caught: 'Seventeen of the forty individuals are being cared for in hospital in Calais while French officials—'

'I don't know what you think you saw on the news—' he began.

'And I found your phone.'

That got him. His smile faded and his eyes narrowed. I felt my stomach rise up into my chest and burn there.

'What phone?' he said.

'See, Dad, I know you. I know what you're like. I forgot that for a while. I thought a stupid wee flip phone stuck under a desk with duct tape was too casual. But that's you all over, isn't it? Nothing on your account, no digital trace. Everything old-fashioned and easy to ditch. That phone was *classic* you.'

'Don't tell your Mum,' he said and relief flooded me from head to toe. 'It would break her heart.' Then he ruined it. 'She meant nothing, Tash.'

I scrubbed my face with both hands. 'Are you seriously going to sit there and pretend that phone was for an affair? Because how do you think I found it? It *rang*.' He was watching me closely now. 'I answered it. And the guy on the other end thought I. Was. Mum. So obviously I don't need to. Tell. Mum. Because. She. Knows.' I felt tears begin to prick at me and I sniffed them away. 'Look, all you need to do today is write your passwords down for me. I know the business. I can take over.'

'You can't seriously expec—'

'You want me to go for my other option? Which is I call the police.'

'You wouldn't.'

'I'd rather not,' I admitted. 'That's why I'm offering you a lifeline. Don't be stupid. Don't be an even bigger moron than you've been. I'm letting you go.' I had thought he'd cave, or bargain. Or possibly explode. I didn't understand why he was being so calm.

'OK,' he said. 'I'll play along. In this fantasy where you've caught me doing something – God knows what! – *why* are you letting me go?'

'Because I don't want BG to go under. I need its money. I need the profit to undo what you did.'

'Still playing along, what does that mean?'

'I'm going to set up a foundation.'

'Who do you think we are? Bill and Melinda—'

'To raise funds—'

'We're a medium-sized transport business, Tash.'

'*We're* nothing, Dad. *I'm* a medium-sized transport business. You're retired.'

He wasn't quite so calm now. His breath was beginning to sound in the back of his throat. I had never understood before what was going on inside his head when he made that noise, but I could make a guess this time. He was beginning to believe me. 'You can't just hand over a business,' he said.

'You can.'

'What about Bazz?' There it was again, that amused look in his eye. Bazz was dead wood. We both knew it and we never said it.

'Bazz can stay on like he is now,' I said. 'Whatever it is you call him.' I would spin that tale to get this done, then I'd cut him loose afterwards. If the only job he was competent to do was sweep the warehouse, he'd be a warehouse sweeper for the going rate. If he didn't like the going rate, he could join the union and fight for more. 'I want the passwords right now, the signed papers in a week and a list of which employees need to be let go with a fat bonus and which can stay.'

'What?' He was frowning deeply.

'I want a list of anyone who falsified a docket. Or drove

one of the lorries. Or even the lads on the wash who cleaned
out after.'

'Tash, I'm not being funny, what are you talking about?
What dockets? Drove what lorry? Cleaned what, for God's
sake?'

And this time I knew he was being absolutely sincere. I felt
the floor shift under me as if it was a boat, as if it was the
bottom of a forty-foot container on a ferry from Calais. Had
I got this wrong? Was he innocent? Was none of it *true*? I
stared at him and my life seemed to drift casually towards me
again, there to be grabbed and lived if I only reached out for
it. My daft dad, my annoying mum, my deadbeat brother all
back again. My ordinary, good enough, infuriating, perfect
family. When I spoke again my voice was shaky.

'I thought,' I said, 'you were bringing migrants in from
Europe. In our fleet. That's what the newsreader said that
night. Forty individuals. The guy on the phone said you were
out in the nick of time and if you didn't believe him you
should watch the news.'

'Tashie,' Garry said and again he sounded amused, 'you're
talking about people smuggling. Lorries full of people getting
smuggled into Britain? Is that what you thought?'

I nodded. I couldn't have spoken. My face was numb.

'BG has never, ever, ever been mixed up in anything like
that,' he said. 'BG is as clean as a whistle.'

I felt my breath go in a long wheezing sigh. If I could have
stood up without falling over I would have gone round his
desk and hugged him. He was still talking.

'Dockets, she says! Cleaning out vans!'

'I'm sorry. I don't know how I got it so wrong. I don't
understand.'

'Me neither.' He was shaking his head at me. And I was
thinking how quickly I could get down to Dumfries and explain
to Ken that I'd left stuff in his files that I needed back. Ply
him with doughnuts until he helped me. Then away to Ayr to
tell the new driver I'd lost my engagement ring and checked
everywhere else, so could I have a wee keek in the luggage
hold of the bus. Then finally to Fraserburgh to clean out my
locker at Icarus and hand back the key.

But then he went on. 'Tash,' he said, his voice heavy with scorn, 'these girls don't come in by the dozen lying in a chilled container.'

'What girls?' I said, tuning back in gradually.

He blinked slowly. 'I thought you said you listened to the report. Those girls. Those women and girls.'

'OK,' I said. 'Yeah, that's right. Women and girls. Because their dads pay for them to leave Aleppo or whatever. Right? To get away from the war. And the men stay and fight. I hated thinking of them paying you to take their wives and children to safety.'

'What about the little boys?' he said. 'Why would it be . . . what did the newsreader say?'

'Women and girls, some as young as twelve,' I said. That *was* what the newsreader had said. I remembered it. It just wasn't the bit that played in my head over and over again. 'Seventeen of the forty individuals' was the bit that hit me so hard. Only, now I couldn't believe how dumb I had been not to see that 'women and girls' was the point. Women and girls changed everything.

'Why wouldn't there be babies and toddlers?' he said. 'Little girls and boys of four and five?'

'I don't know,' I whispered.

'Because, Tash,' – he was enjoying it. He always enjoyed it when he got the chance to lecture me about something – 'these girls should never have *been* smuggled. That's not how it works. These girls come on holiday, or for a bit of cosmetic dental work, or engaged to a citizen – so they think. They come on planes, one at a time. Sending bloody forty of them over in the back of a wagon was ridiculous. People smugglers get caught all the time and that's why.'

'People smugglers,' I said. 'Which you're not mixed up in and never have been. As opposed to . . .'

'Trafficking,' said my dad. 'Smuggling is transit. Trafficking is logistics. They're both supply and demand but otherwise – totally different game.'

'Trafficking,' I said. My vision clouded, a haze coming in from the edges until only his grinning face was still clear. 'You're a trafficker.'

'Was,' he corrected. 'I'm out.' He shook his fingers as if he'd burned them and laughed. 'Those girls that day were all from towns where we'd been doing business for years. If that lorry load had been coming to us and got caught at Calais . . . Aiyeeee! But they weren't because we'd got out.'

I tried to blink away the haze in my eyes, but it only thickened and it was spreading. Even his face was hazy now. 'Out,' I said, 'of trafficking. So it's . . .' I said, before my breath ran out. I was literally gasping for air. 'It's just a coincidence? That BG is transport?'

'No,' he said, lifting his chin. 'It's a big FU to the do-gooders. Transit gets a bad name for being dodgy so we're whiter than whiter than white, see? Hiding in plain sight, Bazz calls it.'

'*Bazz* calls it? Bazz knows? Bazz?' I was dizzy.

'Bazz knows more than you ever gave him credit for,' my dad said sternly. 'He's designed an app and there's more than us uses it now. "Click and collect".'

'Collect . . .' I said and that one word used up my whole breath. I heaved in another one. 'A girl? From . . . a street corner?'

'Come on, Tash!' he said. 'Don't be stupid. Bazz is better than that. Pop-up shops. You're in and out before the neighbours start mumping. Airbnb mostly.'

'Pop-up shops to buy . . .' Another breath. 'Girls?'

'The thing is a lot of them think they're coming to work in factories and they're happier—'

'No!' The anger was instant, like a petrol spill and a tossed match. It cleared my vision. 'No way, Dad. Tell yourself that crap if you like but don't smear it on me.' I stopped and breathed my way back to calmness again. 'So Bazz is a pimp, is he?'

'Don't be a bitch,' Big Garry said. 'Bazz is a tech innovator.' He paused then. 'His customers are pimps. *Were* pimps. I told you: it's over. We're out.'

'But how do you get "out" of something like that?' I said. 'What happened to all the girls?'

'We sold it. You know we sold it, Tash. BG Europe – the front business – and the rest of it too. Got a good price as well. Russians. *They* were the ones who had to write off a loss because some twat used a single lorry instead of forty commercial planes. Not us. Somebody up there likes me!'

'So *what* happened to all the girls?' I said again.

'They've still got their jobs. New bosses, but the same old game. Unless that shitshow with the lorry did for them. Clueless buggers. They don't deserve my good business if they've got no more sense than that.'

'Your good business,' I said. Suddenly he seemed to be a long way away. Maybe I was going to faint. But at least the distance helped me see him clearly. 'Why are you telling me all this? After keeping it secret so long?'

'You were halfway there anyway. Up a hell of a cul-de-sac – people smuggling! – but getting there.'

'And what do you think I'll do now?'

'Eh?' he said. 'Do? Come home. We thought you'd found out and "taken the vapours".' It was one of my mum's expressions. 'But here you are back again. Overreacting, I might say. But at least you're home.'

'It's all documented,' I said. 'And I've written a statement. The cops won't care that I said "smuggling" instead of "trafficking".'

'You've not written anything.' He spoke in a drawl.

'I have. And I've planted it. Along with everything I could find. Anything I could lay my hands on.'

'No, you haven't,' he said. His smile was broad enough to show the gaps from his missing molars. He said he kept the holes in his mouth to remind Bazz and me how cushy we had it compared with when he was a boy. The truth is he was scared of the dentist. He was a coward like most bullies. 'Don't lie to me, Tash. You haven't planted anything. Not at Icarus, not at RoundnRound in Dumfries, not anywhere in the system of the South Ayrshire Health Trust.'

'You *knew* where I was?'

'Of course we bloody knew.' He banged the sides of his fists on his desk, irritated, as if I was an insect he couldn't quite manage to swipe away. 'Bazz found you every time and he'll find you next time too, wherever you go. Shetland, Cornwall, London. The reason I know you've planted nothing is that Bazz found every log-in and every email.'

I shouldn't have smiled, but I couldn't help it. He grew very still, watching me.

'I didn't know about Bazz,' I said. 'You're right. I underestimated him. But that's not why there's no log-ins and no emails to be found. There's nothing online, because I'm your daughter, Dad. And I wanted to present you with something you'd understand. Paper and ink.'

He did understand. He wasn't laughing or drawling now. He wasn't affronted or annoyed. He was breathing like a bull and the look in his eye turned my blood to jelly.

'I'll find your paper and ink,' he said. 'Wherever it is you've stashed it.'

'Where do you think I've stashed it, Dad?' I said. 'Which one of three places would I have picked?' He hadn't cottoned on, so I drove it home. 'Eh? Which *one*? Out of *three*?'

'You stupid—'

'Me?' I said. 'For doing what you always told me? Belt, braces and glue? Belt, braces and three big tubes of superglue? You might talk your way in once, Dad. Two's less likely. But three? How long would it take you to get in and out of three different places when you don't know where to look?' I said. 'Longer than the time it takes me to dial nine-nine-nine?'

'You wouldn't,' he said.

'Try me,' I said. 'I dare you. Or, if your brain's firing on all cylinders, give it up now. And I'll retrieve everything and destroy it.'

'You're breaking my heart, Tashie,' he said. And every one of my hairs lifted and bristled. Because I believed him. It was breaking his heart to do what he was going to do. Leaving his company and moving to Mallorca would have pissed him off and embarrassed him. Letting me go to the police and drag his name through the mud would have enraged him. What he was planning to do – I was almost sure of it – was heartbreaking.

'You wouldn't,' I whispered.

'Try *me*.'

FIFTEEN

I t was neat and it was simple. They both came to the outside
door. One of them opened it. Kate came into the anteroom,
said 'Won't be long, Gail', and got locked in. She opened
the inner door, entered, delivered the food and left again. She
locked the inner door and shouted 'Let me out, Gail!' Which
Gail did. Every day. Five minutes every day to clamour and
beg. Five minutes to bargain and wheedle and argue. And all
of the other minutes of all the other hours to ache.

And to question.

'What do they want?' That was what Martine kept coming
back to, like Laura came back to 'When will someone come?'
and Ivy herself came back to 'Why didn't she kill us, with
her little knife?'

Only none of them said it out loud now. The pain of arguing,
of being at one another's throats, had been unbearable when
it happened out of the blue one day.

'Shut up!' Laura had screamed suddenly, when Martine was
talking about her hotel room, comforting herself, not doing
any harm to anyone. 'Shut up shut up shut up!'

'Don't pick on her!' Ivy had said.

'Your little clique,' Laura screamed. 'Your cosy little
twosome. You make me sick, both of you.'

'No wonder you needed a dating site,' Martine said calmly.
'You're a stone-cold bitch.'

'No wonder your father ran for the hills,' Laura said. 'Who'd
want an anvil like you round his neck.'

'Don't be such brats,' Ivy said. 'Don't be such poisonous
little brats.' She thought it would make her feel better to give
in and say it, but it only put a lump of cold misery in her
chest, as if she'd swallowed a stone, and she started sobbing.
She and Laura cried for what felt like hours, while Martine
banged her head over and over, against the wall behind her,
then she cried too. They cried until they were sick and shaking,

until their sweat had turned bitter, until their voices cracked and their eyes dried.

Then came hours of silence.

At the end of it, Ivy leaned sideways and picked up a water bottle. She took a swig and passed it to Laura. 'Taste that,' she said. She waited. 'I think they've run out.'

'Let me taste,' Martine said. She swilled a mouthful of water round her mouth. 'You could be right.'

'But why would Igor stop slipping us the Valium, or whatever it is?' Laura said.

'Igor?' said Martine.

Ivy saw the flash of irritation cross Laura's face. Any time she was reminded how young Martine was, that look swept over her. As if age mattered now. 'Frankenstein's lab assistant,' she said. 'Good one, Laura. It suits her better than "Kate".'

The next day, Ivy took the first sip from the water bottle after it was brought in and when she tasted the bitterness there she felt a warm surge of relief and then of rage at herself.

She passed the bottle to Laura who took a deep swig. 'Thank God for that,' she said. 'And how pathetic is it that I mean it with all my heart?' She passed the bottle to Martine, saying 'Little something for your nerves, madam?' Martine drank thirstily too.

So maybe they *wouldn't* have ended up at each other's throats again. But still they were wary. They passed the baton carefully. One could be low at a time, no more. Round and round they passed it – tears, and rage and hope and despair – but always keeping those three questions quiet, like a prayer.

They took turns for everything. It was Ivy's turn to choose what to ask for today. Kate didn't always comply, but often enough to make it worth trying. They'd got a toothbrush, and a plaster for Martine's cut hand when she had scraped it on the frame of the fanlight, scrabbling for a way to find the edge of the thick cloudy glass and knock it out.

'One toothbrush,' Laura had said. 'I could weep. Or I could file it to a point and stab her.'

'You can have it,' said Martine. 'I don't mind using my finger with a baby wipe wrapped round.'

They'd got the baby wipes, Ivy thought. That helped. They

washed with them, wiping their own fronts and having each other scrub their backs, eking out every last bit of clean smell and moisture. Then they hung them over a pipe that crossed the cellar at head height and when they'd dried out, they went over to the drain, folded in a pile.

That was another thing they'd fallen out over. Ivy saw Martine wipe after a pee and before she knew what she was doing she had burst out scolding like a monkey. She couldn't help herself. And Martine lashed back. Now they had the drain she wanted to be clean. It was different before.

'Yes,' said Ivy. 'It was quieter.' The drain was high above the sewer it fell to and it was right in the middle of the floor. It was upsetting to squat there while two strangers listened to the stream that splashed into the pipe so far below and the farts that rattled out of them all whenever they squatted, from the terrible food they ate and the lack of exercise. Whenever it was more than pees and farts the other two would go as far as they could get and talk as loud as they could, only returning to the cardboard and the bit of light when they heard the scraper and the rumble of the metal sheet being pulled back over the hole.

There was nothing down here that could be used as a screen either. Not so much as an old curtain or even a bin bag they could slit up the sides and open out. Mind you, if there *had* been a curtain, it would have been too useful as a cover for their cardboard bed, or as a blanket, to waste it as a screen anyway.

The drain was a find all the same. Laura chiselled the cover off with her shoe heels and, once they recovered from the disappointment that it wasn't a trapdoor, they put all the used paper and rags in there and closed the lid back down on them. It still smelled unspeakable when the cover was lifted but they breathed through their mouths.

And they treated themselves to a fantasy of leaving it off, and of Kate tripping over the edge of the open hole and falling in, breaking her neck, lying there at the bottom, bent like a hairpin, begging for mercy.

'You couldn't really do that though?' Ivy said.

'*Could* I not?' Laura spoke so boldly, Ivy never could tell when she was serious and when she was just giving herself a boost.

'She's as much the vict—' Ivy began, but Laura snorted.

'Come off it, Ivy,' she said. 'Not the Nuremberg defence.'

'But what's she supposed to do when Gail's right outside with the keys?' Ivy said. She really did feel pity for Kate. She hadn't wanted to go in and deal with poor little mice in the dark larder. Probably Kate didn't want to come in here and deal with the three of them either, but Gail didn't give her much choice.

'She went up to Fraserburgh and came down to Lockerbie,' Martine said. 'She could have gone to a police station instead and said . . .'

'My sister's a homicidal maniac and she needs locking up in a padded cell,' Laura supplied.

'You don't know what it's like,' said Ivy. 'Not to be the strong one, not to be able to stand up to someone.' She saw Laura open her mouth to say something Laura-like but Martine got there first.

'Don't mention yourself in the same breath as her, Ivy,' she said.

'I'm just saying I understand why she's scared of Gail.'

'We all do,' Laura said in a small voice. 'I don't know what's worse. Night or day.'

The first time they had heard Gail at night, the quiet slap of bare feet and the tick-tock of her knife, they had huddled together and whimpered. Ivy didn't know what the other two were thinking, but *she* was thinking: 'this is it; here it comes; now she kills us.'

Only she didn't. She went away. And she went away the next time and the time after that. So now, when they heard her – tick-tock, slap-slap – they put their hands over their ears. Sometimes, Ivy noticed, Martine still had her fingers stuffed in her ears when they all woke up in the morning.

'I never know whether I wish I'd seen her or I'm glad I didn't,' Laura said, like she always did whenever they talked about Gail. Ivy wanted to add it to the list of things they weren't allowed to say. Instead, she patted Laura's arm. 'What are you going to ask for?' she went on.

'Why?' said Ivy, thinking she heard an odd note in the question. 'What do *you* want?'

But Laura shook her head. 'I'll get my turn tomorrow.'

'And what will you ask for then?' said Ivy.

'Tomorrow,' Laura said, 'I'm going to ask for a hip bath, a Thai massage and a cannabis cookie.' Ivy felt a flare of gratitude. Sometimes one of them could start joking. When that happened they all tried to keep it going as long as possible.

'Have you ever had a cannabis cookie?' Martine said. 'Have *you*, Ivy?'

'Me?' Ivy said. 'I've never even had vodka.' She knew they'd pity her, but they'd laugh too. And so she did her bit. 'I've had wine and beer and Pimm's one time at a brass band concert in a park, and I've had port and brandy to settle my stomach and whisky on toothache. But not vodka.'

'Mushrooms?' said Laura.

'No,' Ivy said, slowly as if she was thinking. 'Ecstasy, though.'

Martine snorted. 'You've never had ecstasy!' she said. 'You're too old.'

'Charming. No, I've never had any of that. Poppers, uppers, downers. And I wouldn't want to start in here. It would drive you doolally if you had hallucinations in here and you couldn't get out.' She had gone too far. No one laughed this time.

'I was in a club in London once, 'Laura said, 'and I put my brand-new bag down on the cistern and it stuck. Vaseline. To stop people sniffing coke off it. Ruined two hundred quid's worth of Italian leather.'

They were all silent then, remembering London and clubs, or at least films about them. Thinking of handbags and bathrooms. Just like that, it had all run out again.

'I'll swap my day with you,' Ivy found herself saying. 'You go next and I'll go after.'

She heard Laura's breath catch in her throat and her whisper of: 'Why?'

Ivy couldn't tell them the truth. If they laughed at her she might disintegrate until she was nothing but a pile of crumbs. Instead, she delved down into herself for a different story, but she was empty. So she took a pinch of the truth and served it up to them. 'Because you're just girls. I'm much older. I want to take care of you.'

It had come to her late last night. She had been dozing, warm at last, with the two of them cuddled up to her on either side. She had dreamed, half-dreamed anyway, of Mother. It wasn't really Mother. It was a woman with Mother's face and someone else's voice, leaning over Ivy asking if she wanted a bowl of soup, or a cup of cocoa. It might have been Glinda the Good Witch, whose voice had been Ivy's favourite sound when she was a child. Then she had opened her eyes and looked at the curve of Martine's arm lying over Ivy's own body and the curl of Martine's hand against Ivy's stomach, how it bumped softly every time Ivy breathed. Maxine's skin was so smooth, even the thin bridge between her thumb and forefinger didn't have a single fold in it. Ivy put her own hand beside Martine's, looking at the elephant's kneecap swirl of her knuckles and the rough ribs of her nails. Martine's nails were little peach shells, each one with a pinpoint of light shining on it. Ivy told herself she was far too old to be thinking about Mother, wishing for the love that never had come and never would come now. She told herself she was nearly old enough to *be* Laura's mother, definitely Martine's. And that was when a thought dropped into her head like a round stone into a still pond. I *will* be the mother; I'll *give* the love: a thought so startling and so complete she ran from it, ruffled and feeling foolish.

But it had come back in the day. That was what she had to live for, instead of pining for death, begging Kate to kill her as she had when she was alone that first month. The thought climbed down from her mind and formed itself into that sentence, pushing an offer out of her mouth, a gift. Like chewed fish in the gullet of a bird, or the rasping reach of a cat's tongue.

Laura was staring at her. She turned to look at Martine, whose eyes were round and bright in the dimness. They were all getting used to the dimness now, the soft grey of day and the soft yellow of night, from the streetlamp's bleary glow through that one tiny window choked with dirt. When they got out, if they got out, the daylight would be blinding.

'No,' said Martine. 'There's no need for that. We're all in this together, no matter what age we are, what difference does that make? I mean, if one of us was a child or was elderly, but we're not. We're all the same.'

'Exactly,' said Laura. 'That said, if you can't think what to ask for, Ivy, how about socks?'

Martine laughed but Ivy bent her head in shame. Laura had been here a week. Her dress was stiff with sweat and dust and her feet were stone-cold all day as she moved around, only warming towards the end of the night when she tucked them close to Ivy's calves and stole some body heat. A real mother would have noticed that.

'I'll ask for three pairs of socks tomorrow,' she said.

Laura said nothing. Not even thank you. And Ivy's fragile little tower of hope collapsed again. Never loved, never loved, never loved, she told herself. So why keep going?

Why don't you kill me? she had asked every day until Martine came. Then, why don't they kill both of us, she asked, until Martine wept and begged her not to. Then when Laura came she asked again: why don't they kill all three of us and get it over with? Wouldn't it be better now they've caught us, just to kill us? Wouldn't it be kinder? If she had to spend another minute in this coal-black larder she would— Cellar, she told herself. You are grown-up, Ivy, and this is a cellar you're trapped in. But still she dreamed of the larder and the mousetrap and the longed-for cat and Mother saying 'Call the plumber. That tap's dripping again!' and 'Even you'd shut up with your neck broken, Ivy.'

She did empty the trap that first day, and the next. And every day until once, walking towards the larder cupboard door, telling herself she was imagining the noise, because it couldn't cry with a broken neck, nevertheless she heard it. It wasn't a squeak exactly. It was too exhausted to be as sharp a sound as a squeak. It sounded more like the last legs of a small battery telling Ivy it needed changing. But as she opened the door, the scuffling started, a frantic scrabbling and, as if the scrabbling recharged the battery, the slow chirps really were squeaks now.

Ivy snapped the light on, half-sure she'd see nothing,

half-hoping it was her imagination turning the scrape of a twig against the window into this impossible noise. But she knew it wasn't. There on the floor, caught in the trap by one bloody back foot, was the mouse, turning the trap over and over as it struggled with its front paws, clawing to get away from the pain and the light and this monster who had come.

Ivy stood frozen, watching the pitiful little drama building to its climax on the floor in front of her. It didn't take long. In a minute, seemed longer but couldn't be, the mouse collapsed, its side fluttering up and down and its paws, save for the one stretched out and bloody, contracting as its eyes closed.

It took another minute, seemed shorter but couldn't be, for Ivy to pluck up the nerve to lift it. She took the dustpan from the nail on the back of the door and, with her face turned away, she shoved it across the tile floor like a snow plough, whimpering when she felt the sharp edge catch the trap and its tiny appendage. Then she tilted it back, whimpering louder to feel the weight slide towards the handle and thump against the metal.

She trotted outside, lifted the dustbin lid and let the mouse, trap and all, fall in amongst the peelings and packets. She heard just one more squeak and told herself she didn't. Told herself it was her shoe leather on the cold ground, or her own voice, still whimpering. For years she told herself it was dead and she hadn't let it lie there in the dark and dirt, in pain and slowly starving. She was grateful to Mother for the scolding she got: throwing away a good mousetrap instead of emptying it! How would she like to rummage in a filthy bin to get it out? She wouldn't, would she? 'No, Mum. No, Mum,' Ivy said and soon enough the harsh words filled her ears and the tiny little dead-battery squeak was silenced forever.

Then, slowly – or quickly, who could say – she grew up. She grew to understand the cost of a mousetrap, five pounds ninety-nine for a bag of ten in the cheap shop with the brooms in buckets and the dusters done up like flower-heads and stacked in baskets. But every night, in her bed, she would imagine she could hear it. Sometimes still, as she slept, she would dream a tiny meeping cry.

Not until Mother was dead did she say to herself, I can have a cat. Now here she was in this cellar, punished for trying.

Kate was there.

She was putting a bag of apples and sandwiches down on the ground.

Ivy hadn't noticed her coming.

She was a different Kate from the chummy, confident little woman who'd bought brandy and stood up to louts in a pub. This Kate was blank and cold, as if she was emptying traps and trying not to hear the sounds of suffering. Even as her feet walked in and her hands put bags of food down, she was miles away, braced against the pleas she would ignore.

But what if Ivy surprised her?

'Thank you,' she said, from the cardboard. 'We do appreciate the food. Even if it's hard to understand why you're feeding us.'

'Sshhhhhh,' said Kate. 'Dead people don't talk.'

The words, delivered so calmly, made Ivy's scalp shrink.

'Dead people don't eat either,' Laura muttered under her breath. 'Oops.'

'Could you bring us some blankets and pillows?' said Martine. 'Maybe even some clean clothes. Socks.'

'Clean clothes?' said Kate, in the same blank voice that lifted the hairs on Ivy's arms. 'Pillows? No. Dead people don't need them.'

'A torch would be nice,' said Laura, as if she hadn't heard. 'Three torches. Head torches. And something to read. Books, magazines . . .'

'Dead people,' Kate said, 'don't . . .'

'Two more toothbrushes and some toothpaste,' said Martine, in a bright voice. The devil had got into her, spreading from Laura. 'And some sanitary pads in the next day or two.'

Kate's head snapped up. 'No! I can't buy . . . those things you said. This shouldn't be happening. Dead people don't need anything.'

'A pack of cards then,' said Ivy. If the other two could find the courage, she wasn't going to let them down. 'A radio? You wouldn't need to buy them if you've got spares.'

'I have to go,' said Kate, shooting a look over her shoulder.

'You don't!' Martine said. 'You don't have to do *any* of this.'

'She's my sister,' Kate said. She opened the door at her back, but before she went through, she spoke again, hissing, 'Don't you understand? How dead do you want to be?' Then she pulled the door shut with a slam. And her voice as she called to Gail was a cold bellow. 'Let me out,' she boomed. 'Now!'

They sat in silence then, letting the sounds pass from echoes into memories. Ivy found it soothing to hear the plastic carrier bag settling with small pops and cracks.

'Interesting,' Laura said eventually.

When Ivy realized it was up to her to answer, she made her voice sound as eager as she could and said: 'Tell us.'

'She didn't mind socks or blankets,' Laura said. 'She'll have them in the house. And she can buy bread and cheese, apples and water. But she hated the idea of tampons and torches. Do you see what that means?'

'Not tampons,' said Martine. 'We'd be dead of toxic shock before morning. No, I don't see what you're getting at.'

'They're buying supplies in shops where people know them,' said Laura. 'Local shops where the assistants would wonder why two women their age need san-pro, or where they'd remember three head torches.'

'OK,' said Martine. 'So what?'

'So,' said Laura. 'Can you think of anything we could ask them to buy that would be suspicious without them knowing? That wouldn't ring their alarm bells but might ring others'? Other people, who'd come. And save us.'

'Oh,' said Martine. '*This* again!'

Ivy had dug her nails into her palms so hard she thought they might be bleeding. Maybe she should make them bleed. Sepsis would work.

'What do you think, Ivy?' Laura said. 'Ivy?' She stretched and nudged her with an icy toe.

'I wish she would kill us and get it over with. Sorry,' she added, at Martine's gasp. 'But there's nothing to work out. And no one's coming to save us. They didn't pick our names out of a hat. They chose well.'

'Don't,' Martine said.

'They chose three women who lived alone and worked alone, at home, for themselves,' Ivy said. 'Women who were all alone.'

'Women without husbands,' Laura said. Her voice broke.

'Women without parents,' said Martine.

'Or children,' Ivy added but, when she saw tears shining in Martine's eyes, she wished she could take the words back again.

In the quiet, Ivy dreamed of her perfect meal. Martine was probably dreaming about her hotel room again. Who knew what Laura was dreaming of but at least she was actually sleeping. Ivy glanced at Martine and both of them smiled, listening to the soft popping snores. Martine stretched Laura's legs out and cradled her feet, and Ivy pulled Laura's head down into her lap and smoothed back her hair. She stopped snoring but didn't wake. Ivy kept stroking her hair back from her head and Martine eased herself back, slower than the seasons, so she could keep Laura's feet safely in her lap. Like that, they waited. When Laura opened her mouth and smacked her lips together, the way she always did on waking, then rubbed her head back and forth as if scratching it on a pillow, Ivy said softly, 'Welcome back, sleepyhead.'

Laura opened her eyes and looked straight up. Then she raised her head and looked down at Martine. 'Have you been holding me?' she said. She screwed her head to the side and stared up at the square of window. 'It's nearly dark.'

'It was good,' Martine said. 'It was time to think.'

'Not again.' Laura's voice was weary but there was warmth in it as well as warning.

'It was what you said, Ivy,' Martine began, 'about them choosing well. Choosing us well. I thought of something.'

Laura sat up and pulled her feet in. 'I need a pee,' she said.

'*You* need a pee?' said Martine, moving at last. 'I've been stock-still with your heels digging into my bladder since lunchtime!' She stood and shook out her legs. 'Ivy wanted a cat and got a sister. I wanted a dad and got a sister. Laura wanted a date and got a woman saying 'Think of me as your sister' or if we're willing to stretch a point got . . . a sister.'

'So?' said Laura.

'So they chose you, Laura, and they chose how to catch you. With the dating agency.'

'For my pathetic sins,' Laura said, shifting the sheet from over the drain and squatting.

'That made sense though,' Martine said. 'And so did I. I was researching my family history and I didn't have a dad on my birth certificate, so the bait they trailed for me was about that. But do you see?'

Laura straightened halfway then shook her behind to dry it. 'We'll all be championship twerkers by the time this is over,' she said. 'See what?'

'The story they told Ivy was completely bonkers.'

'I wouldn't go that far,' Ivy said. She was interested in spite of herself.

'Of course you wouldn't,' Martine said. She was squatting now. 'You fell for it.'

'Ohhhhh,' said Laura. 'I see what you're getting at. A story about a singles dance for someone looking for partners . . .'

'Right,' said Martine. 'Makes sense. Like a dad for a father-less child. But where did that come from that they told you, Ivy? You wanted a cat. And you got a sister.' She was finished and had bent to slide the metal over the drain, but Laura pushed her away. 'I'll get that,' she said. 'Your hand's not healed and with the best will in the world a plaster's not a magic wand.'

Martine rejoined Ivy at the cardboard, plopped down and stared at her. 'They told you you were one of them. Swapped, Ivy,' she said 'And it was nothing to do with you and your life. Like Kate said. Nothing to do with you.'

'So?' said Laura.

'Well, if it's nothing to do with Ivy – this sister-swap – then it's something to do with them.'

'*So?*' said Laura.

'There's something I remember,' Martine said. 'I heard it, but I was half-asleep.'

'No! Gawd, not the podcasts,' said Laura.

Ivy shushed her. 'Try and remember,' she said.

'True crime,' said Martine. 'I think. Or extreme . . . it might have been Oliver Sacks. I keep thinking *carpe diem*. But it's nothing to do with that. It's something to do with family. If we could work it out. Work out what it is they want. What it is they're doing.'

'I'm sorry, Martine,' Laura said. 'But you're clutching at straws. What we need to do is send a sign to someone who'll come and find us.'

If they'd let her be what she wanted to be, Ivy thought, she'd agree with both of them, comfort them, make it all better, like a mother should. But she'd got the message loud and clear. She wasn't wanted. They didn't need her. So instead she spoke her mind. 'What we've got to do,' she said, 'is face facts. We can sit down here going meep-meep-meep till our batteries run out and it won't change a thing. We're going to die.'

SIXTEEN

I stood at the window and followed each drop on its race down the glass to gather at the transom and swell the drip drip drip on to the stone sill. There was a crack at the inner angle and moss growing where the putty should be. I imagined, standing there, that one day the block of stone would split off and fall to the ground. Then the next rain would seep into the fabric of the wall and show as a stain on the plaster. Soon the floor would rot too and this building, so solid-seeming, that had stood here a hundred years, would be gone.

Good red stone slumping like a sandcastle at the high tide wasn't really what was troubling me. Only, when nothing felt sure any more, and every step was a step towards the unthinkable, it was no wonder that even stone and glass, wood and plaster, concrete steps and iron banisters felt like a little house of straw.

I had been here for two days, five left, and I still didn't know if it was genius or madness, precaution or paranoia. How far would Big Garry go to shut me up? Should I just give in and call the police? On the little burner I'd bought ten minutes after fleeing BG that horrible, skin-crawling, insane, impossible day?

Calling the cops would mean giving up the takeover, the reparations, the whole plan to balance out what he had done; so much worse in the end than what I thought he'd done. Him and Lynne and Bazz.

At the thought of Bazz, I nearly smiled. I'd never have come up with Airbnb if I hadn't heard about his pop-up 'shops'. My dad had given me the rest of it, though he didn't know. Shetland, Cornwall, London, he'd said, taunting me. Hiding in plain sight, he'd said, bragging about Bazz's cleverness. And so here I was, in a flat in West Lothian, twelve miles from home.

I changed my mind every ten minutes about whether it was bold or idiotic to be so close to where I'd been born and where

I'd lived throughout my childhood. Twelve miles from the town where my dad was the biggest employer after the supermarkets.

But while I kept watch out of the window, I checked for faces I knew and I had come to see that this town might as well be another world, with a different high school where kids made different friends and a different police station where different neds got a reputation with different coppers. Every one of these little towns, I thought to myself, was so turned in on itself, even if they were joined on nose to tail these days. There was no cross-fertilisation, because there was no destination in any of them that would pull people from any of the others. Each had its own chippy and Chinese, its own Turkish barbers and pet groomers. And no one would dream that the butcher two towns over would offer better cuts than the butcher right here who called them by name and remembered their mum.

I was trying hard not to think about why there was an Airbnb here. I refused to imagine what might have happened in this flat before I got here, between the faded, bobbled sheets of the only bed, on the flattened, darkened moleskin of the couch, even on the hard, washable floor of the cheerless bathroom. Instead, I looked out the windows, not dwelling on what I was looking for, what I was frightened of. My dad wouldn't . . . to stop me. Would he?

I leaned my head against the glass and looked through the raindrops, trying to find distraction. The yards of the shops below were tucked too tightly against the back wall for me to see whatever went on there, although I heard them banging in and out underneath me, taking flattened cardboard out to store it till bucket day, the folk from the chippy humping big bins of old fat over the slabs. If I opened my window, I'd hear the two girls from downstairs out for a smoke, sitting on the old coal-bunker lid, joshing and plotting. I wished I could go and join them. It had been a lonely few months. But even if I booked myself in for an appointment, I wouldn't get out the back for a fag break.

I peeled myself away at last and walked the length of the room towards the front. This room, through and through from the street to the back garden, was the best bit of the flat and the reason I had rented it. There wasn't much else besides: just a barely double bedroom with a painted-over fireplace nipping off one corner; a cold bathroom with chips in the bath and a permanent line round the toilet bowl, and a galley kitchen in an offshoot, where a gutless extractor whined uselessly and never managed to stop the smoke-alarm going off before the toast was ready. But this room was different. The skirtings were deep and the cornicing and centre rose were fancy enough to have made it worth picking them out in a different colour of paint. And sometime in the history of the house, a tenant or maybe an owner had sprung for a good wool carpet in dark red. It had survived the seventies, when it might have been ripped out and replaced with beige and the eighties when it would have been lifted to sand the boards, and now it felt warm and proper under my feet. A good dark red wool carpet with flecks of black in it, no stains and no burns for a wonder.

At the front window I brushed aside the curtains. These weren't survivals from a moment of prosperity in the lifetime of the flat. These were landlord specials: thin cream IKEA, hanging from not enough curtain rings on a squint rod that was held to the wall by half-extruded Rawlplugs.

There was no one down there. I was being paranoid. He wouldn't, would he? But then he was probably telling himself the same thing – she wouldn't really, would she? And I would. I was going to. Just like he had done what he had done, him and Lynne and Bazz too.

I knew more about it now, from googling on my cheap little laptop with the pay-as-you-go dongle I'd bought – for cash – at the nearest Argos that blood-chilling, bone-chilling, heart-chilling day. *That*, I was nearly sure, was total paranoia. Nearly.

Maybe I'd be more sure I was paranoid if he *had* been smuggling like I thought, fleecing folk for a quiet arrival, folk that wanted to come. Maybe then he'd have taken my deal, and retired to the sun. Maybe that man, crooked and greedy, would have bitten my arm off.

But my dad wasn't that man, I knew now. I knew now that they signed papers in English thinking it was for visas. Then it didn't matter what the papers actually said. They'd believe whatever they were told: six months to pay off the airfare; one more job then back home with a bonus; just till a college place opened up. I still couldn't believe I had missed the crucial bit of that news report. 'Women and girls.' I didn't think I would ever get it out of my head now: 'some as young as twelve'.

What broke me, once I started googling, was knowing that often as not they loved their handlers. They loved a man and trusted him and couldn't believe he wasn't what they hoped he was, couldn't believe he was what they watched him be. Not so different from me really, wising up too late. I bet their plans looked quaint to them too now, just like my plan to raise money for migrant shelters and make up for the smuggling.

How would I atone for what had really happened? A business, click and collect, supply and demand, Russian bosses. I was too late to help any of them. Maybe I was even too late to help myself. Maybe I'd be just one more girl who went away. (He wouldn't, would he?)

There was no one down there except a drunk at the bus stop. Or maybe not a drunk, maybe just a guy having a can till his bus came. A retired couple came out of the pub – the Paraffin Arms it was called, unbelievably. They were dressed in matching fleeces and matching trainers but they were arguing bitterly, glowering at one another as they turned into the stair of their flat. A dog trotted past, all alone. It stopped to sniff up at the litter bin but there was nothing lying around it except Coke tins, all the chip papers neatly inside. So it lifted its leg and trotted on. I watched the empty street for a while, until the drunk finished his can, crushed it and dropped it. Then I set off back through the flat to the kitchen window again.

Over the high wall from the shops' bin stores, nothing was moving. There didn't seem to be any kids on the side street that stretched away behind the flat, which was a waste because the gardens were far longer than anything a modern house would ever get, as the builders chunked up the land. They were left over from the days there'd be a drying green and a vegetable plot, a pig at the end and a stable beyond. Most of the stables had been flattened and replaced, but a few had survived, bare brick and dusty windows, garages now.

I rolled my head the other way. Considering it was a stone's throw to a bookie's, a chippy and a nail bar, this street was fairly posh, although one of houses had a broken window in a kitchen offshoot, stopped up with cardboard behind the bars. Cardboard aside though, it was cute, a little cottage squeezed in beside a bigger villa, with a steep roof and a bit of fancy ironwork along the peak. It had a cellar door down a set of mossy steps that dropped without railings from the edge of the lawn, just a dark hole against the back of the house. A death trap.

Maybe it was the months of driving a patient transport van and a special needs student bus but it bothered me to see the homeowner running up and down those steps, no safety rail, doing whatever it was she did in there. Washing maybe, or getting stuff in and out of a chest freezer. She lived alone, I reckoned, because I hadn't seen a husband at the back door or in the long grassy garden. There was just that one little woman, in her slippers on the wet grass, up and down, up and down, like a pigeon at a lever.

But watching a little old lady pottering round her garden wasn't going to help anyone. Wearing a track in the carpet between the front windows and the back either. Am I going to the cops? I asked myself, standing back so I could see my reflection instead of the view. No. Because too many people will lose their jobs. Am I going back in five days to see if he blinks? Yes. Do I really believe he would . . .? I looked hard at myself in the glass, watching the rivulets track down through my reflection. No, but . . . I'll make sure I'll be missed if I suddenly disappear. In case I'm wrong. In case he would. In case he means to.

When I was showered and dressed, I let myself out of my front door, clattered down to the street door, and stepped out into the drizzle, hunching my shoulders and pressing the Velcro shut on my coat for the scoot across the road.

The newsagent's was nearest so I made for it with my head down and my hands jammed in my pockets, hopping over puddles. Inside, it was dark and crammed with tat, the air thick from decades of newspaper ink. The look I got from the man behind the counter was the one he'd give any woman between sixteen and forty that came through his door but he wasn't a bad sort; as I made my way towards him he straightened his face out and pasted on a customer-service sort of smile.

'Hiya,' I said. 'I'm just moved in across the road. Above Hollywood Nails.'

'Aye? Looking for work? Because this is my uncle's place and I've got seven first cousins all married and—'

'A paper,' I said. 'Do you deliver?'

'Deliver! Where have *you* been living? There's not been a paper boy in the Haw since I was at school, earning thruppence ha'penny for mine.'

'Oh,' I said.

'And you're only across the way.' He pointed. 'You could lean out your window.'

'No, it's not that,' I said. 'It's just so's I'm not taking my chances there's one left. Ideally, I'd like a paper every day and a couple of mags.'

'Aye, no bother. I can order in for you and keep them back. You'll need to pay as you go or pay in advance a wee month or two, mind. No offence but I don't know you from a hole in the ground.'

'None taken,' I said, feeling my heart lift as he twisted round and grabbed a ledger from behind him. He thumped it down on to the counter and licked his thumb.

'A *Scotsman* every day, please,' I said. I'd rather have had a *Herald* but I didn't want to put his back up and I wasn't sure which side of the continental divide this was. 'And a *Women's Fitness* and a *Better Homes and Gardens*.'

I couldn't have made myself read either cover to cover but they were nice and pricy and the newsagent would wonder why I wasn't picking them up, if I stopped.

'Name?' he said, looking up at me with his pencil hovering.

'Natasha Dodd.' I wondered if it would light a spark, twelve miles from Big Garry's kingdom, but he just bent his head and printed it in the ledger. 'Tash for every day,' I added.

He put the pencil down, held out a hand and smiled. 'Adim. You know they're cheaper online, don't you? And *they* deliver.'

'Your uncle would string you up if he heard you,' I said.

'Your *Scotsman*'ll start tomorrow,' Adim said. 'There's a couple there if you're after one today.' He pointed to a low rack with papers stacked on it. I took one, picked up a Twix and a Coke and handed over enough cash to charge a month's worth of reading. Feeling stupid, I'd taken out a good wedge, after the burner shop and before Argos. Bazz couldn't hack a bank, I told myself, even as I keyed my pin.

Adim's eyes widened at the sight of the money. Should I say something? Tell him I was hiding from an ex with a joint bank account?

'I'm trying out this strict budget trick,' I went for in the end. 'Take out a month's cash and make it last. No impulse-buys with your contactless.'

'Not very strict if it covers *Better Homes*,' Adim said.

One of the girls in Hollywood Nails looked up from her phone when I opened the door. The other was at a delicate stage in the application of strip lashes.

'Hiya,' I said. 'I've been meaning to come and say hello. I've just moved in upstairs.'

'We saw you looking out the window,' said the girl who'd already got her lashes on. Her face was mesmerizing. She wore foundation so far from skin-tone it was almost green and she'd shaded her nose, jaw and temples with stripes of dark brown; highlighted her forehead, cheeks and chin with streaks of sparkling bronze. Her eyebrows were an inch deep and so perfectly square she must have used a stencil to paint them. Her lips were invisible behind thick matt lipstick the same colour as her foundation.

'We were thinking of grabbing you and tying you down,' said the other one. She looked up from her mirror and batted both sets of lashes. She was a more normal colour for a white girl, with bands of deep peach simulating rosy cheeks and lips stained red and glittering with shimmer gloss. They each, I, noticed, wore a selection of the nails on offer, ten different patterned and textured acrylics.

'Yeah, I've let things slide a bit,' I said, feeling my spirits, which Adim had already lifted, really start to soar. 'I was thinking of booking myself in for a regular . . . depends what you do, actually.'

'Mani, pedi, threading and massage,' the chalky green girl said, waving her arms around as if the chairs and footbaths, the tables and counters, should speak for themselves.

'Massage would be fantastic,' I said. 'But is it weird to do it to people you know?'

'We don't know you, though, do we?' said the peach and red girl with the tarantula lashes. 'I'm Aisling, that's Renny, by the way.'

'Tash. Natasha.'

'And no, anyway. It's not weird. Thanks for asking. I wish it was, number of randoms we went to school with coming in on the mooch.'

'Were you at school together then?' I said, accepting a printed menu of treatments and looking it over.

'We're sisters,' said Aisling. 'Duh.' I loved them both for that 'Duh'. I hadn't realized, in Fraserburgh, Lockerbie and Ayr, how much I had missed my own people, hard as nails, dry as biscuits, impressed by absolutely nowt.

I took a closer look and, right enough, the bones were the same and the pale blue eyes.

'Well, I'd love Friday last thing,' I said, 'but I'm guessing that's a busy time of the week for you, so how are you fixed on Wednesday afternoons?'

'We could squeeze you in,' said Renny. 'Wednesday morning would be even better.'

'Lunchtime?' I said. 'How about every Wednesday at one o'clock and I'll rotate, hands, feet, back and brows?'

Both the girls perked up at the sniff of such regular business and I found myself hoping Hollywood Nails wasn't on its uppers.

'Can I ask though,' I said. 'Can you really do massage? And the rest of it?'

'How?' said Aisling.

'With your nails, I mean.'

'God, listen to Granny!' Renny said, flushing under her green make-up. 'Next you'll be asking if we paid good money for our ripped jeans!'

Aisling laughed and took up the theme. 'What are those tattoos going to look like when you're an old woman, though?'

'Any more piercings and you'll start leaking!' Renny said.

'Aye, aye, aye,' I said. 'Jeez, you're worse than Adim.'

'Adim asks us if we're warm enough!' Renny said. 'How old *are* you anyway?' She had stopped laughing and was giving me a hard stare.

I couldn't have said how old this pair were. They had puppy fat still but the drag-queen make-up aged them. 'Thirty,' I said. I felt eighty.

'Huh,' said Renny. 'We thought you were young and just didn't bother. You're lucky to be wearing so well. If your skincare regime's anything like your make-up and nail regime you should look like Mother Teresa by rights.'

'Wow,' I said. 'Right well, put me down for Wednesday lunchtime and you can decide what's the biggest emergency. OK? Tash Dodd.'

Again both the girls broke out into spurts of laughter.

'Tash Dodd?'

'Oh, you poor cow!'

'Tash Dodd! It sounds like . . . like . . .'

'Baked Spud,' said Renny, screaming with laughter at her own wit and making Aisling choke.

'How, what's your name that's so glamorous?' I said, knowing I sounded huffy.

That sobered them both. 'Hollywood,' Renny said. 'Duh.'

'Well, I'm away now,' I said. 'I might go to the health club, see if they've got a resident masseuse. So I might be down to two Wednesdays in four. And if you need a cup of sugar anytime . . . I'm sure Adim'll sell it to you.'

'Sarky bitch,' said Renny with a smile. 'We're going to be besties, "Tash Dodd".'

'And the *masseur* at the gym is a handsy wee creep – always was – and he only went into massage because it means you can't stop him.'

'Don't tell me,' I said. 'You were at school with him, yeah?'

I didn't drive to the gym, though. I just moved my hire car on to the side street with the open parking. A hire car! As if

Bazz could hack the police computer to find my own one –
this was pure paranoia, like the burner and the dongle and the
cash. (He wouldn't, anyway. Not my dad. Would he?)

I was outside the front garden gate of the fairytale cottage.
It was even more unreal-looking from here, with a garden full
of apple trees, just moving from pale pink blossom to the
softest little yellow-green leaves. And it had a round bay
window with a turret on top. It was so out of place that it
unnerved me. I had chosen Hephaw to hide in for its anonymity.
Stupidly – but I wasn't going to beat myself up – even this
tiny pocket of noticeable character, this one pretty house,
diluted my perfect bolt-hole. I shrugged the thought off myself,
as I made my way down to the mouth of the main street and
my own front door. I'd chosen well. Hephaw was a grey town
where nothing happened. It was perfect for me.

SEVENTEEN

'To . . . the . . . time I farted on a first date,' Laura said. She was trying to get a game of I'd Go Back started. But Ivy said nothing and Martine couldn't think of a single sweet, or funny, or outrageous example. 'Marty? Got anything?'

'No,' she said. But inside she started listing. I'd go back to before Kate brought those chairs. She couldn't stand the feel of the thick plastic against her skin and the squeaking shredded her last nerve. So now she was alone on the pile of cardboard, looking over at Laura on one and Ivy, sitting on another with her feet on the third, the one that should be Martine's if she could bear to touch it.

They were both worried about the state of Ivy's legs. Her ankles had been swollen for weeks but they were dark red and shiny now and when she took her shoes off the marks lasted for hours.

'Keep them above your heart,' Laura told her. 'Skootch right down. You'd be best to lie on the floor and put your legs on the seat really.'

Ivy wriggled down and Martine had to dig her nails into her thighs not to scream at the screech of the plastic. I'd go back, she told herself, to crying on the school bus, getting stood up, getting sacked for no reason and them daring her to question it.

I'd go back to the worst time of my whole life, she thought, to those endless days of raw early grief. She'd learned then why *raw* was just the right word. She felt flayed, as though she'd been scrubbed of the top layer of her skin. The wind was too cold and the lightest breeze would set her shivering. The sun baked her even in its springtime weakness. Her clothes irritated her, cotton scraping and wool like barbs, so that she checked every night for blood as she undressed. If she'd had a father, she remembered thinking, lying in the dark one night in the long bleak trough of time after the funeral was past, the cards taken down, the flowers wilted. If she'd had a father, she wouldn't have felt this way. This couldn't be how human beings were meant to feel when an old woman died. The trouble was she wasn't properly formed. She should have had a father and a real mother. That was the reason she was floored by the death of her gran.

But she also remembered telling this to a Samaritan one night down the phone. It was early hours, with the sky changing colour and sleep as far off as ever. She explained it to the woman with the kind voice, about how she stayed at her mum's as long as she could, hoping to hear something, asking all the right questions, then she'd go back to her gran for rest and clean clothes. But she'd never heard his name. And so when her gran died, she wasn't a fully formed person rolling with the blows like she should be. Instead, she was flattened by it. Flayed by it. She felt as if she walked around under a personal spotlight, exposed. Or as if she had a sword sticking out of her chest through her clothes, a sword that no one mentioned and no one looked at, until their silence and averted eyes made her think she was going to scream.

'It's only natural,' the Samaritan said.

'No,' said Martine. 'It's because of my dad. If I had my dad I wouldn't be in this state.'

'The pain you're in,' the Samaritan said, 'is the bill you pay for the love you got.'

Martine repeated the words, like a little tune played with two fingers on a toy piano. But they didn't make any more sense for all her going over them.

'If I'd ever had a father—' she began again. The Samaritan interrupted her. She told Martine all about grief counselling and support groups. She advised a trip to the doctor, as if that could help, and suggested a new hobby and some exercise out in the fresh air.

'I thought you'd just listen,' Martine said. 'Aren't you supposed to just listen?'

The woman had the grace to laugh. An awkward little laugh. 'Within reason,' she said. 'But if you were hitting yourself over the head with a frying pan, I'd tell you stop.'

Martine thanked her, said she'd think it over and hung up. She was smiling. She saw herself in the mirror opposite her bed, smiling at a stranger on the phone who wouldn't even listen to her.

After that, she waited it out, because everyone said time healed all ills. They were right. When a year had passed, her skin got all its layers back and she could walk along a street and stay as anonymous as a hippo in Dumfries could ever be, no spotlight shining on her, no sword sticking out of her and no endless crawling questions about why everyone she passed pretended they couldn't see it.

But it wasn't time that did it; it was podcasts. It was puzzles playing in her ear, teaching her that anything she could make sense out of she could cope with. Anything understandable was bearable. It was the senseless that was terrifying.

Martine let her head fall forward. Believing she'd work this out was the only thing keeping her sane now. She shouldn't mind whatever the other two used to help them. Even if Laura's fantasies about someone coming made Martine want to scream and Ivy's death wish made every day harder.

'I'd go back,' she said out loud, 'to cross-country in PE.'

'I'm glad you said that,' Ivy piped up, 'because I've been thinking.' She paused as if to get their attention, as if there was anything else vying for it. Martine dug her nails into her thighs again. 'We should all exercise,' Ivy said. 'We can see well enough. We should be walking twenty minutes several times a day. Fast enough to get puffed out.'

'You've changed your tune,' Martine said.

'Yes,' said Ivy. 'I realized I shouldn't be letting the two of you rule the roost.' She paused and then said, 'Mother knows best.' Another pause. 'Just kidding. But if we let ourselves seize up we won't be able to take that chance when it comes. If it comes. If Laura's right and someone opens the door. Or if you're right and we work out something that helps us. Somehow.'

Even more shame flooded Martine, like it hadn't since she was a child, out with her drunk mum, people seeing. Ivy was trying so hard to be kind. 'The thought of working up a sweat though,' she said. 'I could cry.'

'I honestly don't think we could smell worse,' said Ivy. 'If we sweated it might even push some of the stale sweat off us. Dislodge it, you know? Like a Turkish bath.'

'I suppose we've got flannels now,' Martine said. 'Better than those slimy wet wipes. More of a scrub.'

'I want a green pot-scourer,' Ivy said. 'Or some wire wool. And a pumice stone.'

'I want a loofah mitt and a bottle of Dove,' said Martine.

'And an Uzi,' said Ivy. 'For next time Gail comes down. Shoot the lock off the door and then take her kneecaps out.'

Martine couldn't help laughing and hoped it didn't sound scathing. The chances of Ivy knowing what an Uzi actually was were exactly nil. 'You really have changed your tune,' she said.

'But ricocheting bullets would be a terrible idea down here,' Ivy said. 'A crossbow would be safer, actually.'

'Kind of hard to blow out a door lock with it,' Martine said.

Laura said nothing.

'So a crossbow for Gail's kneecaps and a machete for the door?' said Martine.

'And a green pot-scourer,' Ivy said.

Still Laura was silent. And it made the other two wind down into silence too. The rhythm was set for three. Whether they were laughing or crying, when they were plotting escape and revenge, when they were planning their television appearances, they were a trio. Without Laura, they ran dry.

'What's up?' Martine said at last.

'The chairs,' said Laura. 'It never occurred to me till right now.'

'What about them?' said Martine. 'Apart from making my teeth squeak.'

'They can't have had three inflatable chairs lying around, can they? Kate must have bought them.'

'Right,' said Ivy. 'And she's buying an airbed right now if she was listening yesterday and the gods are smiling.'

'So why didn't they just bring chairs down from the house?'

'Because dead people don't need furniture?' said Martine.

'I thought it was maybe because they were lighter to carry,' Laura went on. 'But I don't think so. I reckon she doesn't want to be seen,' Laura said. 'Everything she brings in to us is in bags, like someone might see her running up and down with our meals or a blanket and get thinking.' Martine watched as Laura screwed her face up. 'I'm trying to remember what was over the garden walls. I wasn't concentrating. I was thinking about roses and freaking out because I thought I saw a ghost. And feeling stupid for getting the day wrong. What's actually there?'

'I was unconscious,' Ivy said.

Martine remembered scuttling away in a crouch, as if there was anywhere to hide in the wooden shelves over the stone floor. Then a blank. 'It's just the back of the shops,' she said. 'Flats, maybe?'

'Whatever it is,' Laura said, 'I reckon someone's watching.'

'They're not watching very carefully if they didn't see her move your car,' Martine said. 'Or mine.' They had agreed that Kate must have shifted the cars round into the old carriage house or whatever it was, at the end of the long garden.

'If they're watching out the back windows,' Laura said, 'from the flats above the shops, all they would have seen is Kate coming out into the garden through that door after the cars were hidden. But they can see everything that goes on at the kitchen door and the steps and the door into here, can't they? So we can send a sign. And then they'll come.' Martine managed not to howl. It wasn't fair to get their hopes up like that and then just say the same old thing. If she could keep it in, Laura could too.

'And I know what sign to send,' Ivy said. Martine raised her head. If both of them started it, she would lose her mind. 'Next time Igor comes in,' Ivy went on, grimly, 'we should keep her. Think about it! If there's a nosy neighbour who watches them come and go, and one day – today, if I've got anything to do with it – Kate comes and *doesn't* go . . . Well then. What would *you* do?'

'I'd watch and see what Caspar did,' Laura said.

'Exactly,' said Ivy. 'How long would she hang about before she came in after her. Or would she go away? Even if she did, she'd have to come back. And then we keep her too.'

'And the nosy neighbour sees that and calls the cops?' Laura said.

'Exactly.'

'But that's two of them against three of us,' said Martine. 'Unless . . . Do you think Kate would come over to our side? If she was in here with us?'

'No,' said Ivy. 'But I'm planning to deal with Kate when it's three against one. Does anyone have a problem with that?'

Her voice was hard enough to make Martine shiver. 'Deal with?' she said.

'Tie her up,' said Ivy. 'Think of it that way if it helps.'

Martine stared at her. 'I was joking before,' she said. 'But you *have* changed.'

'Finally,' Ivy said. 'It took me long enough. And I chickened out once. But yes, I have.'

'Hang on, though,' Laura said. 'If we've got both of them down here with us . . .'

'No food,' said Ivy. 'I know. So maybe it can't be this afternoon. Maybe we need to do a bit of stockpiling in advance. Cut our rations and save some.'

'Would Caspar ever come though?' Laura said. 'Would she get her hands dirty?'

My turn, thought Martine. They've both had theirs. 'I don't think that much dependence can all go one way.'

'Oh great! Dr Freud's back,' said Laura.

'Sacks,' Martine said. 'I wish you would help me remember, instead of undermi—'

'You're right,' Ivy said. 'Shoosh, Laura. She's right. We need to send a sign, like you said. *And* we need to understand them, like she said. *And* we need to be prepared – like I said – to do what needs to be done.'

'To "tie Kate up"?' Laura offered.

Ivy smiled. Beamed. 'Exactly,' she said. 'Tie her up good and tight.'

Martine wondered how Kate could miss it on Ivy's face, later that day when she came in with their food.

'Airbed,' Kate said, putting a black bag on the floor with a thick slapping sound.

'Just like dead people use?' said Laura.

'And more,' Kate said, almost as if she hadn't heard. She

had though, Martine thought. She was shaking her head, slow as a charmed snake. Her new way of pretending they weren't really here. Or *she* wasn't. Her new way of pretending it wasn't actually happening, this nightmare she had helped into being. 'Sweatshirts and trousers,' she said. 'Fleece.'

Laura was closest and she lunged towards the bag and lifted out a jumble of grey and black clothes, throwing them up in the air as if she was playing in autumn leaves, as if she was turning hay in the sunshine.

'Hal-LEE-lujah,' she said. As she stood, she grabbed the hem of her dress and pulled it over her head. Standing in her bra and pants, she screwed the dress up in her hands and threw it towards Kate, who stepped aside sharply. 'You can bin that,' she said. Then she plucked a sweatshirt from the pile and pulled it on. She put on a pair of socks, hopping around on one leg and the other, then took a set of bottoms and tied them round her waist, like a wrestler's belt.

Kate was staring at her. 'What is it?' she said. 'You seem different.'

Martine could almost pity her, caught between Gail and them, waiting just as much up there as they were down here. Then Kate turned and shot Martine a look that could shrivel someone much stronger and less exhausted. Martine looked away. 'There!' Kate said. 'You too. What is it?'

'What do you think it is?' Ivy said. She was standing too now, creaking and staggering a bit. Martine thought she was right about the exercise. Ivy was tearing off her cardigan and unbuttoning her blouse. Underneath she had on a bra, solid and massive, the sort Martine didn't know they made any more. The flesh of her stomach below it and above her waist-band was marshmallow soft and the colour of porridge, with little tags of skin, here and there, like pulled stitches in an old jumper. 'We've got a bed and clean clothes!' Ivy said. She was wriggling out of her skirt now, shucking it off and booting it over to where Laura's dress lay crumpled on the floor.

Martine hugged her knees into her chest. 'They're getting stir-crazy,' she said. Kate drilled her with another stare. 'We all are. You can't be surprised.'

'Why are we in here?' said Ivy. She was standing in

sweatshirt and socks too now, like Laura, both of them looking like elves to Martine, their pink flesh like leggings and the thick socks like bootees. 'What do you want? What are you going to do with us? Why did you pretend we were your sisters? Why are you keeping us here?'

'I'm not keeping you here,' Kate said, looking at the wall above their heads. 'And I didn't pretend anything.' Then she brought her gaze down to their faces. 'You should be careful how you speak to me,' she said. 'Don't you ever wonder why it's always me who comes in?' She was bundling up their discarded clothes in her arms. 'You should be grateful.' Then, walking backwards, feeling behind her, she made her way to the door.

'Why?' Laura said.

'Because I think you're dead enough. But you're not dead enough for my sister. And she's almost ready to choose.'

Ivy moved quicker than Martine dreamed she could. She stood in front of them, with her arms spread wide. 'She doesn't need to choose,' she said. 'She can have me.'

But the door was already open and, in a moment, Kate had locked it behind her again. 'Gail!' she shouted. 'Let me out.' The key was rattling in the lock before the words had left her mouth.

The silence she left behind her lasted a good long while. Laura broke it.

'That's not the deal, Ivy,' she said. 'All for one and one for all.'

'She means "thank you",' Martine said. 'Me too.'

'And what got you stripping off and flinging your clobber like we're all on a hen night?' Laura said.

'You started it,' Ivy said. 'But we need to be careful. She picked up on the new mood in here. We need to try to be the same, while we prepare.'

'And thank God she did,' said Martine, 'because it rattled her. She let things slip.'

'Did she?' Laura said.

Martine nodded. 'I've nearly got it.' She put her fingertips against her forehead and balanced her head on them. She could feel the sharp poke of her untrimmed nails on her skin and it made her feel as if she was forcing her brain to work, pinching it awake. 'She denied *she* wanted us in here. She denied that *she* was keeping us here.'

'Right,' said Laura. 'She's just Igor. Gail's the boss. Getting ready to choose.'

'And she said *she* wasn't pretending we were her sisters. We know she didn't prepare for us staying. As if she didn't think beyond getting us here and handing us over for inspection.'

'Try, Martine!' said Laura. Martine ignored the flare of anger at the heel-turn and managed not to say: make your mind up.

'Sisters,' she said. 'She pretended we were her sisters. It's right on the tip of my— Got it!' She had been at the gym, on the rowing machine, entranced by the voice describing something so bizarre and so invisible, the opposite of a normal person standing out like a hippo: it was a normal-looking person so far departed from reality it made Martine feel sick. It made her scared to remember the times in her life that she'd seen a random middle-aged Black man on a city street and wondered about him.

'Capgras syndrome!' she said. 'It *was* Oliver Sacks. I think it's a . . . I don't know what it is. An illness? It's a delusion. Where someone thinks strangers they've never met are people they know. Thinks the people they know have been taken away. This is it! Gail keeps telling Kate not to speak to her, not to feed her, doesn't she? She doesn't believe Kate's her sister any more. She wants a new one. She's going to choose a new one!'

'Choose one to kill?' said Laura. 'Or choose one to keep?'

'And kill the other two?' Ivy said. 'And I pushed myself forward! I had no idea. I thought I was protecting you.'

'Shoosh,' said Martine. 'Of course you did. None of us knew.'

'But how can Kate go along with it, instead of just getting a bloody doctor?' Laura said. 'Why's she pandering?'

Ivy found herself answering. 'When you live a small life, turned in, you can get a long way down a road without ever knowing.'

Martine heard the break in her voice. 'Don't upset yourself,' she said.

'And put your feet back up,' Laura added.

'I couldn't see beyond a cat!' Ivy wailed.

'Ssshh,' said Laura, making Martine's flesh crawl at the memory of Gail. Sliding about in her bare feet, whispering and shushing.

'Sorry,' Laura said. She'd noticed Martine shuddering.

'A cat!' Ivy said again, with a deep sob in her voice.

'Don't,' Martine said. 'You are nothing like her. She's not just dependent, Ivy. She's parasitic. She's fused. She's like a twin from a horror film. She's a . . . perversion.'

'You don't know what it's like,' Ivy said again. 'Mother. The things I did because of Mother. I killed a mouse. I let it die in agony.'

'Would you have killed a cat?' said Martine.

'No.'

'A child?'

'*No!*'

'And look what you're willing to do for Laura and me. Sacrificing yourself.'

But Ivy wouldn't be consoled. 'I thought I was but I got it wrong. What if I've made it worse?'

She'd have to try something else, thought Martine. 'I tell you what,' she said, sticking her nose up and pretending to sniff the air. 'A bit of adrenaline hasn't helped us smell any better.'

Laura wrinkled her nose, held open the neck of her sweat-shirt and poked her face in. 'It's a complete waste of these clean clothes.'

'No!' Ivy said. She said bolt upright, the sobbing gone. 'We have *got* to stop caring about being dirty. It doesn't *matter.*' Laura winked at Martine. It had worked. Ivy was back on the warpath. 'How long were those miners underground in wher-ever it was?' she said. 'And astronauts. It *doesn't matter.*'

'Agreed,' said Martine. 'We exercise and we concentrate on feeling strong and capable. We need to stop giving a toss about anything else.'

'*You* do for sure,' Laura said. Her face was solemn. 'Because when we get out and you see your hair you're going to scream and run straight back in again.'

Martine's mouth dropped open and she was silent for a long beat. Then the laughter bubbled up from her belly and burst out of her. The other two joined in and before long all three of them were gasping.

Upstairs, in the ladies' withdrawing room, Kate stood in the deep shadow at the side of the window and watched her sister's chest rise and fall.

'I told you,' she said. 'Something's changed. Listen to them. They're *laughing*.'

Gail said nothing.

'You need to . . . I mean, it's up to you, of course. But if I could . . . I'd say, if you're ready—'

'Ssssshhhh,' Gail breathed, her lips hardly moving. She was propped on the chaise longue with her net curtain draped over the headrest and covering her to her waist. 'Let me rest. Please, ssshhh. Leave me be.'

EIGHTEEN

I came awake with my limbs flailing and found myself upright in bed, heart hammering and hair sticking to my scalp. I had been back in my parents' house, locked in my room, and my room was a train carriage, rocking, slack and sway-bellied, as if the couplings were loose or the rails were the wrong gauge. Shaking, I reached out and put my bedside lamp on, half-expecting to hear the furtive scuffle of someone creeping around my flat, trying to find me. There was only silence, the soft sound of the wind in my draughty windows and the tick of my heating. He wouldn't, would he? And anyway, how could he find me? I'd ditched my car, my phone and my laptop. I hadn't used my cards.

A woman couldn't just disappear. Adim and the girls would kick up a stink. And anyway, he wouldn't.

I tried to forget the way he'd looked at me and spoken to me, scorn turning his voice sour and his face ugly. 'Try *me*,' he'd said. 'Check out your Brownies and Guides ideas about life, Tash. Go on. You need to learn that the world isn't the pink sherbet place you think it is.'

'You've got a week,' I'd said.

He pushed his lips out and shook his head very slowly from side to side, staring up at me through his brows. I didn't like looking at him when he did that. I stood up and backed off, putting distance between us. I didn't know whether it would be an open-handed slap or a blow from his fist. Maybe it would be both hands round my neck and those small eyes looking coldly into mine until my vision faded.

'Don't test me, Dad,' I said. '*I've* got nothing to lose. Yet. I've done nothing wrong. You're not safe till I've taken over and bleached the books. *Then* I'll have to keep my mouth shut or face jailtime along with you. But right now, you've got nothing on me. So get a clue. And quick.'

He was rising to his feet. He looked stupid with meanness,

small-brained and frightening. He looked like someone who couldn't be reasoned with or even bargained with. He was just a sack of dull meat, angry and bewildered by this new feeling of not getting his way. When I scrabbled my way out the door and slammed it behind me, I expected to hear him fling himself against it, like a rabid animal. I expected to hear him pawing and scratching.

'All right, Tash?' said the manager I passed on the stairs. 'You've been a stranger.'

I ignored him, scurrying past fast enough to feel my feet slip on the metal edging of the steps.

'OK there, Tash?' said the girl on reception. I had spent one Christmas works night out in the women's bogs with that girl and a bottle of tequila, moaning about boyfriends and cracking each other up about maybe just marrying each other because how bad could it be.

On watery legs, I clambered out of bed and felt my sweaty feet slide on the carpet tiles my bedroom floor had been covered with, the cheapest available, flat from wear but still with the odd stiff fibre that could stick to my skin and make me instantly itchy. I dragged my feet to clean them once I got on to the laminate in the hallway, feeling the sprung edges from its cack-handed installation dig into my insteps, not caring. I poured myself a glass of tap in the kitchen then took it to the back window to look out into the night.

Nothing was moving. Not so much as a cat or a fox disturbed the glitter of the garden walls and the grass beyond as the temperature fell and the dew formed. On the long stretch behind the fairytale cottage, there were footprints on the grass. I could see them in the harsh moon shadow, as if they had been added by an artist to finish off the scene. I looked upwards to the blue-black velvet of the sky and the shimmering disc of moon, one night off full, maybe two, outshining the stars so they only winked instead of dazzling. I was almost glad I'd had the nightmare now. So few clear nights had a moon as bright as this one that let you see colours. Or was it my imagination, I wondered as I turned my gaze down again, that the grass had a green cast and that the walls were pearly grey.

I leaned my head against the windowpane, letting my breath cloud it and clear, cloud it and clear. Then I held it.

There *was* someone down there. Someone was moving in the shadow of the stable wall at the far end of that long blank garden. I pulled back, but I knew it was too late. If he was looking, he'd have seen me. So, instead of running for my phone, or even for my keys and down to my car, I stood still and kept watching.

I didn't understand what I was seeing, as the figure broke away from the shadow and moved out on to the grass again. Only that it was too simple a shape to be a real person. It fluttered at the edges as it moved and it had no head or arms. It was just a long column of soft grey, flitting up the garden towards the back of the house.

I don't believe in ghosts, but I came closer in those few moments than I ever had before. Another minute showed me it *was* a person after all, a woman, wearing something long and shapeless that skimmed the ground and a veil that covered her to her waist, hiding face and neck, hands and arms. And, if I had any lingering doubts, I could see the set of new prints in the grass from flesh and blood feet, and the dull glint of some app or other flashing on and off on the phone she held in her hand.

At the house, the figure turned away to open the door in the offshoot then slipped inside. I could see through the veil then, in the harsh light cast by a bare overhead bulb. Underneath, the woman had long hair hanging down her back and her veil was actually a net curtain, still with the doubled hem for the curtain rod weighing it down on one side.

Was that the same woman who dotted about in her slippers and was forever tidying her cellar, up and down with bags and boxes every day? She seemed taller. Or maybe everyone would looked taller dressed as a grey ghost on a moonlit night. It was none of my business and I had more to worry about than what my neighbours got up to. Except if I went round and introduced myself to the woman – women? – and said I had seen a prowler, that was more folk to agree with the police that I had disappeared. *If* I disappeared. He wouldn't, would he?

I made a huge, grinding effort to stop the thought from replaying. I could drive myself over the edge and end up like that mad bat in her net curtain if I kept going at the same thing like a hamster on a wheel. So. Never mind if he would. *Could* he?

I picked up my laptop and climbed back into bed, clicking the light on and looking out at the streetlamp glow beyond my window, wondering if I needed to draw the curtains, wondering if anyone else would be up in Hephaw at this time of night, and if seeing the top of my headboard and half my wardrobe mirror would matter even if they were. Then I tucked the blankets in round my knees and typed *missing girls*.

Six hundred and eighty-one million results. China, Canada, eight hundred and forty-one in Africa, one in London on Valentine's Day. *Missing women*, I typed. Eight hundred and ninety-seven million hits. I let my head drop back with a soft knock against my headboard and looked up at the dark Artex paint beyond the glow of my bedside lamp.

Think, I told myself. You already know more than you ever wanted to about trafficked girls, bonded servants, and modern slavery. What you need to know is how big a deal it would be if *you* went missing.

It came to me as if someone had whispered in my ear. If I wanted to know how likely it was that a woman like me would go missing from where I was, and how big a fuss would get made if I did, I knew exactly what to search for.

Missing woman, Hephaw, 2018 gave me nothing. I cast my mind back over the year and tried again. *Missing woman, Fraserburgh, 2018.*

'Bingo,' I whispered to myself. 'Got one.'

The *Press and Journal* had written about the case regularly while it was fresh and then kept reporting on the search for a while afterwards. I clicked on the first story.

'Aberdeenshire police are seeking information about fifty-four-year-old Ivy Stone who has been missing from her Fraserburgh home for three weeks. Miss Stone, who works at home as a bookkeeper, lives alone. Her postal carrier raised the alarm after becoming concerned about delivered mail, visible through her letterbox. William McKay, who has been employed on the same mail route for seven years, spoke to our reporter. "Ivy's not the sort to disappear and leave a mess," he said. "She stops her post whenever she goes a wee trip anywhere. You could set your clock by her. She picks up her parcels, she tips at Christmas, and she hands back anything that's not got her name on it. I knew there was something wrong when I could hear her letters hitting the day before's envelopes instead of hitting her carpet."

'The CID sergeant in charge of Miss Stone's case, however, had this to say: "Her phone's gone and her laptop's gone. She didn't clean out her fridge but that's not against the law. She's a low priority according to Police Scotland's metrics. She's in good health and there are no signs that she left home anything but voluntarily. We urge Miss Stone to get in touch and reassure us of her well-being, but we are not pursuing the case as suspicious."'

I read the story over again, thinking. I was dead right to make my routines common knowledge then. But no one had paid any real attention to Ivy in any case, had they? The story ran, shorter and shorter, further and further from the front page. There was just one more snippet, so brief I nearly missed it. Two weeks later, the same reporter had interviewed a committee member from the Nine Lives League. 'We didn't get her name and address, but she was here at our meeting a week or two before they say she went missing, even though she wasn't a member. She was only here to meet a friend. And I reckon she knew she was leaving town because she wouldn't give us her details.'

'God Almighty,' I muttered. 'Stray cats?' It probably wasn't fair but this Ivy in her fifties wasn't really the Fraserburgh equivalent of me, was she? Surely I would leave a bigger hole than that if I suddenly vanished.

I cleared the search and cleared out my history too, a habit I'd worked hard to get up and running in the last year.

Lockerbie, I typed, *missing woman, 2018.*

There were two this time, one poor cow who'd run out on her husband and kids when she couldn't take another day of depression and the shit of waiting three weeks for an appointment to speak to a knackered practice nurse to get on the waiting list to see a knackered psychiatrist with a twitchy prescription finger. She'd run away to Skye and spent the family's entire capital – not much – in a B&B before the cash ran out and she used her debit card. She was back home now, even more stressed from lack of money but bumped up the waiting list for a therapy appointment probably.

The other one was more promising. Martine MacAllister was thirty, a freelance grant-writer who lived alone and disappeared from home, with her phone and laptop, leaving clients in the lurch. She had set up automatic adverts to run in email newsletters, some of them to the same clients she was letting down, which pissed them off, understandably.

The *Dumfries Standard* had managed to get a spin on the story off the back of that. Martine's car had pinged an ANPR on the M8 near Livingston, but the reporter took pains to point out that plate recognition doesn't show drivers' faces. And he managed to tie that to the emails:

'—supposed to be genuine contact, but when they're still landing in your inbox after the person's hooked it and isn't answering the complaints they're getting, it shows how false our online relationships really are. How faceless our society has become.'

This Martine had never turned up, or not that I could find out anyway. There was a letter to the paper from something called Family Forest, probably some nutty church. 'We miss Martine,' the letter said. 'She was a welcome presence at our meetings and she had made a new friend that last night she was with us. We have set up a Facebook page – Find Marty – to share all information.'

Find Marty hit me in the gut like a piledriver. The picture looked blurry and strange, as if Martine had been accidentally in the background of some other shot, and the solemn group all holding candles that made the header for the page were the only ones who had ever posted. Seven of them there were, two retired couples and a younger pair, along with a man in his fifties who was looking off to the side as if waiting for the photo-shoot to be over.

I scrolled down a bit, until the repeated messages of concern and pleas for information were getting so over-familiar I couldn't bear it any more. Some of them were cut and pasted from another page, Martine's name showing up in a different font where it had been added in.

'Regular attendee at Family Forest'

'Enthusiastic Forester'

'Great loss of expertise'

Expertise? Maybe Martine was in the choir or arranged the flowers. Except the background to the seven po-faced members with the candles looked more like a pub function room. I scrolled back to the top and studied the woman's face again. She was solemn but eager-looking, well-polished with shiny hair held back in a clip at the nape of her neck and a small gold ring in the ear I could see. She was surely sitting in that same function room, with its loud patterned curtains and tasselled lampshades on the wall sconces, and she was sitting forward in her chair as if whoever she was talking to was holding her rapt.

Maybe *that* person would have more to say about Martine than that she was a regular attendee and a welcome presence. Maybe that person, holding her attention like a magician at a kid's birthday party, would have photos of Martine that were posed with her own sweet face in the middle of the frame. Or maybe this was the last night and the interesting person was the 'new friend'. Maybe Martine was just dead polite and pretending to be fascinated by some bore.

Things go in threes, I told myself, clearing the search again and punching in a new one. *Missing woman, Ayr, 2018.* Maybe because it was the seaside, the kind of place people ran away to, with plenty cheap B&Bs empty in the off-season, there were four this time.

One of the missing women in Ayr wasn't a woman. She was a girl of seventeen and I felt a bitter hit of adrenaline as I read through the newspaper reports. This was different. The *Record* and the *Herald* both cared about this one. And Police Scotland categorized her differently too. Seventeen years old meant a dedicated search and a team.

She turned up. The report was bald but, between the lines, I thought there was a man involved. I'd have put a wedge on the teacher in his forties who appeared days later in Ayr sheriff court, charged with unlawful detention of a minor.

Two more were a pair of widows who had walked away from a pyramid scheme and made it to Spain. I half-remembered the story. 'Gilt-edged Grans' was the Ayr paper's headline.

The last of the four women was something else again. She was a professional running her own business. I read and re-read the descriptions of it but couldn't work out what the business *was* exactly. There were a lot of businesses like that these days. This woman – Laura Wade – had disappeared from Ayr while I was still working there. She had gone out one Saturday in May, all dressed up for a date, and had never come home. I read the address with a strange prickling feeling up the back of my neck. Surely that was where Siobhan, one of my old patients, lived. I had probably been right there at those flats a dozen times picking her up and dropping her off. It was a horrible thought that a woman had been abducted right from that very spot.

I kept reading. Laura Wade *hadn't* been abducted from her flat, in fact. The woman's car was missing, which at first had seemed like a sign that she'd gone somewhere voluntarily. But then it never turned up. It wasn't illegally parked, racking up fines, and it hadn't been clocked at a port taking her through the tunnel to France. It had been tracked up the M77 to Glasgow and on to the M8, then it had vanished along with its owner.

I scrolled some more and found another follow-up story. The police were inclined to think Laura Wade had done a runner, because her phone and laptop were both gone. But I was beginning to lose faith in that as shorthand for all being well. Hadn't the other two women, in Fraserburgh and Lockerbie, both taken their phones and laptops with them too?

I shook my head, feeling muzzy, and glanced at the time in the corner of my screen. It was getting on for three o'clock now. I sank back against the headboard, wishing I hadn't looked at any of this. Because there was no denying it now. Whether or not he would, he *certainly* could. Women disappeared from towns all over Scotland every month, and no one ever found them. No one even tried to.

So I would get up in the morning and go to the police. I'd tell them everything. I'd say my dad was filthy and the only way to prove it now he'd got out and covered his tracks behind him was to put a forensic accountant into BG. Which would tank it. Egger would lose his job and his pension, and the manager and receptionist I'd scuttled past the other day. Every last one of them. And all that filthy money would pay for a great lawyer, and Garry and Lynne and Bazz would all get off. Then I would disappear anyway. If he meant it. If he would really do it. If.

I scrolled back to the top of the page and was just about to delete everything when the picture of Laura Wade in the news story snagged my attention. It was a security cam still, taken overhead, showing the woman letting herself out of the door of a block of flats. I stared at it.

Then I moved the mouse, watching the cursor jig around in obedience to the way my hand was shaking. 'Images'. The news disappeared to be replaced by a chessboard, all over the screen and disappearing off it at the bottom, a Warhol print of that same overhead security camera shot, over and over again. A woman in a floating summer dress, peach coloured, with cream ruffles, letting herself out of a glass door with a bulky compression hinge. And reflected in the open door, I could see part of a bumper and half a number plate, a pair of thin legs in corduroy standing at the kerb between the carpark and the walkway.

That was Siobhan's husband, Kenneth, in the cords. And that bumper and number plate was my ambulance. My patient transporter. I had seen the woman. I had seen Laura Wade leaving her flat.

Siobhan had said how nice she looked and the men had made some daft jokes about romance and love. Something like that anyway; I couldn't remember the details. But I remembered the dress. Peaches and cream and ruffled like something for a summer wedding. I had seen Laura Wade on the last day.

NINETEEN

aura managed to hide the flash of pure fury that shot through her. She was an expert at it. Not like the other two, saying exactly what they thought as soon as they thought it, letting every bubble of gas that got to the top of their brains just come blasting out of their mouths. They had no idea how hard she was working here. It had started with the socks. She had pointed out the completely obvious to Ivy – that she needed a pair of socks – and Ivy had flat-out said she'd ask for 'three pairs of socks', one for her that needed them and two more to keep it even. Could anyone be as clueless as the pair of them? They had tights on and shoes and she had bare legs and cardboard sandals she'd made herself.

And they'd been happy enough for her to use her real sandals as a hammer and chisel to open up the drain. Of course she'd agreed, but she wasn't sure they had actually ever said thank you.

About the socks, she had said nothing and the anger passed eventually. It even helped. It tired her and she slept better. Not that saying nothing was always a good idea. She was pretty sick of their silent moods, the pair of them: Ivy staring at her red, shiny ankles, Martine with her eyes closed. But if she asked them what they were thinking about, she knew what she'd hear from Ivy.

'I've never eaten much Japanese food. Or any Japanese food. But I think a big bowl of clear chicken broth, with some lime and some chilies would be lovely. Prawns floating in it maybe. And sushi. It looks so pretty and so dainty. I think I'd like to try it. Not the raw stuff. And they make a salad with . . . what is it?'

'Green papaya?' said Martine. 'But that's Thai. And it's very sour.'

'I'd like something very sour,' Ivy said. 'Sour and clean on my palate. Even the apples are mushy now. They taste of nothing. And I never want to eat another piece of bread in my life. They don't eat bread in Japan, do they?'

'Of course they eat bread in Japan!' Laura couldn't help it sometimes; she wasn't a saint. 'They eat M&Ms and Kettle Chips and Burger King in Japan. We probably eat more sushi in Scotland than the Japanese now.'

'Do you think they eat more haggis than us?' Ivy said. She was too easy to wind up. There was no fun in it.

Laura still tried though. She did all the heavy lifting when it came to jokes and games and keeping up spirits. She even asked Martine about her bloody hotel room occasionally.

'What's the nicest hotel room you've ever been in for real?' she said.

'After a wedding at a place at Fort William,' Martine said. 'The telly was disguised as a mirror. A bit racy but better than that ugly big black flatscreen staring back at you. In my dream hotel, the telly would come up out of a slot when you need it and then slide away again.'

Laura wanted to scream: will you have a crinoline lady over the toilet roll too? But instead she said: 'How about you, Ivy? What's your favourite hotel? Got anything to add to Martine's wish list?'

'I've never stayed in a hotel,' Ivy said. 'We always went to a caravan or a chalet when I was a wee girl. And bed and breakfasts don't count, do they?'

Laura caught Martine's eye. 'But haven't you ever travelled on business?' she said. 'And stayed at a Best Western?'

Ivy shook her head. 'My clients were all in Fraserburgh,' she said. 'I went on a training course to Glasgow once, but I stayed with my cousin. Her spare bedroom had a basin in it, mind you. But no, no hotels.'

Laura took three deep breaths in and out, feeling a hitch in her chest. That was unbearable. So selfish. She could at least have lied to them. She must have googled the Ritz and Claridge's like everyone else.

'Well, when we get out and I go to *my* hotel,' Martine said, 'you come with me and take first pick of the rooms.'

'Speaking of which,' Laura said, amazed by her own

patience, not reacting to being left out of this plan, 'I do believe I hear room service.'

They all fell silent, listening to Kate's voice and the key in the outer door, the grating judder of the door on the stone as Gail wrenched it open. Then Kate was edging round the inner door with her carrier bag, re-locking it behind her. She walked halfway over the floor and set the bag down, then walked backwards until she was pressed against the wall. She had one of her little cardigans on and under it, one of her little blouses. Where did anyone even buy pencil skirts with kick pleats these days? Maybe she ran it up herself on a Singer with a foot pedal. The silence stretched, all three of them staring at Kate who stared back.

Laura broke it, doing the work again, as usual. 'What?' she demanded. 'Are you waiting for one of us to look at what you've brought us and say thank you?' She pulled herself to her feet, not bothering to straighten all the way and risk making her back spasm.

'It won't be you,' Kate said.

'What won't?' said Laura.

'That she chooses. She's almost ready, you know.'

Laura reached and swept the bag up in one hand then opened it. 'Sandwiches,' she said. 'Apples. Water. What a complete lack of surprise.' Ivy and Martine had told her that one day before she arrived there had been a banana and a pear, as if it was almost shopping day and supplies were running low, but it had been sandwiches, apples and water every day she had been here. She could hardly blame Ivy for dreaming of sushi really.

'You're not thinking clearly,' Kate said. 'Upsetting me. Annoying me. After Gail chooses, I'll be tidying up. I'll be deciding what to do with the leftovers.'

Laura threw the bag down again. When someone came, when they were rescued and got out of this, she would take Ivy to Martine's hotel with the mirror tellies – it was probably Inverlochy Castle – and she would personally see to it that there was a Japanese option on the menu that night. She'd sleep with the chef if she had to.

'I'll bear that in mind,' she said to Kate. 'Was there anything else you needed?'

Kate's mouth was a white line, her cheeks two quivering pouches around it. 'I'll enjoy it,' she said. 'Clearing up after *you.*'

Neither of them even said thanks, once Kate had left. Ivy had the nerve to criticize. 'Do you think it's maybe not a good idea to antagonize her quite so much?'

Laura's silent scream was long and, in her head, deafening. 'Antagonize?' she said, when it had finally dried up. 'You're planning to "tie her up", Ivy.'

'And soon too,' said Martine. 'If Gail's nearly ready to choose. We need to act quickly.'

'Not really,' Ivy said. 'I don't care if it's Gail or Kate who comes in.'

'Gail's got a knife,' Martine said. 'Remember?'

'I've got surprise and right on my side,' said Ivy. 'And something I don't want to tell you.'

'Hang on,' Laura said. 'Wait. What did you just say, Ivy? You don't care which one of them comes in? First. And which one has to decide when to come in after her?'

'Right,' Ivy said.

'I need to think this out,' Laura said. 'We've missed something.'

'Don't upset yourself,' Martine said. And they shared a look then, the two of them. Had they been discussing her? She thought she had heard them whispering away when she was at the drain late last night but she'd assumed they were trying to cover the sounds she was making, to spare her feelings. As if she cared. The painful, watery mess that fell out of her bowels wasn't what was worrying her. It was when she went for a pee that she could feel a little burst of panic. She knew she was getting cystitis. It was all she could do not to cry out with the pain of it when the flow started, and it was even worse when it stopped. Of course she was getting it. She had to be careful, especially on her period, not to drink too much wine and to bathe twice a day, and even then at least twice a year she asked her doctor for an antibiotic when the warm water and cranberry wouldn't shift it. She must have been mad to try to keep her water intake down, testing to find the bottom edge of the dose and see if she could get under it. Idiot.

'You OK?' Ivy's voice floated over. She must have whimpered.

'Fine,' Laura said. There was no point worrying them. Maybe if she drank her water ration in one go tomorrow she could flush it through, even if she ended up off her gourd. And if she saved up her baby wipes till she'd stopped bleeding she could have a proper wash, stop any more infection.

'Are you in pain?' Martine called.

'No, just pissed off,' Laura said. 'Just . . . you know.'

The next day, she chugged the bottle in one long gulp and curled up under a blanket to meditate it away. Laura was a big believer in positive imaging. She used to imagine every detail of the life she was working towards: the house, the kid, the husband, the car, the office, the wallet full of platinum credit cards, the white-gold ring with the cushion-cut diamond. Now she imagined the water falling through her, collecting germs – little cartoon germs, like you used to see on adverts for cough mixture. Maybe if she stayed curled up she'd be able to get properly warm. Maybe if she slept, she'd be able to fight it off.

But Martine wouldn't let up. On and on and on about her podcast and the amazing thing she knew if only she had remembered. As if it mattered what had brought them here.

She was nearly grateful when Ivy started on about her training regime to get in shape for overpowering Kate. Laura had to admit there was sense in that. The inflatable chairs had given her a bad fright. They were delivered in flat packets and it had taken a whole day to blow them up, taking it in turns. Laura was shocked at how little air her lungs seemed to have in them. They were gunked up with the foul air and the damp, but she knew it was lack of exercise too. Ivy was right: they had to get moving.

But not today. She would start tomorrow when she had thrown off this irritating little threat of infection. Nothing to worry about. Just annoying. To take her mind off it, she decided she'd pipe up too, for once. Ivy had had her say about exercise and Martine had given her podcast obsession an airing, so Laura deserved a turn.

'Even without sending a sign,' she began, then she sat up

a bit to make her voice sound less wobbly, 'someone might come at any time. Some copper's going to notice that my car headed west to here and your car headed east to here. God, Ivy, if only you'd used a card to buy your ticket for the train.'

'Some copper who's got a corkboard covered in string and thumb tacks?' said Martine. 'In Brooklyn. Well, supposed to be Brooklyn but it's filmed in Hollywood. Like that, you mean?'

'OK, not the police,' Laura said. 'Vigilantes. People who don't care who's laughing, they'll never give up. We've no way of knowing who's looking for us, have we?'

No one said anything.

'My parents might be trying to get in touch. They live in Spain and we're not all over each other on a weekly basis but you never know. I'm a bit sorry, for once, that my business is set up to tick over so smoothly. I won't have clients on the rampage. How about you, Martine?'

'What about me?'

'Who'll be heading up the search effort, fundraising, stapling posters to lampposts? '

'For me?' Martine said. 'Pass. My mum died years back and my gran died not long ago too. My neighbours might be wondering.'

'It's lovely to have good neighbours,' said Ivy. 'My stair's not the sort of place people take an interest any more. When I was young, when my dad was alive, we would all first foot, up and down the whole street, and we'd run in and out with plates of cake and extra scones if we'd made too much. Mother was a great scone hand.' Laura really did try to find something to say to that, but she was still casting about for it when Ivy went on. 'My cousins in Glasgow might be wondering. I usually write to them both on their birthdays and I've missed the dates. Then there's all the people who saw me at the NLL meeting. With Kate. Everyone who saw us in the pub. No end of people when I think about it.'

Laura could feel her eyes start to swim and she turned her head away in case the other two could see the tears shining as they fell.

When Kate brought the airbed and warm clothes and had her little blurt and it finally shook the magic word out of

Martine's memory, Laura felt better than she had for days. Her head was swimming and her eyes were gritty, but she danced around in her underwear while she was getting changed and made them both laugh. She wasn't cold either, even in her knickers and socks. She was toasty warm. She was hot, actually. Her cheeks were hot and her breath felt hot when she exhaled. She hadn't managed to pee away the infection after all; she'd just wasted two water rations and ended up thirsty in the night. It wasn't so sore any more though, or not in the same way. The nipping and burning had stopped, but there was an ache deep inside her, at the bottom of her back, she was trying not to think about. And she couldn't imagine helping Ivy jump on Kate and subdue her. She would have to let them do it without her. How long would Gail leave it before she came in, anyway? Ten minutes? Or would she go back upstairs? How long before she came down again? A day? Half a day? Then how long would it take with them both down here before— There it was!

Laura sat up, making the chair squeal against the stone floor, making Martine go into her usual routine of shuddering and rubbing her arms as if she'd heard nails on a blackboard.

'What is it?' Ivy said.

'Tell me if I'm going mad,' Laura said. 'Or if this makes sense.'

'Go on,' said Martine.

'We overpower Kate,' Laura said. 'And Gail comes in – then or later – to see if she's OK. Right?'

'And we overpower Gail and then we wait until the neighbour that watches them notices they've disappear—' Martine said.

'No,' Laura said. 'Because when Creepy Caspar comes in to see what happened to the minion she'll either have to leave the doors open or she'll have the key with her.'

There was a moment of complete silence.

'No,' said Martine, 'You're not going mad. As soon as we get Gail inside both doors, we get out! We get out!'

They sat stunned. Laura was still scared to look too closely at it in case it dried up and blew away.

Ivy spoke first. 'It can't be that easy. There must be something we haven't thought of.'

'Like what?' Martine said. Laura felt a surge inside her to hear Martine so fierce on her behalf.

'They wouldn't – Gail wouldn't – have left such an obvious way out,' Ivy said. 'After all the planning.'

'Yeah but Ivy,' Laura said, 'her planning was all about getting us here. Getting to know us, lurking on cat sites and genealogy sites and dating apps, setting us up to get here. Sending Igor out to fetch us. She didn't have any plans for after. Like we said.'

'Cats,' Ivy said. 'You're right. Kate was so sloppy when I got here. I said I was surprised she didn't have a cat and it was like she forgot she should have. Like her auntie in Aberdeen too.'

'And her brother-in-law,' said Martine.

'And don't forget Myra!' Ivy said. They had had enough time now to pore over everything, even the name of Ivy's friend who never turned up, the employee of Fairytale Endings, and the frequent contributor to RoyalBlood who pushed Martine to go to the Lockerbie meetings.

'And then there was the way she asked me to bring my laptop,' Ivy went on, 'but forgot to ask you two.'

Laura shook her head. She wished Ivy would stop gabbling. It was going through her head like a drill.

Martine laughing was even worse. 'She knew she didn't have to!' she said. 'She knew we'd never leave home without them. And if we had, Gail would just have gone back in and wiped them remotely.'

Ivy was silent a while. 'You know Kate sat there in the pub with me that first night and told me I shouldn't have let someone take over my keyboard? Did I tell you?'

Martine nodded. 'Same here,' she said. 'Asked me if I didn't worry that the tech support person would lurk in there forever. And all the time Gail was doing just that to both of us.' She glanced over at Laura. 'All of us.'

'Look,' Laura said, 'we all took the bait; we all ended up here. Let it go. What matters now is getting out again.'

Ivy's face was etched with pain. 'It really *is* that simple to escape?' she said. 'Keep Kate till Gail comes then walk out the door?' She sobbed, a huge belch of misery. 'I could have done that the first day I got here. What a moron. What a pathetic waste of space I am, sitting here for months in my own filth. Mother was right about me.'

'Shoosh-shoosh,' Martine said. 'Come on. *We* never thought of it when it was you and me either, did we? And I never thought of it even today. That was you, Laura.'

Laura stirred herself. 'No, it wasn't. It took all three of us to get there. Martine worked out what Gail's doing, Ivy's the one who's tough enough to take Kate down, and I just worked out the last bit. The three of us did it together.'

'And I'm really glad you did work that bit out,' Ivy said. 'Because you were wrong about the neighbour. There's no one to send a sign to.'

'What about the inflatable chairs?'

'Same as the airbed. She's been careful not to give us anything we could use as a weapon. That's why they didn't carry kitchen chairs down for us. That's why we were on cardboard instead of camp beds.'

'When did you work all this out?' Martine said.

'While you two were sleeping,' Ivy said. 'I was thinking of how I would "tie her up" and how there wasn't much to use.'

'Is there anything at all?' said Martine.

'Yep,' Ivy said. 'I'm going to "tie her up" with the drain cover. I'd fight you both for the privilege. I want to hurt her. I'm *glad* it's an essential bit of the plan. I've never wanted to hurt anyone before.'

'And when will we do it?' said Martine. 'If we're not stock-piling food we don't need to wait. We could do it tomorrow.'

'We could,' said Laura. 'But I don't think I can do it tomorrow. I'm not . . . I didn't want to worry you, but I'm actually not feeling all that fantastic.'

Ivy looked over, then she stretched out her hand and laid it on Laura's head, gasping for some reason.

'Oh, that feels good,' Laura said. 'Your skin's so cool. Don't take your hand away.'

Ivy swapped hands once Laura's hot skin had warmed the first one. Then Martine took over. By the time the cloth dipped in water was placed, she was unconscious. She only felt it in her dreams.

TWENTY

'Ehhhhh, Nettie, it's grand to hear your voice. We didn't know where you'd gone, taking off like that.' Siobhan sounded tired and I could tell from the rumble in her throat that she was lying down, but she hadn't had to grope for the memory of who Nettie Dunn was. Thankfully.

'It's complicated,' I said. 'You wouldn't believe me if I told you.'

'Are you in trouble?' Siobhan's stomach might be slowly killing her but there was nothing wrong with her intuition.

'Not me,' I said. 'I'm helping someone else. How are *you*?'

'Kenneth's not been so clever. It's his knees. He's putting off having the first one done till . . . well, till it's more convenient, but it's getting tricky.'

I could see my reflection in the back window and I shook my head at it. I was bugging someone whose poor old husband was hoping not to have his knee replaced till his wife was dead and didn't need him anymore.

'But never mind that. I'm glad you're OK. You were the best driver we ever had, you know. Never minded stopping off at the shops. This new one's a right stickler and he can't park for shit.'

I gasp-laughed, choking myself.

'Sorry,' said Siobhan. 'It's the pain. You wouldn't believe the pain and if I take any stronger pills I'll be off my pins, talking to the wallpaper. So my language has gone right downhill.'

'Oh, Siobhan,' I said. 'God, I'd forgotten what you were like.'

'Come back and tell them all at the church when I'm gone. Them that sees me every day think I'm a bit of a misery guts lately.'

'Speaking of people you see every day,' I said, 'this is why I'm phoning actually.'

'Oh?'

'It's about your neighbour, Laura Wade,' I began.

Siobhan took it and ran before I could even get the question out. 'You've never found her, have you? Is that who you're helping? Oh my God, wait till I tell Kenneth. He's popped out for a swiftie but he'll not be long. He was very fond of the girl, you know. She used to be out most days by the time the bin men came round so Kenneth always took in her wheelie. And she was very grateful. Always rang the bell and said thanks and then gave him a nice bottle of something at the year's end. She was a bit stand-offish with me. A man's woman, I reckon: the way she dolled herself up any time she went over the door. I always thought she was hoping to meet Mr Right.'

'I haven't found her, no,' I said, taking the chance while Siobhan drew breath.

'But you're looking?'

I hesitated. I wasn't looking. I wouldn't know where to start. I was just getting through this endless week thinking about Laura Wade instead of about me, trying to convince myself a woman couldn't just vanish and Big Garry knew that, and so he *wouldn't*. Would he?

'I'm just interested,' I said to Siobhan. 'I think we saw her, you know.'

'Oh I *know* all right!' Siobhan said. 'The police were here time and again asking me. I'm surprised they never came after you to ask. I couldn't tell them much, only what time it was and what she was wearing. You'll have seen the photos in the paper, have you? See what I mean? All dolled up to the nines.'

'But they didn't pursue it,' I said. 'Not for long anyway.'

'Budgets,' said Siobhan. 'Bloody politicians. I told them there was no way she would take off. She was young but she was steady. You can tell from the shoes.'

'Shoes?'

'And bags. No cheap finery for Laura. She had one or two good bags and she always wore driving shoes to save her high heels, serviced her car, packed away her winter clothes, shampooed her own carpets.'

'How do you know what she did with her winter clothes?' I said. 'Were you that close?'

'She used to borrow our cylinder Hoover to do her vacuum-packs. She had an upright.'

I nodded. I was watching the little woman from the fairytale cottage again. It was a major clear-out today. She had been down to the cellar twice already with bulging black sacks. I couldn't imagine what was in them. They didn't weigh much, evidently, from the way she hefted them.

'Are you listening?' Siobhan said.

'Yes,' I said. 'No. Sorry. What?'

'I think she's been taken. Laura. I reckon whoever she was off to see in her pretty dress that day has got her locked up in an attic somewhere, like that madwoman in that thing. Or those kids. You know how it is.'

I knew more than I'd ever wanted to by now. The numbers of missing, found dead, found alive and never found. America got in the way when you googled it, of course. And America was huge. There were prairies and deserts and thousands of miles of forests. If someone made a decent effort to hide a body in America the chances were it would never be found. Scotland was different: too many people and not enough wilderness. And where there was wilderness, there were hardly any roads crossing it. I laid all this out to Siobhan now.

'Plus the roads cross sporting estates,' I said. 'Which means – I didn't know this but I've been reading up – the game-keepers take a note of all the number plates of cars they don't recognize. For poachers, you know.' I was lying about reading up on it. My dad had told me when he was trying to put me off going to a rave in Deeside one time. I hadn't questioned how he knew. He was my dad; he knew things. But now I wondered if he'd had cause to learn which Scottish roads the gamekeepers watched and which ones were unguarded. 'And the soil's about an inch thick over solid rock most places. So if the worst *has* happened, she'll turn up. Probably. Poor thing.'

'She might be in the sea,' Siobhan said. 'Picked clean and her bones halfway to Finland. I tell you what though, Nettie: it's a relief to get to talk to someone but Kenneth about it. He gets on at me for being morbid. I think it's him can't cope with talk of death. Which to be fair, I'll be gone, won't I? I'm not going to be looking into a coffin and trying not to toss my Shreddies.'

'Right enough,' I said. 'Poor Kenneth.'

'And anyway,' Siobhan went on, 'being put in a shallow grave *isn't* the worst at all.'

'Are you sure?' I said.

'You need to read the papers. It's all over.'

I knew what she was going to say before she started and maybe all the talk of graves and coffins had rattled me. I could feel my stomach start to churn.

'Sex slaves.' I wondered what paper Siobhan read. 'I've been hearing that if we go back to a proper border, there won't be all these lorries coming through with forty girls hidden in the back.'

I felt my blood drain. 'That was only once,' I said. 'And they got caught. Forty folk in a lorry is usually people who want to come. They're coming to skin fish, or gut chicken or pick cabbages, but willingly. The girls come on planes, Siobhan. One at a time. They think their pimps are their boyfriends.'

'Rotten sods,' Siobhan said. 'But they can't come through a hard border is my point. So who's next to get nabbed? Stands to reason – Laura Wade.'

'At least she can speak English,' I said. 'If she gets away and finds a passer-by at least she'll be able to say what's happened to her.'

'S'pose. Mind you, you'd have to be as thick as two planks not to know what's what just because some girl's jabbering away in Double Dutch, eh no?'

I said nothing. I couldn't speak about it. I could hardly bear to think about it. I'd read the stats on the end-users. In my world, the world of BG, with drivers doing long-distance runs away from home, I had to know dozens of them. I must have sat on their knees when I was a kid and joked around with them as a teenager. I had probably signed their leaving cards and given money when they were in hospital. I tried to hope they all went to world-weary single mums working out of their own council flats and socking away enough for Disneyland, but I wasn't a fool.

'Nettie?' Siobhan said.

'Yeah,' I said. 'I know. You can't wrap your head round it, can you?'

'Not if you're half-normal. And they say it's everywhere. Right under our noses.'

'Hiding in plain sight,' I agreed.

'I've told Kenneth, for after I'm gone. He's to get himself back to the choir and the whist club and snag himself a nice widow. There's no point in pretending he isn't what he is – they all are – but there's ways and ways of dealing with it.'

I was watching the little woman let herself back out of the cellar door again, without her bulging bags of stuff. Maybe she was collecting jumble for a sale at the church. She looked churchy. Maybe I could go round with a bag of my own and strike up a passing friendship with another neighbour, someone else to talk to the cops. A woman of that age, living alone or even with a funny friend in a net curtain, was usually the sort to keep a close eye and take a keen interest. Mind you, if I set the stereotypes aside, I had to admit that this little woman kept her head down and scurried around like a wee mouse, more like someone who didn't want to be seen than someone who wanted to do the seeing.

I was still thinking about that long after the end of the phone call, when I left the flat and went down to do a sweep of the gang who – even though they didn't know it – were building an expectation of my steadiness, ready to swear blind I'd never leave. For afterwards, if the worst happened. If he would.

'Wednesday already?' Aisling said. She was dusting the basket of reduced-price nail polish on the counter, lining up the little bottles by shade once she'd wiped them.

'I've got a question,' I said.

'We can do it with your knickers on if you insist, but we might miss some,' Renny said. 'Am I right?'

'No,' I said. 'And neverinamillionyears, by the way. No . . . what it was was I wondered if you know the people in the first house up the side street.'

'The fairytale cottage?' Aisling said. 'Nope. Bunch of weirdos.'

'Yeah,' said Renny. 'Definitely Billy Goats Gruff or Little Pigs. Not Snow White or Cinderella.'

'I don't know about Cinderella though,' Aisling said. 'Them at the post office reckon the parents always kept the girls on a right short rope. It's a shame when you think about it.'

'Yeah but the parents are passed away now,' said Renny. 'Or in a home. For sure you don't see them. And "the girls" haven't exactly burst out and started pole-dancing for fun and fitness. Why, anyway?'

'Nothing,' I said, when I realized she was asking me. I was thinking weirdos weren't the ones to watch. It was normal that was dangerous. Under our noses. Everywhere. 'Can I ask something else?' They waited. 'Speaking of short ropes. You ever had girls come in . . .?' I paused, not sure how to word it. 'Groups of them together.'

'Hen nights?' Aisling said. 'Not enough. Why, are you thinking of having one?'

'We gave one as a prize for the foster home fund at Christmas,' said Renny. 'Some bint and her book club won it. It wasn't exactly a riot. I like a hen night with a bit of you know.'

'Crying on the stairs, puking in your handbag,' I said.

'Exactly.'

'But speaking of the foster home,' I said, trying again. 'Or not really, I suppose, because it's after they leave really. When they get to London and step off the bus.'

'What is?' Renny said.

'I was just thinking, something I saw on the news. If a guy brought in a load of girls to get fancy nails and likes of the knickerless waxing, would you find that strange?'

Both girls stopped what they were doing and turned to face me.

'Trafficked girls, you mean?' Renny said. Her greened and contoured face couldn't change colour but it fell. My stomach lurched and I nodded dumbly.

'We went to a talk about it,' Aisling added. 'They went round the country. Police Scotland, I think it was, or it might have been some government lot, but we both went. They'd never get them out again if they brought them in here, would they, Ren?'

'So you know what to look out for?' I said.

'Not knowing the date, not knowing how long they're here for, not knowing the name of the town they're in, not knowing the name of the person they're staying with, pretending not to understand even when they do. Not having their own money, or a phone. Not having a handbag. Yeah, we know.'

They knew more than me, I thought. 'So it's probably daft to say this, but if anyone tried to get one of you to meet him somewhere quiet, you wouldn't go, would you?'

'Us?' said Renny. 'Ash and me? Come on! We're the Rohypnol generation. We've been at Defcon One since our trainer bras.'

'Right,' I said. 'Right, right. Course you have.'

'Are you on a case?' said Aisling. 'Are you like undercover investigating something?'

'No,' I said. 'Not exactly. I mean, it's probably best if I didn't talk about it.'

'In the Haw?' said Renny.

'My flat,' I said. I had lain awake for hours last night, couldn't get the thought out of my head. 'You know it's Airbnb, right? Have you ever seen folk staying there that made you worry?'

'Seriously?' said Renny. 'In the Haw? Upstairs from us?'

'I'm just asking.'

'Aye right, you are,' said Aisling. 'Naw, it's mostly scientists. Mostly. Biologists. They're looking at stuff growing on the shale bings. Some big project. They'll be spitting tacks you've nipped in.'

'They'll have to stay at the Paraffin Arms,' said Renny. 'And it's not as posh as it sounds.' She took a breath and shared a look with her sister. 'Is there?' she said. 'Something going on.'

'I really can't talk about it,' I said. 'But if I go away suddenly, don't let anyone tell you I meant to, eh?'

'Wow.' They spoke in chorus and I left them standing, owl-eyed, gazing after me.

'Adim,' I said, putting my *Scotsman* on the counter and a packet of sugar-free gum on top of it. 'Do you ever get anyone in here you're worried about? Customers that set off your alarm bells.'

'Like you are now, you mean? What you on about?'

'Stop it, I'm serious. I mean customers you worry about, in case they're not OK.'

'All the bloody time,' Adim said. He had been keying open crisp boxes but he let his key-ring snap back to his belt on its spiral cord and rested his arms on the top of the box in front of him. 'I worry about that pair above the pub, going home legless up those steep stairs at their age. And I worry they're going to put a chip pan on and burn us all to the ground.'

'They usually have a carry-out when they're sploshed,' I said. 'Sorry but they never shut their curtain and I live alone.'

'And that's another thing,' he said. 'You live alone, fair enough. You're young and strong. It's the old ones that worry me. All on their own with a nurse coming in the morning and meals on wheels. I'll never understand that about you lot.'

'Us lot?'

'I mean don't get me wrong, it drives me insane having my mum sitting there in the corner. My wife never gets a minute's peace from the old dear and it's only three years since *her* mum finally popped her clogs. But we know when it's us it'll be just the same, sitting in the corner of our daughter-in-law's living room driving her up the wall. Not parked in a home somewhere wishing for visitors. Like you lot.'

'Right,' I said. 'Like us lot.' Like the parents of the sisters at the fairytale cottage, Aisling and Renny said. Tidied away. 'You're dead right, you know.'

'I know.'

'But it wasn't old people I was thinking of.' I stopped and considered Adim, his open face looking back at me, his arms crossed on the top of the crisp box, sleeves rolled up, good watch loose on his skinny wrist, nails short and dirty from grubbing around with cash and cardboard all day. Why was I hesitating? I took a deep breath. 'It was girls I was thinking of. Mind you, I don't suppose they'd be trolling about buying papers.'

'Girls?' Adim said. 'You mean like Eastern European girls?'

'Exactly. I've been reading about it and it's . . .'

'It's everywhere. I know. I've never seen anything round this way but there was a government roadshow came through and they wouldn't have stopped here if it wasn't worthwhile, would they?'

I shrugged.

'My cousin said something once.' He frowned, remembering. 'There was this guy. A right low-life. Nothing you could pin it on but just a bad vibe, you know what I mean? Of course you do. This was Penicuik and one of his kids had been at school with the bloke, knew him. Said he lived on his own in his dead mum's house. Three bedrooms, end of terrace. But he definitely lived alone. Only, he was in and out of my cousin's shop and he bought magazines. *Cosmo*, *Hello*, *Seventeen*, *Shout*.' Adim swallowed hard. 'He bought Jackie Wilson. And sweeties.'

'What did he do? Your cousin, I mean.'

'Called the cops on a tip line. Never found out what happened but he never saw the guy again. We all watched the papers, but there was never anything reported on it.' He had been staring at the counter, lost in his memories. Now he looked up. 'Is that why you're here? Is that what you're doing?'

I felt myself flush. What *was* I doing? Trying to save my family business instead of phoning a tip line and letting it sink. The Hollywood girls, Adim and his cousin, even Siobhan, thought more about the girls, those endless nameless faceless girls than I had until this year, when I was already too late to save them.

'It's all right,' Adim said. 'If you can't say, you can't say.' I gave him a serious look. He meant it. He knew men like Big Garry were real and I wasn't crazy to be scared, to be hiding. Briefly he put his hand over mine and squeezed it. 'You know where I am if you need me.'

I wanted to tell him everything right there and then. Not him really. Not Adim. Just someone. I'd been on my own with this far too long.

Instead of going straight home, I wandered up the side street and in at the gate of the fairytale cottage, scuffing my feet in the browned apple blossom on the path. I knocked hard on the front door and waited. No one answered so I turned and walked away.

I was filling my kettle when I saw the little woman coming out into her garden again with yet another bundle of something to store in the cellar, and I tried not to be annoyed that I'd been left standing on the step. If a person doesn't want to answer her door she doesn't have to. She wasn't elderly. Not frail. And hadn't they all just decided, Adim and the girls and me myself, that it was young women who needed someone to watch them and worry, not nice wee wifies in cardies like her down there.

TWENTY-ONE

'I don't know if she can hear us,' Martine whispered. 'Is she sleeping or unconscious? She's so hot, but she's not sweating. Her skin feels dry.'

Sssshhhh. Laura thought she said it out loud.

'She might be able to hear everything,' Ivy said. 'We should talk to her.'

'Laura,' Martine said gently. 'It might hurt when we move you but we want you out of harm's way.'

Please don't hurt me. Laura screamed it. It hurts so much anyway.

'I don't think she can hear us,' Martine said. 'Ivy, do you throw your medicine out, like you're supposed to? You know how you're supposed to? Everyone says they do, like flossing your teeth, but do you?'

'I've still got some of Mother's,' Ivy said. 'It's not like the old days, big brown bottles of castor oil. Those pills are inert and you can google them. It would be a waste to chuck them out, time it takes you to get an appointment at the clinic sometimes.'

'That's what I thought,' said Martine. 'Kate's bound to have a decent stash up there, isn't she? Antibiotics.' They both looked at Laura for a while, watching her breathing. 'Did you really take castor oil? I thought that was for your scalp.'

'It's a laxative,' Ivy said. 'Mother . . .'

'Say it.'

Sssshhhh. Laura wished neither of them would say anything.

'OK, I'll go first,' Martine said. 'You said we should talk to her? Here goes. Laura? My mother was a selfish, clueless mess. She did her best but it wasn't nearly good enough. She was always about the new boyfriend, the one that was going to sweep her off her feet and take her away from it all. Laura? If you can hear me. It hurts my heart that you're just the same.

You're clever and funny and pretty – why are you just the same?'

'It's only natural to want to be loved,' Ivy said.

'*I* loved her!' said Martine. Then she bit her lip, shocked at how loud she'd spoken. For a while she sat in silence, watching Laura breathe. Ivy was doing her circuits, she noticed after a while, trotting round and round with her arms pumping. 'I really did love her,' she said. 'But she was absolutely bloody hopeless, Ivy. You've no idea. The place stank like bin juice all the time and we had ants in the cupboards because she'd never put anything in containers. It was just a big pile of packets with ants rummaging around inside them. So then she'd buy a new packet and shove the old one to the back. But I did love her.'

She tried once to make it better, Martine remembered. God knows where she got the money but she decorated the bathroom. She stripped off the old mouldy paper and washed the walls with a bottle of sugar soap from the ironmonger. She painted them pale pink and got matching pink curtains that crossed over and tied in bows. She carried an off-cut of pink carpet home over her shoulder, singing, and cut it to fit with kitchen scissors, added a fluffy bathmat and seat cover. There were candles.

'It took less than a week for the black mould to shine through the new paint,' Martine said. 'And the carpet curled up in the damp. God, Ivy, the look on her face when she rolled it up again and stuffed it in the wheelie.'

'Your poor mum,' Ivy said, panting a bit. 'And poor Laura too. That's not much of a bedside story.'

'It's got a happy ending,' Martine said. 'She went out and got legless and it's a lot easier to clean wine sick off bare floor than damp carpet.'

'Oh sweetheart,' said Ivy. She was back beside Martine and Laura now and she sat, letting herself drop into the squealing inflatable chair. 'How old were you?'

'Don't worry,' Martine said. 'I wasn't a kid. I was at high school.'

'The thing is,' Ivy said, then she drifted off. She did that a lot. She would start talking then disappear inside her own head, deep into her own memories, completely forget that there was someone waiting to hear whatever it was she wanted to say. Sometimes Martine poked her to keep talking, but today she let her drift.

Laura sank into the peace and drifted too.

'The thing is,' Ivy said again. Typical. Laura needed the silence and so of course Ivy was back. 'I can see it from both sides,' she was saying. 'I've been the one who was hopeless and disappointing. *And* I've been the one who was disappointed and stopped hoping.'

'My mum didn't feed me or wash my clothes and I had to teach myself how to do my hair from an article in a magazine,' Martine said. 'I bet that's not what you mean.'

'I don't want to go over it all again,' Ivy said. 'She's gone where she can't hurt me. Oh! You mean how was I hopeless? How did I disappoint her? I was always fat, clumsy, bad skin, couldn't sing, shy, no good at tennis, my teeth were yellow, I was hard on my shoes.'

'You were what?' said Martine.

'I was hard on my shoes,' Ivy said. 'They had to get re-soled a lot.'

'Your mother blamed you for gravity?'

Ivy was silent for a moment, then started laughing. 'She did! That's right. She did. Oh Martine, I'm going to say it. I really am going to say it.' She took a huge breath. 'I'm so glad she's dead. And I never thought I'd be able to tell anyone. Whatever happens to us' – she broke off and they both looked over at Laura again, watching her chest lift and drop – 'I'll never be sorry I met you. And I'm going to tell you something else now.' She paused and took a few more breaths to calm down. 'I've only ever wanted someone to love me, someone to care about me. I wanted to come first with someone. I never had that and I always thought it sounded lovely.'

'I had that. With my gran. It *is* lovely. I'm sorry you missed it.'

'I don't mind,' Ivy said. She was determined to have her say this time. She wouldn't be shouted down. It *mattered*. 'I really don't. See, I was still thinking like a child. Fifty-four and I was still a child. I wanted someone to love me and care about me. I was ready to settle for a cat. And instead I got you. And then Laura. And I'm so much older than you. You never understood what I was getting at, when I said that. You shouted me down.'

'Still don't. Still would.'

'The thing is it doesn't matter which way it goes. In or out. Loved or loving. It feels the same. Actually, I think it feels better to love because you're in charge of it never stopping. *Now* do you understand?'

Laura could feel tears welling up and spilling down the sides of her face.

'Oh my God!' said Martine. 'Look! She *can* hear us. She's conscious. Ivy, she must be in so much pain.'

'All the more reason to stick to the plan,' Ivy said. 'We get Laura safely out of the way, I take the drain cover and go behind the door, when Kate comes in I whack her with it. OK?'

'What do I do?'

'Stay safely tucked away,' Ivy said. 'Precious girl.'

When Martine knew she could talk again without her voice breaking, she said: 'Can I ask her about antibiotics first though?'

'Ask her today. And tomorrow we'll do it. Unless Gail comes down to "choose". But either way we'll do it. I'll do it for you. For both of you. And you do something for me? All right? You let me.'

'What's wrong with her?' Kate's nose was wrinkled and her voice sounded guttural, as if she was so disgusted by them she might gag.

You'd smell just as bad if someone kept you down here for weeks on end, Martine thought.

'A kidney infection,' Ivy said. 'She had a bladder infection and now it's gone up into her kidneys. She's got a high temperature. Very high. I wouldn't be surprised if she starts having seizures.'

'Renal failure?' Kate said.

Martine felt a slow roll of utter revulsion go through her. The woman sounded excited. There was no other word for it.

'So, what we thought,' she said, 'was maybe you could bring down a flask of warm water for her to drink and maybe if you had any antibiotics lying around in your medicine cabinet. Anything would do. Are you prone to it yourself? It would be great if you had just the right thing, obviously.'

'Kidney chills?' said Kate. 'No, we are not. What a thing to say to a person.'

Martine blinked at her.

'That's a nasty, dirty thing to let yourself get,' Kate said. 'Honeymoon disease, they used to call it. Gail and I have never been in the way of anything like that.'

With one last glare, she turned to Laura and leaned forward. Martine remembered her leaning over Gail, spilling stovies on the floor, and had to look away. 'Oh,' Kate was saying. 'I can feel the heat coming off her. I've got to report this to Gail right now. She'll be very interested in this.'

'So if you could bring down what you've got, we could see if anything helps her,' Martine said.

Kate straightened and turned. 'I'll ask,' she said. 'But I don't think so. I don't think Gail would want me interfering.'

When she had left, Ivy and Martine went through the carrier bag of food. 'Sandwiches, apples and water,' Martine said. 'I'm not hungry. She's taken my appetite away. What did she mean?'

'By "interfering"?' Ivy said. 'I don't know. And it doesn't matter whether or not you're hungry, you need to eat so you can run without fainting. I'm going to see if Laura will take some sips of water. You choose an apple. It's your go.'

Martine ate an apple, then a sandwich. So did Ivy. Laura swallowed some water, coughed some back out again, and fell into a deeper sleep than ever.

The next day, Ivy and Martine shared the third sandwich. They saved the third apple.

That night, as they were settling down to sleep, Ivy beside Laura, feeling the heat of her fever, they finally admitted the truth to themselves and each other.

'Interfering with Laura being so ill,' Ivy said.

'Interfering with Laura dying,' said Martine. 'That was our last chance. And I wasted it begging for help. We should have—'

'Too late now,' Ivy said. 'You weren't to know.'

'Ivy! Ivy!' Martine said. 'What are we going to do?'

'Shoosh, shoosh, shoosh,' Ivy said. 'Let me think. Leave it to me. I'll think of something, I promise you.' Martine burrowed into her like a nursing kitten. She didn't seem to mind the rank onion stink of her, just as bad as ever now after the new clothes had given them a fresh start . . . how many days ago was that now? Ivy stayed awake until Martine was snoring, then she let herself sleep too.

And was woken by the key in the lock. It was the dead of night, black as ink and not a single swish of distant traffic on the road.

'Marty,' she breathed, and felt Martine stiffen as she woke too.

But no one came in, not Gail finally making her move, not Kate out of her routine. Instead they heard a rattling sound, fast then slow as it got near them and the door locking again.

'What was that?' Martine whispered.

'I think,' said Ivy, wriggling out from between the two girls, 'at least I *hope* it was a bottle of pills. Help me find it, eh?'

Holding it five minutes later when they'd traced its trajectory over the lumpy floor to where it had stopped, Ivy shook it. 'Sounds quite full.'

'But of what though?' Martine said. 'It could be diuretics. It could be to finish her o— Make her worse.'

'It could be,' Ivy said. 'If we wait till daylight maybe we could read the label.'

'If it's even the right pills inside.'

'But think about it,' said Ivy. 'If it's a trick, why didn't she bring them in the daytime? Maybe she waited till night so Gail didn't find out.'

'But it's Gail's time,' said Martine. 'The middle of the night. So it's a trick.'

They were silent for a while, listening to Laura's ragged breathing.

'What choice have we got?' Ivy said at last. 'If we crush some up in her water and she . . . I can't say it . . . we'll never know anyway. If we don't, we'll never know. If it's good stuff to help her, she might get better and she might not. The only thing we do know is urine goes to kidney goes to sepsis goes to . . . What choice have we got?'

In reply, Martine took the bottle out of Ivy's hands, shook a couple of pills into the lid and ground her knuckle down into them, wincing.

'Don't hurt yourself,' Ivy said. 'We could use . . .' But there was nothing. An old stiletto heel? The corner of a drain cover? 'Here give me a turn too.'

Then they waited. Round and round, convinced she was better, convinced she was worse, thirsty, scared for themselves, starting to feel the hunger bite too. Laura was going to die, Ivy thought, and they would never know if they'd killed her. Then what? Would her body be left down here? Could Martine bear it? Could Ivy comfort her enough to take *that* horror away?

'I've got it,' she said, sitting up so abruptly Martine slid sideways. She'd been so relaxed curled up at Ivy's side. 'I hope Laura's completely out, because otherwise this is going to be awful, but I've thought of a way to get the Kate in here and restart the plan.'

She gave Martine one last squeeze then wriggled away and stood up, pacing as she laid it out.

'We're going to pretend Laura's dead.' Martine was looking at Laura and didn't see so much as a twitch. If she had she'd never have agreed to it. 'Now, I know this house is solid,' Ivy was saying, 'but if we wail and scream at the top of our lungs they'll hear something, don't you think? They'll hear the tune if not the words. Can you make mourning sounds? Can you keen? Can you kneel at her side, hold her hand, and cry.'

'Of . . . course?' Martine said. She stroked Laura's cheek. 'I really hope she's completely out or this is going to be a nightmare.'

It took them a long while to gird themselves for it, even so. They talked, on and on and on, and they rested, as much as they could bear to, with the plan surging in their veins, making their muscles shiver like horses' flanks when flies land. They even took some sips of water, even though for days they'd been giving most of it to Laura, thinking the extra sedation would help with her pain, watching her swallow weakly, spluttering.

She was peaceful as they rolled her on to one side, then the other, pulling the filthy blanket out from under her. They took it over to the drain and spread it for her to lie on. Then, trying not to let their hearts sink at how weak they felt, and being as gentle as they could be, they slid Laura over the floor and arranged her on it, folding it over her, covering her from top to toe.

'Oh God, oh God,' Martine muttered.

'I know, I know,' said Ivy, stroking her back. Then she slid the drain cover clear, gagging deep in her throat at the stink. Staggering a little, she hefted it up and put it under her arm then stepped away from the other two and gave it a couple of swings.

'OK?' Martine said.

'Fine,' said Ivy, grimly. 'There's a kind of ridge I can get my fingers under. I won't let it go. And it's good and heavy. One swipe, as long as I do it right.'

'And then we wait for Gail.'

'And then . . . we're out.'

Martine gave Ivy a long steady look, then put her head back and, starting low in her throat, she began to wail. 'Nooooo. Nooooooo. Laaaauuuurraaaaa! Come baaaaack. Don't diiieeee. Noooooooo!'

Ivy crept over to crouch behind the inner door and send her own bellowing roars of grief up to the stone ceiling.

It seemed like hours until the sound of the key, but it couldn't have been. Martine couldn't have howled for hours without losing her voice. Ivy stood up, knees bent and arms raised, the good honest weight of the drain cover giving her strength, rather than taxing her. When the inner door opened, she steadied her feet and got ready.

Kate was shouting before she was in the room. 'Is she dead? Is she dead?' She was swinging a torch around, the unfamiliar light skirling over the dank stone, making it sparkle.

Martine stopped crying, struck dumb, Ivy thought, by the tone of the words, simmering close to hysteria. Kate stopped the torch full in Martine's face, her mouth open and her eyes wet. 'Is she dea—' then she shrieked, like an animal. 'Get away from there. Get away from there!'

Martine, helpless not to, flicked a glance at Ivy. Kate spun round on her heel, sending the torchlight wheeling again, saw Ivy standing there, arms over her head, but then – unbelievably – turned back and went charging to where Martine was crouched at Laura's side, began beating her over her back and her head with the torch. 'How dare you? How dare you? That's mine! That's private!'

Ivy, the plan forgotten, went rushing up to help, dropping the drain cover, reaching Kate and grabbing for the sickening zigzag arc of light, trying to catch the torch as it came down again and again on Martine's back.

Then strong hands were pulling her back and sending her sprawling on the floor, her elbow cracking hard and an instant rose of pain blooming.

Gail loomed over her, jabbing at her with her blade, pressing Ivy back and back and back.

They were going to die: Martine bludgeoned to death and kicked into that stinking hole; Ivy stabbed; Laura, if she wasn't gone already, soon to sink into the blackness.

'I'm sorry,' Ivy whispered, as her bowel and her bladder and the last of her hope all let go.

TWENTY-TWO

One day left, but every minute felt like an hour to shovel past me, nothing to do except tell myself he wouldn't, then tell myself he would, then tell myself to go to the cops, then tell myself to save the jobs, then start at he wouldn't again.

Even the bit of drama at the fairytale cottage didn't last. She had taken two days off her clear-out, not a single trip to the basement with a bag. Then early one morning, both of them – cardi and curtain – went rushing down and charged inside. Half an hour later they came trailing out again. Maybe it was a gas leak.

There was even less to see out the front window, just Hephaw High Street sweltering in the sudden arrival of summer: wasps round the bins, hanging baskets flagging outside the Paraffin Arms, the drunk in the bus stop – he wasn't waiting for a bus; I knew that now – down to his T-shirt with his boots unlaced.

I had twenty-three hours to get through before I went back to Grangemouth to see if Big Garry would fold, if he would blink. I was kidding myself that anyone would notice a woman like me vanishing.

Laura Wade, I wrote on a pad of paper. Twenty-fifth of May.

Martine MacAllister, I wrote on a new line. The blurry woman who went to the Family Forest church in Lockerbie. Then I swung towards my laptop to see if I could pin a date down for this one. Third weekend in March was as close as I could get it from the scraps in the *Dumfries Standard*.

And what about Ivy Stone up in Fraserburgh? I went back to my history and found the story from the *Press and Journal*. Twenty-third of February.

When I clicked the windows down and went to the calendar in the corner of my tool bar my finger left a streak of sweat on the mouse pad. My heart was rat-a-tat-tatting against my ribs and I could feel my pulse in my neck. The third weekend in March was the twenty-third and twenty-fourth. I sat back and stared at the little box with its grid of dates.

Jesus. I had a finger pressed into the base of my throat between my collarbones, so when my blood gave a sudden sickening extra lurch I felt it inside and with that finger too.

One a month.

It wasn't that women disappeared every month. It was more like, every month, a woman disappeared.

I rubbed my hands on my jeans to dry them then put my fingers back on my keyboard. I had forgotten Big Garry for the first time in six long days.

Missing woman, Scotland, April 2018, I typed and sat back as the screen filled with irrelevant nothing.

With *Scotland* crossed out, I got stories of missing women from all around the world. With *woman* crossed out, it was stories about lost dogs in April, missed planes that wrecked Scottish hen nights, and a hundred other irrelevant reports of runaways who'd turned up, and girls taken overseas by divorced dads. Even Laura, Ivy and Martine popped up once I was a few pages deep in the search results, with *April* gone.

Maybe, I said to myself, just maybe, they tried in April and failed. But tried what? There was no pattern to the three disappearances. Laura left her flat all dolled up for a date. Martine was last seen at her funny church, and Ivy hadn't been seen anywhere after she'd turned out for an animal charity. Where would you even begin to find the missing corner to make that a square?

Family Forest, I typed. Because, not to be prejudiced or anything, but a weird little church no one had ever heard of struck me as the dodgy bit.

Except, as the hits filled my screen I could see it wasn't a hole-in-the-wall operation at all. It was international, with branches from Utah to Adelaide to Lima to Hong Kong, professional-looking pop-ups and pictures of happy groups of people hugging each other and all with photo stock copyright protection overlaid.

When I added *Lockerbie* to the search, it got a bit more low-key: just a single page dedicated to that branch on the main website and not much more information than that they met at the Cross Keys Hotel, once a month on a Tuesday. I sat back. They were meeting tonight. They were meeting in four hours. I had my keys and my bag and was halfway out the door before the spinner had stopped, before the last of the pictures was loaded.

At Hollywood Nails, Aisling and Renny were cleaning, going at the place with gloves and mop slippers on.

'Cos I think there's a smell,' Aisling said. 'Can you smell a smell, Tash? Renny says it's nothing.'

'I never said I couldn't smell it,' Renny said. 'I said it's nothing to do with us. It's the drain out the back that's gone a bit whiffy. You can't smell it in here. Can you, Tash?'

I took a deep sniff and then cleared my throat. The gel nails and acrylic dust, added to the girls' perfume and that cocktail of cleaning products on their wipes and mop feet made a powerful blend. 'Smells lovely to me,' I said.

'What did you want anyway?' Renny said. 'Don't suppose you came in because you've finished all your housework and you still feel like scrubbing.'

'I just came to say I'm going to be out for the rest of the day. But I'll be back tonight and I'll see you tomorrow.'

They had been skidding around, toeing into corners and wiping any surfaces that came within reach but when I said that, they stopped and turned to face me.

'Are you OK?' Renny said.

'Hope so.' I tried for a cheery tone. Their faces told me I'd missed by a mile. Same as with Adim, I felt myself longing to tell them, felt it like a physical pull towards them, a knowledge that if I could get it even half out of my head and into someone else's, I might be able to sleep, and breathe, and laugh again. 'So,' I said, 'see you tomorrow.'

My car was still parked up the side street and, as I turned the corner, I caught a sudden trace of the smell the girls had mentioned. More than a trace. It was strong enough to make me put my hand up to my face and cover my mouth and nose.

'Comfortable rooms, home-cooked food', the sandwich board on the pavement said, as I spotted the Cross Keys and pulled into the carpark three hours later. And suddenly it felt good to be so far from Big Garry. I could stay here tonight and go straight to Grangemouth tomorrow. So I checked in.

When I climbed the stairs, let myself through a couple of fire doors and found my bedroom, it wasn't as bad as I'd feared. The furniture was eighties flat-pack but the carpet was clean and the towels were fluffy. There was even a packet of shortbread near the kettle and a flask of milk instead of little tubs of creamer. I splashed my face and went back down to the bar to order myself a plate of the fish and chips I'd seen someone else eating, waiting till half past seven came and the start of the service.

'Are you here for Family Forest?' I asked the woman who came up beside me. It was a guess but she looked more churchy than pubby. She wore a sweatshirt with a complicated decal on the front – something medieval or fantastical, maybe both – and long unkempt hair brushed down over her shoulders so it looked as if it was sticking to the cheap polyester. It made my neck itch just looking at it. 'I've come from up by Falkirk.'

'We're honoured,' the woman said. 'How are you getting on with it?'

'With what?' I said.

'Your family tree,' she said. 'I'm back to before the parish records on mine.'

'Ahhhh!' I said. 'Family history.'

'Genealogy,' the woman said. 'Different thing altogether.'

'I thought you were a religious organization,' I said.

'We must come across that way to the uninitiated,' the woman said. 'But once you've started, you'll understand. I can help you out tonight. If your parents are living, or even your grandparents, young as you are, the best first step is to pick their brains. Get names on all the photos as soon as you can and see what they can remember about what their elderly relatives told them, away back in their early days.'

'No,' I said, breaking in. I couldn't stand thinking about chats with my family. I'd probably never have another normal conversation with either of my parents again and I could only be grateful that three of my grandparents were dead and would never know what their children had done. I couldn't bear to think about my granny when she found out. 'I mean,' I went on, 'I really thought Family Forest was a church. I'm not interested – no offence – in doing my family tree.'

'You say that now—'

'No really. I'm interested in Martine MacAllister. And what happened to her. Where she went. Why. This seemed like the only place where people might know.'

The woman was changing colour, a deep blush flooding her cheeks and steaming crescents into the bottom of her glasses. 'It wasn't us,' she said. 'We're a friendly group. We take all-comers, just the same. It was her that was stand-offish. Snooty, you would say if you weren't scared of getting called on it. A right snob, actually. Looking down her nose at the rest of us. And then she just stopped coming. We weren't to know she was "missing". All we knew was that she didn't come any more. And if we weren't sorry, well shoot us.'

A waiter appeared from the back just then with my plate of fish and chips and, in the little bit of bustle it took to set me up with cutlery and vinegar, the woman in the decal sweatshirt took her chance to slip away.

The barmaid was still standing there, though.

'Was she?' I said. '*Was* Martine snooty and snobby and stand-offish? Did you ever meet her?'

'You didn't hear it from me,' the barmaid said, 'but I think she was snobby . . . considering.'

'Jesus.'

'Yeah. And then so when she finally made a new friend, at the last meeting, they decided the friend was the problem. Cleared their conscience.'

'And this friend,' I said. 'Was he a stranger? Did no one else know him?'

'Her. Martine bought her a glass of wine. I was on that night too, as it goes. "Did anyone know her?" Search me.'

'*Her* though,' I said. 'So probably she was nothing to do with it.'

Then the barmaid was called away to the other end to serve a customer there and left me with my thoughts. Martine had come to her genealogy club and made a friend. And Ivy Stone, back in February, had gone trotting along to the NLL to meet a friend too. Still jabbing up chips with one hand, I dug out my phone and started searching the *Press and Journal* mobile app for that story with the quote from the committee member. God bless journalists. There she was: Carole McGann, 62, of Fraserburgh. The age didn't matter – I had never understood why papers did that – but Carole McGann of Fraserburgh wouldn't be too hard to track down surely, even if she wouldn't be in the phone book like the good old days.

She was on Twitter, though, and she followed back within minutes. I sent her a message, playing it straight, telling Carole I was looking for Ivy Stone and wanted to follow up on what I'd read in the paper. Could we perhaps WhatsApp? I typed, but Carole had pinged back her mobile number before I could even start setting up a one-off ID. I tapped the number and tucked the phone under my chin as it started ringing, standing and signalling that I was finished with my plate and could they put the bill on my room. I let myself through the fire door into the back corridor and the stairway.

'Carole?' I said, when someone answered.

'Speaking.' The voice was so eager it sounded breathless.

'My name's Tash Dodd.' Here, definitely, was another stranger who would have plenty to say if I suddenly went missing. 'I'm looking for Ivy Stone, as I said, and I wanted to see if you had said anything to the *P&J* reporter that didn't make it into the article. You never know what's going to be helpf—'

'Anything that didn't make it?' Carole's voice was tight with indignation. 'Just a bit. We talked for forty minutes and he put two sentences in. What is it you want to know?'

'All of it,' I said. I took the phone away from my head to look at the time, then tucked it back into my chin again to open up my room. The Cross Keys wasn't swanky enough to have stationery but there was a Gideon Bible with a flyleaf doing nothing. I put Carole on speaker and propped myself up on the bed, stuffing thin pillows between me and the head-board, making it reasonably comfy.

Carole regaled me with a lot of details about animal cruelty and fundraising legalities that I no way needed to know. None of it could be relevant to the night in February when Ivy Stone attended the meeting. Surely. 'She didn't sign up as a member, or even to receive our newsletter. We work hard on that news-letter. We still do a physical one if people prefer. Most branches are online only.'

'Good for you,' I said. There had been a pause begging for me to fill it.

Carole sniffed. Maybe I had guessed wrong; maybe I was supposed to have asked to be put on the list. 'Well, anyway,' she went on, at last. 'God knows why she was there.'

'To meet a friend, wasn't it?'

'Yes, but if you'd let me explain. What I mean is God knows why they decided to meet at ours. Miss Ivy Stone the Cat Killer went rushing out before the end.'

'*Cat* killer?'

'In favour of it, yes. Not a very nice woman, even if you're not supposed to speak ill of the— So anyway, she rushed out and the friend went after her.'

'I know you can't give me Ivy's friend's details. From your sign-up. But could you get in touch and tell her I'd like to speak to her?'

'I'm afraid not,' Carole said. 'She was another walk-in. No genuine interest in our work. Like I said, I don't know why they met there at all.'

I looked at the time. The Family Forest meeting would just be starting.

'Well, thank you, Carole,' I said, breaking into the flow. 'That's all very helpful.'

'What is?'

'I might be able to find out where they went when they left together,' I said, plucking it out of the air for something to say.

'They went to the Boat. A few of us repaired there for a late drink and we saw them, thick as thieves. They sat together, talking, and left the pub together. They hugged in the street.'

'Hugged?' I said. 'You mean, like a romantic hug?' That was a bit more hopeful, if you were looking for the point where a quiet little life started to unravel. A misunderstanding about the nature of a drink? Maybe.

'No, not at all,' Carole said. 'More like one of them was upset. Couldn't say which one. But it was a sort of a "there-there" hug. Bitter-cold night it was.'

'Thank you,' I said again. 'Thanks for filling in all that missing detail. I'm going to have to go now. I'm following up another lead right now actually. But you've been very helpful, even if you don't think so. Thank you very much.'

'You're as bad as the reporter,' Carole said. 'You can't do that. You ask a thousand questions and don't answer a single one.'

'Another time,' I said. 'Sorry, but I really have to go.'

I hung up before Carole could get in any more objections, then stood, smoothed over my bed – if there was anything more depressing than a cheap hotel room, it was a cheap hotel room with a messy bed – and went to put a bit of lippy on or at least brush away the salt, in time for the meeting.

It hadn't really got going, as near as I could tell. Only half the little tables in the function room were occupied and groups of people were chatting. There was a podium set up as if for a speaker but no one was anywhere near it. I put my shoulders back and made a beeline.

'Hiya,' I said, lifting the mike. It squealed and I moved it back. 'Sorry. And sorry to interrupt.'

The conversations died out as everyone turned to listen.

'My name's Tash Dodd,' I said. A few of them were frowning. 'I'm here tonight because I'm looking for Martine MacAllister.' Now some of the people were looking down at their laps or exchanging glances. 'I don't want to disrupt your meeting. I'm just going to sit in the bar and if anyone thinks they've got anything to tell me – no matter how small or even if you don't know how it might be relevant but it's just bugging you, you know? – I'll be there all night and you could just stop by. I'll buy you a drink and I'll listen. Thank you.'

A man in a blazer with a badge on the lapel was coming my way at a fair clip so I dropped the mike back on to the podium. It boomed as it fell and half the people gathered in the room put their hands to their ears and winced. I scooted out through the open arch back to the bar and didn't stop until I was on my stool with the friendly barmaid to look out for me. A minute later I saw someone bearing down, and turned.

'What can I get you?' I said. He was in his thirties, dressed in a Scotland top and a baseball cap, beefy turning flabby.

'Bottle of Becks, hen,' he said. 'And a packet of prawn.'

Pushing it, in my opinion, but I nodded at the barmaid anyway and she bent to the beer fridge.

'So?' I said, when the guy had taken a long suck from the neck of the bottle and stuffed a greedy grab of crisps into his mouth, wiping the flavour dust off on his jeans afterwards.

'So?' he said. His resting face was close to a leer. Amused, anyway.

'Martine MacAllister. What have you got to tell me?'

'Show you,' he said. 'It was me that took the photo of her on the last night. The one the papers used.' He was already flicking pictures across the screen of his phone with a stubby finger, still crusted with prawn flavour.

'And why were you taking pictures of Martine?' I said. 'Was she a close friend? Or did you take them of everyone?'

'Close friend?' he said, hissing a laugh down the sides of his teeth. 'You'll get me shot. No, she wasn't. I was taking a picture of my beautiful wife and her new hairdo. Martine MacAllister just got herself in the background.'

That was right. I had forgotten. I'd been doused in pity for the woman when I'd seen the photo in the newspaper article, side on, pixelated, accidental.

He had found it and he passed his phone over. It was the original of the shot I'd seen; a beaming woman in the fore-ground, looking coquettishly over one shoulder to show off her undercut. Out on the top left of the frame, there was Martine, leaning forward so eagerly towards the person she was speaking to.

'So this is Martine talking to her new friend?' I said. 'Is *she* here tonight?'

'She's not,' the man said. 'She only came that once. Never been before. Never been since. She came to meet Marty, we reckoned. No clue why they did it here though. Wouldn't catch me, if I had the option.'

I stared at him, Carole's words echoing behind his, then I bent to the picture again, zoomed and repositioned, zoomed again, until I was looking at the right-hand side of the wife's head. Martine's companion was tantalizingly out of view. I could see her feet, tucked back behind the spar of her chair, neat little feet in high court shoes, and I could see the woman's left hand resting on top of Martine's on the table-top, but the rest of her was hidden.

'Can I scroll?' I said. 'Have you got more?'

He shook his head.

'Really?' I said. 'I always take twenty to get one half-decent one. Can I check?'

'I keep my phone tidy,' he said. 'Learned that the hard way.'

'Can I send this one to myself?' I said.

'More than my life's worth,' he said. 'What do you think I'm doing here, digging up grannies' names? She caught me, didn't she? The wife. Borrowed my phone and caught me out. So no I wasn't close to Martine and no you can't put your number in my phone. I'm only here talking to you because she's at home on her bad week tonight and I'm off the leash.'

I studied the picture in the few moments I had left. The woman was small, I was pretty sure, the feet looked small and the hand was tiny on Martine's. Not young, I didn't think, from the ropey look of the back of her hand and from the fact of the court shoes and tights. Martine's gaze was directed downwards too, looking into a small woman's eyes, unless she was staring at something the woman was showing her.

'That's them starting,' the man said, as the mike in the function room squealed again. He shook my hand then left, taking his bottle of beer and his half-eaten bag of crisps with him.

'Carole?' I said, when I'd rung and waited and the call had been answered. 'I should have said this before: can you describe the woman who came to meet Martine?'

'That's what you get for being so rude. Practically hanging up on me like that.'

'Sorry,' I said. 'Can you?' I was betting she'd not be able to resist it.

'Hard to say,' came grudgingly at last. I kept quiet. 'Not young and not old, one of those types. Spry enough but dressed very formal. Looked like she might work in a bank maybe.'

'A uniform?' I couldn't help the leap of hope in my voice.

'No. Just heels and tights and a skirt. V-neck cardi, blouse.'

'And what about her hair? Eyes?'

'Her *eyes*?' Carole said. 'I never got close enough to see her eyes. Her hair was fair. Fine. Thin, actually.'

'Was she tall, short? Thin, fat?'

'Not a picking on her. Poor-looking wee thing.' I would have put money on Carole being a woman of fairly comfortable build.

I turned to the back flyleaf of the Bible.

Small thin woman, fair hair, well-dressed.

Family history/cats/first date(?)

It wasn't much to go on to find out what happened in April. Different towns, different methods, totally different victims.

There was always the police, I thought. I wouldn't have to tell them what I was looking for when I had found the three women's stories and put them together. Everybody spent their nights trawling online for nothing these days. It had completely taken over from aimless driving. I could go right now to the Lockerbie police station and ask to speak to a copper.

At that very moment I lifted my head and looked into the mirror on the back of the bar. I had to bite my lip to stop myself from laughing. He was off-duty and out of uniform, but from the precision parting in his hair, through his Kangol jersey and his ironed cords, all the way to his polished slip-ons, that was a polis, sitting there, ordering a drink and giving me a sideways look.

No wedding ring, I saw. So not necessarily a scumbag, despite the looking. I turned from the mirror and smiled at him. 'Evening, officer.'

'Jesus Christ,' he said. 'Just as well I'm not undercover.'

'Don't beat yourself up,' I told him. 'Lucky guess. Listen, can I pick your brain about something if I buy you a drink and a bag of crisps?'

'I'm off the carbs,' he said, patting the front of the Kangol jersey. 'And when you say "pick my brain" . . . you know I can't get you out of speeder.'

'It's nothing like that,' I said. 'It's something I've found out, and I'm going to burst if I keep it quiet any longer.'

'Can't have you bursting on this nice carpet,' he said. 'I'll buy the drinks, though. Keep it on the right footing. OK?'

'OK,' I said, thinking here goes then; here we go.

TWENTY-THREE

I had moved so much in the last year that waking up in a strange place didn't faze me any more. I lay looking at the slice of light spilling across the ceiling from the gap in the curtains and let my mind range lazily back over my room at home, my room in Aberdeen, studio in Dumfries, bedsit in Ayrshire, and the flat in Hephaw, not awake enough to wonder where I was this morning. It was when I stretched my legs out and felt the warmth of another body beside me that I came to fully, with a snap that kickstarted my hangover.

I turned my head carefully, feeling my neck twang, and saw the profile silhouetted on the pillow beside me. Ty. A policeman. Never married. Born in Carlisle, moved here for a cheaper house and quicker promotion. I turned back and faced the ceiling, raising my arms carefully out of the covers and pressing the heels of my hands into my eye sockets. Ty. He'd been surprised, shocked nearly, when I'd put a bottle of wine on my room bill and asked him if he wanted to join me. And the barmaid had given me a look that made me hope she wasn't on breakfasts today. Ty. He had condoms in his wallet and didn't consider for a second not using one, and he'd taken it away to the bathroom afterwards, wrapped it and binned it. Good manners and kind to marine life. Ty.

Whose second name I didn't have a clue about. Which meant I'd just broken one of my own lifelong rules. Never mind that I might not have long to regret it. (He wouldn't, would he?) I took my hands away from my eyes and opened them. The dark sparkles blinded me but I knew without looking that he was awake now.

'Hiya,' he said, his voice thick with sleep and the after-effects of that shitty wine.

'Hi,' I said. My voice was no better, gravelled and gluey.

'How you feeling?'

I considered the question. Physically, I had a headache and

a birdcage mouth, but no nausea. And I was in a pub with a full fried breakfast waiting downstairs if I could stand the smell of a bar in the morning. On the self-respect front, I hadn't led Ty on. I hadn't tricked him or used him. I'd had an open conversation with him and issued an unrelated invitation. One that he'd accepted. And the bit between the end of the bottle of wine and the start of the night's sleeping had been pretty good for a first try. I wasn't sorry about it.

So how *was* I feeling?

'I'm going to have to shoot off,' Ty said. 'But you've got me interested, I'll tell you that.'

I turned my head sharply to look at him, making my brain slosh against my skull. Last night, even after a skinful, he hadn't said a smarmy word to me.

'Not that!' he said. 'I mean, yes that, but that's not what I meant. I *meant* you've got me interested about this missing woman in April. The not-missing one. I'll see what I can dig up when I get to work and then . . . Can I phone you later?'

So how did I feel? I put a smile on my face and pushed myself up on to my elbows. If the ends didn't justify the means, what did? Someone said that and this morning I agreed. For one thing, if this was my last day, I deserved last night.

The bed dipped as Ty swung his legs out and stood. I watched him on his way to the bathroom. Just one shoulder tattoo. Long-faded tan lines. Once he was behind the door he turned and looked round it. 'Just so you know,' he said, 'I'm going to put my keks on and go downstairs, but I'm coming back. Can I bring you a decent coffee if they've started breakfasts?'

'Why are you—?'

'Because that bloody wine has gone for my guts like an old kebab and I don't know you well enough to stink up your bathroom,' he said.

I laughed and put my head under the covers to hide my red face till he'd gone.

I knew I should use the time to pee, brush my teeth, or even dress, but instead I propped myself up as best I could on all four thin pillows and tucked the covers under my arms, going over the conversation from the night before. No one else from

Family Forest had come near me with any titbits about Martine, so there'd been plenty time to convince him.

'Three women have disappeared round about the same day of the month in the last four months,' I'd told him. 'Two of them after meeting a short, thin woman no one knew, who made a beeline. It happened here in March and it happened at an NLL meeting in Fraserburgh in February. The third one disappeared after going on a first date in Ayr in May.'

'With this skinny woman?' Ty had said. He'd only reluctantly agreed to listen at all, but when I started talking he couldn't help himself. He was like a beaver hearing running water.

'Well no,' I had said. 'Actually, I'm only guessing it was a first date, because she left home all dolled up and she didn't have a boyfriend. It was the right time of the month though. All three of them. They disappeared with their phones and laptops, and two of them with their cars, but they hadn't cleared their fridges or put those holiday messages on their emails.'

'At work?' As he listened, he kept stretching his fingers and then curling them, as if his hands were itching for a pencil and notebook.

'They all work for themselves. And they didn't prepare their businesses for walking away.'

'What businesses?'

'Martine's a grant-writer,' I said, hoping he wouldn't ask for details because I had only a very hazy sense of what that meant, 'and Laura's . . . it's hard to say what it is. One of those businesses, you know.'

'A tart, you mean?'

'No! Jesus. Content design and retail, I mean. Something like that'

'I was kidding.' He smiled at me, waiting for me to laugh but I didn't play. These three missing women were real to me now, no laughing matter.

And give him his due he sobered quickly. 'So they're all quite isolated,' he said. 'Living alone, working at home.'

'But your lot never put them together,' I said. 'As far as I can tell anyway. They were all pegged as low priority, not vulnerable or anything. I suppose resources are stretched for you same as anyone.'

'Missper's stretched certainly,' he said. 'And we're not even keeping up with traffickers. Not even scratching the surface. Independent women who take their laptops with them are right at the back of the queue. Are you OK?'

I hadn't realized that my face had fallen. I hid it in my drink, taking a big glug.

'Fine,' I said, when I surfaced again. 'It's just a horrible thought, isn't it? So, I was saying, the police never connected them. One of them, Ivy, hasn't got a car, doesn't drive. That's fair enough. But Martine's car was tracked between Edinburgh and as far as sort of Livingston way on the M8. And Laura's car was tracked up the M77 to Glasgow and then – same thing – halfway along the M8 in the other direction. So, you see? It's like they converged on the same spot.' But he had screwed his face up and was shaking his head. 'What?' I said.

'When you say "tracked", you mean plate recognition? Yeah, well that's the thing, see. ANPR only covers the M77 and the M8.'

'Seriously?'

'And a wee bit of the A726.'

'Where's that?'

He laughed. 'It joins the M77 to the M8.'

'Seriously?' I said again. 'That's pathetic.'

'So it's not really significant that they were clocked there. They could have been going anywhere but there's no way of knowing after they peeled off the motorway.'

'Yeah,' I said. 'Jeez, this country.' He frowned at me. 'Half of it's empty and everyone's jammed in beside the same couple of roads. It's like the whole population's living in a layby.'

'Keeps the nice bits nice,' he said. 'Where is it you live?'

I laughed. 'Grangemouth. You've got a point. But listen, that's all by the by. Even if Ivy went somewhere in February and Martine went somewhere else in March and Laura went somewhere else again in May, the thing I actually wanted to pick your brain about? Is April.'

I waited to see if he would twig, without knowing exactly why it mattered. I wasn't even sure if I hoped he'd find the whole thing ludicrous and so give me roundabout permission to stop thinking about it, or if I hoped he'd pounce on it, proving he had a working brain, not dulled by checklists of risk.

'Let me get this right,' he said. 'You think three women have been lured away from home by the same individual – this wee skinny woman – and you think it's happened once a month since February, all over Scotland, but in April the target . . . ?'

'Didn't bite,' I said.

'Or got away,' he added.

I shook my head. 'No, definitely didn't bite. If she'd got away she'd have reported it, wouldn't she. I reckon she just backed out before it came to the bit.'

'You'd be surprised,' he said. 'You'd never believe how much shame counts for. If she thinks she made a fool of herself, swallowing some crap someone's peddled, she could easily not have come in and told us. I've seen it a thousand times for things worse than this.'

'Worse than what?' I said. I hadn't meant it to come out so aggressive but how could he rank how bad things were when we didn't even know what had happened? 'The three of them might be dead in a ditch.' I stopped as my brain caught up with my words. 'Oh God. The fourth one might be dead in a ditch too, only no one's missed her yet. Like that girl in London. That was years.'

'What's got you so interested?' Ty said then. Taking back control, I told myself. Showing me who was boss when missing women and possible death were the topic.

'I saw one of them on her last day,' I said, lying smoothly. 'And I wondered how common it was. I stumbled on the dates by accident.'

He said nothing for a while, drank his drink. 'You seem more bothered than that would make you,' he said at last. 'Are you worried for yourself? Has something happened to *you*?'

I had drained my glass, so I couldn't use it as a mask again, and I knew my face was naked as I looked back at him. 'Maybe I am worried,' I said. 'I live alone. I work for myself.'

He was shaking his head. 'Forewarned,' he said. 'You'll be

OK. I can send you the best stuff we've got about keeping safe though. What's your email?'

'Ha,' I said. 'You're smooth. I'll give you that. You're a smooth one.'

But I had handed over my email address and my phone number, thinking it wouldn't hurt to have a cop's alarm going off if I vanished. And with him assuming I was too clever to get caught, I was flattered enough to invite him up to my room. Now here I was eight hours later.

As I heard the key in the lock, I pinched my cheeks and bit my lips, hating myself for doing it but doing it anyway. His eyebrows rose as he edged round the door with the coffees only just balanced.

'Still there, eh?' he said. 'I've got to get cracking.'

'Oh my God!' I said. 'Talk about an ego. I'm not revving up again, sunshine. I'm just a lazy cow in the morning.'

'Right, right, right,' he said, handing me a cup and sitting on the edge of the bed with his own.

'And anyway, what kind of sweet nothing is "I'm away downstairs for a shit"?'

He was laughing now and maybe he was even blushing.

'Listen,' I said. 'I'm not going to hold my breath. I know you're busy and you can't just go digging where there's no reason to, instead of doing whatever you're supposed to be doing. But what is it you're going to look for? In April.'

'I won't be digging at all,' he said. 'I'll be passing it up. Same as if you phoned a tip line, only they'll take a bit more notice seeing it's me.'

'Right, but what will it be *they* go looking for? Where would you even start?'

'The date's good,' he said. 'Best guess is they'll trawl ID theft through false pretences. It's not really ID theft but all the other frauds get you miles deep in financial stuff.'

'What about kidnapping?' I said. 'Is that a real thing?'

'Mostly child abduction by non-resident parent,' he said. 'Anyway, it's not up to me – I'm not a detective; I'm a plod.' The way he swigged his coffee had a rounding-off air about it. I could tell he was itching to leave. I'd never been clingy and it bothered me that he wouldn't know that about me, that he might want to scrape me off like burnt porridge on account of how I was spinning this out. But I could hardly tell him I wanted clues, not cuddles.

'You couldn't fling me my shirt before you go, could you?' I said, nodding at the pile of clothes heaped over the back of the desk chair on the other side of the room.

'That's not fair,' he said. 'I got up and gave you a floor show.' But he was standing and rootling through the pile. He faked a scare when he picked my bra up then handed my shirt over and turned his back.

'Not the same thing,' I said, wriggling into it. 'I was half asleep and I was naked too, under the covers. This is completely different.'

'Aye, aye,' he said. 'Listen, I'll phone you later. I'll not wait till there's news. I'll phone you. OK?'

'I might pick up if I'm not busy,' I said, scooting past him and then locking the bathroom door behind me. 'See you!'

'Cheeky cow,' he called, then I heard the room door open and shut.

I stood under the water, slightly hunched to let it stream over my head, and thought about April. There was something, just out of reach, like trapped wind. Nine Lives League in February, Family history research meeting in March, hook-up in May. What was I missing? Or was I putting two and two together and getting five? Maybe Laura Wade was dressed up to go to a genealogy talk, or a cat-lovers' do. Maybe I should scour the internet for all the NLL and Family Forest chapters and talk to all the secretaries, the way I'd talked to Carole.

I angled the showerhead so it was hitting me in the middle of my back and wiped my wet hair off my face. And there it was again, half an idea just out of reach, like seeing someone mid-morning you'd dreamed about the night before.

I cracked open the miniature bottle of shampoo and squeezed the whole lot out into my palm. By the time I'd rubbed my hangover away and managed to get rid of the excess of lather – I'd forgotten how soft the water would be down here – I thought I had it. If Laura Wade had set off on a date but never made it then somewhere there was a pissed-off man with a red carnation who didn't want to admit it.

I picked up the little bottle of conditioner and squeezed it out on to my hand then ran the long wet tail of my hair through my fingers, over and over. How could you find a man who so clearly didn't want to come forward, when you had no idea where he was? The ghost of half an idea floated by again. Was it *about* him not coming forward? Laura's picture had been on the news and no one had admitted to being the other half of the arrangement, slapping on aftershave and ironing his best shirt to go with her floaty dress and high heels.

Of course, he might be married. Keeping his head down and hating himself, but not hating himself as much as he loved his kids, even if he didn't care much about his wife these days.

If he existed.

He had to.

Why else would a woman be leaving her house dressed like that on a Saturday teatime, too late for a wedding and too early for the evening do.

I had coiled my hair up in a slimy pile on top of my head, but I didn't notice as it slipped down again and the hot water started stripping all the conditioner out of the ends.

If it was too early for the evening do at a wedding, it was too early – I saw it now – for a date. So he wasn't local. And that went with the high heels in her hands and the driving shoes on her feet. She wasn't just nipping round to the nearest bistro. She was in for quite a drive. To meet this guy.

So how did she know him?

When it broke over me, I shivered in spite of the hot water. Then, making no attempt to rinse the roots of my hair, I got out, wrapped myself in a towel and trotted back into the bedroom, ignoring the fluff sticking to my wet feet and not caring how see-through the net curtains might be. I found my recent contacts and hit the button to call Ty.

'Talk about playing hard to get,' he said, sounding delighted.

'Yeah, yeah,' I said. 'Never mind. Listen. It was an online dating site. I bet you a much nicer bottle of wine it was a dating agency that hooked Laura Wade in May, so it might have been the same scam in April. It might still be operating now. Maybe.'

'Talk me through it,' he said. I could hear his indicator and then the quieter sound as he pulled off the road and parked to give me his whole attention.

'I'm convinced she was off on a date when I saw her,' I said. 'And call it woman's intuition, but I think it was a *first* date. And she was setting off on a long drive – she had driving flats on, stilettoes to change into – and there was just something about her . . . it's hard to explain.'

'Try anyway,' he said, sounding distracted.

'She was definitely looking forward to it but not like she knew it was going to work, not like a date with a man she knew she was into. But not a break-up date either.'

Ty said nothing.

'I'm probably making something out of nothing,' I said.

'I don't think so,' he said. 'I'm looking at the security cam still now – I've just googled it – and I think you're right. She's half-excited and half-wary.'

'So she's going on a date with someone she doesn't know,' I said. 'And unless it's a blind set-up from a mutual friend that means a dating site.'

'People do go on blind dates,' he said. 'They still hook up at the bar in a pub, as it goes.'

'Ha-ha,' I said. 'Yeah, they do. But why wouldn't the pal who set them up have come forward?'

'We can't interview every man in Scotland who's got a profile up on an online dating service, Tash. We'd need to call in the army.'

It sounded like the voice of experience. I wondered how hard he'd been trying to meet someone before he gave it all up for a quiet night at the Cross Keys on a Tuesday.

'Here's what I think,' I said. 'He doesn't exist. No matter what he said about himself online to get Laura in that frock, I think the truth is he's a skinny wee woman that dresses like a secretary and lands three out four fish she casts for.'

'Or four out of four and one of them hasn't made a ripple,' Ty said. 'This is good stuff, Tash, and I'm going to pass it on and keep your name out of it. I'm going to look like a genius! But I need to tell you, no one's obliged to admit they had Laura Wade on their books, and if we go in saying a kidnapper passed herself off as a hot guy they're going to try even harder to hide that they were involved.'

'Huh,' I said. 'That's disappointing. I mean, I'm glad it's not North Korea and all that. But.'

'I will pass it on though,' Ty said. 'Cybercrimes have got a lot of pull one way and another. And God bless Austerity Britain, eh?' I had no idea what that meant. 'You can still get work as a CI. So I wouldn't be surprised if there's some string they can tug somewhere.'

'If it's even a real site,' I said. 'I mean, it might be and I hope they do the decent thing if it is. But it might be a *total* scam, you know?'

'If she piggy-backed on the NLL and the Family Forest,' he said, 'chances are she piggy-backed on a real lonely hearts too.'

'Yeah maybe,' I said. 'What's a CI?'

'Confidential informant. Like you.'

'Me? I'm a concerned citizen.'

'Nah, you're a CI. I paid your room bill.'

'That makes me something right enough,' I said. 'Why did you do that?'

'Pass,' he said. 'So.'

I roused myself. The guy was parked at the side of the road getting late for his shift and I was standing dripping on the carpet.

'So,' I agreed. 'Right then, let's crack on. Sorry. You're not late, are you?'

'I *meant*,' he said, 'so is there any chance you're going to tell me why you're digging into this?'

I did hesitate. But in the end I went with 'No. Sorry.'

And he said, 'I hope you won't be.'

TWENTY-FOUR

I meant to head straight for Grangemouth. But the A89 turn-off caught me by surprise and I told myself I could go the back roads just as easy as the motorway. Maybe Ty letting me know that no one was watching the back roads made them more appealing. Or maybe it was the sun hitting the red slope of the shale bing full-on, making me think of those scientists, all the flowers and insects somehow managing to thrive in the slag. I flicked my indicator and headed for what, somehow, after a week in an Airbnb, felt like home.

I was right to come, because my little corner of downtown Hephaw was a shot in the arm this morning: someone had watered the hanging baskets at the Paraffin Arms, and it was too early for the bus-stop drunk. Hollywood Nails even had customers in both pedicure chairs.

I slapped yesterday's paper and today's, a pint of milk and a packet of bacon on the counter at Adim's.

'Has anyone been looking for me?' I said. 'Anyone asking?'

'Not so far,' Adim said. 'If they do I'll say you've been in and done your walk of shame and now you're going up to cure your hangover.'

'What are you on about?' I said, unconvincingly even to my own ears.

'You were in here for juice and crisps for your wee road trip yesterday before you set off,' he said. 'Or did you forget?'

'I'm wearing jeans and a black shirt,' I said. 'Walk of shame!'

'Same earrings and you've never dried your hair with your own drier, state of it,' Adim said. 'Don't look at me like that. You were the one telling me to pay attention.'

'Are you gay, Adim?' I said, for revenge on him.

'Am I shite!' he said. 'I've got four girls. There's nothing I don't know about straighteners. It's a conveyer belt on school mornings, and I'm a ninja with them.'

'Four girls?' I said, feeling my face fall.

'So whatever it is you're doing,' he answered, 'more power to your elbow.'

I've always been a sloppy drunk and even worse the next morning. That and the deadline roaring up towards me at last, after months of preparation, forced two fat tears out of my eyes. 'Sorry,' I said, swiping at them. 'I'll be taking over the title of local weirdo from them at the wee house.'

'Who?' he said. 'Oh, the fairytale cottage wifies. Yeah, right enough, Goldilocks would pass on *their* porridge.'

We both laughed and then both fell silent.

'I'm going away again,' I said. 'I need to do something. I think. If I'm not in for my paper tomorrow . . . don't keep it.'

'Are you sure?' He rubbed his arms under his shirt sleeves as if my voice had made his flesh creep.

I couldn't tell which bit of it he was even talking about, so I answered: 'I don't know.'

At Hollywood's front door, I sniffed the air, wondering if I was imagining something rotten nearby. Maybe there *was* a bad drain. Or maybe that faulty gas line I'd suspected was right enough.

Inside the salon, I met a wall of air freshener so aggressive I coughed. Aisling and Renny were still busy with what looked like a mother and daughter, so I sat and flipped through a *Hello* in the reception seats until they were free. I didn't know what I was doing in there. I couldn't bear to think I was saying goodbye.

'And don't come back!' Aisling said, turning the sign to closed and locking the door after the women had waddled off in their complimentary flip-flops.

'Toenail fungus?' I guessed. The mother hadn't seemed the sort for a pedicure, with her bristly mottled legs, the imprint of her sock elastic still showing even after a massage.

'Yukko. No, just crap tips and they sat sniff, sniff, sniffing the whole time,' said Aisling. 'I felt like asking them to try it my end. Who comes for a pedi with cheesy feet?'

'They're going to her hen-do at a spa,' Renny said. 'The mum told me. Told me right out. They didn't have the brass neck to take those trotters away to a posh hotel so we got the prize of chiselling off the top layer.'

'Bloody cheek,' I said. 'That plus the sniffing.'

'Can *you* still smell it?' Renny said. 'We've got an asthma hazard of Glade going on in here and I'm sure *I* can still smell it.'

I shrugged. The truth was I didn't know. Once you've convinced yourself there's a smell you can't stop. 'Have you worked out what it is yet?'

'We've worked out *who* it is,' Renny said. 'Or at least where it's coming from. It's that funny wee house with the freak sisters.'

'That's not fair,' Aisling said. 'The wee skinny one's normal. Nearly.'

I felt a buzz under my skin like a low-level electric shock. I wouldn't have been able to say what it was. 'Sisters, are they?' I said. Then added: 'I can see their back garden from my flat.'

'Well, they need their drains seen to,' Aisling said. 'It smells like something died in their basement.'

'I do think they might be hoarders,' I said. 'She – the wee one – is forever up and down with stuff.'

'What kind of stuff?' Renny said. 'We could get the council on to her.'

I gave it a thought, going back over what I had seen. 'Hard to say. It's all in bags. Small stuff. Not furniture and that.'

'Probably food for the fighting dogs. Seriously, Tash. There is something not right in there.'

'Ignore her,' Aisling said. 'She's got a basement phobia. I lived in London for six months so they're dead normal to me, but it is weird to have one round here, right enough. And I'm telling you, it's the drain, not the basement. Their garden shares a wall with our back bit and there's a grating too big to cover with a bin. That's where the guff's coming from.'

'We're pouring bleach down it night and morning like it's punch at a party,' Aisling said, 'but it's not helping.'

'I'm with you about basements, Renny,' I said. 'I was at a party one time with this guy and I was sure he'd gone off and left me. So I schmopped off too and broke up with him in a text. Six months later I found out he was downstairs playing snooker. I dumped him for nothing. Nice bloke too. Nice bum.'

'Don't worry,' Aisling said. 'You're in the hungry gap. They're all married and none of them are divorced again yet. But just wait: soon they'll be dumping their wives and you'll be laughing. Still got your figure and all that.'

'How old do you think I am?' I said. 'Cheeky mare.'

'Thirty,' Aisling said. 'You told us already. Memory problems?'

They both cackled and I didn't have the heart to bring them down again, dropping hints, so I just reminded them that I'd be in after lunch, prayed it was true, and left.

How could a house look so frowsy just for being empty overnight? It wasn't as if I cleaned every day. I filled the kettle and waited, gazing out the back window, watching the cardigan sister wipe her clothes rope with a cloth before starting to hang a load of washing.

Quick cup of tea, I thought, change of clothes, drive to Grangemouth, pick up the signed papers and back for my massage. Because he wouldn't, he wouldn't, he wouldn't. And even if he wanted to, he knew he would get caught. Like I'd caught him once already, even though I was too late. Like Ty and 'missper' were going to catch whoever it was that tricked Ivy, Martine and Laura. Not too late. Please God, not too late for those three.

My phone rang. Smiling, thinking of Ty on his coffee break or maybe even with news, I answered it.

'Are you in?' It was my dad.

'Am I *in*?' I said.

'I just want to talk to you, Tashie.'

'I'll be there in ten minutes,' I said. 'Give me fifteen. Safe side.' And hung up. Because the only way to make sense of that question was if Big Garry was outside, right now. Otherwise he'd have asked 'Where are you' or even 'Are you at home?'

I sidled along the hallway to the bedroom window, where the thick nets hid me from the street. And there was his car parked across the road outside Adim's. His door was opening.

The passenger door was opening. He had brought my mum! I let out a long shaky breath. But it wasn't Lynne who stepped out of the passenger side. It was Wee Garry. That was a joke, of course. Wee Garry had a head and a half on my dad and surely a few stone too, none of it fat. He wasn't dressed in his warehouse ovies today. He had on a black leather blazer over a T-shirt and a pair of bad jeans, so new and stiff the hems stuck out on either side of his blinding white trainers. He looked ridiculous, like his mum had dressed him for the part, but low in my gut I felt last night's cheap red wine and greasy chips moving. He might well look ridiculous, but he also looked like what he was. Muscle.

I stumbled backwards away from the window and flew to the front door. But they'd be in the close before I could get out. So I dropped the snib and put the chain on, wishing the bolts weren't painted open, then I ran to the kitchen, to the end of the offshoot.

I'd been kidding myself all week that he wouldn't, but only on the surface. Underneath I'd known all along, and now that knowledge took over, sharp and smart. I jumped up on the draining board and prised up the sash, recoiling at the roll of foul air that came in. The top of the wall dividing Hollywood's yard from the chippy's was only five feet down at a guess. If I dangled, I could get steady on it before I had to let go with my hands.

It looked so easy when people did it in films. But when I took hold of the taps and started to climb out I felt the cheap aluminium of the inset sink buckle and, when I lowered myself, the windowsill dug into my forearms. Plus it was miles more than five feet. I was as low as I could go, and my toes were still waving in mid-air, when I heard the fierce, drilling buzz of my entry phone. My first ever visitors. I tried to look over my shoulder. Then, at a second buzz, I let go.

Only an acrobat could have landed on the single course of bricks that made up the top of the yard wall, but at least I hit the flat top of the chippy bin and, even though I kept moving, it slowed me enough that when I dropped to the ground, knees bent and arms out, I stayed on my feet.

The chippy wasn't open yet. It wouldn't be long – this

wasn't the sort of town where the takeaways stay shut at lunchtime – but I couldn't wait. I stacked up a stairway of fat-pails, groaning at the weight of them as I dragged them across the slabs and strained to lift them, then I pulled myself from the top one back on to the bin lid and up on to the wall.

I was balanced there, gathering myself to slither down into Hollywood's yard, when I glanced over into the garden of the fairytale cottage, at the washing hanging on the rope.

Then I forgot I was standing on a narrow brick wall at head height from the hard ground. I forgot about the foul smell. I forgot everything and stared at the clothes line. It was crowded with T-shirts and blouses – all different sizes, underpants and bras – all different colours, looking like the stock for a jumble sale. And in amongst them was a peach and cream summer dress, fluttering on the line the way it had fluttered on Laura Wade as she left her flat on the last day.

I walked along the wall, steady as a rock, then turned and scrambled down, landing in a crouch. I let my legs stretch out in front of me and settled myself, not minding the wet grass under my bum or the rough stones at my back, scratching me through my clothes. I studied the washing, putting it together into outfits. Three of them. A summer dress in May. A suit and blouse from March, and the sort of socks that you wear as boot liners. A cord skirt and complicated jumper from February, ribbed tights.

Three different sizes. None of them a good fit for either sister.

A skinny wee woman, Renny had said. *That* was what had bothered me, making echoes boom in my memory.

One of the echoes was Carole's voice. *Not a picking on her*, it said. *Poor-looking wee thing.*

It smells like something's died in their basement. That was Aisling.

So I was too late. I felt a pain in my chest like my heart was literally breaking. I was only just too late. They had been right there, being fed every day, then being left alone a couple of days to weaken, and then, on that one day of high drama I thought was maybe a gas leak, being killed. Now they were mouldering. I was too late. I was so close, but I had missed them.

The house door was opening. I didn't even try to move. I couldn't have anyway. When she came out, the skinny wee woman, loaded up with more bags, we stared at each other, one frozen in the doorway, one slumped on the grass.

'Myra?' The woman's voice was light with wonder.

'What?'

'You came.' I said nothing. 'My sister's sleeping. You'll have to wait.'

'Can I ask you a favour?' I said. My voice surprised me with how steady it was.

'Anything. I can't believe you came. You just . . . came. I tried so hard to make you come. Three times I tried to make you come. I should have waited. Here you are.'

'Can you have a look up at the windows of the first-floor flat there,' I said. 'Is there anyone in there? But do it subtly!'

The woman pushed her hair back off her head and used the gesture to hide a sweeping glance along the top of her garden wall.

'A large man,' she said. 'Did he try to stop you coming?'

I was on my hands and knees now, Keeping close to the base of the wall, I made my way up to the corner. 'Unlock the cellar door and leave it open,' I said. 'When you tell me no one's watching, I'm going to run inside. OK?' Because I had to see them. I didn't know why, but I had to see them with my own eyes. Then I would phone nine-nine-nine. And I would phone Ty too. And Adim and the girls in the nail bar. What could this tiny little woman do? However she caught the others, she was no match for me.

She opened the door and left it ajar. She threw another glance at the sky as if to check the weather. Then she trotted back up the steps, walked over to her washing and started working her way along the rope feeling the clothes. I had seen my mum do it a thousand times. I had done it myself: judging how dry the washing was and how certain the rain was. It was the perfect cover for looking beyond the rope to a neighbour's windows.

When she was halfway along, actually letting the floaty dress run through her hands, she said, 'Now!'

I squirted forward, covering the space in three sprinting

strides, then threw myself down the steps. I grabbed the door-jamb and swung myself round into the dark, out of sight, stopping, panting in the close blackness.

The air seethed with the smell of death.

The last thing I saw was the woman trotting down the stone steps to lock the door behind me.

The last thing I heard was the distant ring of my phone lying in the grass, where it had fallen, at the base of the garden wall.

TWENTY-FIVE

I came round slowly, gagging on the air and blinking into the darkness. I'd never fainted before. I was in a tiny room, the door I'd come in locked on the other side, but another door with a key sticking out of it facing me. I knew what was behind it. I wanted to see them. Too late to save them, still I wanted to see.

I turned the key and pushed the door. I couldn't see much in the dimness, just a pair of silhouettes. But they were sitting up. One of them was standing up now and coming towards me. I gasped.

'Martine?'

She pulled in a sharp breath.

'I thought you were dead,' I said. 'I thought I was too late.'

The other one stood and came forward. 'Who are you?' she said.

'Ivy?' I said. 'Where's Laura?'

They parted then, moving to either side to let me look past them to where a figure lay stretched out on an airbed on the floor, covered in a blanket to the chest, but propped up and smiling at me.

'All present and correct,' she said. Her voice sounded weak and her face was skeletal, her eyes invisible in their deep sockets and her cheeks sharp as flint.

'Who are *you*?' Ivy said again.

'Tash Dodd. I can't believe you're all here. I thought I was too late. I thought they had killed you.'

'They tried,' Ivy said. 'My elbow's definitely broken and Martine's got a gash on the back of her head. But we fought them off, didn't we?'

'What happened to *you*?' I asked Laura.

'Urine infection,' she said. 'Kidney infection. But I'm doing some fighting off too, after – let me tell you – a couple of pretty hairy days. Look, never mind that. Have you got a phone?'

I shook my head. 'Dropped it,' I said.

'But what are you *doing* in here?' Martine asked me. 'If you knew we were in here, why did you come? Why didn't you phone for help? I don't understand.'

What could I say? Arrogance, ignorance, panic? All of the above. 'I'm sorry,' I went for in the end. 'But I've got a lot of people outside all set to kick up a stink if I go missing,' I said. I had been leaning on both my hands but I couldn't stand to breathe this air any longer. I lifted one and used it to hold my T-shirt hem over my nose.

'Rude!' said Laura. 'Are you insinuating things about our housekeeping?'

'Sorry,' I said. 'You must be used to it.'

'It's worse than it was,' Ivy said. 'There used to be a metal plate over the drain where we squat, but then I tried to kill Kate with it and Gail took it away, so now it's an open sewer.'

I took my hem away from my face and sniffed, trying not to gag. 'But that can't be sewage,' I said. 'It smells like . . . bad meat.'

'It is,' Martine said. 'Well, it's blood anyway. It's periods.'

'Jesus,' I said, with another sniff. 'For real that's just a bit of period blood?'

'On old newspaper and bits of cardboard, yeah,' Martine said.

I let my head fall back against the wood panels of the door and watched the three of them from under my lashes. Trying to take it in. Ivy Stone had been in here for months, squatting over a drain, cleaning herself with newspaper, fed by a madwoman bringing carriers down every day. And there was nothing in here. Absolutely nothing. Just dank walls, a few flakes of old paint hanging off them, a concrete floor covered with moss and dirt, and a collection of furniture gathered under a grimy fanlight that looked so pathetic and so insane I could feel a sob in my throat. Three bright pink plastic inflatable armchairs and a coffee table made of empty water bottles and a sheet of cardboard. The sob escaped me.

'Which one's Kate?' I said. 'The wee twittery one or the one in the net curtain? I've been watching them from the window of my flat.'

'Ha!' said Laura, but she didn't explain.

'Kate's the little one that comes inside,' said Martine. 'Gail's the grey one that unlocks the door.'

'We call her Caspar,' Laura said.

I managed a dry laugh. 'And which one . . . or is it both?'

'Kate's Igor,' Laura said. 'She's the minion. She does the dirty work. But Gail's the one with the flick knife. The one with the keys.'

'Stanley knife,' said Martine in a voice that told me she'd said it many times before. 'That's bad enough.'

'I saw her once,' I said. 'I thought it was a phone in her hand. But it was dark. It was the middle of the night.'

'What do you mean?' Martine said. I frowned at her. 'What do you mean you saw her "once in the night"? I thought you said you were watching Kate come and go.'

'Yeah,' I said. 'So? Well, actually I saw her in the day once too. But only once. What's the problem?'

'She unlocks the door,' Martine said. 'She waits for Kate outside, in the daytime. How come you've never seen that?'

'She doesn't,' I said. 'Kate comes and goes on her own, bringing stuff. What is it – food? Clothes?'

I didn't realize what I had done until Martine started sobbing. 'She wasn't *there*?' she said. 'She was never really *out* there? Kate had all the keys with her every time?'

'All what keys?' I said.

They told me then, about the double doors, the two-lock system they'd believed in. The story that had tricked them.

I waited a while to let the waves of truth and shame and anger settle. When they were all breathing easy again, exhausted with it maybe, I asked the big question. The real question. 'Why are you here?'

'Kate brought us,' Martine said. 'For Gail to choose one.'

'One what?' I asked.

'Sister,' said Laura. 'One more sister. To kill or to keep. Which, is something we *don't* know.'

'Why?' My voice had gone to a croak.

'Because there's something really wrong with her,' Laura said. 'And Kate's completely under her thumb. Not even that. Kate's just her little shadow.'

'But none of that matters now,' Ivy said. 'She's too bloody late.' She sounded like iron filings. It made me shiver. 'Tash,' she went on, the smile back in her voice, 'you look like a big strong girl. No skin breaks and two working arms?' I stared at her. 'Good. Because we've got a plan.'

'It's the happy ending of our last plan,' Laura said. 'The dumb one.'

'What happened?' I asked them. I was still reeling, still couldn't believe these three names had sprung to life, out of their photos and the news reports, and were right here talking to me.

'I was lying in wait for Kate to come in,' said Ivy. 'She was going to come in, see Laura trussed up like a corpse and Martine bending over her, wringing her hands. That was going to distract her, or upset her, then I was going to whack her with the drain cover.'

'What went wrong?' I said. I was clambering to my feet now, to let them go back to their little lounge instead of kneeling on the hard floor beside me. They had nothing on their bottom halves except pants and socks. Maybe they were long past noticing, but it was bothering me.

'That's the question,' Martine said. 'It took us ages to work it out. Gail finally appeared for a start. With her knife. That's quite distracting when you're not used to it. And then we got hurt – the two of us. That knocked everything off as well. But really it was because she didn't do what we expected. And we couldn't see why.'

'Basically,' said Ivy, 'Kate went ballistic when she saw the open drain.'

'But not because she was worried she might get whacked with the cover for it,' Laura said. 'She didn't care where a massive metal plate had gone. Oh no! She only cared that the drain was open.'

'And she said,' Martine chipped in – they were *enjoying* telling me this – 'she said . . . . "Get away from there. That's private."'

'And even when she saw me actually with the drain cover raised over my head to bash her brains in,' said Ivy, 'she was still more bothered about Martine being near the hole.'

'Which is bonkers,' Martine said.

'So,' said Laura, 'we think there's a way out. Through the drain.'

'I think so too,' I said. 'I think you're right.' That set them off like a flock of parrots, flapping and chattering. When they'd quietened again I went on: 'There's a nail bar, on the corner – Hollywood Nails – and in the last few days the girls that run it have been talking about the smell. They even worked out it was coming from here. I thought . . . I really thought . . . Never mind. If the cover was taken off at the other end and the air's moving, that would explain it. How big is it at this end?'

'Like a manhole,' Laura said. 'A womanhole.'

'The Hollywood girls said there's a grating in their back yard that's too big to cover up with a bin,' I told them.

'We've made a rope,' Ivy said. She leaned to the side and lifted a thick grey plait. 'It's our tracksuit bottoms. Not Laura's because of her kidney infection—'

'Just call me Marie Antoinette,' Laura chipped in, giving a royal wave with the one hand that was sticking out from under her blanket.

'And I was going to go down it,' Martine said. 'I kind of still want to even though you're here, Tash.'

'Except no way,' Laura said. 'Because for one – open wound on the back of your head. And for two – if there's four of us in here and the only Black girl gets dropped down a sewer to save three whiteys we are going to get roasted alive in the papers. So just no.'

'Right,' said Ivy. 'We don't care about *you*, Martine, we just want to make sure we can get paid for glowing articles about us in the posh magazines.'

'You're sick,' Martine said. 'Tash, we decided all this before you got here. We've made a pact to talk all together or not at all.'

'Otherwise Laura would be showing them round her pent-house and I'd be in the black-and-white pages at the back,' said Ivy.

I stared at them, one after the other. They were kidding. They were actually joking around. They were laughing.

'I know what you're thinking,' Laura said. 'What a bunch of brain-dead zombies.'

'I wasn't,' I said, stumbling to get the words out fast enough.

'Yeah, you were,' Laura said. 'We're not, though. We're just demob happy because we're getting outta here!'

'And because Laura didn't die,' Martine said. 'That's always nice.'

'Plus – to be fair – they drug us,' said Ivy.

'Yeah, all three of us are off our heads on some kind of sedative or something,' said Martine. 'It's in the water.'

'And when we get out and I get this pair hooked up to a lie detector . . .' Laura said. The other two laughed but it was hollow. 'You look puzzled, Tash,' she went on. 'The thing is that while I was ill – really ill – they gave me nearly all the water and I can't work out if they were trying to put me out of my misery or just keep my kidneys flushed through.'

'I keep telling you,' Martine said, 'I heard on a podcast about deep sedation letting people fight infection. And maybe it worked.'

'Maybe?' I said.

'Yes, maybe,' Laura said. 'Because Kate gave us a bottle of pills, with the label too faded to read. And this pair of Florence Nightingales – or Harold Shipmans; who can say? – fed them to me anyway. We've saved one to get it tested if we ever—'

'Once we're out,' said Ivy.

'Yeah,' said Martine. 'Once we're home.'

'So anyway, Tash, there's Flurazepam in the water. That's why we're all loopy.'

'I wasn't thirsty anyway,' I said, trying to sound as calm as they did without the help they were getting. What a total head-wreck of an idea: to know that your mind was being controlled by the water you had to drink to stay alive.

'Actually, that's a good idea,' Ivy said. 'Don't drink unless you have to.'

'Well, when's zero hour?' I said. 'When's go time?'

'We *had* said tomorrow,' Ivy said. 'To let Martine's head scab over. But since you're here, we could go right now.' She beamed at the others and then at me.

I thought again of Wee Garry stepping out of my dad's car and the sound of the entry-phone buzzer. For the first time, it struck me that this was perfect. My dad must be going crazy out there, knowing I was close – the warm kettle, the open window, even the stairway of fat pails if he looked out and noticed them. He would be climbing the walls, not knowing where I'd got to.

'Actually,' I said, 'right now might be very bad for me. Tomorrow would work much better.'

They shared a look. 'Interesting,' Laura said. 'Makes me wonder all over again what you're doing here. How about we tell you our sad tales, if you tell us yours. In fact why don't we start?'

I listened. It seemed like they talked for hours. About a cold mother, a missing father, a long-lost sister, a hoped-for husband; cats and photos and roses. The light changed while I listened.

'You probably think we're pathetic,' Ivy said when Laura had finished her bout of talking and dried her tears. 'Well, we are. I am anyway. We're as bad as those girls who think they're going to be nannies and hand their passports over.'

And so to make them feel better, when I started to talk I told them everything. Big Garry and Lynne and Bazz, BG Europe and the eager Russian buyers, the collapsing foundations of my life. I told them about the burner phone and the stomach bug, my decision, all my preparation, my ultimatum, my seven-day wait, and the sight of my dad out in the street, coming to get me. Then I pushed the button to light my watch face. 'Gone eleven,' I said. 'I can't believe it.'

'Time's weird down here,' Martine said.

'Let's rest,' said Ivy. 'And try to sleep. We've got a big day tomorrow.'

'Tash, can you put that light on again a minute?' said Laura. 'Sounds daft but we haven't had a light. It's nice.'

When we'd all squatted over the drain in turn and the three of them had drunk some water, giving me an apple instead, we settled down, them like sardines on their airbed and me across two of the plastic chairs.

'Are we ready?' Martine said. 'It's my turn. Tash, someone tells a bedtime story every night. Ivy started it but we help now. You listen and if our plan doesn't work maybe you can take a turn tomorrow.'

If it doesn't work, I thought. Tomorrow. When I'd had

some of the water too. Then I tuned in to what Martine was saying.

'. . . is a hotel that pays test guests to come and stay. I'll have a tower room with a view over miles of countryside, treetops and fields full of lambs, and windows on all four sides that I can leave open and feel the night breeze and hear owls. Laura's got a room downstairs with a balcony facing the sea, so you can hear seagulls and smell the ozone. Your bath is sunk in the floor, Laura, and it's got jets of water and there's a pot of salt scrub. Ivy, you're in a suite with a full kitchen and a log fire, so you can bake crumpets in the oven and then toast them on a fork and then we'll come down and eat them with you, dripping with butter and blackcurrant jam.'

'Strawberry,' said Ivy, her voice already gravelly.

'Strawberry,' said Martine. 'And when we go to bed, I'm on cool linen sheets and a goose-down duvet and Laura's bed has got satin and no blankets at all because the room's so warm, and you've been to the waxers, Laura, so your legs don't snag them – See? I do remember – and Ivy's bed has got red flannel sheets and real wool blankets and a Tiffany lamp on the bedside table so you can sit up with your cocoa and read.'

'What am I reading?' Ivy's voice was slurred.

'The new Ann Cleeves. They sent you it early because you're such a superfan. And it's her best yet.'

'What am *I* doing?' said Laura softly.

'His name's Jaden,' said Martine. 'He's a trainer, but he's also a trauma counsellor. He volunteers at the Samaritans on a Saturday night. That's their hardest night. But he's in a rugby club too. He's got a scar through one eyebrow from a bad scrum. And I'm Skyping Idris because he's filming in LA. But he'll be home tomorrow.'

'You get Jaden and Idris and I get cocoa?' Ivy said. 'Is Bill Nighy dead in this dream?'

'Shoosh,' said Martine. 'Don't make us laugh. We'll all wake up again.'

'What did we have for dinner in the hotel?' Ivy said. And Martine started talking.

TWENTY-SIX

It wasn't exactly light when I woke but the darkness had a different quality, dusty instead of silky, muffled. I had moved to the airbed sometime in the night and now I lay on my portion of it, trying not to move or breathe differently in case I woke them. I'd had one night to take. Ivy had been in here for months. Any time they could sleep was surely a blessing.

'Do you think Ty's looking already?' Laura said.

'And Adim?' Ivy said.

'I was going to run to his shop the day I came,' Martine said. 'When I realized my bag was gone with my phone in it. But they'd locked me in already.'

'How long have you all been awake?' I asked.

'A while,' Martine told me. 'We didn't want to disturb you. I remember waking up the second day.'

Two pairs of tracksuit bottoms hadn't looked like a very long rope but it stretched to double when I tested my weight on it.

'No sound of stitches ripping though,' Ivy said. 'That's good.'

'And if the pipe to the other drain is too small you'll come right back,' said Martine.

'I will, but I'll have to sit away from you all or you'll all puke.'

'No way,' said Ivy. 'It's a waste of food.'

'Five metres,' Laura said when I shone my watch light down the shaft, moving it gradually, lighting the dark brick walls and only letting it settle a moment on the jumbled mess at the bottom.

'Fifteen feet,' Ivy said.

'Same difference. And I'm five foot five. I can do that. If you think you can counterweight me so I don't drop, Martine,

I can do that easy.' I didn't feel as brave as I was trying to sound. Not nearly. What did I know about letting myself down into a deep hole in the ground without dying? I'd seen it in films but they always made it look like nothing. 'Were any of you in the Brownies?' I asked. 'Because I haven't got a clue how to climb down a rope. Not a single clue.'

'Don't climb down the rope,' Laura said. 'Walk down the wall. More control that way.'

I bit my lip on the answer that sprang to mind but it was easier than I expected, once Laura – never a Brownie, but once a gymnast – had explained the basics. It was mostly trust and there was no way these three were going to let me fall. Martine took most of it, her knuckles shining bony on the pale grey twisted cotton and a grim set to her jaw, but Ivy was there with her one good hand, pale from the pain, and Laura insisted. Still, the first step off the horizontal on to the face of the shaft was terrifying. Everything felt wrong – new muscles working, fighting gravity, the threat of my feet slipping on the wet bricks. It was better when both feet were flat in front of me and I was passing the rope up through my hands, slowly shuffling down, grabbing, releasing, shuffling again, keeping going. When I felt the big knot in the rope end pass between my legs I was shocked to look up and see how far above me the edge of the hole was, even more shocked to look down and see the filthy floor of the drain only a few metres below. 'It's really stretched,' I called up to them. I took a breath, held it, and let my legs drop away. Then, sending up a prayer, I let go.

'Are you down?' It was Ivy. They must have felt the tension leave the rope.

'I'm down,' I said. 'Standing on solid ground. But oh my God the smell.' The base of the drain was bigger than the shaft, like the bulb in the bottom of a test-tube, but it was still close enough all around to make me feel trapped and panicky. It *couldn't* be piss and shit and a bit of dried blood. I didn't believe it. It was too thick and far too sweet.

'Is there an opening?' Martine shouted. 'Just tell us and then come back up. I'll take over.'

'No!' I shouted. The air down here felt like poison, bitter

and stinking in my nose and my mouth. Martine with that gash on the back of her head couldn't come down here.

'Tash, I'm flinging the wet wipes to you,' Ivy said. 'See if you can't make a mask. See if that helps.'

'Don't waste them!' I said. 'I'm fine. I'm sorry. I just . . . I'm fine now. I'm going to put my light on and have a look.'

I turned my wrist and hit the button, turning in a tight circle, peering at the bottom of the blackened brick walls all around me, then suddenly a section that was striped and shining. The moan escaped me helplessly. 'Nooo.'

'What?' All three voices came booming down.

'There's a grate over it. It's covered.' I dropped on my knees and put my hands round the bars, shaking them more out of frustration than hope, but I felt them give and I fell back, sprawling flat with the square of grating on top of me.

'Shit!' I spat. 'Bloody hell.'

'What?' It was Ivy. 'Tash, we can't see a thing up here.'

'The grate's loose. It's off. It came away in my hands. But I've sprawled on my arse and I'm covered in crap.'

'How big's the hole?' Laura shouted. 'Put the light on.'

But I knew without checking, because I'd heard the crunch, that my watch was a goner. 'There's no light now,' I said. 'I'm sorry. The grate fell on it. But the hole's . . . about the size of one of those wee IKEA tables. The square ones.'

No one said anything for a moment, then Martine spoke up. 'It's your call. That sounds pretty tiny to me.'

I slid until I was lying flat, trying not to think about the wetness at the back of my head. 'Yeah but if I skootch right down and look along it,' I said, 'I'm pretty sure I can see light and it doesn't look that far. I mean, how far can it be? Twenty feet? I really can see light. It must be from the grate in the yard at Hollywood. I'm going.'

'Wind the rope round your waist in case you need it at the other end,' Laura shouted. 'And be careful. Feel your way. Don't get jagged on anything. Or anything.'

'The bottom's soft,' I said. 'I think there might be litter or something. And there's a blockage. It's all gathered in a pile halfway along. I'll need to shift it.'

'A pile of what?' said Ivy. 'I still think you should make a mask.'

'I don't know,' I said. 'Leaves? Maybe someone at the other end swept them down the drain and they got blown along the pipe?' Or maybe, I was thinking, something crawled in there and died. It would explain the waves of stink. But that pile was far too big to be a dead animal. I sniffed again. 'Oh Jesus.'

'What?' Another frightened chorus.

'Smell,' I managed to say. 'It's really bad. It's much worse in the pipe. It's not good.' I tried to laugh and failed completely. 'I'm taking that tower room at the hotel, Martine. And Jaden. And the cocoa. I'm just saying.'

It wouldn't have been so terrible if I could crawl, but there wasn't enough clearance so I dropped on to my front and, grabbing my cuffs in my fists to save my arms getting scraped, pulled myself forward into the pipe, wriggling my bum and pushing with my toes. I made a good six feet of progress that way, panting hard, feeling the closeness press all around me and thanking all the gods I wasn't scared of small spaces, or the dark. And at least panting made me breathe automatically through my mouth and stopped me smelling maybe half of the evil stench down here. I could still hear them shouting encouragement from up in the cellar, even though I had no breath to spare to answer them.

Now I was at the bit where that heap of litter blocked my way. I would have given anything for my watch light back again. Instead, I had to feel ahead in the dark to see what the blockage was and how I might get over it or move it aside or something.

'A shoe.' I said it out loud to myself. Why the hell would anyone hide old shoes down here halfway along a sewage pipe? That's private! they said Kate had blurted out. But why would even a madwoman – even a madwoman's minion – stash shoes here? I grabbed it and tugged, expecting to chuck it behind me but it didn't move, as if it was stuck on something. I felt around, trying to understand the strange texture of the flakes and strings that were shifting under my hands, dropping away from my touch until I felt a sudden unyielding rod like a . . . like a . . .

And I was moving backwards, ten times faster than I had crawled in, screaming, my screams booming in the shaft.

'What? What? Tash!' I could see the dim outlines of their heads above me.

'Throw the rope up. We'll get you up.'

'What's wrong? Untie the rope and throw it up to us.'

I had crawled right through the heap of waste at the bottom of the shaft and found myself sitting pressed against the far wall whimpering. 'It's a body. There's a body. It's a corpse. There's a corpse in there. I felt its foot. There's a dead person in there. It's a body.' I wasn't cold – I was hotter if anything, from the close air and exertion and adrenaline – but I was shivering hard, my teeth clacking together and my limbs shuddering.

'Come up,' Ivy said. 'Come away up. I'm so sorry.'

But I couldn't move. I could barely hear her soothing words and Martine's echo of them, like a lullaby. It was Laura who got through the shock and reached me.

'Fucking hell,' she said. 'No wonder she said it's "private".'

I clambered to my feet, trying to untuck the end of the trackie-bum rope from my waistband to unwind it, but I stopped before my numb, fumbling fingers had got even half of it free. 'But the thing is I can definitely see light,' I said. 'I can see daylight.'

'Tash, you can't crawl over a corpse,' Laura said.

Could I? To get out of here? To get them out of here?

'No,' I said. 'But I can tie a rope round its legs – *his* legs. I think it's a man's shoe – and drag him out here out of the way.'

'Do you ever pray?' Ivy said.

'I just started again,' I said. 'Two minutes ago. I'm not going to stop you, that's for damn sure.'

'Do you want a hand?' Martine said. 'Do you want me to come down and help you.'

I opened my mouth to say no, but found myself crying. 'Yes. Oh my God, yes I really, really do.'

And after all the business with the rope and the abseiling, Martine just lowered herself off the edge of the drain above and put her feet into my hands as I reached up then slithered down the rest of the way. We hugged, fierce enough to creak, for a long moment. Then Martine stepped back and literally spat on her hands. I could see them glisten.

'Right,' she said. 'Who's going in to tie the rope to him and who's staying out here?'

'I'm going.'

I was back at the shoe in a second or two, prising apart the twist in the trackie-bum rope and clamping it over the ankle, trying not to think about skin and tendons, about overcooked ends of turkey drumsticks, about how easily bones, supposedly knitted together, could break apart. I knew if I had to come back in here over and over again and pull him out piece by piece I would lose my mind.

'Give it a tug,' I shouted back, then 'Whoa!' as the shoe started to move towards me. I wriggled out and put my hands on the rope beside Martine's.

'It is a man,' I said. 'An old man, I think. He's got brogues on.'

'Here goes,' Martine said.

It was quiet. I had expected bumping and scraping, but he came out with only a whisper of sound but with a bulging engulfing roll of stench that made Martine retch and made me cry again.

'Oh God,' Ivy said, above us. 'I was hoping you were wrong.'

'No,' I said. 'Right then. Let's get the rope off him and get along to that light, eh?'

Marine had stopped spitting into the tiny pile of bile and vomit she had made but she was still on her hands and knees. 'Look,' she said, nodding along the pipe. 'There's another one.'

There were three. The man in brogues and a woman in a skirt and jumper that I had to drag out by a wrist because I couldn't bear to reach over her sharp ribs and the mess of the cavity under them to reach her foot. Then there was a second woman, with bare feet, in a nightdress that rode up as we hauled her out. The three of them filled the bottom of the shaft even with me piling them up, folding their bones over and tucking them under. There was always something sliding and crunching, no matter how hard I tried.

I was sobbing helplessly now. Up above, Ivy was still praying and Laura had joined her. Martine was breathing in long ragged heaves, as she kicked at the bones to clear space for us to crouch down, but she hadn't been sick again.

When the naked one, with her nightie round her neck, was finally well clear of the pipe, we could both see it, round and empty, and that tantalizing dazzle of light at the end. It looked so close.

'Who's first?' Martine said.

'Doesn't matter,' I said. 'You go if you like.' I couldn't take my eyes off the light. It sparkled like drops of water. It *was* drops of water. I was looking at a stream of clear twinkling water. I bent my head and gasped as I caught a whiff of it too. Then I plunged into the neck of the pipe, shouting at the top of my lungs. 'Aisling! Renny! Aisling! Renny! Help! Help! Help me!'

At the other end I started to cough and there was no way to stand, no clear shaft here to climb up, just a bend in the pipe to the grating above. I didn't care. I rolled on to my back and laughed as I choked, staring up at Renny's face staring down, the bleach bottle still tilted in her hand.

POSTSCRIPT

They owned the doctor's house and lived there with their three daughters; quiet, ordered, comfortable lives. The little place next door, the doctor's ballroom, was a charming Wendy house for their girls, Kate, Gail and Myra.

The trouble started when they signed it over, one Christmas, as a special present: a two-bedroomed fairytale to share between three. Kate wanted to keep it just the way it had always been; Gail wanted to make it a home and live there; Myra wanted to sell her share and move away.

Myra died on the twenty-fifth of January, sedated into deep unconsciousness and then slit open with a short blade, from her right wrist to her right elbow. Gail 'died' days later.

'Cotard's delusion,' the medical expert said, on the first of the reports, when they moved back to the studio from the outside broadcast, from the reporter standing solemnly at the end of Loch Road where the tape was stretched over as, behind him, the techs in their blue suits carrying bagged items out of the fairytale cottage and into their vans.

No one knew what Cotard's delusion was then, not even Martine. Everyone knows now, now that there's been such a famous case of it, such a notorious crime.

'A belief that one has died,' I'd said, reading it off my phone. 'Gail instead of Myra. She coped with her grief by deciding *she* had died and her baby sister was still living.'

Ty shook his head. He was off-duty and sitting beside me in the hospital waiting room, holding my hand. 'And then the other one ups and thinks if Gail can decide she's dead instead of Myra, why not make another switch and get her back again?'

'The other one.' I nodded, staring at the hospital corridor floor. Everyone thought she was the minion, the Igor. Everyone thought Gail with her nets and her knife was running the show, when really she was grieving, treasuring the knife that took her baby sister away like she treasured the pictures of her family in their little case. 'I'm not denying that Gail's ill,' I said to Ty, 'but Kate is absolutely off-the-charts insane.'

'You think?' Ty said. 'She must have killed the mum within days, else why was the sister not buried? And then she killed the dad. And when that didn't work she started looking around for better fake sisters.'

'So I'm going to go with "Yes, I think",' I said.

'Not me,' said Ty. 'They don't reckon Myra was suicide.'

'How does the body count rising make Kate saner?'

'Because – under the cone, right? I'd lose my job – but Myra had been to a lawyer to see about getting her share out of the house. So . . . no, I don't think Kate's insane at all. I think she's greedy and selfish and – don't laugh – evil.'

'Evil,' I said. I thought I'd enjoy having a source of inside gen, while the fiscal and the CID started to piece it all together. But now, after only three days, I was beginning to wish I didn't have to hear it, didn't have to know, didn't have to think about the difference between evil and madness.

'What a bloody stupid thing to do,' Ty said. 'Forking over a glorified gang hut for your three daughters to fight about, when one of them's a psychopath.'

'Families,' I said. 'Maybe they didn't know. Maybe they thought they were all dead normal. Like everyone does.' I really wanted to stop thinking about it. I knew I'd have to face it sometime – madness and badness and greed – but not today.

'Here they come,' Ty said. Martine was walking, with a bandage on her head, and Laura was on her feet too – 'chockful of monster antibiotics and fresh from the renal clinic' as she'd put it – but a nurse was pushing Ivy in a wheelchair. The others hadn't realized she'd been eating so little, giving them so much. They doled their daily rations out in so many tiny servings, she'd managed to hide what she was up to.

'Who's driving?' the nurse said.

'Me,' said Ty standing up.

'Well, I'll hand them over, officer,' said the nurse, making him roll his eyes and getting the first giggle out of me since I'd laughed up at Renny days ago.

'And you're going to the hotel,' I said to the three of them. 'No arguments. Ty's dropping you off and then leaving you to it, right?' Ty nodded. 'I'll stay if you need me, or go if you'd rather.'

'Even Ty can stay,' Martine said. 'You, definitely.'

'Because he was coming to rescue us!' Laura said. 'I was right.'

'You were,' Ty said. 'I was. Once Cyber found the report about April – Hazel, actually – and found out the lonely-hearts scam was based in Hephaw, it was only a matter of time. It could have been days though. Even with Aisling and Renny phoning every hour and Adim chipping in. And if they'd stopped feeding you again after Tash got locked in . . .' He shook the thought off. 'Nah, this is your hero. This one here.' He rubbed my arm with his knuckle.

'No way,' I said. 'The plan was hatched. I was just the grunt. Worker bee, that's me.' I turned to the others. 'It's not on a clifftop but it's dead nice and it's dead close. Suite for Ivy, big bath for Laura, best view for you, Martine. They know it's us and they're determined to keep the press away.'

We came back for Ivy's anniversary in February, and in March for Martine, in May for Laura and then again in May for the day when I ran from my dad and found them.

Every time, we ate and drank and bathed but mostly what we did at the hotel was talk. We talked a bit about the sisters. Gail was recovering slowly in a nice place in Perthshire; because she had rolled a bottle of Septra over the floor and saved a life that way. Kate was in a locked ward she wasn't likely to leave anytime soon. We talked about Idris and Jaden who stayed imaginary, and about Ivy's real widower who didn't know why she called him 'Cocoa'. We even talked about the time in the cellar. We managed to laugh. And of course we talked about the survivor centre, nearly ready for its grand opening, at number 1a Loch Road, Hephaw. Nice and handy, halfway between the two cities, where all the people are. We talked about the girls – and boys – who'd come there. About the translators and counsellors and the lawyers who'd work there. About the good that would be done there. Sometimes I talked about the other ones too, the ones I dreamed about. The ones I was too late to help. The ones whose names I'd never know.

The only thing we don't talk about, on the hotel weekends, is work. Morrigan Movers – formerly BG Solutions – doesn't need discussion. We changed the name but we stayed put. Yes, I'm still here, but not – this time – because it's handy. I'm here because I've tried the sparkling granite and the wild water of the North Sea now. I've seen the soft southwest and the rolling border country and this is where I want to be. Where rare orchids grow on the steep scree of a shale bing as if to say 'life's tough but we're tougher'. Where I never have to worry about people finding out, because everyone knows. Where I can forget Big Garry saying he came from nothing and agree with my granny that he and I were both lucky to come from this.

He squandered it. But I'm not going to. Morrigan Movers survived the scandal that followed so close on the heels of all the great publicity my so-called heroics had brought. Oh yes, there was a scandal. I never meant to let them get away. Garry and Lynne and Bazz. I always meant to report him once I had the business off him, once the drivers' jobs were safe and the firm was working well under my leadership. All that guff about retiring to the sun was just to get him to sign.

He swore blind he had come to Hephaw to hand the business over and turn himself in. But he didn't have any paperwork on him and he hadn't been in touch with his lawyer. He swore on his mother's life that he hadn't known about the business behind the business at BG Europe, that he'd got out as soon as he found out, that he kept it quiet to protect jobs. Yes, he stole *my* true story and spun it into lies to cover him.

It didn't work. The flaw in Big Garry's innocent act was how I'd been missing for months and he'd never tried to find me, never reported it. He could hardly admit he knew Bazz was tracking me, since he'd sworn on his own mother's life that Bazz was working alone, that Big Garry himself had been shocked to find out what Bazz was doing. So there he was: no way to hide how much he didn't care about girls who never came home.

He went quietly in handcuffs to his jail cell, the court, his prison cell and his endless appeals, throwing Bazz under fleets of buses. I avoided the papers while the case worked through and I try not to think about him these days. I channel my granny. Since he lied on her life, she's done with him. She hasn't got a sentimental bone in her wiry wee body.

As for my mum, she managed to keep out of it, didn't get arrested, wasn't convicted. But she lost her house and her car and her cushy life. I honestly think having to live in my auntie's spare room in the loft conversion and visit her husband in prison is punishment enough. Especially since she goes on the bus like the other wives and none of them speak to her. I can feel myself softening sometimes so I try not to think about her either.

I don't have to try hard not to think about Bazz in Bali. Oh yes of course *Bazz* got away. Scum floats, Ty says, and tells me to forget all of them.

Which I do, mostly, although Big Garry crosses my mind whenever something he always did one way gets changed and gets better. Slicker, more efficient, fairer, more flexible.

Laura's unlike any operations manager I've ever encountered before. And Martine on logistics is unstoppable. Ivy's happy enough running the payroll for a living, and running the book club, the charity wing and GirlsatWork for fun. They've saved me – by balancing me. Everyone thought I was probably in the trafficking up to my neck but got away with it. But the same everyone all agree that Ivy, Martine and Laura are pure as the driven snow, beyond reproach. If those three trust me, maybe I'm not so bad – I think that's how it goes. And I can't blame anyone who doesn't trust me, not really. Because when people ask why I didn't stash the evidence in a deposit box or leave it with a lawyer, I have to tell them the truth. If I'd done that, I might have crapped out. Stuffing photocopies in my locker and the student files and the bin full of papers in the Cancer Express meant that sooner or later I'd have to deal with them, before my luck ran out and somebody found them. 'So, you might have let him get away with it all?' Renny said, when I tried to explain it one time. 'Shut up,' said Aisling. 'She didn't. Get off her case, eh?' But she gave me a hell of a look.

All four of us still get a lot of looks. At work and every-where else, and a few questions from people too clueless to know better. But the three of them, at least on their good days, are all OK pretty much, after four months, and three months and a week when she nearly died.

I was only there overnight and it's me that's still seeing the doc, writing letters and not sending them. Writing this. 'It wasn't one night,' Dr Norman tells me. 'It was five months and one night.'

They do have their bad days, the three of them. But on days when Martine wants to hit her head against a wall, when Laura wants to wrap herself in a blanket and shake, when Ivy locks her office door and puts the light out, they've got each other and they've all got me.

When it's really bad we've got the hotel, whichever hotel someone's found this time. We'll never give up hoping for one with a tower *and* a sea view, a kitchen *and* a fireplace. There's never going to be a day when it's over.

There's never going to be a day when any of it's over.

There's always going to be a girl reading a sticker inside a toilet door at a motorway services and nicking a phone to call the number. There's always going to be a girl getting out of the house because they thought they'd broken her spirit and they stopped making sure she was locked in there. There's always going to be a girl rolling out of the car when it slows at the lights and getting away before they can catch her, picking the right door to knock on, finding kindness behind it. There's always going to be a girl. And I'm in time for some of them. Knowing that and keeping on is as close as I'll get to an ending.

FACTS AND FICTIONS

The general geography of Fraserburgh, Lockerbie, and Ayr are as depicted here, but none of the people, buildings or organizations I've written about are drawn from life. It wouldn't take a super-sleuth to work out which West Lothian town Hephaw is based on, and there is a house quite like 1a Loch Road there, but the Doctor's Ballroom, Adim's, Hollywood Nails, the Dodds and the sisters are absolutely imaginary.

ACKNOWLEDGEMENTS

I would like to thank: Lisa Moylett, Zoë Apostolides and Elena Langtry at CMM Literary Agency; Kate Lyall Grant, Rachel Slatter, Natasha Bell, Penny Isaac, Jem Butcher, and all at Severn House; my friends and family in the UK and the US who helped me through the three or four drafts I was expecting and then the rest of the eventual eleven drafts it took; and the people of Scotland's central belt, whose necessary toughness and well-disguised cheer grow more and more precious to me the older I get and the longer I spend far too far away. I miss youse and this is a love letter, eh.

And thanks, Neil. It must have felt like a hundred and eleven drafts to you.